MARRYING THE BILLIONAIRE SINGLE DAD

L. STEELE

1

____

#DamianSavage can I have your babies?

#DamianSavage you're my baby daddy, so what if your last album sucked?

Damian

"Shaving foam," I hold out my hand.

Riley clambers onto the chair and gets the can. She shakes it, then piles the foam into my outstretched palm.

"Thanks, Poppet." I slather it on, then smear the residue across her face.

She shrieks, "Ugh, Daddy." She wipes the foam off of her face and makes a gagging sound.

I laugh, then wipe my hands clean before gliding the razor up my chin.

She perches on the bathroom counter, "You're so handsome, Daddy."

I chuckle, "You're biased, sweetheart." I tilt my head and run the razor up the other cheek.

"I'm not." She shakes her head. "Even my teacher thinks so."

"Your teacher?" I narrow my gaze on her.

She jerks her chin, "She's always asking me about you."

"She is?" I frown. That's what comes from being famous; everyone seems to think they have a claim on you. And because I'm a single dad, every woman seems to want to use Riley to get to me.

She scrunches up her nose, "I think she wants to kiss you."

Wha — I lower my razor and stare at her.

How does she know about kissing? Is it normal for a five-year-old to know about that? Who could I ask about it? Not my friends; none of them are single dads so they'd have no idea what I'm talking about. Add that to the list of queries I need to investigate online. I blow out a breath. Why the hell is she growing up so quickly?

"Do you have to go?" She pouts.

"I promised Uncle Weston I'll be there for his Christmas Party."

"B...but," she purses her lips, "I want you to stay home and watch Frozen with me."

Frozen? *Again.* I wince. "You can watch it with Meredith." The only person I'd trust to babysit my precious little girl. Hell, she'd rightened me out when I was at my most rebellious. If anyone could take care of Riley, it would be her.

"But she's not as much fun as you, Daddy," Riley whines.

I frown at her. "Don't trouble Meredith while I am gone."

She juts out her lower lip. Uh-oh. I know that look. It means trouble. My daughter has an unbending spirit, which is all too familiar, for I was the same way. Still am. Dare me not to do something, and hell, if I don't want to rush in to prove a point. *Not much fun from the other side of the fence now, is it, ol' chap.* I heave out a sigh. "Riley," I warn, "promise you'll behave."

She huffs, then winds the hem of her dress about her fingers. "When will you be back?" she asks.

"Not until later." I glance at my reflection in the mirror. How the hell am I going to manage her at fifteen if she is such a handful at five? Maybe I need to get her to socialize more with kids her age. Is it spending so much time with me that is making her grow up so quickly?

"Will you be home in time to tuck me in, Daddy?" she whines.

"I don't think so." I shoot her a sideways glance, "Remember, I was going to stay out tonight while Meredith takes care of you?"

"But I don't want Meredith." She folds her arms over her chest, "I want you, Daddy, you."

I take in her scrunched-up features, her too bright eyes, and a part of me wants to give in, to agree that I'll be back in time to tuck her in. Would that mean I am giving in too easily? Wouldn't I be spoiling her if I agreed to her demands so quickly?

"Maybe..." I wipe the remnants of the shaving foam from my face with a towel, "Maybe just today, Meredith could tuck you in?"

Her chin trembles. "But I want *you* to read to me at bedtime."

I swallow the lump in my throat, then rinse the razor under the tap. "I did read to you yesterday," I remind her. "It's just one evening Riley."

"But...but, I don't want to wake up and not find you at home." A tear slides down her cheek, "I feel safer when you are here, Daddy. Otherwise, I have nightmares. Please, can't you come home tonight?"

I take in her pinched features, her furrowed forehead, and a hot sensation stabs at my chest. This little girl has me wrapped so tightly around her finger, I'd do anything for her. No way, can I stand to see her unhappy. I'd give anything to put a smile on her face. "Fine." I heave out a breath, "Fine, I'll be back home tonight—"

"Yay!" She claps her hands together.

"On one condition," I hold up my finger.

"Uh-oh." She folds her arms over her chest, suddenly looking more like a teenager than ever. "Am I in trouble, Daddy?"

"Not yet," I grab a towel and wipe my face, "but you will be if I come back home and I find you still up."

"B...but..." she blinks, "don't I have to be awake for you to read to me?"

I gape at her. What the—? Did she just try to twist my words around? When did she get this clever? "I said," I pronounce my words slowly, "that I'll be home at some point tonight, *not* that I'll be home in time to read to you."

"But I want to see your face before I go to bed, Daddy," she pouts.

"Riley," I warn her. "Didn't you say that you are all grown up? Grown up girls go to bed on their own. They don't wait up for their fathers to come back home before they go to sleep."

She blinks rapidly, and her shoulders slump, "Guess I'm not grown up then." She peers up at me from under her eyelashes. "If you promise to be back in time to read to me, I'll promise not to trouble Meredith."

What the—? The little imp is bargaining with me? Only this little girl could get away with something like that.

"Why you little monkey." I scoop her up and pretend to tickle her.

She shrieks, "Daddy, stop, stop—" She bursts out into peals of laughter. "Daddy, please..." She giggles and my heart blooms.

Just like that, everything is right with the world.

I hold her close and press my forehead to hers. "I'll be back home tonight, but I don't want you to wait up."

She pouts, "But Daddy—"

"Or I can be home in time to read to you and then you don't get pancakes for breakfast Sunday morning."

"But I loooove pancakes," she protests.

"You gotta choose, Riley." I tilt my head, cross my fingers mentally. "Which one is it gonna be?"

She sighs, a big gust that blows her hair up from her forehead. "Fine, I'll let Meredith read to me tonight."

"And you promise not to trouble her, or stay up until I come home?"

She pouts, and I hold her gaze, keep my features calm.

"Okay, fine, I won't stay up until then."

"And you won't cause trouble for her?"

She lowers her chin.

"Riley," I warn her again.

She purses her lips, "I won't cause trouble for her." She peers up at me from under her eyelashes. "But I get to choose the book she reads."

I open and shut my mouth. Jesus, was I this difficult growing up? This stubborn? At least, I know where she gets it from. My daughter's a chip off the old block. Warmth fills my chest. I've delivered many chart-topping hits in my career, but my proudest creation is, without doubt, this lively little bundle right here.

"You don't want pancakes?" I tilt my head and hold her gaze.

She juts out her chin, then, "Fine, fine." She throws up her hands, in a very grown-up gesture. "You choose the book, just as long as I can see you when I wake up."

2

____

Julia

"Did you know that hating someone feels disturbingly similar to loving them?" the female radio announcer asks her co-host.

"You mean when your stomach twists at the thought of that person and your chest hurts?" The man responds.

"Oh, so you do get it?" she exclaims.

"I thought that was heartburn." He chuckles.

She groans, "Wolfbane you suck, you know that?"

"It's Wolfe, and PS, that's only one of my many talents, darling Poison Ivy."

"It's Ivy," she retorts, "and if you're listening, don't forget to tune into the next episode of this guest edition of the Daily Date, where we invite you to speed date on air. Send your application via email to—"

I switch off the ignition of the Volkswagen, and the radio shuts off. Speed date...and that, too, on-air? Who'd set themselves up for that torture, huh? The only thing worse will be walking into this party where I don't know most of the guests. I glance up at the imposing building that overlooks the Thames. What the hell am I doing here?

I should be back at my apartment—okay, technically my friend, Amelie's apartment. Right about now, I'd like nothing better than to be tucked into bed and sleeping; instead, I'd accepted Amelie's boyfriend's invitation to a Christmas gathering because… Well, I don't want to disappoint them. Besides, I do want to see her, and if that means having to put up with a bunch of strangers, well then, guess I'll simply have to suck it up.

I get out of the car, walk into the reception area of the apartment block. The porter glances up at me.

"Julia Andrews here to see—"

"I know." He smiles. "They're in the penthouse." He jerks his chin toward the bank of elevators, "I was told to expect you."

Right. And of course, it had to be the penthouse. Where else do full-of-themselves, upper-class prats live, huh? Okay, come on. So maybe I shouldn't judge them before meeting them. Yeah, best save that for later. I chuckle as I ride up the elevator to the top floor. I step out, and straight into a living room filled with so much natural light that I blink. Talk about being on display, huh? The floor-to-ceiling windows at the far end reveal a view of London that makes me catch my breath. I walk forward, then pause when I spot Amelie, and next to her, a familiar face. Wha—? No, it can't be, can it?

He glances in my direction and my pulse begins to thud.

He stares at me and the full blast of those arctic blue eyes slams into my chest. I gulp; my stomach twists. The rays from the setting sun casts the lower half of his face in shadow. His shoulders bunch as he glares across the short distance that separates us.

He tilts his head, and I take in the hollows beneath those cheek-bones, the hooked nose, that prominent jawline, that beautiful throat with tendons that flex, the hollow at the base of his throat, and that sculpted chest… That gorgeous eight pack, which obviously, I cannot see through his T-shirt, but I know is there because the last time I saw it was on the celebrity gossip sites. I blink. No, it can't be. Is it…is he who I think he is? I frown; he glowers back.

He props his hands on his hips and his biceps stretch the sleeves of his leather jacket, which only enhances the breadth of his massive shoulders.

He widens his stance, drawing my attention to those narrow hips, the powerful thighs clad in jeans with the kind of distressed look that he must have paid thousands to get just right.

He slides his hand into the pocket of his jeans, outlining the length of what he's packing… And trust me when I tell you that all of those accounts by the paparazzi don't do justice to Damian 'Big D' Savage. Bad boy rock star, famous for his onstage tantrums and offstage dalliances. What's he doing here?

I move forward. Damian's scowl deepens. What's his problem?

He rakes his gaze down my face, to my chest, down to my hips, my ankles, then says something to Amelie.

Amelie frowns at him, then jerks her chin in my direction.

Gah! Are they talking about me? No. No way. He can't be interested in me, can he?

I drag my fingers through my shoulder length hair. My fingernail catches on a knot. Damn. I should have, at least, made an attempt to freshen up before coming here, huh? Except, I couldn't be bothered. Not after the debacle that my life has turned out to be.

I'd gone to Australia, excited to be with my boyfriend and looking forward to exploring an entire freaking new continent. I had returned heartbroken, with no savings and in urgent need of a job to pay my bills. Welcome to my sorry-ass life, peeps. That's why I've sworn off men. And that includes hot as hell, macho rock icons as well... Right?

I straighten my spine, hitch my backpack over my shoulder, then proceed toward Amelie. She pulls her hair to one side of her face and blue fire flashes on her left ring finger. Well, hell, so her boyfriend proposed, huh? Good for him. Unlike my ex, who'd decided he'd rather have sex with another woman, never mind that I was bound to walk in on them. Yep, my life is one never-ending cliché.

"Julia doesn't suffer fools gladly," I hear her tell Damian.

"And rock stars?" Damian grins back at her. "What does she think of them?

What the hell—? Why is he talking about me as if I am not in the room?

"Why don't you ask me directly?" I challenge.

Damian jerks his chin up, "Better still, how about I show you...?"

"Show me, huh?" I plant my hands on my hips, "You ain't got nothin' that I haven't seen before."

"Don't bet on it." The too-full-of-himself asshole stares down that hooked nose at me. His blue gaze narrows and those cerulean eyes seem to bore into my soul. A shiver runs up my spine. This man? His presence is potent. He leans in close and the heat of his body slams into my chest. All of my nerve endings seem to fire at once. Damn him. Why am I so drawn to him?

"I don't bet." I school my features into a mask of indifference. "I prefer certainties—a path to my goal, one from which I never veer."

"Is that a challenge?" He curls his lips, and that smirk... OMG. That upper lip of his seems to thin further. Combined with that puffy lower lip, that square jaw, the tendons of his gorgeous throat that stand out in relief and highlight the hollow at the base of his throat... Hell... He's lethal, all right. And too handsome to be real. Guys like him exist on the covers of magazines, in online memes that I drool over in secret. Nah, he occupies a different world, a rarefied space I have no intention of joining. So what, if I am attracted to him?

"Take it any way you like." I raise a shoulder. "I don't care."

There is an indrawn breath. I turn to find Amelie staring at me with huge eyes. She shakes her head, moves toward me, only her fiancé pulls her back. He whispers in her ear. She blinks and her cheeks turn pink. He pivots her around and they walk off, leaving me alone with this reprobate of the first order...aka, this big, grumpy male who glares at me with... Something like intent in his eyes.

The hair on the back of my neck rises. My stomach trembles. "Ah... I... I guess I should circulate among the guests. Uh... Don't want to seem impolite or anything, know what I mean?"

I turn to leave, take a step forward, then another. Okay... Maybe this is going to be fine. I'll just sidle out of here and— Warm fingers encircle my wrist. I am pulled around, and hauled up against the massive chest of the afore-mentioned douche canoe... My breasts are plastered against those ripped abs, which I can feel through the T-shirt he wears under his jacket. I gulp and my knees tremble... They bloody tremble. "Let go of me," I demand.

"Make me."

"What?" I narrow my gaze on that sinful-as-fuck face. "You release me right now or else —"

"Or else?" He peels back his lips and his teeth gleam against the tan of his sculpted features. At my silence, he continues, "You were saying —"

"That this is a misunderstanding." I huff. "I am not interested in you."

"Neither am I in you." He widens his stance.

"Doesn't seem that way from where I am, buster."

"How much control on your anger can you muster?" He tilts his head.

"Just because you think — mistakenly — that you're superior?" I flip my hair over my shoulder.

"I am going to break through your tightly controlled exterior."

"Wait." I gape, "Did you rhyme your words to mine?"

"So did you."

"No, I didn't."

"Yes, you did." He grins and my stupid heart stutters. It bloody stutters.

He peers down into my face, his blue eyes glittering. "So much sass," he growls. "I wonder how it would be to peel back the mask you wear to the world, to unveil the passion that lurks under the surface, to show you how it could be if the right man were to touch you in your secret places, the ones you think you have hidden away," his voice lowers to a hush, "but which I can see, feel, touch, suck..."

My core clenches. I swear my panties self-combust.

"I don't care for self-obsessed, insufferable, prats," I declare. "You've got the wrong woman."

He lowers his head until our eyelashes tangle. "I don't think so, baby."

"You're no Johnny," I stammer.

"Huh." His forehead wrinkles, "Dirty Dancing?"

"Oh," I blink, "you…you placed the reference?"

"Rock star, remember?" He relaxes his hold and I put some space between us.

"Like I could forget. Though, considering you are not on social media anymore, I'm beginning to think that you want the rest of the world to."

"You've been stalking me?" His lips curl.

"Of course, not."

"So how did you know that I pulled my social media accounts?"

"It was, uh…all over the news."

He stares at me.

I redden. "You couldn't miss it. Biggest news of the decade: the rock star who decided to disappear from the media's eye, cancelled his concert dates, decided to focus on —"

He tilts his head.

"On his personal life," I mutter.

He glares at me. I throw up my hands, "Yes, fine. Okay, so I did read up on everything I found, but only because I loved your earlier albums—" *Hello. Understatement of the year. I've downloaded all of his music and I listen to it on repeat. Not that I'd ever confess that to him.* "I admit, I wondered what happened, that you decided to go into hiding..." And how I'd love to help him find his mojo again. He can use his mojo on me anytime. In fact, he can use the other parts of him too, especially the one that's rumored to be eleven inches long. At least, meeting the rock star has improved my sense of humor. I snicker.

He frowns. "Do I look like I am in hiding?"

I am more interested in what you have hiding in your pants. Gah! I hope he's not a mind-reader. I step back. He grabs my shoulder and holds me in place, then lowers his head to my neck and sniffs.

"What the—?" I gasp, "Did you just sniff me?"

"Your scent," he rumbles. "It reminds me of clay and vanilla; soft and creamy, yet so spicy." He frowns, "Why the hell do you smell of playdoh?"

"None of your business."

"You work with clay," he accuses me. "Are you a potter?"

"I'm a clay artist, you idiot." In my own time, and when I'm not too busy being a nanny, but he doesn't need to know that. Not that being a nanny is not something to be proud of. It's just, he's an artiste…and famous, and hell, if I don't want to match up to his creative level.

"Hmm." He takes in my features, then leans in closer, closer. He drags his tongue up the side of my cheek.

My breath catches. That was bold, and weird, and okay, such a dominant gesture… My belly trembles. "You…you…."

"You taste bloody delicious." He smacks his lips. "Can I lick you again?"

Yes.

Yes.

"No." I splutter, then snap back my shoulders. "How dare you?" I blink at him. "How could you — ?"

"You can say it." He lowers his voice to a hush.

"What?"

"Tell me how much you want to touch me, put your hands on me." He smirks.

The blood rushes to my cheeks, my fingers tremble, and my toes curl. What the hell? One flirtatious glance from him and I'm melting into a puddle of slurry. One more second in his presence and I'll likely throw myself at him and beg him to play me like his favorite guitar. *Ugh, get your mind out of the gutter… Or rather, out of his pants.* A chuckle bubbles up and I swallow it down. "Keep your distance," I insist.

"Or what?"

"Or," I hold up my fists, "I'll unleash my Krav Maga powers on you."

"Krav Maga?" He blinks. "The form of self-defense favored by the Israeli secret service?"

I nod. "I've learned it, I uh…" I move back; he follows.

"Have you now?" He lowers his voice to a hush and my thighs clench. Whoa, this is not good. I shouldn't have this over-the-top reaction to a man I've just met… In real life. In reel life — on screen and online… Well, that's a different matter altogether. Not that I am going to reveal that. No way. Best I leave while I have some dignity intact.

I angle my body away from him, "I… I have to go."

"No," he snaps.

"What?"

"You're not leaving," he tells me.

"What the—?" My jaw drops. "Of course, I am."

"Oh?" He tilts his head and his eyes gleam. "Don't challenge me." He looks me up and down, and damn it, I'm instantly wet. My knees tremble, my toes curl, and a rush of heat sweeps up my spine. What the hell is this reaction to this… Full-of-himself, hot-as-Hades, larger-than-life male? And why did I just think all of those adjectives in one sentence? That's it, I've gotta get out of here. *Now.*

"Goodbye." I turn; then squeak when he grips my shoulder and yanks me around and to him until I am pressed to him from toe to thighs to chest.

Something hard stabs into the cradle of my core. I draw in a sharp breath. Hell, did I say eleven inches? Nope. No way. This is surely bigger. The man's seriously packing a monster something in his pants and nothing I've read has done any justice to the real thing. So, this is what they mean by *there are three of us in this relationship?* I chuckle, then turn it into a snort.

His frown deepens, but there's a twinkle of amusement in his eyes.

"I shall call you lover, and you're welcome."

"I'm not and... For what?"

"Not yet," he corrects me, "and...for the kiss." He smirks.

"What kiss?" I scowl, "And you have some ego presuming—"

He swoops down and closes his mouth over mine.

3

Damian

The sweet scent of eucalyptus fills my senses. The taste of her, like lush oranges, coats my tongue, fills my lips, drips into my bloodstream. My head spins and my groin hardens. I tilt my head, deepen the kiss. She moans at the back of her throat and the sound wraps around my ribcage. My heart begins to race. I drag her up, widen my stance to take her weight, then wrap my arms around her slim body and nip on her lower lip.

She gasps, opens her mouth, and I swoop in.

I dance my tongue over hers, splay the fingers of my palm across her waist, down to the curve of her butt. I squeeze her arse and she shudders. I suck on her essence, draw breath from her mouth, and offer her mine in return. I bend her backward and push my hips forward, intent on taking her, right here, right now. A growl rips out of me. I tear my mouth from hers, "Bedroom. Now."

She stiffens. "What did you say?"

"I don't repeat myself, sugar." I allow my lips to kick up. "I want inside of you."

"And I want..." Her lips—swollen with the pressure of my kiss—tremble. She flutters her eyelids… "...want…" She inhales.

"What is it?" I glare at her. "Say it."

Her gaze narrows, "...to kick you in the nuts."

I sense her bend her knee, and twist my body aside; I pivot her around at the same time, flip her over to my front so her hips are flush against my crotch. I wrench her arms in front of her and shackle her wrists with my fingers so she's imprisoned in the circle of my arms.

"You were saying?"

"I wasn't," she snarls. "And you're overstepping your boundaries."

I laugh, "I haven't even started. And isn't it time you were honest with yourself?"

"About what?"

"About how you find me irresistible. It's natural, after all."

"Is it?" She glances up at me.

I nod. "It's normal for someone like you to find my presence over-whelming."

"Overwhelming?" She opens and shuts her mouth.

"Yep." I take in her flushed features, the spark that lights up her green eyes, turning them into pools of gold-tinged fire. "I mean, it happens. After all, my charisma, my larger-than-life persona—"

"Your smaller than normal weenie, for which you are clearly compensating with your words."

I smirk. "Aww, come on baby, you and I both know that this—" I push my hips forward, ensuring that every inch of my throbbing length is imprinted against her curves, "is the opposite of small and unlike anything you've seen before."

"A status I mean to keep." Color smears her cheeks.

Is she blushing? She makes a choking sound in her throat… Okay… Oops, maybe not.

"You don't mean it." I smirk.

"I do," she says through gritted teeth, "and if you don't let go of me right now, I'll—"

"You'll?"

"Hey, you two. Are you coming into the kitchen to taste the dessert Amelie created?"

I jerk my chin toward the entrance to the kitchen, where Weston glances between us.

"Unhand me," she huffs.

"In my own time."

"Julia," Amelie calls out from next to Weston, "you okay?"

"Yes, she is," I reply.

"What the hell?" she splutters. "She's speaking to me, not you, you…you…"

"We'll be right there. Why don't you go along? We'll follow," I tell them.

"Jules?" Amelie frowns, "Should I wait?"

"Tell her you're fine, and that you'll be along soon enough," I command.

"Why should I lie?" She glowers.

"Because it's the truth," I lie.

"Not."

I click my tongue. "That's the first thing you're changing, this inability to speak your mind."

"Oh, I am more than capable of saying what's on my mind. And right now, you don't want to read my thoughts, trust me."

"On the contrary." I release her, take a step back, only to circle her wrist with my fingers and tug.

She squeaks, but her body follows my direction as I twirl her around to face me, bend her arm behind her, and curve her back. I lean in close enough for us to share breath. "I want to know every last thought of yours, your deepest most intimate secrets, your fears, your desires, what you hate, what you run from…" I frown. "What are you running from?" I lock my gaze with hers, peer into the depths of her green gaze, past the golden embers that crackle and swirl. My breath catches in my chest and sweat pops on my brow. *The hell? What am I doing? Why am I holding her captive?*

She can do as she wants. I don't know her. I have no claim on her. If I want a woman, all I need to do is snap my fingers and she'll throw herself on the floor, part her legs and offer up everything I desire… Except, I don't. The thrill of success, of fame, of easy lays and meaningless shags that took a piece of my soul with every inter-action… All of it pales in comparison to the vital, feisty woman I hold in my arms. How curious. How not what I need right now. What an irritation this is getting to be.

Why the hell had I kissed her in the first place?

I release her and she stumbles back. "Not that I care." I flick my fingers over the front of my leather jacket. "Have a nice life." I brush past her, head toward where Amelie and Weston track my progress. "Your friend was just coming." No pun unintended. I compose my features into a polite facade.

"Rockstar," her voice reaches me.

I swagger forward.

"Aren't you forgetting something?"

Likely not. I always pay my debts, never let another get in the way, nor play with my emotions, so no, I don't think I am. I move forward.

Footsteps sound behind me, then she draws abreast.

"Stop," she demands.

I chuckle. No one tells me what to do. Definitely not my friends. Absolutely not this chit of a woman I've just met.

"If you don't, you'll never find out about the proposition I have for you."

4

Julia

"Proposition, huh?" He stiffens, then pivots and fixes me with the full force of his blue eyes. Storm clouds before the rain falls, the depths of the sea that I had gazed into, on a trip to Byron Bay. I blink and the mirage clears.

"Wouldn't you like to know?" I force out the words through a throat gone dry.

A slow smirk curls his lips. He bends to thrust his face into mine, "You tell me, babe." He drags a finger down my cheek, "Would I?"

"I think…" I tip up my chin, "you're intrigued." I tug on my earlobe, then shuffle my feet.

"Is that what this is about?" He hooks his finger in the V of my blouse, "You trying to catch my attention? If so, you have it, sugar."

What am I doing? I should have let him walk away, then left here and begun job hunting in earnest. I should be searching for my next job as a nanny, while working on my clay artistry skills. And then what? A lifetime of taking care of others' children…? Not that I don't thrive on that. When I am with little ones, something raging inside of me quietens. This need to give, to nurture, that is so much a part of me, finds an outlet.

Other girls dream of being doctors and pilots… Me? I want kids of my own, a large family, a husband… None of which is looking likely very soon, so… Considering I caught the eye of this… Man, who is definitely out of my comfort zone… My one chance to live voraciously.

To throw caution to the wind and indulge myself in all the ways he'd offered. I mean, why not? I've walked the straight and narrow, and look where that has gotten me? Single, with no prospect of a relationship in sight, while my friends are settling down. Not that it is any reason to offer myself up to this god-like man… Ugh, I am pathetic, putting him up on a pedestal.

So, he is a rock star…and tabloid fodder, a face that launched a thousand memes… And me, the stupid woman who tilts her chin up and declares, "One night."

"What?" he frowns.

"You heard me." Thank god, my voice doesn't tremble, "Give me one night; you and me."

He takes in my features. "You're serious?"

I curl my fingers into a fist at my side, "Why? Are you scared about the earlier reaction you had to me?"

"Reaction, huh?" He tilts his head, "I am sorry to tell you, babe, that kiss did nothing for me."

"So what was that column in your pants when you were plastered to me?"

He looks me up and down, "A physiological reaction brought on by my nearness to a woman, who," he smirks, "just happened to be you, in this situation."

Jerk.

He chuckles, and heat flushes my cheeks. "That's not true and you know it," I mutter.

"Is that right?" he drawls.

I draw in a breath, then jut out my chin, "Prove it."

"What?"

"Prove that you didn't feel anything when you kissed me." *What are you doing? Did you just ask him to kiss you again? What the hell, you complete idiot.* But do you blame me? That kiss...was something. And how the hell can he deny that it affected him? Maybe I'd imagined that crazy reaction to him. The only way to be sure is to kiss him again, right?

His glance drops to my mouth, "You sure?"

No.

No.

"Yes." I chuckle, "Wouldn't be asking otherwise, now would I?"

"I don't know." He leans in, gets in my space. "It seems to me, you are a sucker for punishment."

"And you're avoiding the challenge."

"Julia?" Amelie calls out, "You guys coming?"

"Two minutes." I hold up my hand.

He smirks. "It will take us a lot longer than that to finish."

I peer at him from under my eyelashes, "Considering you haven't even started—"

He lowers his head until his lips are almost on mine. Almost. His shoulders block out the sight of the room. Heat from his big body pours over me, cocoons me, pulls me in closer, closer. Or maybe it's he who closes the remaining distance between us. Our noses bump, our eyelashes entwine. His lips part; I lick mine.

Then he straightens, "Sorry, not sorry, babe. You're not my type. No offense." He turns away, heads into the kitchen.

I blink, sway for a second. *What the hell? How dare he?* He's toying with me, is he? I pivot, march into the kitchen, "You stop right there, Rockstar—" Six faces turn to glance at me.

"Uh..." I flush. "Hey…" I clear my throat, "I mean, hello. I mean, I didn't mean it that way. I mean…" I bury my face in my hands. "Forget it. Rewind. Maybe it's best I leave... Come back in and start all over again," I mumble, then backtrack from the scene of my humiliation.

"Jules." Amelie hurries over, and grabs my arm. "Everyone, meet my friend Julia." She turns me to face the crowd of interested people.

There is a chorus of hellos.

I raise a limp hand, "Hi." I wave. "I'm Julia. Call me Jules," I shuffle my feet.

"Lovely to meet you, Jules," a woman with dark hair flowing to her waist calls out. "It's good to have you with us for Christmas."

I jerk my chin, "It's, ah, nice to be here too." I cringe. Nice? Couldn't I have come up with some other adjective? Anything else to enliven the status of my boring life?

Thankfully, the rest don't seem to notice. They turn away to talk amongst themselves. Everyone, including the rock star, who turns his back on me. Is that good or bad? At least, I am not at the receiving end of those glowering glares of his…the panty-melting kind, I mean… Which, I admit, I miss already. Damn it, why am I so shaken? I rub my fingers on the fabric of my jeans-clad thigh.

"I think it's best I leave while I still have some dignity intact," I mumble. "Not that I have any left. What the hell was I thinking earlier?"

"I don't think you were thinking at all." Amelie chuckles.

"You're right about that." I scowl. I had reacted to the presence of the dominating, larger-than-life male who prowls over to join the other men clustered on the other side of the island. And why the hell am I still watching him. "I… I shouldn't have come."

"What nonsense." Amelie winds her arm through mine, "I want you here with me. After all, it's not every day that a woman gets engaged, huh?" She holds up her hand and I stare at the sapphire that glitters on the ring around her finger.

"It's gorgeous," I say sincerely, even as my heart twists inside of my chest. Shit, I will not be envious, will not. She deserves all the happiness in the world. I turn and throw my arms around her. "Congratulations." I squeeze her shoulders. "How did you meet him?"

"We met at Summer's wedding, then ended up double-booking the same cottage over the festive season."

"No," I gasp.

"Yes." She nods. "I thought the sparks between Weston and I were pretty explosive, but I've changed my mind."

"Oh?" I lean back, peer into her face, "Why's that?"

"Because, the chemistry between you and Damian is enough to set this house on fire." She stares at me meaningfully.

"Hmm." I glance away, unable to meet her eyes. There's something between me and the rock star, all right. Some crazy connection that's throwing me off kilter and making me act so out of character. *One night.* Had I actually propositioned him? What the hell had I been thinking? My cheeks flush. Good thing he'd snubbed me, huh?

The same woman who'd welcomed me earlier totters over to us in her stilettos. "Hi," she says in a breathless voice, "I'm Isla."

"Jules." I shake her hand.

She pulls me in for a hug, "Soooo nice to meet you." Her embrace is warm and effusive.

"Hey," I pat her back, "so, you're Amelie's friend, huh?"

"As are you." She leans back, her face wreathed in a big smile, "Which makes us friends-in-law, huh?" She giggles.

I blink. Wow, the optimism pouring off of this woman… No wonder, she and Amelie get along. Unlike me… The cynical, non-believer in love, or men, for that matter. Hell, I so don't belong here. "I need a drink," I declare.

"That's my girl." Isla grabs my arm and drags me to the corner of the room…opposite from where the rest of the crowd—including the rock star—is huddled. "What do you fancy?" She rubs her hands together.

"Why don't you let me do this?" I reach for the bottle of tequila, pour it into the blender, follow it up with the lime juice, the orange liqueur. I add in the agave and the syrup, followed by kosher salt, then blend it all together.

"You've done this before," Isla comments.

"Yep." The one thing good about being in Australia... I had partied my ass off…when I was not working. Which had been a surprise. I was—am—a loner, but being in a foreign country had been freeing. I could let go of my inhibitions. Somehow, it had felt like I wouldn't be judged.

I pour the mixture into the margarita glasses that Isla helpfully provides, then top them off with garnish. "Here you go."

"Ooh, this looks good." Isla gulps down a mouthful, then smacks her lips, "Woman, I almost came from that sip."

I giggle. "If only it were that easy."

"Tell me about it." She shakes her head, "Have you ever come with someone fingering you?"

"Never," I shake my head.

We both turn to Amelie, whose cheeks redden.

"Oh, don't even ask her." Isla tosses her hair over her shoulder. "Bitch has a new fiancé, who is a surgeon, so he's clearly good with his fingers, in more ways than one."

"Who's good with his fingers?" A woman in a pink onesie with glitter down the front saunters over to join us.

"Nothing you need to worry about, Summer," Isla scoffs. She leans in close to me. "And another who clearly has had too many O's, courtesy of her rich bastard of a husband," she says in a whisper loud enough for the rest of them to hear.

"Not my fault that the Seven are men of many talents." Summer chuckles.

"The Seven?" I tilt my head.

"That's what the media calls the guys." Amelie nods toward the men. "And that includes your rock star." She smirks.

"Not my rock star."

"Oh, are we talking about the encounter between Damian and Julia?" Another woman, a brunette in a perfectly-tailored dress, glides over to us.

"We are not," I snap.

"Yep," Isla confirms.

"Totally." Amelie nods.

"Gosh, that was some kiss, huh?" Summer fans herself.

Heat sears the back of my neck. Of course, they'd all noticed that. I offer the brunette a glass of the cocktail, and she declines. "I'm sticking to water." She points to her glass. "I'm Victoria, by the way."

"Are you also pregnant?" I joke.

"I am, actually." She nods.

I splutter, then cough and place my drink back on the island. "Jeez, sorry."

"No worries." She chuckles, "I'm still getting used to the idea, myself."

I glance at her flat belly, "Are you in the first trimester?"

"I am." She nods. "I'd have preferred for the others not to know until later, but the Seven are so close…"

"Or maybe they just like to pretend that way," Isla scoffs. "The way they get into arguments with each other, you'd think they were enemies."

"Wanker," a male voice rings out from behind us as if to punctuate her words.

There's the sound of something crashing into wood. I glance up to find Damian and another man as tall as he is, with dark hair and piercing eyes, engaged in arm wrestling.

"The other one's called Sinclair; he belongs to me," Summer chirps. "Who do you think will win, by the way? Yours or mine?"

"Mine," I reply, then press my lips together. "I mean, he's not mine." I jerk my chin toward the rock star."

"Freudian slip, huh?" Isla exchanges a glance with Summer.

"Freudian nothing," I scoff. "I'm simply punch drunk with jet lag, is all." And maybe a little bit worried about finding my next job. Okay, I am very worried about my situation. The money in my bank account will barely stretch to a few more weeks. No way, am I going to borrow from my family. My mum had warned me against taking off with my boyfriend. I'd ignored her, to my detriment.

Wouldn't she love to say I told you so, now. My shoulders sag. That's not fair. She's not like that, but I'm too embarrassed to tell her. As for borrowing from Amelie? Nope. She is already doing so much for me. No, I need to find a job quickly, though the agencies I'd called prior to travelling home to London had warned me there weren't any live positions at the moment. None had sounded very hopeful about an assignment coming up soon either. And hell, if I don't need a job quickly.

"Or maybe you're reeling from that kiss, huh?" Isla chortles.

I groan. "Can we pretend that never happened?"

"Nope." Summer laughs.

Isla chuckles. "Remember, I've seen each of the women here

succumb to one of the Seven. Once they set their sights on you, you don't stand a chance."

"And you?" I frown. "What about you?"

"I'm busy building my wedding planning business." She gathers her long hair over one shoulder. "I don't have time for such shenanigans."

"Like we did?" Amelie snorts. "But trust me, when you know… you know."

"That's how it was for you and Weston, huh?" I ask.

"I met him and I had this sinking feeling…" She presses a hand to her stomach. "I was hot and cold all at once, know what I mean?"

"Isn't that normal in London weather?" I say dryly.

She laughs, "Oh, trust me, it's a completely different sensation." She looks me up and down, "Is that how you felt when you saw Damian?"

"Nope," I lie, then chug down the rest of my margarita, cough, and place the now-empty, soup-dish proportioned glass back on the counter.

"Prove it," Isla challenges.

"What?"

"Show us that whatever is between the two of you didn't affect you."

"What are you talking about?" I half laugh.

"You heard me, girlfriend." She taps a finger on her chin. "Demonstrate that he doesn't make your knees go weak and your pussy all moist."

"Isla," I scold. "Mind your, uh, p's and q's."

Isla chokes on her drink.

Amelie slow blinks, "Keep up the bad jokes and you'll have won all of us over in no time."

"All of whom?"

She makes a circular motion with her fingers, "The collective."

"Is there a collective?"

"Given you've already caught Daddy D's eye, I'd say you are on your way to becoming one of us," Victoria adds.

"Daddy D?" I frown, "Why do you call him that?" That's not how the media refers to him, at least.

Summer, Victoria and Amelie exchange glances. Then Summer pipes up, "It's because he's the oldest of the Seven."

"He's not that old." I scoff, "He's what, thirty-two?" That's what his Wikipedia page indicates. What? So, I sneaked a peak, or two, at it.

"He's closer to thirty-five," Amelie offers.

Isla wrinkles her nose. "Though you have to admit, the years sit well on him. Imagine you could be bratty with him," she waggles her eyebrows, "and Daddy D would be only too happy to dole out the punishments, huh? Bet you'd enjoy that too."

I throw up my hands, "Seriously, you guys need to stop with the trying to get us together." Speaking of, I turn back to where Damian and Sinclair are arm-wrestling.

Damian's neck ripples with tendons. He leans in, jaw clenched. The biceps of his arm bulge and he growls deep in his throat. A shiver runs down my spine; moisture laces my core.

Gosh, the rock star going all caveman-like is bloody hot. And somehow, so different from what I expected him to be. His social media used to be about him on stage performing, or recording in his studio, or else on the red carpet, accompanying one celebrity or another. There isn't much more of his personal life in the scene I am looking at right now. So why does it feel so intimate? I am merely a stranger who ran into him by chance. Providence. Kismet. Whatever you want to call it. *And what are you going to do about it, huh? You going to take fate into your own hands and do something with it?*

Damian's shoulders stretch the width of his T-shirt. A vein throbs at his temple, then he smashes Sinclair's fist into the surface of the island. "I won," he fist-pumps in the air.

Sinclair straightens in his suit, which seems to have been tailor-made for him. There is so much designer wear in the room—the kind you don't normally see on catwalks because they are created exclusively for the kind of men that these Seven are.

"Where are the others?" I frown.

"Others?" Isla enquires.

"You all referred to Seven. I count four in the room."

"Baron's the secret one. No one knows about his whereabouts," Summer muses.

"And Arpad and the Father aren't here," Victoria supplies.

"Hold on." I turn to her, "Did you say Father?"

Isla nods. "Edward's a priest," she replies. "The incident impacted him so much, it urged him to find his calling, apparently."

"The incident?" I tilt my head.

Amelie nods, "The Seven were kidnapped together and held for ransom when they were in their pre-teens. And that kind of shared experience… It binds you together for life. Know what I mean?"

"I let you win this round. Doesn't mean I'll go easy on you next time," Sinclair's cold voice cuts through the space.

Damian chortles in response.

"Excuses, excuses." He pokes a finger in Sinclair's chest, "You're getting soft, you wanker. Admit it, the old ball and chain is weighing you down."

"Perhaps it's giving me a purpose?" Sinclair glances past him at Summer. His features light up in a smile that's so open, so real, so everything, that my heart thumps in my chest.

He prowls past Damian, and heads to her. Summer meets him half-way and the two kiss.

The women behind me ooh and aah. A ball of emotion blocks my throat. Damn it, what's wrong with me? It's just a man kissing his wife, and pulling her to him and ravaging her mouth thoroughly. Jesus, that's hot as hell, and now I feel like a voyeur. I glance past them to where Damian watches, a bored look in his eyes.

"Go get a room, you guys," he taunts.

Sinclair straightens, then grins down at Summer. "I think I might do just that." He swoops down and tosses her up over his shoulder.

She yelps, "Sinner, what the hell?"

Sinclair raps her on her backside and she squeaks, "Sinner, behave."

"Not what you told me the last time I took you over my knee, my darling wife."

My cheeks heat.

He marches past me, carrying the now-giggling Summer. No doubt, to make hot, heavy love to her. My belly knots and sensations ripple down my spine. Damn it, there is way too much chemistry between the couples in this room, not to mention all that testosterone from the gathered men.

"Well, look who we have here." A new male voice sounds behind me. I turn and have to look up, all the way up, to meet the piercing gaze of another man.

5

———————

Julia

"I'm Arpad." He holds out his hand.

"You're one of the Seven." I place my palm in his much larger one.

"My reputation precedes me?" He smirks, then bends to kiss my knuckles. I blink. Gosh, each one of the Seven is more lethal than the last. I mean, put them all together, and honestly, no woman stands a chance. It's like having a range of delectable thoroughbreds preening and vying for attention. Not that any of them are horses… Well, okay, they are stallions, all of them, especially the man who's glowering at me from the sidelines. Continuing to ignore Damian, I focus my attention on Arpad, "So what are you doing here?"

"Yeah, something I want to know as well." A hard voice sounds from somewhere behind and above me. Heat sears my back, curls around me, rolls straight down to the triangle of heated flesh between my legs. I shiver.

Arpad looks from me to the man standing behind me. "Rockstar," he drawls, "something bothering you?"

"You," Damian snaps.

I gasp, turn to shoot the rock star a glance.

He glares at Arpad, who chuckles. "I see all that time you've spent on R&R isn't doing much for your disposition. Not that I blame you, considering your Christmas single flopped."

Damian growls. He actually growls. "Fuck off, Beauchamp."

Arpad's lips twist, "If you fancy a fight, I'd be only too happy to oblige."

"Oh, yeah?" Damian steps up to stand chest to chest with the other guy. "Don't think I'll back down."

"I'm counting on it." Arpad flicks open the buttons on his long-sleeved shirt, then rolls up his cuffs.

Damian shrugs out of his leather jacket—Why the hell did he put it back on?—and hands it to me. "Are you really going to do this?" I hiss.

He doesn't reply. Typical. I grab his jacket— Why the hell am I doing that? I should simply throw it down on the floor and walk away. Instead, I slip it on. It's big enough to dwarf me, and his scent… Oh, his spicy, dark essence envelops me, and I swear, my ovaries spasm.

"Step back," Damian orders.

"What?"

He turns, leans in toward me, and I skitter back.

His lips kick up in that smirk that would give Billy Idol a run for his money… And Damian Savage has far more presence.

"Good." He nods. "Now stay there."

"What the—?" I scowl, take a step forward, when Isla grabs my hand.

"Stay," she insists.

"But."

"Trust me." She lowers her voice, "You don't want to poke the beast right now."

I stare at her, "You make him sound like some primitive species."

"Which is what they are. Primal to the core, especially when it comes to their women."

"You have much experience?"

"Only from the outside," she firms her lips. "It's also why I've sworn never to be mixed up with them."

"Famous last words," Amelie drawls. "That's what I told myself, and now look." She waves her left hand in the air.

Isla makes a gagging sound. "I'm so tired of all my friends falling for one of the Seven, which is why I am so pleased you are here, Julia." She hooks her arm with mine.

"You are?"

She nods. "You're not going to get caught up with that self-entitled rock star."

"I'm not?"

She shakes her head. "You have too much common sense to become another of his conquests."

I frown, "You mean, I'm not his type?"

"You are the kind of woman who'd rather take things into her own hands, and set your own terms."

"So, I should go after him, rather than the other way around?" I muse.

"All I'm saying is, don't give in too easily," Isla urges. "Rock star or not, make him work before allowing him close to you."

"Only, don't think it's easy to get one of the Seven out of your mind, once you get involved with them." Victoria slips onto one of the barstools, places her glass of water on the island. "I set out to seduce Saint—but then I fell too." She jerks her chin in the direction of the large glowering man who stands with his arms crossed over his chest.

"I don't see you protesting much, girlfriend," Isla huffs.

"At some point, I realized it was best to give in and enjoy the ride." Amelie looks at me. "Know what I mean?"

"Are you trying to tell me something?" I frown.

"What I am saying…" Victoria smiles—with that soul-deep contented smile that only those who have found their other halves seem to wear like it is some kind of secret, which I admit, from where I am standing, it is.

"You're saying...?" I prompt her.

"That you best not underestimate what entangling in any form with the Seven means," Victoria replies. "Once you step into their circle of influence, you won't be able to catch your breath. The force of their personalities will overwhelm you, and by the time you come to your senses, it'll be too late."

I clear my throat, "You make it sound like they are some kind of cult."

"Not a cult." Her features grow serious. "But they are a tribe. These men are wild beasts who wear a veneer of sophistication so they may pretend to fit into society."

O-k-a-y.

"They may fight with each other, but because of the incident, they'll always be united in ways we can never understand," Amelie adds.

"So," I turn to where Damian and Arpad circle each other in the space that the rest of the men have cleared, "they are still hurting from the trauma of the past?"

She nods. "Which means, when the right woman comes along... Well, let's just say, it accelerates the healing process in a way that is life changing."

Damian throws a blow, Arpad ducks, then drops down and kicks the rock star's legs out from under him. I draw in a breath, take a step forward, but Damian springs up to his feet and lands his fist in Arpad's pretty face. Blood explodes from Arpad's nose and he staggers back. Damian cracks his neck, raises his arms in mock victory, "You're going soft, Beauchamp."

Arpad shakes his head, says something unintelligible.

Damian laughs, "Guess the round is mine then."

"Now's your chance," Isla coaxes.

"What?"

"If you want to take your future into your own hands, instead of allowing the Seven to get to you, this is your opportunity."

Too late. Damian has already made an impact on me. The chemistry between us is off-the-charts crazy. She's right about one thing, though. I am done being an onlooker to my own life. This time, I am going to steer my own fate. I am going to throw caution to the wind, live life to the fullest, and then walk away with my ego and my heart intact.

One last dalliance before I find a good man to settle down with and live my quiet, boring life.

I hitch my bag over my shoulder, then walk forward, still wearing his jacket. "Hey, Rockstar," I call out. "This is your last chance to accept my challenge. You in or out? Do you have the balls?"

Weston whistles.

Saint snickers.

Damian jerks his head toward me, "Balls, huh? I'll show you my balls all right, sugar. I—"

That's when Arpad closes the distance and lands a punch to Damian's head.

6

Damian

I come to with a start to find I am on my back on the floor of the kitchen of Weston's apartment. "Bloody hell." The pain ripples down my spine. I raise my hand and my knuckles throb; my shoulder screams in protest. "What the hell happened?" I open my eyes and her green gaze clashes with mine. Delicately arched eyebrows, an upturned nose, pink lips that curve in a bow so perfect it should be illegal. She flicks out her tongue to lick her lips and I feel the tug all the way to my groin. "Juliet?"

"You are no Romeo," she scoffs.

"You don't know that yet."

"I know that you can't hold a fight." She frowns.

"Only because you distracted me," I sneer.

"Not my fault that you have the attention span of a child."

"Child is the father of man, after all," I mutter. *What the hell? Did I just say that out loud?* Clearly, that blow to my head ruffled up my brains, not to mention my thinking process.

"And Daffodils are my favorite flower," she grouses.

"Not bad. You got the Wordsworth reference." I smirk.

Damn it, my cheeks hurt, and clearly, I am a bloody mess.

"Didn't take you for the poetic kind." She sniffs. "And, actually, I do prefer the Bard to Wordsworth."

I open my mouth and she frowns. "Don't say the obvious."

"You don't know what I was going to say," I point out.

"I do," she grumbles, "and yes, my mother loved his plays. She wanted to call me Juliet. My dad thought Juliet a bit much, so they settled for Julia." She smiles a little. "It's one of the things my mom and I like to do together."

"What else do you do together?" I peer into her face. "Other than read Shakespeare?"

"None of your business."

"You sure?" I look her up and down. "After all, you're the one who challenged me, despite being a stranger."

"Hardly a stranger," she huffs.

"Just because you see me on tabloid headlines doesn't mean you know me."

"Just because I look like the quiet, mousy kind—

"You, and mousy? Have you seen yourself in a mirror?" I laugh, then wince when my right eye throbs, "Ouch."

"Frozen peas." She glances up, speaks to someone out of my line of sight, "Is there a bag of frozen something to put on his bruised eye?"

"Arpad, asshole," I groan. "I am going to get you for this, mofo."

Arpad thrusts his face into my line of sight, "Looking none the worse for wear, Savage." He grins, "Apparently, I upgraded your pretty boy looks."

"Apparently, you don't value your life." I swipe out with my fist; he swerves.

"My, my, getting beaten didn't do much for your temperament, I see," he muses.

"Sod off." I lurch up to sitting position, the world sways, my stomach churns, and... No fucking way, am I going to be sick. I shake my head and the ringing in my ears worsens. How the hell did I manage to get myself into this situation?

"Here, let me." Julia reaches over with a bag of frozen peas in her hand. I snatch it from her, hold it to my aching eye. The pain instantly recedes. I pin her with my open eye. "This is all your fault," I glare at her. "If you hadn't called out to me, I wouldn't have turned and given this joker here an opening."

"Don't flatter yourself." Arpad chuckles, "I would have beaten you anyway, though I confess, your girlfriend's presence sure helped distract you."

"Not my girlfriend," I protest.

"He's the last person I'd choose for a boyfriend," she snaps at the same time.

I frown up at her, "Not the impression I got earlier, babe."

"The proposition I had in mind was not of the relationship variety."

"Oh?" I lower the bag of peas, "Funny, I'd put you down for the rainbows and unicorns and shit kind of woman."

"Umm." Arpad stares between us, "You two sure you don't want to borrow one of Weston's spare rooms? He has enough of them, god knows. And by the way, do you promise to name your first born after me?"

"Shut up," I say at the same time as her.

She scowls at me.

I glower back at her.

Arpad rises to his feet. "Uh, I guess I need to see a man about a dog."

"Don't come back in a hurry," I call out after his retreating figure.

"I think Victoria needs me." Saint prowls away in Arpad's wake.

"I'll be right outside, Jules," Isla calls out. "You need any help—"

"She won't," I snap.

"Uh, okay," Isla says brightly, "but, you know, if you want back-up…"

"I don't." Julia turns to her. "In the state that the rock star is right now, I doubt he poses any danger to me."

What the hell? How dare she dismiss me that easily?

"Hold on a second." I lean forward, then groan when my hurt eye chooses that moment to set off a series of spasms that thud against my brain. "Ow," I groan.

"Like I said," she nods to her friend, "I think my virtue is safe for the moment." She smiles.

Isla pivots and leaves.

"I'll show you how safe you are with me," I reach for her with my free hand.

She scoots back, shakes her head. "Now, now, you're hardly in a position to misbehave, Rockstar. At least, wait for the swelling of your eye to go down."

"The only thing swollen is between my legs, and trust me, it's not going away. As for anything going down..."

She sucks in a breath and flushes, then shakes her head. "Stop joking around."

"Who's joking? I'm being very serious." I look her up and down. "Since I met you, you've been a pain in my side, and in other parts, and by the way, that proposition of yours? It's unacceptable."

"It is?"

"Yeah." I nod. "I don't need a night. Give me an hour and I'll draw enough orgasms from you to last you a lifetime."

"My, my," she scoffs, "someone has a big ego."

"Not the only thing that is big —"

She opens her mouth to respond.

I raise my hand. "And you know it's true, considering you've been stalking me online."

She reddens. "I haven't."

I click my tongue. "Don't lie now, and by the way, the answer is yes."

"Yes?"

"To the question you have in your mind."

"Which is?"

"That it's eleven inches."

She drops her gaze to my crotch. "So, *not* in competition with Dirk Diggler, then?"

"Very good, though if there were a competition, I'd win." I nod. "Not that I'd have expected you to have watched Boogie Nights."

"Because I'm female?" She scowls.

"No, because it's considered porn in polite circles, and also, you're welcome."

She jerks her chin up, her cheeks fiery. "For what?" She clears her throat.

"For the chance to touch it." I smirk.

"Aargh," she makes a gagging sound, but her cheeks go pink, "As if I want to do that." She swipes her hair over her shoulder.

"Sure, you do." I toss the bag of peas aside, hold out my hand.

She glances at my palm, and her features grow wary.

"I won't bite," I assure her.

"I wouldn't bet on it."

"You're right," I tilt my head, "I can't make that promise where you are concerned. In fact, I am sure by the time the hour is over, I'll have eaten you out many times over."

"What the—" She throws up her hands. "Can't believe you said that out aloud."

"Believe it, baby, and I am just getting started."

She stares, then firms her lips and shakes her head. "Maybe this was a bad idea."

"Maybe you're getting cold feet."

"Maybe..." Her gaze narrows. "Maybe I finally realized how uncivilized a man you are."

"Maybe that's what attracts you to me." I reach toward her.

She evades me, then springs up to her feet.

I grab her ankle, and she tumbles straight into my lap.

"What the—?" she splutters, her hair about her shoulders.

"Well, hello there," I purr.

She pushes against my chest.

I wrap my arms more tightly around her. "Lost your nerve, hmm? Didn't take you for a coward."

She tips up her chin and her green eyes glow with an inner fire. There she is. There's the fighting spirit in her that has made this encounter so much more enjoyable from the beginning.

"Didn't take you for a…a…"

"Handsome, charismatic, larger-than-life personality?" I offer.

"More like an obnoxious, over-the-top, sleazy douche."

I allow another smirk to curl my lips. "I think the lady doth protest too much."

"Do you always speak in such archaic prose?"

"Only when I am in your presence." I chuckle.

"Hmm." She peers up at me from her position in my lap, and yeah, we are both on the floor of Weston's kitchen, considering I'd gone down like a light when Arpad, that bastard, had KO'd me—a favor which, by the way, I am going to return with compounded interest. You can count on it.

"Well?" I tilt my head. "You have until I count to five."

"Five?" She wrinkles up her forehead. "What do you mean?"

"Stay and be kissed, or run away, and we'll forget that you chickened-out on your so-called proposition."

She pouts, her lips twisting into a sexy 'O' that has my groin tightening further.

"Five." I start the countdown.

She scans my features, her gaze landing on my lips. "I think…" she swallows, "I think that—"

"Four."

She licks her lips, glances left, then right.

"Three."

She wriggles her bottom against the thickness that tents my groin.

A growl rips up my chest. "Two."

I lean in; she gulps.

I hold her gaze and her pupils dilate. Her chest heaves. The pulse at the base of her throat increases the intensity of its pace.

I lower my mouth to hers, stop when there's less than a millimeter that separates us. "One." I press my lips to hers. That's when my phone pings.

7

Julia

"Your phone." I gasp and sidle back.

"Fuck that." He swoops down, clamps his fingers on my neck. "You had your chance to leave, Flower. You lost it; now, you're mine."

"And you are what, a cave man?" I huff.

"Only when it comes to you." His eyebrows knit; he scrutinizes my features. "What is it about you, that makes me want to tear through your tightly controlled veneer and expose the passion that seethes under the surface?"

"Who uses verbs like seethe?" I scoff.

"I'm a song writer, and a rock star, remember?"

"You forgot the 'has-been' part," I retort.

His jaw tics and a vein throbs at his temple. His blue eyes blaze with silver sparks that flare and coil, then fade away, leaving a mirrored coldness in their wake.

"So, the flower has thorns, huh?" He peruses my features. "I have you in my grasp. May as well make the most of it, hmm?"

He lowers his face. I turn my head, or try to, only to find I can't move, because he tightens his grasp on my neck, so I have no choice but to meet his kiss head on. I clamp my lips shut.

He swipes his tongue across my mouth. A shiver runs down my spine, my belly trembles, my limbs shake, and damn him, but this nearness to him… It's potent—a drugging, mind-melding kind of force that draws me to him, that coaxes me to open myself up, throw myself at him and ask him to lick the lips between my legs too. Gah, what the hell? Now I am thinking in pornographic detail, something I don't normally indulge in. Clearly, it's his proximity that's affecting me. "Please," I whisper against his beautiful mouth. "Please …"

He brings up his other hand to cup my cheek. "What is it?"

Heat sinks into my blood, arrows to the space around my heart. My core clenches, my toes curl… Jesus, somehow his gentleness is even more potent than his brute force.

I raise my hand, wrap my fingers around his wide wrist. The rough hairs abrade my skin. Goosebumps pop on my forearms.

He stays quiet, his lips so close to mine that if I lean in a millimeter more our noses will bump. He stares into my eyes, holding my gaze, searching inside of me, finding the parts of me I have never before revealed to the world.

"Please," I whisper. "Please…don't."

"Don't what?"

"Don't stop."

He closes the distance between us, fits his mouth to mine. I open my lips, and he thrusts his tongue inside, draws on my breath, sucks on me like I am the last note in one of his songs. I close my eyes, tilt my chin up, grip his shoulder and move in closer. Push my breasts into his chest. A shudder grips him. He tears his mouth from mine, "Leave here with me."

He meets my gaze and my mouth dries; my belly trembles. How can his smirk be so hot, so filled with a promise that I don't dare acknowledge?

"I don't do this normally," I tip up my chin. "I'm not that kind of a woman."

Why the hell do I care what he thinks of me? I'd all but told him that I was up for a fling, so why the hell am I delaying now?

"What kind?" He frowns.

"You know… The kind who sleeps around?" I mumble.

"There's no chance of either of us sleeping tonight." His lips curl.

"Oh."

"Keep your mouth open and I won't be able to resist stuffing it." His grin widens. "And it won't be with Christmas pudding, either."

My core clenches and my pulse thuds at my temples. Why the hell is his crudeness such a turn on?

He drags my hand to his crotch, massages his impressive length.

I squeeze his hardness and he draws in a sharp breath.

"It's gonna feel even better when I'm inside of you," he growls.

"I really never jump into bed with strangers," I feel compelled to say.

"And yet it was you who proposed we spend a night together," he points out.

"About that..." My cheeks heat, "I've never done that before; this is the first time I've been this bold."

"I know," he rumbles.

"You do?"

He nods, "But then, you also know a lot about me, don't you?" He stares into my eyes and heat flushes my cheeks.

"You…you're right," I mumble. "I may have, uh, had a small crush on you."

He stares.

"Okay, fine, so maybe I followed your coverage in the press."

He clicks his tongue.

"Fine, fine." I throw up my hands. "I stalked your social media. I know you have a type that you go for."

"What type is that?"

"Blonde, curvy, willowy."

He looks me up and down, "You'll do."

"Jerk." I scramble away and jump to my feet. "Forget this conversation ever happened."

"A bit late for that, Flower."

I grab my backpack from where I'd dropped it on the floor earlier, then turn to leave.

He wraps his fingers around my ankle again. "One hour," he repeats. "Give me one hour, and if, at the end of it, you are still standing, you can leave."

I glance down to where his thick fingers shackle me. "Is that a threat?"

"A promise."

"One hour?" I purse my lips.

"Starting now." His eyes gleam. He releases his grip on my ankle and rises to his feet…and keeps rising.

"Just one hour?" I search his features.

"That's all I'm asking for." He holds out his hand. He sounds sincere; bet it's all an act though. I stare down at his hand, then back at his face.

"Well?" he coaxes, lips curved in a smile that could charm the panties off of many a woman. And has. The bad news—my knickers are damp too. Damn it, I can't accept. And if I refuse? I'll never forgive myself for passing up the opportunity to find out what it was to be brought to orgasm by Big D alphahole himself. Besides, I'm the one who'd started this insane sequence of events. I can't back out now, can I? I jerk my chin.

"Is that a yes?"

I nod again.

"I need to hear you say it."

"Yes." I swallow, reach for his hand, when he pulls back.

"I changed my mind."

"What?" I blink, as he bends his knees, then scoops me up and throws me over his shoulder.

"Hey," I squeal, "put me down."

"You promised me an hour. Now we do things my way."

"What if I don't…want to?"

He stalks toward the door of the kitchen. "Trust me, Flower. I promise, you won't regret it."

8

Julia

"Famous last words." I glance around the apartment on the 65th floor of The Shard. Bloody hell, this has to be the only apartment at this level in London. I mean, I had no idea there were apartments in The Shard—the tallest building in London—but there you go. You learn something new every day. Like…the fact that I hadn't resisted him as he'd hauled me out of Weston's apartment and into the elevator. We'd ridden down in silence and then he'd led me to his bike.

Yep! The big bad rock star drives a road hog… A massive Harley, which had been pure sex between my thighs… Okay, almost as sexy as having Mr. Grumpypants Rockstar there… Gah, stop thinking about that.

He'd made a smooth exit from the Christmas Party. I have to give him credit for that. Not that I'd wanted to be there a second longer. Not when almost everyone there had seemed to be in love, or one half of a devoted couple, not to mention the level of bromance that exists between the men… They hate each other, and clearly, would also do anything for each other… The kind of circle of friends I've always longed for…and never had. Well, except for Amelie, who is one of the few who's survived the transition from childhood to adulthood. So, there's that.

Both she and Isla had stepped in as Damian had carried me out. They'd asked me if I was okay, and I'd assured them I was in full possession of my faculties and was leaving with Damian of my own free will… Ha! If only that were true.

I dig my feet into the lush carpet in the apartment. This is bloody prime real estate in the heart of London. I knew this guy was successful, but somehow, being here in his place…brings home just how out of my league he is. I walk over to the floor to ceiling windows that comprise an entire side wall of the bedroom. London stretches out below me… Picture postcard perfect… Unlike my bloody life, which is turning out to be the fodder of a B-grade romance movie… Minus the happy ending, which this association with out-of-my league, sexy–as–hell rock star guarantees I will not have.

I place my palm against the glass, which feels cool to my touch. Why the hell am I so feverish? Besides… I pull out my phone from my backpack. Forty minutes of the allocated sixty have already passed, and I haven't orgasmed once. Maybe he changed his mind, huh? Perhaps this is just a way of… What? Showing me the inside of his bedroom? I shake my hair back from my shoulders. Nah, that doesn't make sense. He'd all but whisked me here, without giving me the slightest chance to reconsider, so where the hell is he?

He'd stepped out into the other room to make a few calls, he'd said, and that had been — I look at my phone — ten minutes ago now.

"Miss me?" Heat sears my back at the same time that his voice sounds from behind me.

I swallow and my knees threaten to buckle. I drop the phone into my backpack, then lower it to the floor. "Of course, not," I stammer.

"Liar." He places his face close to mine. "You can leave anytime."

"I know."

"I'm not keeping you here."

I start to turn my head, but he clicks his tongue, "Keep looking ahead."

"But—"

I sense him shake his head. "Eyes forward," he orders.

"I am not your possession...something that you can manipulate," I protest.

"You sure about that, Flower?"

"I hate that name."

"Lying again?"

I stiffen, "Of course, not. Why would I? I—"

He steps away. The heat of his body recedes and a chill crawls up my spine. I shiver, stay poised, forehead pressed into the long floor-to-ceiling windows.

"Why are you here?"

The rough edge of his voice wraps about my shoulders, sinks into my blood. My toes curl. Hell, why am I turned on by the harsh edge of his tone, huh?

"You know why," I mumble.

"I didn't hear you." I hear the smirk in his voice. Jerk.

"I said, *you know why*," I repeat, a little louder this time.

"Do I?"

"Of course, you do," I snap.

"Then say it aloud. Ask me for what you want."

I bite on the inside of my lip. I want to ask him. I do, but damn him, he knows why I am here, so why is he making me repeat it? "No," I mumble under my breath.

"What's that?"

"I said, *no!*"

Whack! Pain grips my backside. "What the hell—?" I howl. "You slapped me?" I turn my head to see his face, ready to rip into him.

He jerks his chin up. "Stay facing forward."

I grit my teeth and comply. "Why...?" I stutter, "Why did you—?"

"You don't get to ask the questions." He spanks me again.

I cry out. "Oh, and you can?" I sputter.

He slaps my butt and the pain blooms up my spine. Tears spring up in my eyes, and moisture blooms between my legs. What the hell? I've never been spanked before... Hell, all of my previous partners have been... Civilized, disciplined... Boring? I shake my head. *No, no, no, don't go there.* I want him to hold the door open for me, just as long as he slaps my ass when I walk past him. What the hell am I thinking? I mean, don't get me wrong. I'd prefer a man who breaks the headboard of my bed rather than my heart, right?

I snicker aloud, then sense him straighten behind me. "What's so funny?"

"Nothing," I mumble.

"Something is." He palms my butt.

I shiver. "You...you...don't want to know."

"Oh, but I do." He drags his knuckles up the valley between my butt cheeks and I shudder. "Damian," I whisper, "please..."

"Please what?"

"Please don't."

He slaps my arse again and I whimper. He spanks each arse cheek one after the other. I groan. He does it again. I press my forehead into the glass, flatten my palm against the glass barrier and thrust my butt out. More. I want more.

He steps back. "Your time is up."

"Bu...but... We spent most of the hour in transit to get here."

"London traffic." He shakes his head. "It can be a bitch, right?"

"But what about my, uh...my..."

"Say it, babe." I hear the grin in his voice. What a bastard. He knows why he invited me here. What does he want me to do, beg for my orgasms?

"That would be a start."

"So now you can read my mind?" I huff.

"I wouldn't be as successful as I am if I weren't perceptive."

"An aptitude you've clearly lost, considering your last two albums were flops, as was your Christmas single."

Silence. A beat, then another. The hair on the nape of my neck rises.

"You're right."

"I am?"

"Of course. It's no secret that my career is in the toilet, but I'll tell you one thing I'm still good at."

"What?"

"Denying bratty women their orgasms."

"No, no, no!" I turn, and this time he doesn't stop me.

"Yes." He nods, then turns to leave.

"Don't you dare, Rockstar," I snarl. "You come right back here and finish what you started."

"Oh, that reminds me. I forgot... One more thing..." He glares at me over his shoulder. "You won't come until I give you permission." Turning, he stalks off.

9

Damian

"What the fuck was I thinking?" I grab my dick and pump it once, then again. The cold water pours over me. I wince as goosebumps dot my skin. Not that any of it helps with the bloody hard-on that I've had since refusing to put her and myself out of this insane misery. Since I'd left the apartment last night, I had jerked off at least four times, but not even that had helped.

I pound my forehead into the wall of the shower.

Pain shoots through my head. Not that it helps with the problem between my legs. I swipe my cock from base to head again. The water beats against my shoulders, runs down my chest, drips from my balls. I'd all but come in my pants yesterday, and that had been from spanking her. The curve of her butt, the indentation between her arse cheeks, the way she'd thrust out her hips to fit into the palm of my hand. *Fuck.* The blood rushes to my groin and my shaft lengthens.

Her scent had filled my senses, her soft hair flowing about her face, reflecting the glow of the city that had poured in through the windows. Good thing I hadn't brought her home. If I had, I wouldn't have been able to turn and leave as I had. Her anger and frustration had been palpable in the hotel room, and her arousal — by god, that sweet, sugary scent of her had been overpowering in that space.

Enough to make me want to turn and march right back and take her against that window. To turn her back to face the pane, part her thighs, and sink into her moist softness. She'd have taken all of me in as I'd pumped into her, sheathed myself in her tight channel, even as I'd strummed her clit, eased a finger into her backhole, and worked my thumb into her mouth. I'd have taken her completely, utterly, thoroughly, have pleasured her and brought her to the edge. Then I'd have pulled out and come all over her clothes. Those tomboyish clothes that she wore — jeans and a shapeless shirt… The kind that made me want to tear them off of her to see what she was hiding. Her curves, her dips and hollows, the contour of her gorgeous waist, the sweet indentation between her thighs. I'd have torn off her garments, dropped on my knees and pleased her with my mouth. I'd have licked her slit from arsehole to the honey of her pussy, pinched her clit, woven my tongue in and out of her, bitten down on her melting flesh and commanded her to finally come.

My balls draw up, my cock thickens, and I climax. I shoot my load against the wall. The water pours over me, washing away the evidence. I stay there, shoulders clenched, thighs so fucking hard that the muscles threaten to go into spasm at any moment.

I turn off the shower, reach for my towel and step out. Wrapping it around my waist, I walk to the door, fling it open and step out. I pull on jeans and a T-shirt from the closet, before I head down to my studio.

I pass my guitar on the stand in the corner, hesitate, then stalk toward it. I lift the Stratocaster, then I notch the strap over my shoulder, fit the beauty under my arm. It's almost as satisfying as strumming the lips of her cunt, playing the arch of her spine as I dip her under… *Mine, all mine.*

A touch, a look, her lust drips down my throat as I devour her soul.
Her body is my damnation.
Her breath my rhythm,
The curve of her belly my devastation,
The sweet flesh between her legs my salvation…
Starlight in a darkened sky,
A spark that destroys,
How far will I go to make her mine…? Only mine.

I pause, the echo of the notes dying away as I hear my daughter's voice come through the baby-cam sitting on the side table.

Shit, I'd been busy jerking off, then composing, while my daughter needed my attention. What kind of a father does that make me, hmm? I place the guitar back on the stand. Then pivot and stalk out of the room.

I race down the hallway and up to the door on the far end, push it open, and walk into my daughter's bedroom. She's sitting up in bed, her hair tumbling over her shoulders, her features pinched. "Daddy," she mumbles, her lower lip quivering.

"Hey, sweetheart." I sink down onto the bed. "What's wrong, baby?"

"I… I had a nightmare."

"The same one as last time?" I frown.

She nods, "I … I dreamed that you left me."

"But I didn't. See, here I am." I wipe the tears from her soft cheeks. My heart twists. "Don't cry, baby," I murmur. "Daddy's here's now." I scoop her up into my arms.

She clings to my shoulders. "Dad," her voice hitches, "I… I don't want to be a baby."

"You're only five, Riley. You're allowed." I pat her back as she hiccoughs.

"B…but I want to grow up fast, so I can take care of you."

I frown, "Take care of me?"

"I know how sad you are that Mummy left us."

I am sad, but not for the reasons she thinks. "I am fine, sweetheart. You needn't worry about me."

How does my little girl always sound so much more mature than her years? Is it because her mother left us, forcing her to grow up overnight? Is it because I was a shit father, too engrossed in my career?

I had tried to manage releasing albums while doing my best by Riley, but I had quickly discovered that being a single father doesn't go well with being a rock star. So, I'd cut down on tours and appearances to stay home and take care of her.

The result… My albums had flopped, and the Christmas single I had been counting on had bombed. It had been a disaster, the kind of low I hadn't experienced since my early years when…

Right after the incident, I had gone on a bender, ready to wreck my life. I had survived it, thanks to music… Question is, would that same music be the end of me? The pressure to deliver another hit is stifling. It's not for the money—of which, thanks to the investments I've made with the rest of the Seven, I have more than enough of. It is about salvaging my ego, proving myself as an artist again.

I have to do it, for myself. For Riley… So when she looks back, she won't remember her father as a failure. If I flop, it would mean all the time I spent away from her wasn't worth anything, and that… that would be too painful. No, the only way I can justify the time I lost with her is to be successful.

Somehow, I have to come through, if not for myself, then for my daughter. I want her to be proud of me.

I rise up to my feet, carry Riley with me to the window. "I am not going anywhere, Poppet, I promise, and you don't need to worry about me."

She leans back and stares up into my face, "Can I have pancakes for breakfast?'

"You bet."

"With strawberries and jam."

I stare, "Who has pancakes with jam?"

"I do, Daddy. I do."

"Hmm." I frown past her at the gates to my home, where I see a car pulling up. What the hell? Who could it be? A woman gets out of the car—a pink Volkswagen. Do they even make them in that color?

The sunlight glints off her hair so dark that blue sparks seem to light up the air. Juliet? What's she doing here? She walks up to the panel by the gate and leans in. The intercom connected to my phone buzzes.

I place Riley on the floor. "Go on, and brush your teeth. I'll see you in the kitchen."

"Okay, Daddy." Riley bustles off in the direction of the bathroom.

I head for the staircase, taking the steps two at a time. Reaching the front door, I depress the button on the side that unlocks the gates, then swing the door open.

I lean a shoulder against the door frame as she parks the car in the driveway. She gets out of the car, hauls her backpack over her shoulder and approaches the house. She notices me, comes to a stop at the bottom of the steps.

"What are you doing here?" She frowns.

"What are *you* doing here?" I scowl.

"I am here for my next assignment."

"Assignment?"

"I am a nanny." She glowers up at me.

"I thought you were a potter?"

"A clay artist." She all but stamps her feet. So fucking cute. My lips twitch.

"Hold on a second," I hold up my hand. "So, you're a potter *and* a nanny?"

She draws in a breath. "Yes," she grits out. "Being a nanny is my full-time job; being a clay artist is my hobby."

"So, you're a nanny potter?"

"You make me sound like Harry Potter," she grumbles.

"Just as long as you're not a pothead."

"Of course, not." She draws herself up to her full height. "I am responsible, and very good with kids. I can provide you with references." She scrambles around in her ragged backpack, the same one she had last night, and which she insists on carrying over one shoulder, and why had I noticed that?

She produces a sheaf of papers.

"Why would I need to see your references?"

"Uh," she scowls, "because I am here to take care of your daughter."

"No." I straighten.

"No?" Her jaw drops. "What do you mean, *no*?"

"I don't need a nanny. Goodbye."

I begin to close the door.

She throws up her hand. "Wait, I'm not making this up. The agency told me I was being sent to take care of the daughter of a well-known celebrity."

"I didn't ask any agency for a nanny."

"But... but..." Her forehead crinkles. "They called me and sent me an email to confirm." She whips out her phone, starts up the steps to offer it to me.

"I'm not interested," I growl.

She pauses, one foot on the step above. "What?"

I peer over my shoulder, then step forward and close the door behind me. "I didn't ask for a nanny."

"Are you sure you didn't ask and forget?"

"Are you accusing me of a faulty memory?"

"I am saying," she takes a deep breath, "that I need this assignment."

"Too many debts, huh?"

She straightens her shoulders. "What do you mean?"

"You certainly left Australia in a hurry after your boyfriend dumped you, and in the middle of the bush, no less. You barely had enough money to buy your ticket back home. And not only do your student debts beckon, but your failed aspiration to be a—what was it?" I snap my fingers. "A potter." I nod. "Your failure to become a potter haunts you."

"Fuck you," she snarls.

"No, thank you."

The color leaches from her face, "How... How do you know all of this?"

"I make it a point to find out everything about those I come in contact with."

Especially when it's a curvy sprite, with wide innocent eyes, who I can't get out of my mind.

"Must be fun to have such a trusting nature." She drops the phone into her bag. "So, I have a few student loans, and a jerk of an ex. Big deal." She swipes her hair over her shoulder and her fingers tremble. "It's not uncommon."

"A £100,000 debt that you'll spend the next twenty years paying off."

"So?" Her chin wobbles.

"So, good luck with that." I pivot, reach for the door handle.

"Stop," her voice is choked.

I allow my lips to twist, then push open the door.

"Wait… You… You are right."

"Oh?" I say without turning around.

"I need this job."

"Hmm."

"If I don't get this position, I am in a lot of trouble."

If you get this role, you are in so much more trouble. I push open the door and step through.

"I…need this assignment," she pleads. "The agency doesn't have any other role for me at the moment. Hell, there aren't any roles going for a nanny anywhere in London, it seems." She shakes her head, a look of disbelief in her eyes. "Trust me, if there were an alternative to this, I'd take it."

I pause, glare at her over my shoulder, "How far will you go to get this job?"

"I'll," she swallows, "I'll do a…anything."

"You sure about that, Flower?"

"It's not like I have a choice, do I?" she grumbles. "I mean, I'd rather go throw myself off a bridge, but then —"

My heart begins to race. I turn, march down the steps so quickly that she pauses mid-step and stumbles. I swoop out my hand and grab hold of her bicep. "What the fuck did you just say?"

"I… I…"

I haul her up to her tiptoes, then lean down and thrust my face into hers. "Say it," I dare her.

"I… I didn't mean it," she stutters.

"Don't ever talk like that again."

"O—okay."

"Good." I peer into her features. I should let go of her. I need to get back inside to take care of my daughter, and yet, with her scent in my nostrils, the curve of her arm under my fingers, those big green eyes that hold mine, the lips that tremble and call to me, to close the distance and close my mouth over hers… I… I lean in close enough for our eyelashes to entwine, for us to inhale a shared breath. *Kiss her, kiss her… Do it. No bloody way!* If I do, I am lost, and she is a distraction I cannot afford. Not now. Not when I need to take care of my motherless child and a career that is fast unravelling unless I do something to turn it around. On the other hand, I've never felt as alive as I do in her presence.

Only one way out. I need to turn this situation to my advantage. If I can use her sweetness, her vitality to kickstart my muse… Then huh, why not? As long as she benefits from it too… Yeah, that would make this a transaction that's beneficial for both of us, right?

I hold her gaze, then lower mine to take in her rose bud lips. "I have an arrangement in mind."

"Oh? You mean being a nanny to your daughter?"

"Only if you pass my test first."

"Test?"

"An hour with me every day for the next six days, doing everything I want."

She stares at me. "What does that involve?"

I glare at her face, then slide my gaze down her breasts, to the space between her legs. By the time I raise my gaze to her face, her cheeks are flushed.

"Well? You did say that you'd do anything."

She tips up her chin, "Anything but that."

"That's not what you said earlier, when I left you at the apartment yesterday. In fact, if I recall correctly, you pleaded with me to finish what I started."

Her cheeks heat; her breathing grows shallow. Bet she recalls how I'd smacked her butt, huh? My fingers tingle, and I curl them into fists at my sides. "So, what do you say, Flower?"

She glances at me, then shakes her head.

"No, thank you, I'll just have to figure this out another way." She turns to leave.

What the fuck? No one turns me down. No one. Especially not this tiny little thing who needs this gig as much as I need to make a success of my next album.

"A hundred thousand pounds for each day you spend with me."

10

Julia

"Excuse me?" I choke out.

"You heard me," he says through gritted teeth.

I pivot to face him, "I... I am not sure I heard right."

"What did you hear?"

"A hundred thousand pounds?" I blink at him. "Per day? One hour per day?"

He nods.

"To be a nanny?" I slowly blink.

"I told you, I don't engage nannies for my daughter."

"Why not?"

"I don't like her getting close to people who'll one day leave her. I want to avoid further heartbreaks in her life."

"Heartbreak?" So, someone else had left his daughter and him... Was it his wife? But he'd never been married. If he had, surely, I'd have heard of it. But then, I hadn't known he had a daughter until just now. How had he managed to keep that from the media? So, who is he talking about then?

"Your daughter's mother," I burst out.

He freezes; his gaze narrows. He regards me with a cool expression. "What about her?"

"Where is she? Isn't she around to take care of your daughter?"

"What interest is that to you?"

I swallow, then hold my papers close to my chest, "I prefer to get all of the facts before I engage in any kind of, uh, arrangement."

He folds his arms, leans a hip against the door jamb. "Very wise." He rakes his gaze across my features, "She's no longer in the picture."

"Hmm." I shuffle my feet, then hitch the bag over my shoulder. For all the media's best efforts to infringe on his privacy, Damian has, apparently, managed to keep his personal life a secret. What else do I not know about him?

The band around my chest tightens.

Shit, why the hell am I jealous now? If I could find another assignment, I would turn him down and walk away, but there's nothing else on the horizon... Except this gig as a possible nanny for the daughter of this irresistible jerk-ass of a rock star... Or not? What the hell is he suggesting with this set-up anyway, huh?

"Well?" He frowns.

"Was she... Is she your girlfriend?"

He hesitates, then replies, "Yes." He rakes his fingers through his hair. "Yes, she was."

Holy shit, so he hadn't married her. And he is no longer with her. A warm sensation blooms in my chest.

"Any more questions?" He glares at me and I shiver. That edge of meanness in his gaze; it's such a turn on. I rub my thighs together.

His nostrils flare, and one side of his lips curls. "So, we have a deal, then?"

"What?" I blink, "No... Not yet... I mean, you're not making any sense. That much money to spend such a short period of time with me? It's—" I shake my head, "it's bonkers."

"Tell me about it," he takes a step toward me and I stumble back.

He grabs hold of my shoulder, and pin pricks of heat sizzle out from his touch. My core clenches.

He rights me, then lowers his hand, and of course, I miss it already.

His jaw tics, he firms his lips, then shoves his hands into his pockets. We stare at each other for a second and goosebumps break out on my skin. The air between us is so charged that if he were to touch me again, I am sure I'd come on the spot. *Ugh, stop that.* "I am really not sure what you're offering me," I finally say.

"It's simple." He leans back on the heels of his feet as if he wants to put distance between us.

Good, I don't want anything to do with this man, either… Except, damn it! This chemistry between us is intense. The kind I've been dreaming about, but which I was sure only existed in romance novels. I mean, there is a 'one' for everybody, right? So what, if the men I meet, including the ones I am attracted to, like the a-hole in front of me, turn out to be douches of the first order, eh?

Daddy Grumpypants looks me up and down, and I resist the urge to wipe my sweaty palms on the front of my pants.

"Trust me. Where you are concerned, nothing is simple," I scoff.

"That's stating the obvious." He smirks. "So, are you in or out?"

"What are you talking about?"

"You rhyming your words with mine?" He drawls.

"Of course not, you…you swine."

He quirks an eyebrow.

"I… I couldn't help it." I throw up my hands, "You are doing my head in."

"You and me both, Flower." His jaw firms. "And this meeting is over." He turns to go.

"Wait," I cry out. "You can't leave me like this."

"Like what?" He smirks over his shoulder.

"You…you know." I flush.

"No." He shakes his head. "I made you an offer; you turned it down. That's the end of our non-relationship. Have a good life." He heads toward the house and every cell in my body snaps to attention.

No, no, no, no. He can't just… Stalk off and leave me hanging. And why the hell had I obeyed his order, huh? I'd spent the night tossing and turning, sure that I had been running a fever. Only...a part of me had known better. I'd wanted to bring myself to climax, but every time I came to the edge, his earlier command had held me back from it. My body seems to have a mind of its own. One which insists on following his direction. It is forcing me to comply... Aargh! *Stop, stop. Tell him what you want.*

"Orgasm," I blurt out.

He pauses.

"At least let me come, please?" I curl my fingers at my sides.

He angles his body. "So," he drums his fingers on his chest, "you want me to give you permission to achieve satisfaction?"

Asshole's gloating, but whatever, as long as I can somehow relieve this burning, clawing sensation in my center. I jerk my chin in his direction and his eyes gleam.

"On one condition," he purrs.

"What?"

"You accept my proposition."

"A…a hundred thousand pounds for every day I spend with you?"

"Which would come down to, normally, an hour a day, which is all I can spare." He nods his head toward the house. "Occasionally, it might be more."

Of course, he has to take care of his daughter.

"No Sundays, though," he adds. "I have a full schedule on Sundays and won't have time for—" he gestures to the space between us.

"Wouldn't it be easier to simply have a trial period for me as the nanny for your daughter—?"

"No." He straightens. "Take it or leave it."

He turns to go.

I call out, "Wait."

He pauses.

"For how long?"

He angles his body, glares at me over his shoulder, "Until New Year's Eve."

"That's…"

"Today's December 26th… Boxing Day," he reminds me.

"I know," I snap. "That's five days?"

"Six including today."

"So, six hours?"

"More or less."

"How many…orgasms is that?"

"That's for you to lose track of." He laughs.

"And you'll pay me for each day?"

"Of course."

"You sure you can afford it?" I frown. He's not poor, but he's going through a rocky patch in his career… Well, okay, this is also me making conversation so I can buy myself some time.

"You sure you can afford to ignore it?" he scoffs.

"No."

"Good. It's a deal then." He holds out his hand.

I ignore it. "What's in it for you?"

He glances down at my breasts, then at my crotch. By the time he glares at my face, my mouth is dry, my pussy wet, my scalp tingling as if someone has run their fingernails across it.

"Right." I nod. "Can I think about it?"

"Nope."

My jaw drops.

"Decide in the next second or this is over… Not that there ever was anything between us."

I narrow my eyes, "I think you protest too much. There definitely is a lot between us—which is the only reason you are suggesting this insane arrangement."

"Oh?" He yawns. "Keep kidding yourself, sweetheart. You're nothing but a convenient hole to wring satisfaction from."

I draw myself up to my full height. "Fuck you, asshole."

"Alphahole." He smirks.

"A-class douche canoe." I tip up my chin, "You know what? You can stuff your stupid-ass proposal in your darkest part."

"You mean my heart?"

"Only you'd say that," I splutter.

"Listen, I have to go attend to my daughter. Why don't you...uh, head on to the greenhouse? I'll meet you there."

"Greenhouse?"

"Yes."

"You want me to wait there?"

"Unless you'd rather wait here?"

"Don't do that."

"What?" He frowns.

"Rhyme your stupid sentences with mine."

"Where you're concerned, that's not the only thing I hope to rhyme with." He snickers.

I make a gagging sound. "That was a terrible pun."

"You're right." He raises his hands. "I really have to get back." He jerks his chin in the direction of his garden. "Go on." He turns to leave, glances back over his shoulder. "Or not...your choice."

Turning, he marches inside and shuts the door on me.

Motherfucker actually had the gall to not invite me inside. I stare at the door a second longer. Maybe I should bang on it and demand that he let me in? And then what? He's only going to refuse me... Or tell me the deal is off. Or worse, he'd allow me in and then I'd be in the same space as him...and his daughter? A tiny version of him, with all of his presence and none of his cynicism. I swallow... Nope, I'd be a goner all over again.

Maybe this is better... I won't risk breaking my heart twice over, for I am very sure that his daughter would be as adorable as he is. Hang on, did I just refer to him as adorable? Jesus, I am tying myself in knots. I turn, head for the greenhouse in the corner of the sprawling grounds when the gates swing open. A car draws up and parks near the house. A woman slides out. She smooths her gray hair, hauls a designer bag over her shoulder, then pauses when she sees me.

"Hello there." She smiles. "Were you visiting Damian?"

"Umm," I hitch my backpack over my shoulder, "I'm still visiting him." I shuffle my feet.

"Why don't you come on in?" she nods toward the house.

"He, ah, asked me to wait in the greenhouse."

"The greenhouse?" She glances over to the structure at the far end of the yard, then back at me. "Hmm." She scrunches up her forehead. "He didn't want you to come in, huh?"

"He didn't," I confirm. "Is that normal?" I ask. "I mean, clearly, you are allowed in…so…"

"I'm the assistant to the Seven, so I came by with some papers for him to sign."

"Right. I'm Julia…Julia Andrews."

"Andrews?" Her forehead wrinkles.

"I know…" I grumble. "No relationship to the actress, at all, or to Julie & Julia, or to Juliet from Romeo and Juliet."

"Of course, not. You'll get your Happily Ever After, unlike her."

"I will?"

"Of course, dear." She holds out her hand, and I take it. "I'm Meredith, by the way."

"Nice to meet you, Meredith." I release her arm. "Guess I should be going along then."

"Julia," she calls after me, "don't be too hard on Damian."

"What does it matter what I think about him?" I turn.

"Just a…" she looks me up and down, "just a feeling." She studies me a moment longer, then finally says, "Just give him a chance, okay?"

I prop my hands on my hips. "Why is it that all of you women seem to think he needs to be handled with kid gloves?"

"That's not what I meant; quite the opposite."

"Oh?" I step toward her. "Explain."

"He'll push you away, ensure that you hate him because of his actions."

"I already do," I inform her.

"It's all a front." She leans in closer. "The incident, you see… It didn't break him."

"It didn't?"

She shakes her head, "He managed to survive it. In fact, he made a complete recovery, after therapy. It was what happened after that, which snapped his confidence."

"You're joking." I chuckle, "I haven't met a more obnoxious, more over-the-top alpha than Damian 'Big D' Savage."

"Big D?"

My cheeks warm. "Just what the media calls him."

"The media?"

"Yeah." I wave my hand. "You know, what I read about in the tabloids on social media…"

She fixes me with a steady gaze that reminds me all too much of my mother. It's probably why I rebelled so much growing up, enough to give up a well-paying position and take off with an almost virtual stranger to the other end of the world... Eek, stop that, don't blame your parents for your lack of a career. I mean, I did want to be a nanny. I love kids, wouldn't have come this far if my natural child whispering instincts hadn't kicked in when I was younger. It's just, I want more. Children of my own, a chance to pursue my creative aspirations. Gah! Stop that self-pity.

"You can't blame me, the man practically invented headline news with his crazy antics—"

"Until he didn't."

"Right." He did go quiet for a couple of years, then bounced back with his disastrous albums. Hold-on-a-sec... "The time when he disappeared from the news, when he was supposed to be off the grid, composing his next release—"

She nods.

"What happened during that time?"

"Not my secret to tell."

"And his daughter?"

"He mentioned his daughter to you?" She frowns.

"Why? Doesn't he talk about his daughter to people?"

"Not to strangers—" Her features clear. "Oh." She looks me up and down. "Oh, so I was right then."

"I don't like the sound of that Oh." I half chuckle. "And what do you mean, exactly, by that?"

"No, no, don't mistake me, my dear." She closes the distance between us, grabs my hand, "This is good, Julia."

"It is?"

Yep." She nods. "Very, very good."

"I… Umm, you're making me nervous, Meredith."

"Don't be." She smiles, and her features light up. "You have no idea how much progress you've made with him."

"Progress?" My head begins to spin. "What do you mean?" What the hell did I miss? Why do I get the feeling there's something very obvious that I'm not getting?

"I mean, he's invited you home, someone outside of the Seven." She taps her foot on the ground. "That's a first."

Oh! "He never invites anyone else home?"

She shakes her head.

"How about the women he's seen with?"

"All a front."

"Really?"

"They were nothing special, not like you."

"Not like me?"

"He asked you home, didn't he?"

"Not exactly." I glance at the door. "Considering he didn't let me in."

"He will. It's only a matter of time."

"What if I don't want to continue being associated with him?"

"Well, that," she glances at the door then back at me, "that would be a pity, but it's your choice, of course. You need to think of yourself first."

"I do?"

She nods. "I mean, he is an overpowering man. All the Seven are. It takes a special kind of woman to catch their attention."

"Right."

"It takes an even stronger personality to hold their interest."

"You mean, I'm not special or strong?"

"Not what I said." Her face grows serious. "You need to think carefully about if you want to be involved with him. The Seven, you see, are the kind of men who, once they set their eyes on their women, will not back down. They will not stop until they get what they want. And you have to be either able to go toe-to-toe with them and hold your own against them or —"

"Or?"

"You may as well cut your losses and leave now."

"Are you asking me to leave?"

"He asked you to stay, didn't he?"

"He did." I frown at her, take in her shrewd gaze, the straight cut of her dress, her expensive shoes. "Who are you to him, anyway?"

"Let's just say, I am the one who helps the Seven to keep their offices running smoothly."

"You are more than their assistant, aren't you?"

"Whatever gave you that idea?" She chuckles, reaches into her handbag, then thrusts a card into my hand. "If you need anything, just call."

"Why would I need anything?" I frown.

"A friendly voice, a need to speak… We could all do with a friend on the other side of the phone, right?"

"Right." I pocket the card. Why do I get the feeling that there's something very obvious here that I am missing?

"I'd better get along then." She heads up the steps, then pauses, to glance at me over her shoulder, "Oh, and Julia?"

"Call me Jules."

"Jules," she nods at me, "it's the ones who are the most hurt who need the most love."

"You mean Damian?"

"I mean," her grin broadens, "don't forget what I told you earlier… Don't let him push you around."

Julia

"You haven't left?"

His hard voice chafes across my skin and all of my nerve endings seem to pop at once. I turn so quickly that a cloud of butterflies rises up from where they'd settled on my skin.

"Oh, you scared me." I press a hand to my chest.

"Were you expecting someone else?" He smirks.

"I was kind of hoping you had forgotten about me," I retort.

"No chance of that happening." He laughs, then swoops out a hand so quickly, I flinch. He scoops up something from my cheek, shows it to me. An eyelash.

"Make a wish." His voice is low and edgy and soft. How the hell can he be so many things at once? I close my eyes, then blow.

When I look up, he's staring at me, his nostrils flared, a look of something like…desire in his eyes. I glance away, then back at him. "Damian," I swallow, "who's taking care of your daughter, while you're here?"

He straightens, schools his features back into that look of indifference I am coming to realize is a mask, one he's perfected over the years, the image he likes to project to the world. Same way as I'd prefer people to think of me as happy-go-lucky, a wanderer... A nanny, always borrowing a family to call her own rather than making one for herself. Does that make me a cuckoo? The bird that lays eggs in another's nest and has them bring up its chicks as their own. No, that's backward. That doesn't make sense.

"Meredith's with her," he replies.

"Does she help out with your daughter?"

"Sometimes." He takes a step back, then folds his arms over his big chest.

"Is that her name?" I jerk toward the cursive tattoo that peeks out from around his left forearm.

"Whose?"

"Your daughter's."

He glares at me, and a shiver runs down my spine. Jesus, when he looks at me, all angry and grumpy, it's so fucking hot. I swallow, hold his gaze. Well, I am not going to run scared from jerk-ass, here. "Go on," I coax, "you can tell me. You won't be struck by lightning if you do."

He doesn't respond.

"It's a joke." I raise my shoulders. "You were supposed to laugh."

"Hmph." He widens his stance. His features take on a strange look before he shakes it off and resumes a look of bored indifference.

Silence stretches, a beat, another. A cloud of butterflies takes wing from the flowers nearby. I follow them as they dance over to another set of flowers in the corner of the green house.

"This place." I clear my throat, "It's beautiful."

"You're beautiful."

I turn my head to find his gaze on my face. I redden. "Uh, thanks." I tuck a strand of hair behind my ear, "When you said greenhouse, I didn't realize it would be so...enchanting. Did you build it by yourself?"

"I had help," he drawls. "And yes, that's my daughter's name."

"Riley is a beautiful name," I offer. "How old is she?"

His forehead scrunches. He draws himself up to his full height. "Have you thought about my proposal?"

I tilt my head. "One hour a day for six days, huh?"

"That's six hundred thousand pounds in the bank at the end of it."

Whew! That's a hell of a lot of money. Enough to pay off my debts, allow my mother to retire from her job, get a fresh start, focus on becoming a pottery artist and not worry about paying my bills. And yet, when I'd wanted to spend the night with him, it had been because... I'd desired him, had felt a connection with him when he'd kissed me. He'd taken that and turned it into something sordid. Something transactional, where he wants to buy me.

It is a lot of money he's offering; but really, is that all I am worth? Can I place a value on myself...with such ease? Besides, I'm not seriously considering this, am I? Would I sell myself, for cold hard cash?

"Well?" His voice cuts through my thoughts, "What do you think?"

"It's not enough," I inform him.

"Excuse me?" He frowns.

"You want me for an hour a day for six days, for some unfathomable reason. Well, it's going to cost you."

"Oh?" He peruses my features, something inscrutable in his eyes. As if I am following a script he already knows, one that I am finding my way through, blindfolded.

"How much?" He drums his fingers on his chest, "Tell me quickly. I don't have all day."

I grip my fingers tightly together and sweat pools under my armpits. "One million," I say under my breath.

He holds a hand behind his ear, "What was that?"

"One million for all six days." I draw myself up to my full height. "Take it or leave it."

"Well then," he yawns, "you'd better get going."

"Oh." I stare at him. Disappointment and something else, a strange sensation like I had missed the one thing that could have changed my life completely, twists my insides. I open my mouth to speak, and he lifts an eyebrow.

"Never mind." I shove my hair back from my face, hitch my backpack over my shoulder. "Goodbye." I brush past him and head for the doorway.

"One million pounds." His voice follows me.

I don't stop.

"Per day."

"What?" I stumble, then right myself. "What did you say?"

His lips twist, "Exactly what you heard."

I pivot to face him, "One million pounds per day, for six days?" I blink, then pull on my earlobe.

His grin widens. "Good." He closes the distance between us, "See you at six pm."

"Hold on. What the hell? I didn't agree to—"

"Sure, you did," he replies.

"No, I didn't."

"You tugged on your earlobe," he points out.

"What?"

"You do that when you've inwardly come to a decision."

"I… I do?"

"Yep." He smirks down at me, "You're too easy to read, Flower."

"Just because I quoted from Wordsworth, once..."

"It's also your eyes."

"What?"

"They're green like the new shoots that come up from the ground in early spring."

"Wow," I breathe, "who'd have thought an obnoxious d-bag like you could be romantic."

"Don't let my words fool you." He half turns, then shoves his hands inside his pockets.

"Your biggest hit was a love song."

He winces, "It was a rock ballad."

"One with some sexy, angsty verses that had everyone going gaga over it."

"Including you?"

"Never." I snicker. "A little too sappy for my liking."

"So, you prefer not to face your emotions, huh?"

"And you?" I close the distance between us. "Do you ever face your feelings?"

"All the time." His features close. "Every fucking time I think I've found peace, something happens that reminds me how everything can change in the blink of an eye."

"Is that why you think money can buy everything?"

"Doesn't it?"

I twist my fingers together, wanting to deny it, but hell if, he doesn't have me there. One million pounds per day for six days. OMG, OMG. My heart begins to thud and my pulse rate ratchets up. That's... Way more money than I thought I'd see in my life... Ever. It is... A lifechanging amount.

I lick my lips, and he locks his gaze onto my mouth, "Open."

"What—"

He shoves his thumb inside my mouth. "Suck on it," he orders.

I swallow, my nipples harden, the flesh between my legs buzzes with anticipation, with recklessness, with need... A gnawing something opens up low in my belly. I close my lips around his digit, suck on it. I swirl my tongue around the pad of his thumb, absorb the salty taste of him. The dark edginess that sinks into my blood heads straight for that churning, yearning pit that gnaws at my core.

His chest rises and falls; his nostrils flare. He presses down on my lower lip, and I open my mouth. He inserts his thumb deeper inside. I swallow. His breathing grows ragged; a bead of sweat slides down his throat along the demarcation between his sculpted pecs.

Moisture pools between my thighs. A moan bleeds from me…
Needy, wanting… A kind of hunger I've never faced before… Will
never again.

Holy hell, what kind of draw does this man…this almost-stranger
have on me? He's barely touched me and I am ready to self-combust.

He draws out his thumb, then brings it to his mouth and sucks on
it. He drags his digit across his lower lip and I can't stop the groan
that spills from my throat.

His lips kick up in a smile. He wipes his finger across the fabric
of his pants. "You'll do nicely."

Turning, he heads for the exit.

I stare after him. What the bloody hell—how dare he? Had
he…? "Don't you leave," I cry. "Not again." I curl my fingers at my
sides. How had I let myself be taken in, all over again? "Damian, you
bastard—"

He pivots, prowls over to me.

My heart begins to thud, my pulse races, and the flesh between
my thighs clenches. He holds out his hand. "Give it to me," he
demands.

"Wh…what?"

"Your phone." He curls his lips. "What did you think?"

"I will not."

"Either you give it to me or I take it. Your choice."

Anger thuds at my temples and something very close to hate
crawls up my spine. "Just because you're bigger than me, don't think
you can bully me."

"Bully you?" He laughs. "I haven't even started, sweetheart." He
crooks his fingers, "Don't keep me waiting, doll."

I frown.

"Your phone." He bends his knees, peers into my face. "Now," his
voice lowers to a hush, the dark edge of his tone sinking into my
blood. My belly trembles. My scalp tingles. I pull out my phone, hold
it out to him.

"Unlock it."

"You mean you don't know my password?"

"Hmm." His brow crinkles, "Good point, I need to rectify that."

"Jesus." I stare. "I was joking."

"I wasn't."

"You wouldn't invade my privacy that way…"

He stares.

"Would you?" Of course, he would. Nothing is beyond the reach of this alpha male. He can have any woman he wants, so why the hell had he extended this stupid-ass agreement thing to me? "It makes no sense," I shake my head, as I unlock my phone.

"Don't try to discern the pattern of a plan that's clearly above your pay grade." He smirks.

My jaw drops. Bloody hell… What an ass. "Why… You…"

He snatches the phone from my hand. His fingers move over the screen, then he slides it back into my open backpack. "All set," he declares, then turns and prowls toward the exit.

"That's it?" I demand. "You're going to leave me here and walk away?"

He raises a hand, "Save the small talk for later, sweets."

My vision tunnels, anger slams into my chest. "Wait!" I call out after him. "Did you place the call to my agency, and then get cold feet when you saw me?" I demand.

He halts, then glares at me over his shoulder, "Why would I do that, hmm?"

"Because you want me at your mercy?"

"I had you at my mercy earlier. I was the one who left, remember?"

Can't deny that.

He strides over to me, then bends his knees and thrusts his face into mine. "I'm not sorry for buying you," he whispers, "and I am not sorry for everything I am going to do to you."

My core clenches. "Is that a threat?" I breathe.

"A promise." His lips curl. My ribcage tightens. Hell, every nuance of his expression is hot and sexy and a bloody turn on. I am fighting a battle I can't win… Not without preparing for it, and right now, I am so out of my depth, it's not funny.

"And by the time I'm done with you, you won't be either."

I raise my hand, intent on slapping him, but he grabs my wrist.

"Let me go," I hiss.

"Don't tell me what to do."

"You're crazy," I insist.

"Takes one to know one."

"Oh, so now we're on the same level?"

"No," he mutters almost to himself. "You're on a different plane, one where we can never see eye to eye, and that's what makes whatever is between us a challenge, one I can't resist. I won't stop until I've broken you down, until I've figured out what makes you tick, until I have you melting and crawling and begging for my mercy, and even then, I won't release you. Not until I have sampled that sweet essence inside of you, bathed in the passion you keep hidden inside of you, until I have used the creativity that you harbor to fire mine, until I have your thoughts, your words, your every cry as you orgasm, trapped in my cells."

"What, the—" I blink, "What are you talking about?"

His lips twist, "Wouldn't you like to find out?"

He releases me so suddenly that I land on the ground, on my arse.

Turning, he stalks off again.

"Damian," I call out after him, "I know you didn't mean that earlier insult."

He reaches the door to the greenhouse.

I wipe the sweat from my face, and scramble to my feet. "This isn't over, not by a long shot. You're not the complete jerk hole you make yourself out to be, you know. You messed with the wrong woman though. I am going to get to the bottom of your secrets. I won't stop until I bring you to your knees," I yell.

He throws open the door. A gust of cool breeze wafts in and goosebumps pop on my skin. I shiver, wrap my hands around my waist.

"Knock yourself out, sweets," he drawls, then surveys me over his shoulder. "Just make sure you're not wearing panties."

11

Damian

You'll do nicely? What the hell was that about? What had I been
thinking when I'd tossed out those words? Not to mention, that
speech about her being a challenge?

I had been as cruel as fuck. No wonder she'd been so furious.
Flower has a temper, all right…and a fighting spirit…not to mention,
impressive negotiation skills. That back and forth there, I hadn't
expected. It had been oddly stimulating too. Pitting my wits against
hers had made me feel alive in a way I hadn't felt for months. I want
to revel in her vitality, draw on it, imbibe it and allow it to fan the
flames of something that has died inside of me.

Doesn't forgive the fact that I hurt her.

A half hour after I'd left her, I'd glanced out the window and seen
her drive off. Thankfully, she'd given herself time to cool off before
leaving. Good. No way, did I want her distracted while driving. It's
the only reason I've put my people on her. They'll keep her safe…
And ensure if she meets anyone else that I'll be the first to know.

I am protecting my investment, that's all. Hey, it is an agreement that we came to, and I intend to honor every part of mine. By the time we come to the new year, she'll be rich and I'll be… Well, hopefully, I'll have managed to write enough songs to fill an album.

I glare at my reflection in the mirror of the rundown dressing room of the gym in central London owned by Jace. A close friend of the Seven, he and his wife Sienna had moved to London from LA when Sienna was pregnant, partly so they could be close to Sienna's sister Bella who is studying in the city.

He was the first to fall for the family trap, followed closely by Sinclair, then Saint and Weston. Shit is going down fast and I don't plan to be part of that particular train. Nope. I have more than enough on my plate, trying to resurrect my career…and taking care of my daughter. Maybe it's stupid that I insist on being a hands-on parent, but I am determined to make up for the time I lost with her. I am going to ensure that Riley will never feel the absence of her mother. Speaking of, I glance up at the clock on the wall.

I have half an hour to work out, before I leave for my six pm with one sexy, hot-as-fuck woman who owes me a few orgasms—or is it the other way around? I chuckle. The look on her face when I had left her earlier…Clearly, she had been turned on and frustrated as hell. Good. That's how I felt too, after all. Though, the lack of fulfillment had clearly sparked me to write, which is a bloody good sign, considering I've been blocked for nearly six months.

Six months since I have composed anything worth stringing into a tune… Six months since I have picked up my guitar… Then, one encounter with her, seeing her writhe under me, spanking her arse as I had brought her to the edge, had seemed to break something inside of me… Or rather, break through the fog I had been mired in, enough to spark the beginning of a song… Something… The first inkling of a star in the night sky, the first scent of bread baking in the oven, the heady sensation of a child's first kick in the womb, hinting at the promise of a new life. Holy shit. I blink, then grab for my phone and key in the words. This is good, bloody good. I sink down onto the bench, continue writing out the stream of consciousness… It's garbled…but it's a start. Get it the fuck down, get down the words…the flow. Ride it as far as you can. Catch the wave, mother-fucker. Don't screw this up.

"What the hell are you chuckling about, asshole?" A familiar voice reaches me from the direction of the door.

"Fuck off," I growl back, then focus on my screen.

The next moment an arm reaches over my shoulder and grabs the phone from me.

"Hey," I protest, "give that back."

"Not a chance in hell, brother." Arpad walks backward, reading through what I'd written. "Holy shit, Savage, this is some emo stuff."

The back of my neck heats. I jump up to my feet, stalk after him. "And you're going to be in some serious shit if you don't return my phone to me."

Arpad glances up, "Lost your balls already, huh?"

"The fuck you talking about?"

"You in love, bro?"

"You lost your mind, *bro?*"

"When was the last time you wrote such sentimental lyrics… hmm?" He pretends to think, "For that matter, when was the last time you wrote anything?"

No shit! "Those are not my words, you prick, and besides, it's none of your bloody business." I reach for my phone; he tosses it over my head.

"What the fuck?" I turn to find Edward has snatched the phone from the air.

He reads the screen and his eyebrows rise. "You wrote this?" He glances up at me.

"Nope." I glower at the Father. "It's. Not. Mine."

"Oh?" Edward scans it, "Where did you find these lyrics, they're…"

I set my jaw. If he makes fun of them, I am going to —

"They're not bad." The Father tilts his head.

"Not bad?" I splutter.

"They're very good, actually." He chuckles.

"They are?" I stiffen. "Is that good good, or bad good?"

"It's bad good, which makes it good good…" Edward tosses the phone back at me. "In fact, it's so good, it makes me wonder what prompted you to write it."

I glower at him.

"Not that you wrote it," he placates me.

Bastard.

"But if you had written it," Arpad picks up the narrative, clever bugger that he is. He raises an appraising eyebrow. "I'd wonder, what sparked it."

The back of my neck heats. Shit, no way. Now I am embarrassed when my asshole friends compliment me on my words. Like I am in kindergarten or something. I glance away, then back at them. "Nothing… Everything…" I raise my shoulders, pocket the phone. "Does it matter how it happened?" I mumble.

"Something prompts you to break your creative block?" Edward surveys my features, "Yeah, I'd think it's significant."

"It's her, isn't it?" Arpad drawls. "She inspired the ol' muse, I take it?"

"Who are you talking about?" I narrow my gaze. "And that's none of your business."

"You know who I'm talking about," Arpad barks a laugh, "and going by your touchy reaction, I take it I was right?"

I glower at him.

"Thought so." He nods, "You going to keep her around a while longer then?"

"Maybe..."

"You come to some kind of an arrangement with her yet?"

"Why does it have to be an arrangement?" I snap. "Why couldn't it be a normal relationship?"

"You and normal?" He chuckles, "Hello, you are one of the Seven. Have we ever done anything in the normal way?"

He has a point there.

"So," the asshole persists, "it is an arrangement?"

"It's not *not* an arrangement," I finally concede.

"Good grief, you're resorting to hiding behind wordplay. Thought you saved that for the stage." Arpad chuckles. "Clearly, the situation is far worse than it seems."

"Oh, fuck off." I crack my neck. "I got inspired, I wrote a few words. Big fucking deal."

"It is, though." Edward walks toward me. His features wear an almost understanding look… Which I'd hate on anyone else, but this is Edward. The one of us Seven to have suffered the most from the incident. No wonder it turned him off life, in general… Though he'd deny it, of course. For him, the church is his calling, serving God is his passion, which is noble of him, of course. If only I didn't get the sense that he is avoiding the real issues at hand. Not that this is the time to tell him, not when I am facing a crisis of my own. And is that what this is, a crisis?

I firm my lips. "Something you want to get off your chest, Father?" I tilt my head.

Edward pauses in front of me. He peers into my features. "It's different."

"What is?"

"The lyrics you wrote?" He purses his lips. "It's the first thing that's you."

"Like I give a fuck."

"Everything you wrote before this came from a place of anger, but this…" His forehead furrows, "It's raw, it's the words of a man who's finding there's more to life than the selfish focus on himself."

"What else is there to life?" I roll my shoulders "Except sex and drugs and rock n' roll."

"Love." Edward's lips kick up.

"Love?" I laugh. "You're not in church, Father."

"Stop trying so hard, Damian," his voice is soft. "Sometimes you need to enjoy what you have in front of you."

"And I thought the Rockstar was getting overly emotional. Jeez, Edward, between the two of you, I hope it doesn't catch on." Arpad glances between us. "Glad things are clearer for me—the open sea, the wind in my hair. I don't need much else."

"It's also called escape." I smirk. "What are you running from, dipshit?"

"The same thing as you, dickwad," he chuckles.

We stare at each other, then he jerks his chin toward the open door and to the boxing ring in the center of the main room, "Wanna fight it out?"

I crack my knuckles. "Thought you'd never ask."

Edward glances between us. "Mind if I stick around to watch two grown men make utter asses of themselves?"

Arpad cracks his knuckles.

I draw myself up to my full height.

"So, you enjoyed the little surprise I sent your way, huh?"

"Wait." I blink. "What are you — ?" I stiffen. "It was you?" I snap. "You sent Julia to me?"

He nods.

"You called up her agency and asked for her to be my nanny?"

"Bingo." He pretends to shoot at me while making a popping sound.

"The fuck?" I growl. "Why the hell would you do that?"

"'Cause the sparks between the two of you that day were intense, 'cause it was the first time I'd seen you interested in something other than your own grief?" He folds his arms across his chest, "Because, apparently, I care about you enough not to see you fuck up your life?"

"Oh?"

"Not that you deserve it, of course," he nods. "In fact, I think I should start by rearranging your pretty features. It may help wring some sympathy from your to-be girlfriend."

"Don't talk about her, you piece of shit."

He laughs "You angry enough to give me a proper fight this time?"

I step forward and bury my fist in his face.

12

______

Julia

Alphahole: Strip.
    Alphahole: On your hands and knees. Arse in the air.
    Alphahole: Don't ignore my commands or you'll pay for it.

"What the hell?" I stare at the text messages on my phone, then around the room. I'm back at the bedroom in the apartment he'd taken me to the first time. It's five minutes to six pm, and hell, I'm early. Not by much, but why the hell couldn't I have waited and made an entrance?

My phone vibrates again.

Alphahole: Why haven't you taken off your clothes yet?

. . .

"What the—?" How does he know what I'm up to? Are there—I straighten, glance around the room—are there cameras here? Surely not. Or... I glance at the mirror on the wall opposite the bed... Hmm... Bet that's where it's hidden. Two can play a game here, huh?

I shove the phone into my purse. Yeah, okay. So I had dressed up a little. I mean, you can't blame a woman for taking care of her appearance when she is going to spend some time with a rock god, huh? Not that it matters, considering the man isn't here... Except for his orders by text messages...which, admittedly, are hot. Hmm. And, of course, I do want those orgasms he promised me... I'm not in this only for the money, after all.

I still don't understand, though. What does he get from this? Unless he gets off on watching me come? I stiffen. It's what he'd implied earlier... Only I hadn't believed him... Maybe... Maybe he is observing me even now? I wouldn't put it past him to have cameras in this place. Perhaps, he has one in this mirror, and is staring at me right now?

I watch my reflection as I raise my chin, run my tongue across my lips, then reach for the strap of my dress. I lower it down one shoulder, then the other, allow it to drop. I let the fabric pool around my ankles, kick it aside. I weigh my heavy breasts, run my hand down my belly to cup the flesh between my legs. This won't do; something is missing. I turn, head for my bag, pull out my phone and switch to one of his songs. The song that wasn't his most famous, but which has always been my favorite.

The strains fill the air. His harsh voice croons out the words; they pour over me, wrap around my shoulders, slither down my chest, into the dip of my navel, down into the hollow between my legs.

I place the phone on the nightstand, walk around to stand midway between the foot of the bed and the mirror.

I grind my hips in tandem to the slow rhythm of the song, once, twice. Narrow my gaze on my reflection in the mirror...knowing, no wanting, him to be on the other side of it.

Look at me, Rockstar. Know what you are missing, every second that you are not here with me.

I reach behind me, unhook my bra and shrug it off. I cup the underside of my breasts, massage them, throw my head back and forth as I pinch my nipples. Then bring the mounds together, imagining what it would feel like if he were to slide his dick in the valley between them. A hot flush spreads across my skin, my core clenches, and moisture beads my center. I drag my palm down my belly, hook my fingers under the band of my panties. I slide them down my legs, and step out of them. Hold up the lacy briefs in my fingers before dropping them to one side.

I straighten, part my legs, and slide my fingers between my thighs to play with my pussy lips. I bring my other hand up to my breast, squeeze the nipple again. A groan spills from my lips; a shiver of lust runs down my spine.

I sway to the music, slide my finger inside my channel, bring my other hand up to my hair. I wrap the strands around my palm and tug. Another moan wells up my throat. My breathing grows ragged. I dig my fingers into my scalp, shudder as goosebumps rise on my skin. I thrust another finger inside of myself, and a third, the girth stretching my entrance. I curl my digits inside like he would if he were here. He'd shove his fat cock inside of me—in and out, and in again, and keep going.

He'd slam his dick inside my pussy, again and again, not letting up, not when my knees tremble, not when my thighs spasm, and not when moisture pools in my core and overflows to run down my thighs. Not when I throw my head back, close my eyes and pant, shake with the pressure that builds at the base of my spine and fills my womb and snaps tighter, tighter, edging me closer to the edge… Closer.

"You will not come."

His voice whips through my mind. *Asshole.* As if he could command me when he isn't here. Why should I obey him anyway, huh? So what, if I am wound tighter than the rock star ever has been on stage in front of his adoring millions? He'd perform duo rhyme and I am performing for him… And for me… Yep, no doubt about it. I am enjoying being able to scrape my fingernails across my scalp, widen my stance as I shove my fingers in and out of my pussy, as I bend my spine backward, dig my feet—still in the fuck-me pumps I chose for this occasion—into the floor and aim higher, higher for that release that lingers on the horizon.

"Your orgasm belongs to me, Flower."

I snap my eyes open.

"Your mind may defy me, but your body knows how to follow my command."

Heat sears my back, envelops me, curls around my waist, down into the hollow between my thighs. "D…Damian," I gasp.

"Were you expecting someone else?"

"N…no."

"Why did you stop?"

"What?" I blink.

"You were giving me a show, weren't you, Flower?"

I stare forward into the mirror, at how his blue eyes blaze as he holds my gaze. His large shoulders block out everything else as he towers over me. He's dressed in a leather jacket and jeans, heavy motorcycle boots on his feet. His hair is tousled. Did he ride here on his bike? He props his arms on his hips, lowers his gaze to my pussy.

"Keep going," he growls. "Fuck yourself for me."

I stare at his features, slide my fingers in and out of myself. Color sears his cheeks; his nostrils flare. He lowers his hands to his sides, curls his fingers into fists. I press my thumb into my clit; his chest rises and falls. I cup my breast with my other hand and squeeze my nipple.

He inhales sharply.

I work a fourth finger into my channel and my entire body convulses. OMFG. He raises his gaze to meet mine in the mirror, his blue gaze deepening to a shade of almost cerulean.

He reaches around to place his big hand on mine. I shiver. Goosebumps dot my skin.

"Damian," I whisper.

He lowers his head to nuzzle the curve of my shoulder and my belly trembles. "Damian," I gasp again.

"When you say my name like that, it fucking turns me on, you know that?" He presses himself against me and the hard length of his arousal stabs into the curve of my hips. I groan, throw my head back against his chest as he squeezes my arse.

I shudder. "Damian," I whine.

"Don't stop," he commands.

I swallow, continue to shove my fingers in and out of myself. His hard fingers engulf mine, making the gesture somehow more intimate, like it is him fucking me. He slides the fingers of his other hand into the valley between my butt cheeks and I groan. He pushes a finger into my backhole. I can't stop the moan that whines from me.

"Damian…please." My fingers tremble and my knees knock together. He tightens his grasp on my hand which is between my legs. The force of it pushes my fingers deeper inside my channel. I gasp. A trembling begins at my toes, flows up my calves, my thighs.

"Oh, Damian," I moan.

"Open your eyes," he orders.

I flutter open my eyelids—when had I closed them, hmm?—meet his gaze in the mirror. His burning blue gaze holds mine.

He presses a kiss to the curve of my neck, then parts his lips and bites down on my skin. Pain pinches my nerve endings, shoots straight to my core. He curls his fingers around mine, pushes them into me, and again. He proceeds to fuck me with my own hand, even as he keeps my backhole plugged with his own. He releases his hold on my neck, only to bend in close. He places his lips next to my ear, gazes deep into my eyes in the mirror. "Come," he growls.

13

Julia

The climax crashes over me; sparks flash behind my eyes. Moisture gushes out from between my thighs. I hear the sound of someone scream… I know it's me… It can't be. Have I ever sounded so unfiltered? So completely consumed by the moment. By him. By the passion that ignites between us, by the heat in his gaze that holds me in place as the orgasm smashes into me. I tip up my chin, thrust out my breasts.

"Damian!" I cry out as the climax recedes, leaving me empty. So empty. My knees give out from under me. I fall into him, slide down, and he steadies me with his hold on my hand and my fingers still inside of me. He holds me upright with his grip on my pussy, licks the shell of my ear, and fuck, that's hot. And erotic. And for all that, he hasn't even fucked me… Not in the conventional sense.

"Jesus," I whisper.

"Nothing to do with him." He smirks. "And you're welcome."

"I haven't thanked you yet," I jut out my chin.

"Oh, you will, before the hour is out. That is, if you have any voice left." He releases me, only to flip me around. He drops to his knees, shoves his head in between my legs, and swipes his tongue up my pussy. I cry out, grab at his thick hair, and hold on.

He squeezes my butt cheeks. I pant.

He slides his tongue inside my melting channel. I moan. My belly trembles and my toes curl. "Damian, Damian," I chant as he tongues me in and out, and in and out. He inserts his finger into my backhole, closes his mouth over my swollen core. I howl, bend over his head, try to close my thighs. A chuckle rumbles up his chest. He proceeds to eat me out, suck on my clit, before shoving two fingers into my channel. "Damian, no," I howl.

His lips curve against my center—or I swear that's what he must have done—for the next moment, he adds two more fingers inside my sensitive core. He curls his fingers and I explode. The climax grips me, and I clamp my pussy around his fingers, grab hold of tufts of his hair as the sensations smash into me, then fade away. Leaving the sound of my heartbeat pumping in my ears. My bones seem to melt; all of my brain cells have surely self-combusted. I can't think, can't do anything except slump against his broad shoulders. I sense him move, crack open my eyes to find he's scooped me up and carried me to the bed. He tucks me under the covers. "Sleep, Flower." He kisses my forehead, then turns to leave.

I grab his wrist. "Stay," I whisper.

He hesitates.

"Just for a few minutes."

"I need to leave to take care of my daughter."

"Of course."

This man, he's the most macho man I've ever met, and yet, every single night, he makes it a point to be home to put his daughter to bed. I'd been so caught up in his media image that this...caring side of him...is a surprise. What's worse, it makes him even more irresistible. And that... That isn't fair, at all. I twine my fingers with his, brush my thumb across the roughened skin of his knuckles.

"You've been fighting again?" I yawn.

"Fucking Arpad," he says without heat. "The man knows how to get to me."

"You two close?"

The song on my phone switches to another; he reaches over to shut it off.

"Why did you pick that one?" he asks.

"It's from your first album. Your earlier work was so much better than your later tracks, not that I didn't like them, but somehow your later songs seemed to—"

"Lack heart?" He winces, then chuckles, "At least, you're honest."

"Your turn." I glance up into his face, take in his features, which seem almost relaxed. Apparently, getting me off, relaxed him too. "You can tell me." I half smile. "I won't tell anyone."

"He and I, we were together through most of the incident."

"You supported each other through it?"

"More like fought each other, and that helped us stay alive."

"Oh?" I frown. "You mean the two of you had to trade blows when you were kidnapped."

"Not only." His features close. Damn it, and we'd been getting along so well.

"I need to go," he insists.

But I don't want you to leave. I bring his hand to my face, kiss the broken skin across his fingers. "There, that should help."

"Is that a fact based in science?" He chuckles.

"You bet." I yawn so loudly my jaws crack. "Damn," I whisper, "apparently, orgasms make me sleepy."

"And even more alluring."

"Did you say alluring?" I frown. "Your vocabulary never ceases to amaze me."

"Now I know why my parents paid for my expensive private school tuition." He laughs.

"Why?" I mumble.

"It was just so I could impress you, of course." He laughs, then bends in to brush a kiss over each of my eyelids. "Sleep, Flower. When you awaken, you'll feel better."

Darkness pulls me under. When I awake, I am alone.

14

Damian

"But Daddy, Salad wants to read Calvin and Hobbes." Riley folds her arms over her chest.

I glance up from the copy of *Alice in Wonderland* that I had been trying to read out loud — 'trying' being the operative word here, for Riley is having none of it. "You're too young for Calvin and Hobbes."

"But Mommy read to me from it."

Ah. I bite the inside of my cheek. How do I tell her that her mom made a mistake? Not that I could come out and admit it openly, huh? So, what should I tell her? That Calvin and Hobbes has the kind of language that is just a little too mature for her.

"Daddy," Riley's bottom lip quivers. "you promised…"

"I promised I'd read to you."

"From a book of my choice," she lisps. She only does that when she's upset. Shit. A tear rolls down her cheek.

"Don't cry, baby." I push the book aside, then scoop her up in my arms. "I promise I'll read Calvin and Hobbes to you, just not yet."

"But…but…"

I cuddle her closely as I lie down on the bed. "Alice had a white rabbit, you know."

"White…white wabbit?" she gazes up at me with her big blue eyes so like mine.

Damn, she sounds so young. Well, she is young. Except, she normally sounds so much older than her years that I forget. Then she lapses into the language of her younger years, and damn, if my heart doesn't almost break. "Yeah, she followed the white rabbit down the hole and that's when her adventures began."

"Ad—ventures."

"Yep, she meets a crazy queen, a mad hatter—"

"What's a hatter?"

"Someone who makes hats."

"You wear a hat…"

"A cap," I correct her. "A baseball cap."

"What's the difference?"

"A cap? Well, uh, it has a rim that doesn't go all the way around, unlike a bowler hat."

"A bowler hat?"

"Yeah, you know… The thing that the twins wear in the adventures of TinTin."

"TinTin?" She sits up, "Who's TinTin?"

"TinTin has a dog called Snowy."

She scrunches up her features, "D-a-a-d, I want a dog."

Shit, no way, can I deal with a dog on top of a kid. Christ, how did we land on TinTin anyway? Weren't we talking about Alice and her adventures?

"There's a dog in Alice's Adventures in Wonderland too." *I think.*

"Really?"

"Yep." I pick up the book in relief. "Here, let me read to you…"

Ten minutes later, she's fast asleep… Shit, there is no dog in *Alice's Adventures*… Fuck, if I couldn't do with my own version of a white rabbit though. The kind you imbibe, not the dildo… Shit, don't think of a dildo when you're putting your daughter to sleep, you ass.

I slide out of the bed. Riley stirs. I freeze, wait until her breathing deepens. Whew! If you'd told me a few years ago that I'd be turning down gigs to spend time with my daughter… W-e-l-l, I'd have laughed long and hard. The final joke is on me, though. I smooth the cover about my daughter's shoulders. Her cheeks are rosy, her cherubic face relaxed in sleep. She's so fucking gorgeous. Fuck, don't swear—not even by way of thinking, in relation to her. Bloody hell, this parenting thing? I suck at it.

I back away from the bed, close the door behind me, keeping it slightly ajar, exactly how Riley prefers it. I head down the steps toward the kitchen. The empty kitchen where Meredith put aside dinner in the fridge, no doubt. She's taken to coming by more and more often. Clearly, she's worried about me. Hell, she treats all Seven of us as part of her extended family. She'd helped us after the incident, given us a place to hang out away from our homes where we could be ourselves without the constant worried attentions of our close families, or worse, the kind of indifference that came from parents who couldn't cope with what had happened. Like mine. They'd been alright though, I suppose. They'd taken me to shrinks, helped me to deal with it. Just… They had never been able to stop treating me with kid gloves. The result? I had rebelled in the typical way…

I had left home at eighteen to form a rock band. It hadn't been easy, but the challenge of it…had kept me going. And the Seven. All of them had encouraged me. Even that fucker, Baron, who'd preferred to leave the rest of us behind as he travelled across the world to wherever the hell he is right now… He'd made sure to send me a letter congratulating me when my first album had been a hit.

Now that I am scraping rock bottom… Yeah—a rock star bottom, I suppose. I can call it that. I snicker—Well, now that I am as close to the starting point as I had been, in terms of being a failure, that is… I have nothing to lose, huh? I can simply follow my instinct, give tune to the kinds of words I wouldn't have been caught dead writing before… At least, I am writing, thanks to her. I walk into my study and make sure the baby-cam is switched on, so I have eyes and ears on my angel.

Then strum my guitar as I begin to compose the rhythm for the words that have been buzzing in my head from earlier.

Space, presence, amalgamation of a lifetime.

I take,

You yield.

My presence fills your void.

Balance...

I claim the openings you leave.

The chase,

The hunt,

The thrill of the beyond.

Taking, moving, taking, moving.

Empty as a dance without a partner.

Demented as a man without his wife…

What the hell? My fingers slip on the chords, the sound jarring in the empty space. Wife? Where did that thought come from? I place the guitar on the couch, then jump up to my feet. Shit, this wasn't meant to happen. This…this itch inside of me, the crawling, damning need that lodges in my gut and aches to get out and I cannot, will not, let it… I hope.

I snatch up my phone and dial.

"Hello, motherfucker." Arpad's voice comes through.

"Hello to you, too," I blow out a breath.

There's a pause, then he switches to video. His face appears on screen. "What's wrong?"

"What could be wrong?" I rub the back of my neck.

"You wouldn't be calling if there wasn't something."

"True," I concede.

"Your stalker bothering you again?" He scowls.

"It's been quiet on that front." I sigh. Maybe too quiet. Not that I am complaining. I'd gone off social media but it hadn't deterred the die-hard fans from trying to track down where I live. One of them had sent me threatening notes, then had been caught trying to sneak onto my property a few months ago. It's why I'd had Karina beef up the security around the house; and why I had cancelled my gigs and all engagements to stay home. No one can protect my daughter the way I can, after all. And no way, am I going to let anything happen to her.

"What are you going to do about it?" He frowns.

"About what?"

"Her."

I scowl, "Why the hell did you have to send her to me?"

"Why would I not?"

"You're deflecting."

"And you're still in mourning."

"Fuck that," I hunch my shoulders.

He pauses, "It wasn't your fault, Damian."

"You don't know that. If I had handled things differently, if I had made more time for my family, things would have been different."

"You can't change the past, but you can affect the future. It's in your hands."

"Is that why you saw fit to steer things around, so I couldn't avoid her?"

He clicks his tongue, "You forget things so quickly."

"What do you mean?"

"Remember, I said that if Weston and Amelie decided to get married, you'd have no choice but to accept the gift I sent you."

I pause. "Motherfucker," I swear out aloud. "She's not an inanimate object you bastard."

"But she is a gift, and she's what you need right now."

"Oh?" I stare at his face on the screen. "The fuck you think you are, playing with our lives?"

"Someone has to, considering you don't want to move on from where you've been stuck for too long."

"Jesus, Arpad." I shake my head. "This…is all wrong. You shouldn't have done this."

"Why not?" he retorts. "You were too much of a loser to take what was right in front of you. Left to yourself, you'd have never seen her again."

"And rightly so. She deserves fucking better."

"That's for her to decide."

"She's better, away from me."

"That's your decision."

"Huh?" I stare at him.

"I've done my part," he raises his shoulders, "the rest is up to you."

15

———————

27th December

Julia

"Bastard!" It's six pm, and once again, I stand in between the mirror and the bed in the same room as yesterday. Only he hasn't texted me yet.

Why hasn't he texted me, yet?

I glance down at my phone, then throw it on the bed. I will not allow him to see how anxious I am. Will not allow him to find out just how pissed off I am that he didn't call me after yesterday. Hell, when I awoke, he was gone. Which I expected, but not even a note left behind. I'd woken up a few hours later to find I was alone and covered in the sheets. The mattress next to me was cold and uncreased so I know he never laid down beside me. He'd simply taken my orgasms—okay, so I had given them to him freely—and he'd gone. "Asshole."

No doubt, if he were here, he'd ask me to call him Alphahole. A title that, strangely, does fit him. Only Damian fucking Savage would have the ego to claim that label, and with no sign of irony either. He'd mean it… He actually believes every single legend the media spins about him. Well, the length of his cock, for one… Not that I have seen it yet… I've felt it, learned the shape of it through his pants…but he hasn't even taken off his clothes yet. Hmm. He's devoted himself to my pleasure, it seems. And not that I am complaining, but that yummy body of his? I definitely want to see more of it.

Just as I want to find out more about the man and his daughter. I could call up Amelie or Isla and ask, I suppose. But somehow that doesn't seem right. I want him to tell me about his life…want to get to know the man who pays for my company better. Hell. If only I didn't need the money. But damn it, I can't turn away from the millions he's dangled in front of me. I'd checked my bank account, and already, the number of zeroes in it had confirmed that Damian is a man of his word—Ha! And if that's the case, why isn't he here already?

I pick up the phone and look at the clock. It's already been ten minutes since I got here. Ten minutes without his touch on my skin, his fingers in my pussy, the imprint of his shaft against the softness of my belly... And damn it, today I want more. I need more. I need to get him to share more of what lurks behind those blazing blue eyes.

I need to do something different. Need to get him to react. But how? I glance around the space—the wide headboard on the massive king-sized bed that takes up most of the room. I run my fingers down the scarf I draped around my neck before leaving home. Hmm… What if I surprise him? Or is that what he expects from me? To do the unexpected because he hasn't asked something specific of me? Maybe… But hell, if I am going to pace the room waiting for him… I am going to take some control of the situation—something he doesn't want, but too bad.

I grab the bedspread, throw it over the mirror. Good, now he has no idea what he's walking into. I head for the bowl of fruit kept on the coffee table by the settee, pick up one, then I walk over to the bed. I shed my clothes, making sure to keep my heels on—yeah, I'd dressed again for that asshole—then I climb onto the bed.

16

Damian

Six-twenty p.m. I'd have delayed it further, except she'd cut off all
visual to the room. She'd thrown the bedspread over the mirror, and
the app I'd been using to track her, courtesy of the camera in the
frame of the mirror, had gone dark. How the hell had she guessed the
location of the camera anyway? The woman is resourceful. And
smart. Of course, she is. It's why she'd intrigued me from the
moment I'd seen her. I use my keycard to let myself into the
apartment.

I walk through the living room, lit by the glow of the city lights
coming into the space, and step into the bedroom…and stop. My
breath catches. Blood rushes to my groin. "What the fuck?"

I stalk to the foot of the bed and glance down at my woman on
her hands and knees, on the bed, facing away from me. I take in the
curve of her arse, emphasized by the light that flows into the room…
The flesh of her thighs, the sweep of her calves, her feet clad in fuck-
me shoes. A growl rips out of me. "What the hell are you doing?"

She glances over her shoulder and I catch sight of the apple she holds in her mouth. Her green eyes gleam. Her pink lips contrast with the red of the skin of the apple. Her neck is arched, her shoulders pulled back.

I take in the unpainted fingernails, her palms pressed into the bed. The globes of her pert breasts mirror the shape of the apple, her nipples dark, their color a contrast to the white of the sheets on the bed. I drag my gaze down her belly to the lushness of her hips and the sight of the ripe flesh between her legs. Moisture glistens against her lower lips and I know she's ready for me.

"How dare you start without me?" I growl.

She draws in a breath and the apple slips from her mouth.

"Don't let go of the fruit, or you'll regret what I am going to do to you even more."

Her gaze widens. A hint of something like fear glimmers in her eyes.

She quickly grabs the apple, puts it back in her mouth. Good.

"Eyes forward!" I order.

She blinks, hesitates. I swoop down and slap her arse.

She cries out, or at least I presume she does, for its muffled by the bloody apple in her mouth…Jesus, what the hell had she been thinking? Why is she offering herself up like that to me? Doesn't she know I am less Adam and more the serpent in the Garden of Eden…?

"Remember what I said, Flower? Don't let the apple fall."

I slap her arse again and again. Left cheek, then right, then left. Pause.

I step back, survey the reddened bloom of her butt, my fingerprints clearly standing out against her pale skin. Moisture drips down her inner thighs. "That turned you on, hmm?"

She trembles. I reach down and kiss the curve of her butt; she shudders. I press another kiss to her other arsecheeks and she shivers.

"Remember," I whisper against her skin, "hold onto the apple."

I straighten, undo the buckle of my belt.

She stiffens, turns her head.

I click my tongue, "Don't turn."

She stares ahead.

I slide out my belt, and the whine of the leather across the waistband is loud in the space.

She curves her back, clenches her butt.

"Three lashes, Flower," I drawl, "and you'd better not orgasm."

She tips up her chin. I snap the belt. The leather connects with her backside. Her entire body jerks. Her thighs spasm. I straighten, then lower the belt again. The crack of the strap against her skin leaves a pink welt across her butt. My cock lengthens. *Fuck me.*

This…thing inside of me, this need to see her ready and open and willing…for me… Why the hell have I never felt it with anyone else before? A hum winds down my spine and my groin hardens. I lower my arm and lay the last lash across her butt. She jolts, the apple rolls from her mouth, and a cry spills from her lips. All of my senses pop. I grab her hips, flip her around, then bury my mouth in her pussy. I drag my tongue up to her swollen clit and she screams out.

She tries to pull away. I grip the backs of her thighs, pull her close, until my face is jammed in between her folded legs. I thrust my tongue inside her melting channel. She grips my hair and tugs. The pain shivers down my spine, and my balls harden. I lick my tongue up her pussy lips again and again, bite down on her clit, and she arches her back off of the bed.

"Damian," she cries out, and fuck, my name from her lips… It's sweeter than the screams of adoring crowds as I face them from on stage.

I tear my mouth from her pussy, rise up and over her, fit my mouth to hers, thrust my fingers knuckle-deep inside her channel, wrap my other palm around the back of her neck, my fingers resting on the pulse points on either side, and kiss her and fuck her with my fingers, in and out, in and out. Her core clenches around my fingers; her mouth opens further as I dance my tongue across hers. She strains against me, pushes her nipples into my chest, parts her legs wider as she tilts her hips, pushes her pelvis up, coaxes me to grind the heel of my palm into her cunt. A groan trembles up her throat. I tear my mouth from hers, peer into her eyes, pupils blown, the green now merely a circle that rings her dark irises.

"Come," I order, and she shatters. Her features twist, her lips part, and her muscles tauten as moisture floods from her center.

I pull my fingers out, ease them into her mouth. "Lick me off," I command.

She wraps her tongue around my digits, in the creases between them, across the junction where my fingers meet my palm. The slide of the wetness sinks into my blood, arrows straight to my cock. This woman... Nothing with her is predictable. Just when I think that I have her tamed, she springs a surprise that completely floors me. She holds my gaze as a tear slides from the corner of her eyes. I bend and lick it up.

She releases my fingers, tips up her chin. "Why did you do that?"

She's come apart under me, and yet, there's nothing timid or submissive about her...yet. "You don't get to ask me the questions." I increase the pressure of my fingers around her neck. She swallows.

"Understand?" I lower my face to hers, until our lips almost touch, "Answer me."

"Yes," she whispers.

"Good." I release her, then slide back and off the bed. Straightening, I tug on my shirtsleeve.

"You're already dressed in your formal clothes?" She frowns.

I glance at my watch. "Don't want to be late." I jerk my chin toward the closet at the far end of the room, "Get dressed, remember we have a wedding to attend?"

17

Julia

"Do you Amelie Elizabeth Abram take Weston George Kincaid to be your lawfully wedded husband?"

Weston glances down at his bride, his features lit up with such adoration that my heart skitters. Jesus, all that love in the air. Is it possible for someone to feel so much love for his wife-to-be?

"I do." Amelie giggles.

Her simple, knee-length, off-the-shoulder, white dress should seem almost too casual, except she wears the glow that seems to often characterize brides.

Damian stands to attention on the opposite side of the gathering, not a single bone in his body relaxed.

The entire wedding has clearly been planned to be a small intimate affair, on the ranch owned by Saint and his cousin Tinkerbell. The weather is freezing, but the space is surrounded by freestanding outdoor heaters, which cast a circle of warmth around us.

"You may now kiss the bride."

Before Edward has completed his statement, Weston swoops down, drags Amelie up to her toes, lowers his head, and kisses her.

Applause breaks out from the assembled group. Sinclair pulls Summer into his side. She tips her head up and he presses his lips to her forehead. The puppy she holds in her arms whines. Summer holds the dog up to Sinclair who scratches the little fella about his ears.

The dog barks, Summer lowers him to the ground, and he bounds over to where a little girl, bends to play with him. Behind her, a tall man frowns down at the scene as if he's not quite sure what to make of it. "That's Liam," Isla whispers to me.

"Is he perpetually angry?" I frown.

"He's scary," Isla shivers, "in a mean, dominant, cold, sexy, tear-your-panties-off and not take no for an answer —" her chest heaves, "obsessive, compulsive, calculating, single-minded," her tone grows raspy, "fuck you until you can't walk straight for days, kind of way."

"You mean he's a high-functioning sociopath?"

"Hmm." She looks him up and down. "More like a sexy, stalker-ish, manipulative, psychopath who just happens to be a billionaire."

"How can you find that hot?"

"I don't." She turns to me. "I mean, not really."

I stare at her.

She blushes. "I mean, come on. Damian's just as controlling, as self-assured, as provocative, as fine a specimen as they come —"

"He's better than that," I mumble.

"As much of a harsh, yummy, vigorous, macho, eight-pack-abbed —"

I snap my head in her direction, "How do you know that he has an eight-pack?"

"He is tabloid fodder." She raises her shoulders.

"Keep your eyes off his abs, his corded forearms, not to mention that beautiful, sculpted, whiskered jaw that leaves rug burn in its wake —"

"Whoa, you did it then?" Isla turns on me so quickly that I retreat from her.

"Woman, you'll get whiplash, if you keep that up," I hiss.

"Admit it," she crows. "You shagged that fine piece of arse. Please say, you did."

My fingers tingle and my sex clenches. "No." I feign disinterest.

"No way." Her gaze widens. "Tell me you didn't pass up the opportunity to test drive that fine piece of machinery."

"Down girl," I mutter. "Let's just enjoy the wedding without getting all hot and bothered."

"As if that's going to be possible when you're surrounded by all of this testosterone. Not to mention, all that dopamine that the couples in love are transmitting all around us."

Next to us, Jace whispers in Sienna's ear and she blushes. Next to them their baby sleeps in his pram.

Saint wraps his arm around Victoria, tilts her chin up to his and kisses her.

Isla sighs. *Yeah, you and me both, girlfriend. Don't I know the feeling?* If only there were someone special out there for me… The hair on the back of my neck rises. I glance up and across the room to where Mr. Smoldering Gaze Rockstar leans his hip against a wall. Clearly, he'd rather be anywhere else but here. Clearly, a marriage—not even one of his best friend's, carries much significance to him.

"The way he eats you up with his gaze," Isla shakes her head. "You sure nothing happened between the two of you, yet?"

"Not…sure," I reply under my breath.

"What does that mean?" I hear the confusion in her voice but don't glance up. I know how that sounds… But hell, how else do I classify what almost happened between us?

"You mean, you guys haven't done it yet?" she probes.

"We haven't *not* done it," I offer.

She huffs. "You are talking in riddles. Like the rest of the women did once they hooked up with one of the Seven."

"I haven't hooked up with him," I insist.

"Of course, the chemistry between the two of you is just a mistake, then?"

"It must be," I mumble, my gaze captivated by the beautiful profile of the man who'd captured my imagination from the moment I'd seen him first perform on stage.

He shoves a hand in the pocket of his beautifully-cut slacks. Surely. they must have been cut to his physique while he was standing in front of the tailor, who, no doubt, wept as he stitched them to fit every powerful muscle of those sinewed legs — *Gah! Stop drooling you idiot.* It's just cloth, fabric that many others wear, except on Damian f'ing Savage, formal pants and button-downs seem to be poetry in motion. *What the hell am I thinking?* I shake my head; he jerks his chin up and locks his gaze with mine. Those blue eyes of his seem to penetrate my heart, my skin, my soul. My throat closes and a bead of sweat slides down my spine.

Around me, confetti rains down on the newly married couple.

Damian straightens and his shoulder seem to bulge. His biceps flex, stretching in the full sleeves of his formal wear. He doesn't take his gaze off of me. My heart begins to thud. He brings up his thumb and runs it across his bottom lip, and bloody hell, my entire body seems to snap to attention. My belly clenches and moisture pools between my legs. What the —? What kind of hold does he have on me?

"Nice dress, by the way," Isla whispers.

"What?"

"Your gown."

"Oh, it's borrowed."

"From whom?"

"Uh, Damian told me to wear it."

"Damian?" she whisper-screams. "So, you did spend time with him, after all?"

"Shh," I grab her arm, "you'll attract attention."

"So I should." She stares at me. "Tell me all, bitch."

"There's nothing to tell." I glance back at the space where I'd last seen Damian, and find the space is empty. Huh?

"Well?" She shakes off my hold, only to grab my arm instead, "So you did shag him?"

"No," I snap. "Uh, we've done stuff, just not that."

"I don't understand."

"Tell me about it." I glance around the space as Weston and Amelie accept congratulations from the rest of the crowd. I should go up and wish her well too. Except, damn it, I can't, not yet. Not when I'm not sure what I've gotten myself into. Not sure if I have a job to go to, either… Shit, a job I needed. Why the hell couldn't he let me see his daughter? Am I so abhorrent to him? A shapeless piece of clay? Well, I certainly feel dowdy, compared to the glowing faces in this room.

"You okay?" Isla hisses.

"No. Yes." I swallow, "I don't know." Tears prick the backs of my eyes. *No, no, no.* "I… I need a moment."

I step back from her and she releases her grasp on me.

"Where are the restrooms?"

"First floor, to the far right." She searches my face, "Want me to come with you?"

"No." I shake my head. "I'll be fine, I just need to get away." I turn, skirt the crowd, and head inside. The sounds of laughter and conversation fade as I walk across the beautiful lounge, head up the steps and to the right of the hallway. Follow it to the door that's partially ajar at the end. I peek inside, then gasp when a warm hand descends on my shoulder. I'm pushed inside so abruptly that I stumble. I turn to find Damian leaning against the door. He lowers his hand to grasp the doorknob and a lock snaps into place.

"Wh...what are you doing?"

He unhooks his belt and the buckle clanks as he pulls it off. My nerve-endings pop. I drop my gaze to his crotch, to where the evidence of his desire tents the fabric of his pants. OMFG, it's not possible that he's as big as he seems, is he? My toes curl. My scalp tingles. I dig my heels into the floor, curl my fingers into fists at my sides.

"On your knees," he orders.

My jaw drops. "You're crazy."

"For you."

I glance up at his face and his lips twist.

"You're joking," I whisper. "Not even you can be that much of a bastard."

"Oh, good, so I don't need to pretend." He wipes all expression off his face. "Do it," he snaps.

My thighs tremble and my knees hit the floor with a thump that sends pain shooting up my legs.

"Touch yourself."

I gape.

He tilts his head, "You don't want me to come there."

I tilt up my chin. "On the contrary," I raise my gaze to his face, and flinch. The skin is drawn tightly over his cheekbones, his jaw tics, and the creases around his eyes seem to deepen. He seems like a man possessed, one who is this close to losing control, and I am not sure why.

"What…what did I do?" I whisper.

"What makes you think it's something you did, hmm?"

"Isn't it?"

"Yours is not to question why."

"—But to do or die?" I joke.

He draws in a breath; the planes of his chest seem to flex.

In two steps, he closes the distance between us, grabs the hair at the back of my head and tugs. Pain lances down my spine, arrows straight to the emptiness that crawls in my core.

"I told you never to talk about dying, didn't I?"

I stare up into his face. His jaw tics, his features twist, and he looks like a man who's seen a ghost. *Oh, hell.* "I'm sorry," I whisper. "I didn't mean to bring back memories—"

"I told you not to speak," he snaps.

"You didn't," I protest.

"It's understood."

"What? Now I'm supposed to read your mind?" I huff.

"Nope, now you take the punishment I am going to mete out to you."

18

Damian

"Show me your pussy."

"What?" Color smears her cheeks.

"You heard me."

What the hell are you doing, asshole? Let her go, get away from her, turn around and head back home — to…my daughter? My life… shorn of all creativity, one filled with responsibilities that weigh heavily on me. A life filled with yearning for something…more.

I love my daughter — the light of my life, the one who makes it all worthwhile… And if I don't work another day in my life, she'll be provided for. But would she be proud of the music I've created so far? Would she see my fall from the pinnacle of success I'd once occupied? Would she remember me as a failure…one who couldn't compose anymore? And the songs I have out there… They are hardly the kind I'd want her to listen to. I have to come up with more, so much more, something that will ensure that she sees me in a new light. The kind of father I've always wanted to be, one she'll remember with pride. With the kind of emotion I'd wanted to feel for my own parents and hadn't quite been able to, given the distance that had grown between us since the incident.

No, I want more for my daughter. I have to do right by her. I have to make her proud of me if it is the last thing I do… And this sassy, proud woman is going to help me with that. She will play a key role in helping me reinvent myself. So what, if I am being selfish about it? I owe it to myself, don't I? I simply have to make sure she benefits from this arrangement too.

"Do it, Flower," I coax her. Where the hell did that come from? I am not supposed to show her any mercy, yet here I am requesting her to fall in line with my plans. I shake my head, straighten my shoulders. "Don't keep me waiting." I lower the pitch of my voice.

She shivers, then slides her hand under her gown, flips it up.

"Fuck." I stare at the pink flesh exposed between her thighs. "What the hell? You didn't wear panties?"

"Neither did you."

I tilt my head. "Not in the habit of wearing frilly underwear, not even for you."

She flushes. "You know what I mean."

"No, I don't."

"I mean…that." She jerks her chin toward my open fly.

"What?"

"You're gonna make me spell it out?"

"Anything to see you squirm, sweetheart." I chuckle.

"Asshole."

I click my tongue. "You know how I prefer alphahole, or even Master would do very nicely."

"Go fuck yourself."

I laugh, "I'd much rather see you fuck yourself.'

"Argh." She throws up her hands, and her dress flows down around her knees.

"Now you've done it."

"What?"

"You disobeyed my command."

"I…I didn't."

I glance down to where her dress covers the sweet flesh she'd exposed earlier.

She follows my gaze, then pales, "It…it was a mistake."

That's for sure. "Oh?" I take a step forward.

She stumbles to her feet. "Honest, I… I didn't mean to."

I move toward her. Her gaze flicks around the bathroom.

"Don't even think about it," I murmur.

"You… You don't know what I am thinking about."

"Don't I?"

"If you did, you wouldn't be standing there talking to me."

I close the distance between us.

She squeaks, dodges around me and makes for the door. She grabs the handle, twists it, then swears. "Why the hell isn't it opening?"

"Guess."

She turns around, then stares at the key I show her. I slip it into the pocket of my slacks.

She swallows audibly. "Oh, hell."

"Indeed." I quirk my finger at her, "Come 'ere."

She shakes her head.

I draw in a breath. "You're making this more difficult on yourself.

"And you're t…talking in riddles."

"Nervous?"

"Of course, not." She hiccups. "Oops." She slaps a palm to her mouth.

"Did you just hiccup?" I frown.

"Not me." She hiccups again.

I chuckle. "Such a little liar."

"I'm not." She glowers at me.

A tiny line appears between her eyebrows. Fucking adorable. Wait. Hold on. Back up. I did not just think of her as adorable. WTF?

"Prove it."

"What…what do you mean?"

"Come closer."

"No, thank you." She folds her hands together in front of herself. "I'm, uh, good right where I am."

"Don't say I didn't warn you." I move toward her.

She squeaks, then darts toward the window on the side.

"What the hell—?"

She grapples with the sash lock of the window pane.

I reach her, clamp my hand around the nape of her neck.

She shudders, tries to wriggle away.

I increase the pressure about her nape, and she lowers her forehead to the glass. "Please," she whispers.

"Please what?"

"Please let me go."

I slap her butt.

She studders, "Wh…what was that for?"

"Lying again?"

"I'm not."

I take a step back, hold her still with my grip on her neck.

"Last chance," I snap.

"For what?"

"To tell the truth."

"I… I don't understand."

I take aim, then bring down my palm with such force on her arse that her entire body jerks. She rises to the tips of her toes. Her hair flows around her shoulders. "Ohmygod," she screams.

"Wrong answer." I spank the curve of her butt again and again.

She howls. "Stop," she gasps.

"Answer me first."

"What's the question."

"Do I make you nervous?"

"Yes."

"Do I turn you on?"

"Yes."

"Will you defy me again?"

"Yes," she stutters, then gasps. "No, no, you bastard, I won't. I'll do what you tell me to."

"Too late, Flower." I hook my finger into the V of the neckline at the back of her dress and tug. The material rips, the sound slicing through the space.

Goosebumps rise on her skin. "What the hell — ?" She turns her head and I tear the flimsy material from neck to hem. The fabric parts, leaving the exposed length of her body from shoulder to hip to the cleft between her thighs to the turn of her beautiful ankles. My groin hardens; my cock lengthens.

She kicks back. I angle my body to avoid her, then plant my thigh between her legs. She wriggles her arse, and Jesus, the warmth of her center sinks through the fabric of my slacks. I lean in, press the weight of my crotch into her back. A trembling grips her. She plants her palm flat against the pane.

Below us, a white mare gallops by, followed by a dark stallion. Nature in action, the dominant and the female with whom he was meant to mate. I place my cheek close to hers, and another shudder rolls up her spine. "Shh," I whisper, "I won't hurt you."

"Oh?" She turns to glare at me, the green of her eyes burning bright, "What do you call this then?"

"Taming the shrew."

"I am no shrew," she protests.

"Sure could have fooled me, sweetheart, for you definitely need a firm hand."

"I don't need anything from you. I don't need you," she snarls.

"Wrong." I lower my head and nip on her lip.

She moans.

I rub my thumb over the pulse that flutters at the hollow of her neck. Her pulse rate ratchets up; the sweet scent of her arousal deepens. I slide my other hand between her legs. "You're fucking soaking." I press little kisses to the corner of her mouth, make my way up to the shell of her ear. I bite her ear lobe and her entire body jolts. "See how you respond to me?"

"That's…uh…. Just physical."

"That's a start."

"For what?"

"For what's coming next."

"Which is?"

I thrust two fingers inside her pussy. She yells. The sound slices straight to my gut, and goddamn me, but I am so hard, and I can't wait any longer. I need to taste her, I need to have her falling apart on my fingers, on my tongue. "I want you helpless and broken and shattered for me to pick up the pieces. Only me. You understand?"

"No," she snaps.

"Yes." I release my hold on her neck, only to sink to my knees between her legs. I squeeze her butt cheeks, then thrust my tongue inside her pussy.

19

Julia

OMG. OMG. He curls his tongue inside of me and I groan. He flicks his tongue across my pussy lips, and I push my forehead into the glass. There's a whinnying sound from far below. I glance down to find the mare prancing about as the stallion stalks her. Jeez, talk about life imitating nature. Or is that life imitating art? Whatever it is, nature unfolds her drama down in the field, and up here, my very own racehorse of an alpha begins to thrust his tongue in and out of me, fucking me with his tongue. "Oh, God," I groan. He picks up speed.

He slides a finger into my puckered hole, then thrusts his wide palm between me and the window pane. He fastens his fingers across my core and I gasp, "Damian." I try to turn. He pinches my clit and I yell, "No, goddamn it, no."

He pulls his fingers from inside of me. Cool air envelops my heated flesh. What the—? I glance over my shoulder to find he's stalked to the shower cubicle. He wrenches open the door, grabs one of the bottles from the receptacle inside.

"What are you doing?"

He pivots. "Eyes forward," he commands.

I take in the bottle of conditioner that he uncorks as he marches over to me.

"No." I swallow.

A smile pulls at his lips, and it's not the good kind. I gulp, "D… Damian?"

"Yes, Flower?" His grin widens.

"You…you won't."

"Is that a challenge?" He stares into my face.

"I hate you," I mumble.

He pauses, widens his stance. "Leave."

"What?"

"You heard me." He jerks his chin toward the door, "Go."

"You…you don't mean it."

"Have I ever said anything that I don't mean to you?"

"N…never."

"Right." He cracks his neck. "So, stay and let me take your arse, or turn and go. Your choice."

Is it though? Considering I have no clothes to wear.

I take in his flushed cheeks, the hard tendons of his sculpted neck, the V of his skin exposed by the lapels of his shirt, the smattering of dark hair that arrows down to the part of him that I haven't yet seen.

"I'll stay."

His eyes gleam.

"On one condition," I force out the words.

"You don't get to call the shots."

"You haven't heard what I'm going to say."

"Hmph." He flattens his lips, "What is it?"

"Take off your shirt."

"That's it?"

"And your pants…"

"No."

"What?"

"I don't undress in front of strangers."

"I'm hardly a stranger, you ass," I scowl. "You've had your tongue inside of me."

He smacks his lips, "And you taste so fucking good, Flower."

I redden, then push my thighs together. Why the hell do I find that so hot? I stare at him and he seems to relent.

"Okay, this once." He unbuttons his shirt and the lapels gape in the front. I take in those cut abs, the hollow of his belly, the massive tent over his crotch.

"Happy?" He smirks.

"No," I grouse.

"Too bad." He jerks his chin, "Face forward."

I hesitate.

"Flower," he warns.

I huff, then turn to glance forward.

"So, you're staying?"

His voice is right behind me. The heat of his body envelops me, and the hair on my nape prickles. I know what's coming, and damn him. I don't want him to do it, and yet, I have to find out how it would be to be taken by him.

"Why don't you want to fuck me?" I demand.

"Newsflash," he growls. "I am gonna fuck your arse." Cold liquid pours down the valley between my butt cheeks.

I shiver. My belly knots. "Th…that's not what I mean. Why don't you want to…" I hesitate, "Want to—"

"Tear into your luscious pussy?"

"Jesus," I breathe, "you have a filthy mouth."

"One you love, admit it."

"You have me there," I draw in a breath. "I don't know why those uncouth words from you turn me on."

"Don't beat yourself about it." He leans in, kisses my shoulder.

The tenderness in that gesture. I blink. Wow. I glance at him sideways. "It's not what I am used to," I mumble. "I mean, I've been with men—"

He slaps my arse.

"Hey," I protest.

"Don't fucking talk about anyone else when I'm with you." He glares at me.

"But I mean—"

He wraps his fingers around my neck in a gesture I'm coming to recognize as the hallmark of his dominance. It's hot, I'll admit. It's what sets him apart from anyone else I've been with… Well, not only, but it's the confidence with which he handles my body, how he massages the cold liquid of the conditioner in between my butt cheeks, and works his finger inside my backhole, then follows it up with a second digit…while he holds my gaze, and intensifies the pressure on the back of my neck just enough so I tip up my chin and push out my butt.

"Good girl," he grunts. And my nipples harden; my pussy clenches. The blue of his eyes deepens.

He works a third finger inside of me and I gasp, "Oh, my… Oh wow, Damian… Oh…"

"How does it feel?"

"F-full," I stutter. "It's too much. I can't."

"You can." His lips curl, "I'll make sure."

A shiver runs up my spine. "What if it hurts?" I whine.

"It will," he promises.

"What?" I gape, "If you think you're selling this to me, you're mistaken."

He lowers his head and bites me on the bridge of where my shoulder meets my neck.

"Ow," I yelp. "That hurts, as well."

"Just priming you, babe."

"I'm not a steak."

He chuckles, "You're softer." He curls his finger inside of me and I snap my head back and against his shoulder.

"Not to mention, fucking hot." He does something with his fingers, a jerky circling motion that sets off a burst of sensation that sweeps up my spine. "And tight. So tight." His voice seems to break. Did it? Nah, not possible.

Sparks flare behind my eyes. "Oh, my god," I gasp.

"I'll take that as a compliment," His chuckle rumbles up my spine. My nerve endings seem to pop, all at once, and moisture pools between my legs.

"I'm so empty." I slap my hand over my mouth. *Did I just say that aloud?*

How is it that when he touches me, I lose all of my filters, all of my carefully planned forward momentum mantras, the ones I picked up from self-help books along the way. Clearly, none of the authors of those books had come up against a real-life obstacle like Damian, someone who'd sweep through all the barriers, who'd get under your skin and turn every preconceived notion you had about yourself upside down. "Do it," I snarl.

"You forgot the magic word."

"Are you serious?" I angle my body to steal a glance at him, but he keeps me immobile with that warm hand of his that's still fixed on my nape, like I'm a bloody kitten. Hell, I feel as powerless and as pathetically needy. "Damian," I whine.

"Say the word, Flower."

I lick my lips. "This is stupid."

"Not the word I was looking for."

He withdraws his fingers, and my stomach clenches; my thighs spasm. That feeling of emptiness multiples — no, quadruples — in my belly. "Fine, fine, whatever," I huff. "Please, Damian, fuck my ar —"

The hard crown of his dick nudges my backhole, then he breaches me.

"Ow," I protest. "It hurts. It hurts." I pull away — or rather try to wriggle away from him, try being the operative word, for he wraps a heavy hand around my center, pulls me flush against his hard chest, then coaxes me to turn my chin up and toward him. "Damian —"

He closes his mouth over mine. He stays as is, his hard length throbbing inside of me, allowing me to adjust to his size… As if that's ever going to happen.

He curls his fingers around my neck again, then reaches down to play with my pussy. He dances his fingers down my core then back up to pinch my clit. I gasp, draw in a breath, and he slips further inside my backchannel. A moan wells up, and he swallows it down. He sucks on my tongue, while his fingers play with my core, and his hard cock… OMG… He pulls out, then thrusts back inside, there's a pinch and I gasp.

"Take a deep breath," he commands.

I follow his direction, draw in a breath and release it, then again. My muscles relax. I unclench and he slips in deeper. He thrusts two fingers inside my soaking channel and I shudder.

Goosebumps flare on my skin and a trembling grips my legs.

I throw my arm up and around his shoulders, hold on as he releases my pussy, only to hook his arm under my knee. He pulls up my leg, presses it into the window.

And the angle of my body allows him to slide in further. The fullness is unlike anything I have experienced before. Not that I have that much experience, but still… This… What he's doing to me… It's different, balancing me on the edge of pain and pleasure, that in-between place where all I can do is moan his name, "Damian," I plead, "Please."

I tip up my chin, meet his gaze. He glares down at me, so close that I notice the dot on his left pupil. It's something so intimate, something only a lover would notice… Or an enemy. "What am I to you?"

"You're mine." He growls.

"Damian," I whisper, then reach up to cup his cheek. "Damian."

His features twist and a vein throbs at his temple. "I hate what you do to me," his voice whispers over my skin.

I frown. "Damian, what do you — ?"

He thrusts in with enough force that my entire body jolts. At the same time, he tightens the hold around my neck, enough that my oxygen peters out. Darkness closes in on the edges of my vision as he begins to fuck my arse in earnest. In and out of me, again and again. My pussy clenches, heat sears my spine, I curl my toes, dig my fingers into his back, and gasp and moan and cry out. He doesn't stop. He pushes into me, all the way in, filling me in a way that I wouldn't have thought possible. *Oh my God, I'm going to —*

"Come." He releases his hold on my leg, thrusts his fingers inside my pussy. "Come all over my fingers," he insists. "Now," he snaps at the same time that he releases his hold on my neck and the climax crashes over me.

My orgasm sweeps up my legs, my torso, as the oxygen inflates my lungs. I throw back my head and howl as blue sparks flare behind my closed eyes. The climax goes on and on, and I hold onto him. Unable to keep my knee pressed into the window, I lower my leg, tightening the hold on his dick. He lowers his head and bites me on my shoulder and the pain shoots down to my belly. A second orgasm slithers up my spine, this one gentler, more mellow as it shivers over me. I slump and he wraps his big arms around me. Holds me as his dick throbs inside me still. Vibrations grip my back, a humming reaches my ears.

"Damian," I whisper.

"Shh." He kisses the top of my head, then pulls out of me.

I glance up and meet his gaze. "You didn't come," I point out.

"I know." His voice is matter of fact.

"I am beginning to think you are never going to orgasm in my presence."

He tilts his head, "Now that you point it out…"

"What are you afraid of?" I scowl.

"Myself." His features turn bleak, the skin stretching across his cheeks, highlighting the hollows under his eyes.

"Who hurt you?" I burst out. "Who turned you into this…"

"This?"

"Unfeeling monster?"

"That the best you can do?" He turns me, then scoops me up in his arms. I glance up at the jut of his chin, the weeks-old growth of whiskers that he'd trimmed for this occasion.

"The Seven, they are important to you?"

"They are family." He stalks over to the bath tub, lowers me to sit on the edge. He leans past me, turns on the taps, the hot water runs, and steam fills the room.

"You okay?"

I nod, glance up at his shuttered features.

"Good." He cleans himself up with a paper towel, then tucks himself inside, and zips up. "I'll send Isla with a change of clothes for you."

Turning, he leaves.

20

Damian

What the fuck was that about? Did I actually call her mine? What gives me the right to do so? Not that gut wrenching orgasm where she had come all over my fingers. Not the way she'd called my name as she'd writhed on my dick, and thrust her butt against my pelvis and thrown her head back and orgasmed, and again when I had bitten into her shoulder. I had bitten her… Fuck! Not once, but twice, and both times her body had fallen apart under my ministrations.

As she comes for me
As she begs me
As she struggles under me
As the world outside stops
As my life ignites
As she calls out my name… All I can think is she is Mine. Only mine.

"Fuck that." *She's not.* She doesn't belong to me. She is merely a conduit for my creativity. The siren song for my muse, the inspiration for my next move. Fuck, now I am thinking in lyrics… an abundance of riches—the poetry that pours out of me every time she climaxes. "What the hell am I thinking?"

"That's what I'd like to know."

I stare down at the man who stands at the bottom of the staircase.

"What the fuck do you mean?" I take the steps two at a time, reach the landing, and brush past Arpad.

He grabs my shoulder, "Not so fast."

I turn on him, "Keep your hands to yourself pal."

"What's gotten into you, man?" He holds up his hands, his forehead furrowed.

"Nothing." *Everything.* Especially that dark-haired witch who's clearly cast some kind of a spell on me.

"What were you doing up there?"

"None of your business," I snap. Good thing the walls of the ranch are thick enough that no one had heard her scream. No one but me, that is. I can't stop the smirk that curls my lips.

"So, it's like that, huh?" He chuckles. "And PS, your belt's undone."

I swear aloud, then fasten my belt. "Get off my balls man." I pivot and stalk forward, Arpad on my heels. "Shit, can't you go fly a kite or something?"

"I don't fly kites… Never did, not even when I was a boy. And neither did you, by the way, pal."

"Yeah, yeah." I stalk forward to the door that leads to the patio where the rest of the crowd are still gathered.

Spotting Isla, I head for her, Arpad right behind. "Jesus, man, cut me a break," I snap.

"Trust me, where you're headed, you need a wing man."

"Go fuck yourself."

"Not interested." He chuckles.

"I forget you have a woman you are too much of a pussy to seal the deal with."

He grabs my shoulder, turns me around, "Shut the fuck up."

"You want a fight, you motherfucker?" I growl.

"I want you to take back what you said."

"No," I bare my teeth.

He throws a punch. I duck. "Hold on, I need to first take care of something else."

I stalk toward Isla. "Julia," I jerk my chin in the direction of the house, "she needs your help."

"What happened?" She frowns.

"She's, uh, up in the bathroom."

"What did you do to her?

"Nothing she didn't want done," I insist.

"I don't believe you." She frowns. "Did you hurt her?"

I stare at her, then look away.

"Motherfucker," she snarls. "Why the hell are you toying with her?"

"I'm not." I slide a finger under my collar. "Look, it's complicated, okay?"

"You bet your ass it is, buddy." She folds her arms over her chest. "I swear, sometimes I can't thank my stars enough that I'm not entangled with a man."

"Is that right?" Liam prowls over to stand next to her. "You sure about that?"

She flinches, then glances at him sideways. "Hello, Mr. Not-one-of-the-Seven."

"Liam," he says through gritted teeth. "My name is Liam."

"Goodbye Mr. Whatever-your-name-is." She flounces off. "And newsflash, I'm not interested."

"What the fuck?" He stares after her.

"What the fuck?" I frown at him. "You sweet on her or something, man?"

"I don't do sweet anything." He turns those cold eyes on me and I bloody believe him. The Seven of us are ruthless and have seen enough to know that life's not easy, and each of us have our ways, albeit unorthodox, to cope with that, but this man…? He was born with the proverbial silver spoon in his mouth and has had a privileged existence, by all counts, so why the hell do I get the impression that he's as tortured as us, if not more?

"Not that I care," I growl, "Except Isla is Amelie and Summer's friend, both of whom married into the circle, which means she comes under the protection of the Seven, so you better not mess with her, man."

"And Julia?" He scratches his jaw, "What about her?"

"Don't talk about her." I widen my stance, "If I were you, I'd stay the fuck away from her."

He chuckles, "And if I were you, I'd duck."

"Why would I?" The hair on my forearms rises.

I angle away, but not quickly enough, for Arpad's fist connects with my shoulder. Liam steps aside. I grunt, then grab Arpad's arm and throw him over my shoulder.

He hits the ground, lays there winded, then jumps up, and turns to me.

We circle each other, as the rest of the men close in.

"Who's the more frustrated, you think?" Sinner drawls.

"I don't know, man. They both look angry enough to kill each other." Saint chuckles.

"Do you think we should leave them to it?" Weston asks. "They deserve it, considering they disrupted my wedding."

"They make for free entertainment, at least," Edward responds, his voice mild.

Arpad shakes his head, "Can you believe this?"

"We're surrounded by married folk," I roll my shoulders, "all ball-and chained up and shit."

"Hey," Summer objects.

I wince. "Present company excluded, of course." I raise my hands.

"You women don't count as women anymore," Arpad offers.

"What the hell does that mean?" Victoria frowns. "What are we, if we aren't women?"

"He means you are the wives and fiancées… So—"

"So?" Amelie glowers between me and Arpad, "Are you guys trying to say that the married slash engaged among the Seven are less because of that?"

"You're right, Edward. This is entertaining," Weston quips.

"Umm." I rub the back of my neck.

"Shit, I can't believe that you hesitated." Sinclair chuckles. "Man, even I am not brave enough to take on the might of a woman."

"See." Summer pats his cheek. "He's changed, hasn't he?"

Sinclair shoots me a look over her head, his features wearing an agonized look.

I laugh, then turn it into a cough. I cover my mouth, "Umm, hey, didn't mean no harm, folks. Honest."

"Yeah," Arpad straightens, "just me and Rockstar here, blowing off steam." He nods.

I step toward him, at the same time that he closes the distance between us. I throw an arm around his shoulders. "See, all made up."

"Aww, you guys gonna kiss or something?" Saint taunts.

"Nope, don't want to make Julia jealous," Arpad retorts.

"The fuck you talking about?" I lower my arm and stare at him.

He rolls his shoulders, "Just telling it like it is, brother."

"There's nothing to tell here." I glare at him, "Not unless you count one sorry excuse of a man, who's carried around his feelings for a woman for years and not dared to confess it."

"That's it." Arpad pivots, hooks his leg around mine, tugs at the same time he shoves at my shoulder. The world tilts. The next moment, my back hits the ground. Pain shudders through me. "Fuck," I swear.

"Get up," Arpad growls from above me.

I spring up, shake my head to clear it, then charge him. I head butt him; he grunts, grabs me in a headlock. We struggle, evenly matched, break apart, then circle each other.

"Haven't seen you this upset in a long time," Arpad bares his teeth.

"I'm not the one carrying a torch."

"No, you're simply too scared to grab what's right in front of you."

"Fuck you," I growl.

"No, thank you," he shoots back.

"Shit," I straighten, "this is pointless."

Arpad rolls his shoulders, "It's bloody confounding, is what it is." He drags his fingers through his hair.

"I need a drink," I mutter.

"So do I." He holds out a hand.

"Don't push your luck, man," I growl.

"What happened here?" Amelie glances between us.

"What?" I frown.

"What?" Arpad dusts off the front of his jacket.

"And I thought women were temperamental?" Summer heaves a sigh.

"Just as things were beginning to get interesting, too," Victoria cries.

Saint wraps his arm around her. "Come on, darlin'. You shouldn't get stressed in your condition."

"I'm pregnant, not sick," she protests, but allows Saint to lead her away.

"What now?" I frown.

Arpad glances past me, "If I were you, I'd definitely get out."

"What the fuck do you mean?"

The back of my neck prickles and all of my senses pop. *What the hell? Is she here?*

"Damian, you motherfucker! You stupid-ass, good-for-nothing loser of a Rockstar." A voice that could only belong to the one woman I'd been trying to get away from rings out.

Silence descends on the crowd. I draw in a breath.

"Turn around and face me, you coward."

Julia's voice sounds closer. Guess there's no rest for the wicked huh?

I turn, just as she plants her fist in my side.

21

Julia

"How dare you?" My fist connects with his hard chest, but he barely moves. He doesn't blink, or seem surprised. *What the hell?* Not even his breathing changes.

"You ass." I punch his side again; pain shivers up my arm. I pull back, then aim for his groin this time. My fist connects with his rock-hard abdomen. He draws in a breath. A reaction, finally. I pull back, raise my fist again. He swoops down, grabs my wrist, then turns me around and hauls me against him.

"Calm down," his hard voice sounds near my ear.

"I will bloody not," I growl, trying to kick him.

He sidesteps but I catch him in the shin anyway. He curses under his breath. "The fuck is wrong with you?" he snaps.

"The fuck is wrong with *you?*" I shove the hair out of my eyes. "You left me on my own after…you…you…"

"I?"

"You know." I swallow, then glance around and take in the

varying expressions of interest among the assembled faces. Bloody hell. Of course, we were the highlight of the afternoon. Likely, we'd usurped the attention from the bride and groom.

"Sorry," I direct my apologies at Amelie, who shakes her head.

"Don't worry," she mouths at me, then glances up at the man behind me who has me pinned to him. "You okay?" she asks me.

No.

No.

"Yeah," I tell them.

"You sure?" She stares between me and Damian, who pulls me closer.

"What? Don't you trust me with your friend?" He laughs. "Rest assured, I'll make sure she's taken care of."

"Hmm." She narrows her gaze at him, then points a finger in his direction, "I'll hold you to that."

I ensure that my features stay calm as she heads into the house, followed by the rest of the crowd; then I turn on the alphahole who restrains me. "Let go," I hiss.

"No."

"I need to get out of here."

"So do I," he agrees.

"I'm not going anywhere with you," I snarl.

"You should have thought of that before you made a spectacle of yourself, and PS, what the fuck are you wearing?"

"What did you expect?" I hiss. "You left me there and walked off. And what's wrong with what I'm wearing?" I glance down at the plaid shirt and the too-short jeans and ballet pumps that Amelie had loaned me, courtesy of Tinkerbell.

"I sent your friend to help you, and I like the fit of these jeans against your arse."

"Should I thank you for that?" I scoff, "And stop talking about my butt."

"It would be a start." He lowers his voice, "And I haven't stopped thinking about it, considering I was your first there, after all."

"And yet you left me?" I bite the inside of my cheek.

"What did you expect? A post-coital cuddle, a kiss, a pat on the head."

"How about simple decency…you…you oaf?"

I swallow the thick lump of something that clogs my chest. What the hell had I been thinking rushing out here? When Isla had found me curled up in the bath tub having a good cry, it had been the last straw. Not that I don't appreciate her consoling me…but damn it! I am tired of being taken for granted by the world, by my life, by this obnoxious grumpypants rock star who, damn it… I still want to shag. Gah!

"The reason I came out here was to dare you," I snap.

"What?"

"I dare you to pose for me."

"What do you mean 'pose for me'?"

"Let me sculpt you."

"What do you mean? Like, out of clay?"

"No, out of toilet paper, you douche." I shake my head. "Yes, out of clay. I'm a clay artist, remember?"

"Thought you were a potter."

"A sculptor, actually."

"Is it me you're looking for?" he asks.

I still. "Did you paraphrase Hello! By Lionel Richie, in which she sculpts—"

"His bust," he echoes my words.

I start; so does he.

He studies me for a moment. "So, do you like eighties music videos, or was that a lucky guess?"

"The first," I mumble.

"Hmm."

"So, will you pose for me?" I tilt my head.

"Maybe."

"Why is everything so difficult with you?"

"Because… It's you?" he offers. "You seem to bring out my dark side."

"You're no Luke Skywalker," I scoff.

"Thank God." He laughs. "I prefer a different kind of lightsaber, Flower."

"Eeugh." I make a gagging sound, "That was so, so, so bad."

"It was," he agrees. "If I release you, will you promise not to attack me?"

"Of course."

He releases me, takes a step back. I turn around and throw myself at him. I must surprise him this time, for he stumbles, then catches me by my shoulders.

"Stop," he commands.

"No." I try to kick at his shins.

He throws his arms around me, pulls me close to his chest, where the warmth of his body pours over me, where I can hear his heart hammer against his chest. Is he as aware of me as I am of him?

"Let me go." I strain in his hold and he plants his big palm around the nape of my neck to hold me captive. I am instantly wet.

Damn it, this shouldn't be happening. He's restraining me, he's holding me back, and I am turned on? What kind of depraved stupidity is it, that I find his ability to rein me in so primitive…so… bloody hot?

No way, am I going to stand for it.

I turn my face into the skin exposed by the 'V' of the lapels of his shirt. I draw in a deep breath, fill my lungs with the musky, cinnamon-laced male essence of his. I lick at the warm skin; he freezes. I bury my teeth in his chest and he laughs. He fucking laughs. I glance up to find his eyes gleaming; color smears his cheeks.

"Shit, that turned you on, didn't it?" I huff.

"Now you're getting to know me better." He grins and his teeth glint against his tanned skin. My belly flutters. Why the hell does he come across as so irresistible, even as he's preparing to take me apart bit by melting bit?

"No," I mumble.

"Yes." He nods. He applies enough pressure on my throat that I gasp.

"What…what are you doing?"

"Making sure that you understand my instructions, and PS, you're welcome."

"For what?"

"For saving you from being bored to death in this terribly august gathering."

"It's not August, you ass."

"You know what I mean," he pauses, "don't you?"

"Of course, I do," I huff. "I can't get over how archaic your prose is though, and I thought I was the only one who loved historicals."

"Hate historicals," he yawns, "but have a weakness for poetry. Comes with the territory. If it weren't for my lyrics, I wouldn't be here, after all, right?"

"Like I care."

"You should, for I hold your future in my hands."

"More like you need me, you bastard. It's why you keep wrenching orgasms out of me, after all."

His features close. "What do you mean?"

"That for some reason you like to… No, you *need* to, see me come. You have this strange compulsion to have me orgasm, to watch me fall apart under your ministrations. Makes me wonder if, in some strange way, it's not fueling your writing."

He glares at me, then releases me so suddenly that I stumble.

"I was right, huh?" I blink. "You really do think that my orgasms help you what—break through your creative deadlock?"

His nostrils flare. "I am not discussing this with you here."

"Then where?"

"You did mention wanting to sculpt me." He scowls.

"I…did."

"So, let's go to your studio."

"I…uh, I don't have one yet. I just flew in from Australia. haven't had time to, uh, set one up…" I bite down on my lower lip. Shit, this sounds like an excuse, but it's true. So why the hell does he narrow his gaze, look me up and down like he doesn't believe a word that I'm saying?

He grabs my upper arm, "Come on." He stalks forward, hauling me behind him.

"Hold on," I hiss. "I am getting tired of being dragged around by you, like I am a sack of potatoes."

"Be grateful I didn't throw you over my shoulder and whip your arse for your impertinence. Oh, wait. I already did that." He chuckles.

I scowl. "Can you get any more abhorrent?"

"Can you get any more cranky?"

"You're calling me cranky?" I yell, "You—"

"Julia, everything okay?" I glance up to find Isla planting herself in our path.

"Yeah, need some help?" Liam prowls up to place an arm around her shoulders.

She shakes it off. "Back off, this is my friend." She sets her jaw.

"And he's not," Liam drawls. "All the more reason I'd be happy to step in, if the situation demands."

"What?" I frown at him. "No, I… I'm good."

"You sure?" Liam glances between us. "Say the word and I—"

"You heard the lady," Damian growls. "Now, piss off."

"OMG," I throw up my hands, "I've had enough of this possessive caveman act."

"I haven't even started." Damian grabs my arm, "We're leaving. Julia's coming with me. End of story. Anyone have a problem with that?"

Silence; the crowd glances at us. Then Arpad scratches his jaw, "Can I borrow your bachelor pad at The Shard, considering you'll be wanting to move to a townhouse in Primrose Hill with the rest of the married folk?"

Damian stiffens, then draws himself up to his full height, "That won't be happening, I'm afraid. This is purely a transactional friends-with-benefits arrangement." He turns to me, "Besides, I've sworn never to marry."

22

Julia

"What the hell was that about?" I mumble into the helmet that the
rock star had jammed on my head, along with the boots, gloves and
heavy jacket—how the hell did he guess my size with such accuracy?
— he'd asked me to don, before shoving me onto the bike that had
been parked in the driveway of the ranch. Apparently, when you are
stinking rich, you can get the hired help to drive your bike an hour
out of the city to where you are, just so you have the pleasure of
driving it home.

"What the hell was *what* about?" Damian's low drawl sounds in
my ear.

I jump. Yeah, another thing you can buy when you're loaded,
these techno-advanced head gear, aka helmets with built-in mics, that
you can use to communicate with each other... While the bike purrs
between my legs, setting off pin-pricks of lust up my spine.

"Jeez, do you have to go scaring me?" I grumble.

"Scaring you, huh?" He accelerates and the bike shoots forward.

I yelp, clamp my arms even tighter around his lean stomach, which I admit, is no hardship; especially since I am plastered to his broad back, with my thighs spread wide enough to accommodate the tight flanks of said Rockosaurus. He leans into a curve without slowing down, and I tighten my grip around him.

He chuckles.

Jerk.

"What's with that proclamation that you are never going to marry?" I burst out.

The tires squeal loudly enough that my eardrums reverberate with the vibration and the scent of burning rubber assails me through the protective covering of my helmet. Shit, either he's mad or this is just how he normally drives. "If you don't want to answer a question you only have to say so. I mean, you may have a death wish pal, but I don't. I—"

He slams on the brakes so suddenly that the back of the bike rises up in the air. I scream, hold onto him like he is the last mooring in a world gone mad. The bike rotates on its front wheel, does a complete 360 turn, before the back tire—the one I am positioned above—hits the tarmac, bounces once, then comes to a stop.

My limbs tremble and a bead of sweat runs down my spine. I bury my helmet-covered forehead into his back and stay where I am, not daring to move. I couldn't if I tried—my legs have gone to sleep, my fingers are frozen, despite the gloves, partly from fear, partly from the cold wind that had buffeted me as he'd torn his way up the road.

We stay there a beat, another.

There's not a house in sight, or another car. We'd been driving up a B road, one of those picturesque thoroughfares that run parallel to the highway. If there had been enough light, I would have noticed the vista of rolling hills and storybook cottages. No, strike that; even if it had been earlier in the day, I wouldn't have noticed the scenery, because I had been too busy reveling in the firm expanse of the back which I had been tucked into all this while—the planes of which clenched and unclenched as if there were a fight going on underneath his skin.

"Damian?" I finally venture. "You…you okay?"

He stays still, the motorcycle's engine throbbing underneath us. Then he switches it off and the silence that descends is almost painful to my ears. I swallow and my eardrums pop. That's better. "Damian?"

"How many times have I told you not to talk about dying?"

"I…I'm sorry."

"I'm not."

"Wh…what do you mean?"

"Get off the bike."

"What?"

"Do it," he snaps.

My muscles uncoil and sensations sizzle up my legs. Is it pins and needles of blood circulation being restored, or the primitive urge to comply with what he wants, when he wants, how…he wants? Holy hell, what's this insane need to comply with his every demand? Even the insane ones… Particularly the insane ones. Like this… I scramble off of the bike, stand next to him. "Give me that." He jerks his head toward my helmet. I take it off. A gust of wind blows my hair about my shoulders. He points at my jacket; I shrug off the protection. Goosebumps immediately shiver over my skin.

He tosses my stuff aside; then removes his helmet and throws it aside as well.

I wince. It's not my gear, but hell, if I don't appreciate the craftmanship that went into it. "Hope the stuff is unbreakable," I mutter.

He doesn't respond. Instead, he lowers the kickstand of the Harley, leans the bike into it. He looks me up and down, then jerks his chin at my shirt, "Take it off."

I stiffen, "What? Here?"

"Where else?"

"Why would I do that?" I scowl.

"You want the job, remember?"

"And this is another…test I need to pass?" I frown.

"Maybe," he shrugs his shoulders, "maybe not."

Asshole's trying to dare me, huh? Is that what this is? Because I challenged him first? Likely, that's all it is. We'll see who blinks first, buster. I unhook the first button of my shirt, then the next. The cold wind instantly seeps down into the space between the fabric and my skin. My nipples tighten painfully… And it's not because he's following my progress…with those brooding, blue eyes of his.

I undo the last button on my shirt. He holds out his hand as I hand it over.

He takes in my bra—thank God I had worn one under the dress, then drops his gaze to my borrowed jeans. "Off with them."

"What?" I cry in horror. "No."

"Yes."

"Not here."

"There's no one here."

I glance around, don't see a single other person, or bird or insect, for that matter. I can do this. I am not gonna give in to whatever mindfuck thing he has got going on here. I lower the zipper of my jeans, then pause. *Shit.* "I don't have panties on," I gripe.

He tilts his head, and I shake my head, "Are you insane? I'm not going naked out here in the open."

"Thought you wanted to get close to nature and all that crap, which is why you went to Australia in the first place?"

"How do you know that?"

"It wasn't hard to guess." He raises his gaze to my face. "It's what women of a certain age do, when they're single and trying to find themselves. All that *'Eat Pray Love'* shit, ya know?"

"You're a piece of shit, ya' know?" I spit out the words, then swoop my nails toward his face.

He laughs, hooks his fingers around my wrist, and tugs on me. The next second I am looking down at the ground, splayed across his thighs and over the gas tank of his bike, which means I'm forced to thrust out my butt, up closer to his face.

He palms my arse—thank God, I still have the jeans on.

A shiver of desire runs up my spine. Fuck me, but nothing new there, I guess. I mean, I do like it when he touches me…anywhere… everywhere…especially on that part of me which is the fleshiest, something which I've hated, but which he, apparently, has an unhealthy liking for.

"I am beginning to think you have a butt obsession," I huff.

"Only with yours."

I still.

Above me, he ceases stroking my flesh, his big palm covers my backside, and I swear, I can discern every single fingerprint of his through the seat of the fabric that separates us. Damnit, I changed my mind. I should have taken off my pants so he'd have easier access to the melting, aching core of me. I squeeze my thighs together, push my crotch into the still warm fuel tank.

"Did you know your figure was the first thing I noticed about you."

"Wha…what?" I blink.

"You're shaped like a guitar."

"You mean I have a big-ass arse?"

"A curvy, sexy, beautiful backside that I wanted to sink my teeth into." He slides back on the motorbike, then pulls down my jeans. Cool air hits my bare arse.

"What are you—?" I yell as he lowers his head and fastens his mouth on my butt, his sharp teeth digging into the flesh of my arsecheeks. I squirm, wriggle, try to pull away. He merely places his heavy arm across my lower back, "Hold still, darlin'. Don't want to hurt you, now."

"You already did that, you cock, when you sank your big dick in my arsehole," I snap.

He laughs, then slides his fingers across the valley between my buttcheeks. "Did it sting?"

"What do you think?"

"I think, you want me to fuck you again."

"I… I…do." I blink.

Shit, didn't mean for that to pop out. Here I am, splayed out across the lap of this rock star, in the middle of nowhere, and hell, if I can't stop myself from pushing my aching core into the smooth metal of the road hog under me and wishing it were something else entirely.

"So, you finally decided to come clean, huh?" I turn my head to find he's wearing an amused expression.

"No thanks to your *Jenny from the Block* routine."

His gaze widens, then he throws his head back and laughs, a full blown throaty, from-the-belly chuckle that rolls down my spine and arrows straight to that space which is constantly needy around him…i.e. my stupid pussy.

"You laughing at me?" I scowl.

"Just appreciative of the scenery." He grins. "And of your sense of humor."

"At least you placed the reference, I'll give you that."

"You mean the part where Ben Affleck bites J-Lo's luscious arse in the music video?" His lips kick up, "What's not to like? It's every teenaged boy's fantasy come true." He lowers his gaze down to my curved flesh, "As is this."

"Don't get ahead of yourself, motherfucker."

"Language." He clicks his tongue. "Not that your potty tongue doesn't turn me on, but I have other, better, uses for it."

My center instantly grows wetter, bloody hell. Everything he does and says is like a green signal to my hormones… Not even that… I simply have to think of him and my ovaries sit up and beg. Okay, not a pretty picture, and I'm definitely getting out of here. "Unhand me." I push against his thigh.

He holds me in place. "I'm not done yet, Flower," he drawls.

"But I am."

"Trust me, you're not." He flips me around so I'm peering up at the sky, arms flung out as I try to hold onto something to steady myself.

He yanks my pants down to around my ankles, then pulls them off.

He leans back, rakes his gaze down my naked body. "If only you could see yourself." His voice grows rough.

Heat flushes my skin, my nipples pebble further, and my core clenches.

He lowers his face to my stomach, then drags his unshaven chin across my lower belly.

I shudder as liquid heat blooms between my legs. I grasp at his hair, tug on it, then push it toward the aching emptiness that coils in my pussy.

"What's your hurry?" His lips curve against my stomach.

"I… I'm not in a hurry."

He slaps my pussy.

I cry out, "What the hell?"

"Thought I told you not to lie."

"I… I'm not…"

He slaps my core again. I arch up and into him, "Stop…"

He raises his head, "Do you want me to?"

I hold his gaze, peer into his burning blue gaze. "I don't know," I whisper.

"Good girl." His voice lowers to a hush, "I am going to eat you out, gonna suck on your sweet, swollen center, suck on your clit, and play with your swollen pussy lips, you get me?"

23

Damian

Her pupils dilate, her breathing grows shallow. "What's stopping you?" she tips up her chin and asks.

I bark out a laugh. Can't help it. This sassy little thing is laid out like a delectable meal, and yet, she can't back down. She's gotta go toe-to-toe with me, gotta dare me. Again.

"You, Flower." I peer into her eyes, "I want to watch how you react when I—"

I grip her waist, then raise her up, only to position her so she's straddling my hips.

"Oh," she gasps. "Wow."

"Is that a sound of appreciation, I hear."

"Just of surprise." She swipes her hair over her shoulder revealing the long line of her throat. I lean in and nuzzle her, right there, in the hollow between her clavicles. She shivers; goosebumps pop on her skin.

"Are you cold?"

"I'm naked, at the height of winter, in the middle of nowhere." She snorts, "What do you think?"

"Time to get you warm, huh?" I scoot her up the fuel tank, then press my palm to the middle of her chest. She obeys, beautifully. She stretches out, her head on the handlebars, her hair flowing over and down the headlight. I drag my hand down the valley between her breasts, over the slight curve of her belly to the warmth between her legs. She shudders, tries to close her thighs. "Don't," I insist, "let me see you open for me, Flower."

She gulps, a flush spreads up her creamy skin, and arousal glints on the inside of her thigh. I scoop up the moisture, suck on it. She gasps.

I slide my finger inside her pussy and her entire body jerks. "Oh, Damian."

And there it is. When she says my name like it's a prayer, when she squints up at me, gaze wide, tits standing up, nipples perky and ready to be pulled and teased and sucked on by me. When I slide a second and third finger inside of her sweet cunt and begin to work my digits in and out of her, and she brings her hands up to cup her breasts and squeeze them together, making an inviting hollow, all thought goes out of my head. I reach down between us, lower the zipper on my pants. A gust of wind blows her hair across her face just then. She reaches for it.

"Don't," I order and she lowers her arm. "Squeeze your nipples."

She locks her forefinger and thumb around each diamond-hard tip and squeezes. A moan ripples up her throat. My dick hardens further as blood rushes to my groin. I grab my dick, take it out and squeeze it from base to crown.

"Damian, please," she groans again.

My shaft goes impossibly hard, my thighs spasm, the blood begins to pump at my temples behind my eyelids, at my wrists, even in my balls. I pull my fingers out of her, replace them with my cock.

She draws in a breath, tips her chin down, "Damian I—"

I thrust forward, breach her in one smooth movement.

She groans, "Oh, my God… Dami-aaan." She tries to wriggle away.

I grip her hips, hold her down "Easy." I glare at her. "Easy now."
"You're...too big."
"Just right for you."
"I... I can't..."
"You can."
I lock my gaze with hers, rub circles with my thumb into her clit, and stay...and stay... Allow her to adjust to my width, as she clenches around my cock. So hot, so tight. I grit my teeth, focus on not moving. Just a little more time, a few more seconds until she's ready.

She swallows, "Damian..." She licks her lips, "More."

My vision tunnels and all of my senses seem to pop. How the hell does she know exactly what to say to me? Something hot stabs at my chest, my ribcage tightens, and my breath catches in my throat. I slide forward, feed another inch of my length inside of her. "You're so beautiful." The breath rushes out of me. "Flower," I growl.

She wraps her fingers around each of my wrists, her touch sparking off a fresh need that swirls down my skin, lodges at the base of my spine.

"Julia," I growl.

"D... Damian?"

I squeeze my eyes shut... Shit, I'll never get used to her calling out my name... Something primal...primeval about it... Something so wrong...so right... So new and yet so familiar. Shit. Fuck... The tension in my balls grows impossibly big, the blood thuds at my temples, the beat growing louder, more insistent.

"Julia," I draw in a breath, "Julia..."

"I'm here, Damian."

I tighten my hold on her, dig my fingers into her soft skin. She's going to wear my marks there... Good. I want that. I want every part of her body to bear evidence of my possession, of how I made her writhe and throb and yearn and cry out as she begged for more of my cock. "Julia," I growl.

"Look at me, Damian. See how much I need you."

I snap my eyes open, hold onto the hunger in those beautiful green eyes. "I...am going to fuck you now."

"What?" She stares, "Bu…but…you are already —"

"I'm not even half-way in."

"Oh," she whimpers, "oh, God."

"Hold on, Julia.'

"No.. Wait…"

I piston my hips forward, bury another inch inside of her and her entire body jerks, the motorcycle shudders, and I dig my heels into the ground to hold us upright. Shit, not the brightest idea, fucking her for the first time astride my bike… But hell, if this isn't another fantasy come true. I lean into her, push the hair from her face, thrust my thumb between her open lips. "Suck me," I command, and she draws my digit inside her hot little mouth as I pull out then pump inside of her, burying myself to the hilt.

She bites down on my digit and holds on, both of her hands wrapped around my forearm, as I begin to fuck her. I thrust into her, filling her, stretching her, feeding my cock inside her hungry pussy. "Fuck, Julia."

She moans deep inside her throat, and my balls draw up, and my groin tightens. I pull my thumb from her mouth, lean over her, hold my lips close to hers, then thrust forward and into her, as I bottom out, against her pelvic bone.

Her eyes roll back in her head, she wraps her legs around my waist, digs her heels into my back and cries out, "Oh. My. God. Damian."

I hook my arms under her thighs, prop her legs over my shoulders, then pull out, and thrust into her again. I propel my hips forward, slant my body and pump into her again and again. Her back arches off the bike; she grabs onto my arms, digs her fingernails into my skin. I'll be wearing her marks as surely as she wears mine.

"Come with me," I command, and she clamps her pussy around my dick. She thrusts her breasts up, nipples stabbing into my chest." Now," I snap, and she shatters, moisture flooding her core.

Shudders wrack her body, and she throws her head back and screams. I watch her as her shoulders jerk and her breasts tremble. I bend, nip at one nipple; she shivers. I kiss the valley between her breasts, lick her other nipple, and she whimpers. "Damian…"

"Shh." I nibble little kisses up her throat back to her lips, kiss her
again and again. Tilt my mouth to hers, slide my tongue inside to
play with hers. My cock jumps, my balls beg for release. I begin to
move inside of her, thrusting into her hot channel, again and again.
She flutters open her eyelids, entangles that soulful green gaze with
mine. "You're fucking beautiful," I pull out then plunge inside her in
one long, smooth stroke that has me buried inside her completely.

"Oh," she gasps.

"Bloody hell." I grit my teeth, hold her gaze, "I'm going to—"

"Come inside me," she gasps.

That's when I remember, I am not wearing a condom, and no
way, am I going to come inside of her unprotected, not even if she's
on the pill.

I pull out and come all over her chest, her breasts, across her chin
and her face.

Her breath comes in pants, in tandem with mine. My heart thuds
so hard in my ribcage, I am sure it's going to jump out. I glance
down, then rub the gooey mess into her skin, about her breasts, into
her nipples, down her curvy waist, and between her legs. I scoop up
some of the mix, hold it to her mouth; she licks it off. I lean down,
then kiss her, taste myself and her, and our combined cum, interlaced
with that honey of her taste, and, fuck, if that isn't the most erotic
thing ever. My dick twitches against her core again. Her gaze
widens, "Again?" she croaks.

That's when my phone alarm goes off.

24

Julia

I watch from the window of my apartment as Damian pulls away on his bike. He'd insisted on escorting me to my apartment door, and seeing me in, then kissed me—on the cheek—before he'd left, without any promises or anything to raise any expectations in me in terms of when I was going to see him next. Not that I had expected anything else…

Well, okay, so I had. I mean, hey, a woman is bound to get her expectations up after that crazy scene he orchestrated on his bike. Holy shit, he shagged me on his bike in the middle of nowhere, then rubbed his cum into me. He also pulled out a bandana and wiped me down before helping me back into my clothes.

We hadn't said a word to each other on the trip back—huh. Is that good or bad? It isn't good, but is it bad? I mean, he had orgasmed too, just not inside me. And he hadn't asked to fuck me again… And I hadn't invited him inside the apartment either.

How could I, when the alarm that had gone off on his phone had been a reminder that he needed to get home to take care of his daughter.

Turns out, when you're dating— Is this dating? Or should I call it fucking? Or perhaps it's the 'Damian's 100 Ways to Get Julia to Orgasm' game that we're playing? Well, whatever you want to call it, it's complicated, more than usual, when the guy in question is a famous rock star and a single dad, to boot.

And why the hell is he still holding me at arm's length from his kid? Doesn't he trust me enough to take care of his child?

I drag my fingers through my hair and encounter a gummy piece of something… I slide it off, glance at it… It's the remnants of when he came all over me… My belly clenches. Why the hell had I found that hot…and filthy…but a turn on? I squeeze my thighs together… I mean, I'd fantasied about kink…but never been part of the kind of escapades the man seems to have in mind every time we meet. Yep, Damian f'ing Savage gets a freaking 1000+ when it comes to being innovative. And he isn't a selfish lover… I mean, he's been entirely focused on my orgasms all through… And when I'd confronted him about it… He hadn't denied that he loves to make me come. He seems to get some perverse pleasure out of it…Maybe more than that.

Why is that? What secrets is this man hiding from me? Why the hell does he come across as all tough and mean on the outside and broken on the inside? Well, shit… The classic combination. The bad boy rock star who's hurting and waiting for the right woman to come along and save him… Ha! I snort. That's one that belongs in romance novels.

In real life, it never works that way.

In real life, the bad boy breaks the heart of any female who dares get close to him. He'll push her away, trample over her feelings, and walk away…

Don't let him push you away.

Shit, that's what Meredith had said. Guess she'd anticipated his reaction—no surprises there. Not that I care… I mean, this entire thing is a transaction, huh? A way for me to make money while I figure out what to do with my life. What do I want to do with my life?

Pursue my non-existent career as a clay artist? Continue as a nanny? Why can't I have both? Why can't I have the career I yearn for and the kids of my own that I'd hoped to have by now. I mean, I am only twenty-six. I'm not old…but hell, if I don't feel my biological clock ticking. Which is crazy. Women have kids into their forties… But me? I'd always hoped to have them early… Only things hadn't worked out that way…yet.

If he'd come inside me earlier… Shit, I'd wanted him to come inside of me. Bloody hell… I hadn't realized, until now, how much I want to be pregnant… And not with just anyone's child. With Damian's child. *No, no, no, don't go there. You stupid idiot, don't fall for him.* Do something else… Anything else… Think of how you're going to spend the money you've already earned. Orgasms in exchange for cash. The deal is crazy, too good to be true.

And I don't, for one second, buy that all this is a test.

It's more. Something more. But what? Shit, I need to find out. I've got to figure out why he's so frustrating, complex, and gorgeous, yet obnoxious and dominant. And yet, I sense, he harbors such a melting heart, which is never more evident than when he talks about his daughter. Just why is he the way he is? What makes him tick?

What does he want out of this weird set-up? Got to find out. Got to… I pivot, head for the bathroom. First things first: a bath, then a call…

The next day, the sun is already dipping down into the horizon, when I lean across the bar at the top floor of the National Portrait Gallery in Trafalgar Square.

"Thanks for coming." I raise my wine glass at the two women who flank me.

"Of course," the petite woman with flashing eyes replies.

The last time I met her, she'd been all business as she'd ensured the flat I occupied was secure from future break-ins. Yeah, when Amelie lived there, a burglar had surprised her. Thankfully, Weston

had been there with her, and according to Amelie, she owed the
burglar, because it was thanks to that incident that Weston had
confessed his feelings for her. Well, bully for her… If only it were
that easy with Daddy Savage, huh?

"So, you want to know about him?" Karina reaches for her glass
of sparkling water.

I blink, "Uh, yeah. I mean… I confess, it's refreshing that you
come straight to the point, but I need something stronger than wine
for this conversation."

I drain my glass of wine, then reach over the counter, "A shot of
tequila?"

"Coming right up." The bartender pours out the golden liquid of
my faithful lover, the one who's stayed with me through thick and
thin, the one who never cuts and runs, who never abandons me when
the alarm on his phone goes off… Not that I begrudge Damian that,
really. I love that he's devoted to his kid. It turns me on, to be
honest… Still, if only there were a way to take up more of his time
without feeling guilty about it. Aargh. I reach for the shot glass,
drain it, then cough.

Isla pats my back, "There, there." She draws soothing circles on
my back.

"Thanks," I swipe my hair over my shoulder. "You didn't have to
come."

She frowns, "Of course, I did."

"I didn't mean to drag you away from your job."

"Pfft." She waves a hand in the air, "This is more fun. Seems even
I need a break from planning weddings. For once, all that talk of true
love and celebrations…" she winces. "It was getting to me."

"Or is the hangover from meeting Liam, yesterday?" I shoot her a
sideways glance.

She freezes, then reaches for her own margarita and downs it.
"Who?"

"You heard me." I stick my tongue in my cheek. "I'm not the only
one with an alphahole-shaped hole in my heart, apparently."

"What does that look like?" Karina places her glass back on the
table; the perfect red of her lipstick stains the side of the rim. Damn

it, why does this woman ooze sex like she owns it? Why the hell can't some of that confidence rub off on me, huh?

"What?" I frown.

"The alphahole-shaped hole," she elaborates.

"Like sex and chocolate and an incomplete shag fest."

Both women look at me, then Isla bursts out laughing. Karina cracks a smile. Whew, this one's a tough cookie.

"Yeah, well, forget I said that," I mumble.

"No, no, no, no." Isla taps into her phone, "I am absolutely gonna use it."

"Fine," I signal at the bartender for another drink, "just don't attribute it to me."

"So," Karina turns to me once I have my grubby fingers around another filled-to-the-brim shot glass, "you want to know about Damian Savage."

"Yeah."

"You know I can't break client privilege."

"So why are you here?" I snap.

"Hey, hey." Isla waves her hand between us. "Be nice, Julia. You know Karina didn't have to be here at all, considering she takes care of the security for all of the Seven, and she has a vested interest, considering her prior relationship with Arpad."

Karina's fingers tighten around her glass and some of the water spills over the side. "I have had prior dealings with Mr. Beauchamp."

"Ooh, it's Mr. Beauchamp, is it?" I lean forward in my seat, taking in the tightness at the corners of Karina's lips. Apparently, Ms. Hoity Toity successful business woman here has a soft spot, or is it an Arpad-shaped spot, in her life.

"Asshole," she snaps, then drains her sparkling water like it was champagne.

"Want something stronger?"

"I don't drink," she retorts.

"Fine," I sniff. "Don't take your frustrations out on me, girlfriend. You didn't have to come. You know you could have simply said that you wouldn't help me."

"But I want to," she draws in a breath, "help you." She reaches for a napkin from her designer purse—Jesus how much did that cost, huh? No wait, I can afford that now that I have money in the bank. So what, if I sold my body to line my bank account? And shit… I don't like the sound of that. Not at all.

I slump into my chair. "Thanks," I mumble. "I didn't know who to turn to, and with my best friend now married… Well," I glance between the two women. "Apparently, and despite my having grown up in this city, it's the two of you I know best, at this stage in my life."

My lower lip trembles and pressure builds behind my eyes. No, no, no I am not going to bawl! Nope. I sniffle, reach for my shot glass, which is empty. "Crap." I signal toward the bartender.

"Go slow, babe," Isla cautions. "We're here for you."

Karina watches me from under hooded eyelids.

"I don't care what you think of me," I burst out at her. "Clearly, you have your shit together and I don't. Well, some of us are late starters, and hell, what the hell is wrong with me, yelling at you, huh?"

I reach for the paper napkin, and Karina grips my hand. "It's okay," she says.

I glance up at her.

"I've been there." She holds my gaze.

"You have?"

"Of course, babe, so have I," Isla offers. "I mean, it's definitely not easy when your friends get married one after the other, and you're left bringing up the rear…"

"Literally," I scoff under my breath.

"I don't understand." Isla squints at me.

"It's… nothing." Definitely need that drink now.

Karina folds her arms in her lap.

I signal to the bartender, who tops up my shot glass.

"Did you mean that he…uh…" Isla clears her throat, "you know…"

"If you mean anal? Yeah." I throw back the drink, then smack the glass back on the counter.

"Oh, hell… And wow. I mean… OMG," Isla chokes on her

drink. "Not that it's unheard of, but so early in the relationship…" Isla's voice tapers off.

"Yeah." I hunch my shoulders, " Why do you think I was in the bath, and why do you think that asshole sent you to help me out?"

"I thought that perhaps the two of you made out, that he got so passionate that he ripped your dress, and then you decided to take a bath and—"

"You thought wrong," I snap at her.

Isla frowns.

I redden. "Sorry, sorry, sorry! So, he fucked me afterward, the right way, I guess, and this time he came all over me."

"Wait… Where?" Isla

"On his bike, on a deserted country road, in the middle of nowhere, and I let him. I'm not proud okay, and you," I stab my finger at Karina, "seriously, why the hell am I spilling my guts in front of a total stranger?"

"Almost stranger," she offers.

"Whatever." I drag my fingers through my hair, "You'd think I had no filter, considering how I seem to lose it in front of Big Daddy D…but…"

"It's kismet," Isla nods sagely.

"What?" I scowl.

"That's what my mother used to say."

"What's fate got to do with it?"

"When two people can't stop rubbing each other up the wrong way…"

"Oh, trust me, it's more than that. The man clearly hates me. It's why he doesn't allow me anywhere near his kid, even though I am a nanny."

"Nanny, huh?" Karina stares at me. "I didn't realize he had a kid."

"Oh, but didn't you do the security for his home?" I drum my fingers on the table, "Didn't you see Riley, then?"

"Maybe she was away." She raises her shoulders, "Anyway, he didn't let me inside the house. The rich can be eccentric that way." She runs her finger up the side of the glass. "He had me boost the security for the grounds and the front door, especially after his stalker broke into his property. Thankfully, he didn't get inside the house though."

I stare at her in horror. "He had a stalker?"

"One of many." She takes a sip of her drink. "It's one of the reasons he unplugged his social media accounts."

"Right." I stare into my glass. "All that's interesting," and every piece of information helps piece together the enigma that's Damian Savage, "but it doesn't change the fact that he doesn't trust me."

"But he does want to offer you a job as his nanny?" Karina probes.

"First, I have to pass a test, or rather, a series of tests...with an 'sssss'." I hiccup.

"What? You mean the shagging?"

"Uh, not only." I hiccup again, then reach for the water.

"How much is he paying you?" Karina asks.

Isla gasps, "Hold on, don't go accusing her..." She glances at my face, "Oh..." She swallows. "OH!"

"Oh, shut up." I bury my face in my palms. "Shit, I've done it now, haven't I?"

"Don't blame yourself," Karina pats my shoulder. "These Seven, they use money to get their way."

"Including Arpad?"

"Especially Arpad."

"What's the story with the two of you?" I stare at her through the gaps in my fingers.

"No story." She raises her shoulders, "Anyway, that's not why I'm here, right?"

I shake my head.

"What did you want to ask me?"

"Tell me whatever you can about Damian—"

She begins to protest and I hold up my hand, "I know, whatever you are allowed to tell me, client confidentiality, notwithstanding."

She draws in a breath.

"I just need to know what I am dealing with here," I plead. "Everything I've read about him in the media doesn't tell me about the real man."

She nods. "You're going in prepared. That's wise."

I tilt my head.

"And this is for the sisterhood, huh?" She half smiles, and her features soften. "I know how it feels to be alone in a city."

"You do?"

She nods. "I moved to London from LA only a few months ago. It takes some getting used to."

"Well, you have me and Isla now."

"Of course." Isla nods, "We single women, we need to stick together, huh? Not that I have anything against our married friends… Just, it's different when you're still searching, ya know?"

Am I searching? What if I've found him, but he doesn't want me? What if he's the man, but he's all wrong for me? What if I am not the kind of girl who's right for him? Shit, now I'm tying myself up in knots.

"So, Damian Savage." Karina leans in, "Here's what I can tell you."

25

Damian

"You want to watch Frozen again?" I stare at Riley.

Last evening, I'd rushed home after dropping Julia off. I wanted to make sure I was home in case Riley woke up at any point during the night.

Today being a Sunday, she'd normally have swimming lessons at the gym, followed by ballet, but when she hadn't wanted to go, I hadn't insisted.

Instead, I'd made her pancakes, as promised. Then we'd played in the pool in my backyard, and spent time in the greenhouse, where I'd repotted some of the flowers and she'd been happy to help. I'd also introduced her to online chess which she'd taken to like a champ. (After all whose daughter is she, eh?)

At dinner she'd happily devoured the mac and cheese I'd cooked, and now we're settled on the couch for her Sunday night treat... Which normally means an hour and a half of watching a movie... Which, apparently, means re-re-re-watching the adventures of Elsa

—no getting away from that four-letter word— and her sister, whatever her name is.

"Daddy, you promised." She pouts, then thrusts out her jaw, in
that expression of stubbornness I am coming to recognize. I should.
It matches my own. Once I set my mind on something, I don't give
up...

Which is why there is no way I am letting that little minx of a
woman get away with the havoc she's creating in my life. I am happy
right here with Riley, and once she goes to bed, I'll have time to
work on the lyrics which have been buzzing around in my head…
Something I have stopped taking for granted.

Clearly, the double orgasm I had wrenched from Flower
yesterday is responsible for this burst of inspiration.

Which means I need to write down the lyrics fast… And that
means… Yeah… "Fine, fine," I grumble at Riley, and reach for the
remote.

"Yay." She dives down into the sofa, cuddles up against me. "I
love you, Papa."

She only calls me that when she's very happy or very sad.

My throat closes as a ball of emotions crowds my chest. This little
girl right here, I'll do anything for her. Anything. Ask me to lay down
my life for her and I'd not hesitate. If anyone dares hurt her, I'd…
I'd… No, don't think about it. She's safe here with me. I wrap my
arm around her, tug her close and she snuggles in. I switch over to
Frozen and the characteristic tune of the opening credits flows over
me. I begin to hum along to it under my breath.

"Daddy," she admonishes, "shh!"

"Okay." I chuckle. I may be a rock star, with fans clamoring to
hear me and see me play on stage, but in my own home, I clearly
come second to the characters on screen. Trust your family to always
take you down a notch, huh?

I settle in to watch the movie. Half an hour later, I glance down
to find her yawning. "You tired, sweetheart?"

She rubs her eyes, then sits up, "No, of course, not." She focuses
on the screen and ten minutes later I find her fast asleep.

I carry her up to her bedroom, tuck her in. I kiss her forehead, inhale the baby shampoo, then head down to my studio. I check the baby-cam on my phone, to make sure I see her asleep, then pick up my guitar.

I still remember the outline of your lips,
the warmth of your touch,
the curve of your eyelashes as you raised them to glance at me...
And then you were gone;
I ache to caress your neck.
If I were to touch you between your thighs
Would you come again —?
I—

My phone vibrates with an incoming call.

Hell, I should have switched it off, except I don't anymore. Not since my daughter arrived, and with her, that unfamiliar sense of vulnerability, the one that has me checking around corners, under the bed, around the house, to make sure that she is safe. The one that makes me want to carry a gun and guard her every moment of every day. For now, she is young and I can protect her. As long as she is under my roof, I can take care of her, ensure no harm comes to her. As long as I can keep her close, I will, which also means I don't let anyone—except the most trusted of my inner circle—near her. Doesn't mean I can't take this call from another woman... The only other person who has penetrated the shield I've put up against the world, hmm?

"Hello," I bark into the phone.

Silence, then her voice comes over the phone line. "D... Damian?"

"Who else?"

"Oh... I didn't expect you to answer the call."

"So why did you call?"

"I—" There's the sound of footsteps, then female voices speaking. The noises recede. "Sorry about that," she mumbles.

"Where are you?" I frown.

"Outside."

"So late?"

"It's... 9 p.m."

"It's late."

"For you, Daddy." She laughs lightly.

My cock jerks. Hell, is it because she called me the D word? Or is it simply her laugh. This is crazy. I have a five-year-old who calls me Daddy, so why the hell does Flower calling me by the same title make me want to reach across the phone line and drag her flush against me?

"Go home," I order.

"What?" she says, breathless, "No."

"Don't defy me."

"Don't order me around." I sense her pout, see those pink lips in my head. And I'm instantly hard. This crazy reaction to her; I'll never get used to it.

"I'll do what I bloody want and you'll obey me, you understand?"

Her breathing grows ragged. Hell, is she turned on by my show of dominance? Of course, she is. The woman's the most natural submissive in denial that I have met, and she doesn't even know it yet.

"Hey, baby," a male voice calls out, "who are you talking to there, when all the man you can handle is standing right here in front of you?"

"Who's that? I can only see a jackass," she snaps.

"Julia," I begin to pace… When the hell did I stand up from my seat, huh? "Julia what the fuck is happening there?"

"Nothing," she hiccups. "Need to teach this guy a lesson."

"Don't," I roar, then dig my fingers in my hair and tug at it. "Don't do anything that will end up with you being hurt."

"Hold on—"

"Don't you dare put me on hold. Don't—"

Crash.

The sound rips through the phone and up my spine. Fuck. Did she drop the phone? I hear the sound of scuffling, "You ass, take that." The sound of someone's palm connecting with a face. Her's? His?

"Hey, you little bitch—" the man howls.

"Julia," I yell into the phone, "Julia, what the hell? Are you all right, babe?"

My heart begins to thud. Why the hell am I not there, taking care of her? Why the hell am I not able to manage everything better? My daughter, my woman… She's not my woman… But hell, if something were to happen to her... Why the hell haven't I done a better job of protecting her? I can't lose another person I am beginning to care about, and when the fuck had that happened? When had I begun to feel some kind of ownership toward her? "Julia?" I roar, "What the fuck — ?"

"Damian?"

A woman's voice, not Julia's, comes over the phone.

"Karina?" I draw in a breath. "You're with her?"

"Of course, you told me to keep an eye on her, remember?" Her voice is calm.

Male groans, a woman's chuckle floats over the phone.

"What the fuck is happening there? Is she okay?"

"Your woman's a fighter." She half chuckles, "I think you under-estimated her."

"You're telling me," I rake my fingers through my hair, "And she's not my woman —"

"Gotta go."

"Don't fucking hang up on —"

The line goes dead.

She hung up on me.

"What the fuck!" I grab my phone and am about to hurl it. Then stop… Nope, that won't help. Not when I have the baby-cam on it as an app. I stare at the screen. At least, Riley is safe. But Julia. What the fuck is Julia doing out? How dare she endanger herself?!

The phone vibrates and I accept the call from Karina.

"Is she okay?"

"She's fine." Karina's steady voice comes through. "And she didn't need my help, by the way. She had the situation in hand."

"Stay with her," I snap.

"Of course."

"Don't let her out of your sight."

"I can't do that without making her suspicious."

"I pay you good money to keep my family safe."

"Wasn't aware she was family."

"She isn't—" I swear aloud. "She's an asset. And her safety is priority."

"Noted."

"You're the best security expert that money can buy. Don't fail me."

So, I've put Karina on the task of keeping tabs on her. What's wrong with that? So, it's creepy, maybe stalkerish. Too bad. I've learned my lesson, and while I can't always be there in person to protect Julia, I've ensured she'll be protected.

"I know how to do my job," Karina murmurs. "And that means, while I can look out for her, if you want her protected a 100% of the time, then someone needs to be with her 24/7, and that can't be me."

"What do you mean?"

"It means, why don't you arrange for her to stay with you? That way, you can ensure—"

"No."

Silence.

"I mean, I can't... I mean." I squeeze my eyes shut. "Fuck, fuck, fuck."

"You okay?" she asks.

"Yes.

No, of course, not. How am I supposed to juggle both? Take care of my daughter while protecting my woman, without hurting either of them?

"Listen, I've gotta go." I hang up the call, ready to hurl the phone again, then stop myself.

Only one way out. I dial Meredith's number.

"Damian," she answers on the second ring, "everything okay?"

"I need your help."

26

Julia

I walk up the sidewalk toward The Shard.

That catch-up with Isla and Karina… It did wonders for my confidence… Oh, wait, maybe that's the alcohol that's running through my bloodstream. The cool night air wakes me up. I'd taken a cab here after Karina had told me what she could about Damian… which was not anything I didn't already know, except for the information about his family.

Seems he has a sister who is married and has a daughter, and he is close with her and her family. His own parents? Not so much. Which isn't unusual. And he dropped out of the public eye about a year ago… And no, she couldn't tell me why… So overall, I am back where I started. Which is why I am here… I mean, no way, am I headed home after what happened today. My own flat, it feels strange… But this apartment—Okay, Damian's apartment, with its view over the city... I feel invincible here. Or closer to him… Okay, that too… And it's past ten pm, and on a Sunday. So what, if he's busy today? I can still come over, right?

Maybe he is waiting here…or not. I snort. Like Big Daddy D would ever wait for anything. God forbid, it might put a dent in that inflated ego of his… Or in other parts of him, which are also inflated… Like his dick. Man, that is gigantic. I've never seen anything like it… And how the hell had he actually shoved that thing inside of me? Gah! Next time, I am going to pay more careful attention to it… That is, if I'm not squirming under him and don't have my eyes shut in ecstasy and in agony and — my sneakers catch in a crack in the pavement and I tumble forward.

A strong pair of hands grips me, "Whoa, there."

I straighten, lift my head to glance into a pair of bright eyes. Tanned skin, teeth flashing against firm lips.

"Hello?" He tilts his head and his dreadlocks dance around him.

He releases me, steps back, "You okay?"

"Y…yes. Thanks. " I grab my backpack, tuck the strap under my arm. "I must be the only woman in this city who loses her footing despite not wearing heels, huh?"

"You were lost in thought." He raises his shoulders, "It happens."

He retreats, then walks around an upturned hat and sinks down onto a makeshift seat that seems to be made out of newspapers. Huh?

"Next time, keep your eyes on the goal."

"Goal?"

"The task at hand; don't let go of the big picture."

"Big picture?"

"Like I do." He snatches up a board that had been facedown and waves it in my direction.

What care I for the wreaths that can only give glory?

"Byron?" I turn to him, "Why Byron?"

　"Why not?"

I scowl, "A privileged full-of-himself, opinionated twat."

"That he was."

"You agree?" I tilt my head.

"Sometimes, you have to separate the words from the man."

I stare, "You've lost me."

"Don't disregard the words because of the man he was. If you separate what someone's saying from what they've made of themself? Well, the words take on a different meaning." He nods towards the prose, "Get me?"

"I'm not sure." I shuffle my feet, "Why do I get the feeling you're trying to tell me something?"

"Me?" He places the board back on the ground, "Not at all. How is it my place to tell you how to differentiate right from wrong? Truth from fiction?"

"Who else but you can point that out?" I look at him, then at The Shard that towers over us, "With your vantage point of all the comings and goings around here, who better than you to tell me the things that I can't see from where I am?"

"So, you'll heed my advice?"

I flip my hair over my shoulders, "Why not? I have nothing to lose."

"Make him sweat."

"Huh?"

"Don't make it easy on him."

"Who?"

"Your man."

"How do you know I have a man?"

"Don't you?"

"Yeah." I lower my chin, "I... I am not sure, actually."

"Bet he's thinking the same thing right now."

"Is he?"

"Only one way to find out."

"What do you mean?"

"Test him, force the issue, do something out of character."

"Like what?" I chew the inside of my cheek.

"What's the one thing about him that you want to find out."

I stare at him. "You mean…"

He nods. "Don't take no for an answer."

"And if he still refuses to divulge the truth?"

"Do something unexpected, something that will catch him off guard…"

"Hmm." I frown.

"Meanwhile, you got a cigarette for me?"

"I don't smoke." I shove my hand in my bag, pull out my wallet and rifle through it. Shit, I have Australian dollars, no pounds though. "Hold on."

I glance around, spy an ATM machine. I stalk toward it, insert my card and pull out a few notes. I spin and walk toward him, drop a couple in his hat.

He glances at it, then back at me, "A cigarette… I'd die for one right now."

"Don't say that." I frown.

He chuckles, "Don't like the big 'D' word?"

"Oh, I like 'Big D' all right." I snicker to myself. "It's just, my boyfriend has a thing about my saying that…" I pause. Why the hell did I refer to Damian as my boyfriend? I shake my head. "I know just the thing."

I walk the other way, toward the all-night corner shop I'd passed earlier. A few minutes later, I drop a pack of cigarettes and a lighter into his hat, on top of the money, which he still hasn't touched. How strange.

His face lights up. He reaches for the pack of cigarettes, tears off the foil and lights up. "Thanks." His lips curl. "He's lucky to have you, you know?"

I blink, processing his words. His accent... Shit, it's definitely not that of a street bum. In fact, it's posh. Not that he couldn't have gone to a private school then dropped out, but still. What are the odds, huh?

"Who are you?" I ask.

"A friend." He grins back, then nods to the side, "Speaking of, isn't that someone you know?"

I glance up the street to find a familiar motorcycle turning onto the road and heading toward me. My heart begins to pound, my pulse thuds, and my throat goes dry. The last thing I want is to be spotted here as if I've been waiting for him. Hold on. I turn to the homeless guy, to find he's not there. Huh? I glance the other way to see him walking up the road, with his sign over his shoulder. His gait is steady, his long legs eating up the distance as he puts more space between us.

"How odd."

The double barrels of the approaching bike cut through my thoughts. I pivot and race toward The Shard.

27

Damian

By the time I park and take the elevator to the apartment, she's
nowhere in sight. Not that I'd expected to see her. In fact, I'd been
on my way to her apartment, but as I'd turned the corner at the top
of road and spotted her outside The Shard, my heart had stuttered. It
had bloody stuttered. What the fuck is wrong with me? For that
matter, what am I doing here?

I had fully intended not to come, but after hearing her cry out on
the phone and knowing that she was in danger... And then, unable to
do anything about it. I'd felt so helpless... Fucking helpless. For only
the third time in my life—three times too many—this is it!

I am never going to put myself in that position again. I am going
to find a way out of this.

I am going to fuck her out of my life, once and for all. I am going
to make her orgasm over and over again, create a stockpile of her
beautiful climaxes so I have enough inspiration to write all the lyrics
I need. Then, I am going to leave her.

I use the keycard to let myself in. The place is quiet; the only light is from a floor lamp at the far end of the room. She stands with her back to me, her back pack on the floor at her side, her jacket placed over it. She's wearing her usual jeans and plaid shirt, dark hair in a cloud around her shoulders, as she stares ahead.

I walk to her. "Julia?"

She doesn't reply.

I reach her, touch her shoulder, and she trembles.

"Why?" she asks. "Why did you do that?"

I follow the direction of her gaze to the potter's wheel, and next to it, a counter that has been set up, complete with all of the tools she'd need for molding clay.

"You said you didn't have a studio."

"So, you set one up for me?"

Her voice is low. I walk past her, switch on the spotlight. The glow bathes both of us.

"How dare you?" She turns on me. "How dare you do this?"

"Hold on." I scowl, "I'm confused. I thought you wanted to work again, that you wanted to sculpt me?"

"I did, but not like this."

"What do you mean?"

"The one thing I want to do on my own, the one thing that's sacred to me, you had to go and spoil it with your money."

"Wait," I hold up hand. "My money's good enough for you to accept in return for sex, but not good enough for me to buy you something to help you pursue your passion?"

"That's exactly right." She curls her fingers into fists at her sides. "This is important to me. It's what makes my life worth living. All this time, people have come and gone from my life, people like you—"

I wince.

"People who I thought cared for me, when actually, they were toying with my feelings. Not even my father cared enough to hang around to find out what kind of a person I'd grow up to be—"

"That's why you became a nanny?"

"What?"

"Is that why you decided to take care of other people's children."

"Maybe" She frowns. "That's not the point."

"Then, what is?"

"When I work with my hands, when I can dig my fingers into a shapeless form, mold it to my liking, breathe life into it, it satisfies something primal inside of me…" She hesitates, seems to struggle with her words before whispering, "Something that I feel only when I'm with you."

"You do?" My heart begins to beat hard. "What are you trying to say?"

She swallows. "That…" She peers up into my face and peruses my features. My pulse rate ratchets up. *Say it, say what's on your mind, Flower.*

"That?" I hold her gaze and she glances away.

"That working with clay is the one thing that gives meaning to my life, other than taking care of kids…" She squares her shoulders, "It's what I do for myself, and you had to go and sully it."

I stiffen, "Because I set up a studio for you?"

"Because you're trying to buy me again."

She tips up her chin and I take in her flushed features, her erratic breath, the color that smears her cheekbones. "Why are you upset?"

"Why am I *upset*?" She throws up her hands.

I nod. "You clearly missed having a space of your own where you could create, where you could give form to your dreams."

"Are you hearing yourself?" she snarls.

I scowl, "You have to help me here, Flower. I thought you'd like this."

She stares at me, then chuckles, "You thought you could simply walk in and occupy the one space in my life which is sacred, which I have kept for myself, the space where I can be myself and not worry about being judged… Or have to pretend to be someone else. You thought you could take over even that part of my life, you—"

"I thought you would appreciate it."

"No, you thought I *should* appreciate it, that you could ingratiate yourself to me, maybe make me dependent on you," she draws in a breath, "but you know what?"

I tilt my head.

"You can't buy me anymore."

"No?" Anger thrums against my veins, my balls harden, and fuck me, this is wrong. I shouldn't feel so turned on. I take a step forward and she holds her ground. Bloody hell, this woman, she has the kind of strength and fire that makes me want to consume her. Bury myself in her and allow her to burn the darkness inside, fill the empty spaces and paint my blank canvas, fill my sheet with the kinds of lyrics I haven't been able to create since...forever.

"No." She closes the distance between us, then shoves her index finger in my chest. "The deal is off."

"No, it's not."

She tips her chin up, meets my gaze head on, "You're not hearing me."

"I am," I glare down at her, "and I'm telling you, we're not done yet."

Her green eyes grow stormy and golden flickers dance in their depths. So real, so vital, so bloody full of the kind of fearlessness that I had forgotten I once had myself. I inch forward until my shoes bump the tips of her sneakers, bend my knees and thrust my face into hers. "Strip."

"What?" She straightens. "No."

"Strip, or I'll do it for you."

"Fuck you."

"Oh, I intend to." I reach for her, she feints to the side, grabs her backpack and races for the door. I pull out my phone and tap the screen. The locks on the door engage with an audible click as she reaches it.

She turns the handle, and the door doesn't open.

She jiggles it, puts her shoulder to it, then straightens, only to kick the door. "Ow," she gasps, then grabs her leg and hops about. Her backpack slips from her shoulder, weighing her down further. "Ouch," she cries out again.

I rush toward her. "Did you hurt yourself?" I reach for her.

"Don't touch me." She stumbles back and her bag hits the floor with a thump. She tumbles over it, then falls on her arse. "Argh," she gasps out a breath, then clutches at her hurt leg. "This is all your fault," she cries.

I can't stop the chuckle that rumbles up my chest.

"Don't you dare laugh at me, you ass."

Me?" I wipe the smile off of my face. "I wouldn't."

"You would." She rubs at her hurt foot, then stares up at me. "Open the door."

"Nope." I hold out my arm.

She stares at me, then up at my face. "You're joking," she snarls.

"Am I?" I tilt my head, "Take my hand, or I'll be forced to pick you up."

"No." She glowers at me.

I stare back at her.

"Fine, whatever." She grabs my hand.

I haul her up to her feet, then tug her so she careens into me.

"Let me go."

I bend my knees, heave her over my shoulder, "Now, where were we?"

28

Julia

"We were... Nowhere." I shake the hair out of my eyes. "You were leaving. No wait, that was me."

"Neither of us is going anywhere." He heads for the bedroom and my stomach trembles; my core clenches. No, no, no, this is not happening. I will not be turned on by him going all hot and dark and caveman on me… Not when he's done something that has completely shaken me… I mean, paying to fuck me is one thing. Not that that is acceptable, in any way… But hell, if it's not a transaction, fair and square, something I can catalogue and put into a tidy box.

But his setting up my studio without telling me about it? It's tantamount to his declaring that he cares for me… Which he doesn't. No way.

I struggle in his grasp, "Put me down."

"No." He increases his pace.

Oh hell, if he places me down on the bed, if he touches me, kisses me… I'll be gone. I won't be able to resist him, damn it. It's not him… It's me, I fear more. I fear the reactions he causes in my body. I fear how I react to him when he holds me, touches me, kisses me… None of it is real. It's simply my body's reaction to his very expert skills, something which I need to put an end to right away.

"Let me go, you…you complete reprobate."

I lock my fingers and bring my fist down on his side and kick out at him, at the same time. He slaps my butt and hell, I'd been expecting it, and yet, nothing prepares me for the flash of lust that pierces through me. Bloody hell, I can't let this happen. I can't! "Damian, no!" I yell.

"Julia, yes." He mocks me as he steps into the bedroom.

"Don't you dare," I snarl.

"Ooh, I am so afraid." He laughs.

Anger ripples up my spine. My belly twists, moisture leaks between my legs. Jesus, this is wrong. I shouldn't be so turned on. I shouldn't. He bypasses the bedroom and heads for the sliding doors that lead out onto a deck I hadn't noticed before. What the hell? I stare as he reaches out to flick on lights. An infinity pool? I gasp. What the hell is a pool doing here on the 68th floor? And it stretches out as if reaching out to the city. "Wow!"

"Like it?"

"I didn't say that."

"Oh, you'll be saying more than that in a second. I hope you know how to swim, Flower."

He marches toward the edge of the pool and I begin to squirm in earnest, "Don't you dare, Rockstar, don't you fucking—"

The water comes up to embrace me, then pours over me, envelops me as I scream and swallow several mouthfuls of chlorinated water as the shock of being dunked smashes through me. What the hell? I come up choking, my hair sticking to my forehead, covering my eyes. "I hate you," I sputter.

"Finally," he sneers. "You're being honest. How's the water by the way?"

I right myself, and my feet touch bottom. At least, he didn't throw me in at the deep end, and the water isn't all that cold… A heated pool. Of course, it is. I swim toward him, hold onto the rim of the pool and scowl up at him. "Asshole."

"Cooled off yet?" He smirks.

"No, but I will, as soon as —" I hold out my hand and he takes it. I tug and he stumbles forward. I yank more; he tumbles over and into the pool. Water splashes over me, over the edge.

He comes up for air, his hair plastered to his scalp, and outlining the shape of his beautiful face. "You've done it now." His voice is hushed.

My nerve-endings crackle.

"Umm…" I push back and away from him. "I… I didn't mean it."

"Of course, you did." He peels back his lips, showing off those sharp, white teeth. I gulp. Hadn't meant to bring out the predator in him. I should have known I'd never be able to outwit him… Doesn't mean I can't try to outrun him… I clamber over the side of the pool; my feet slip, I cry out, then right myself.

"Come back, Flower."

"No." I take off for the sliding doors, hear a thud, glance over my shoulder, then gasp when I find he's in hot pursuit. His leather jacket drips water, and what I can see of his shirt outlines those sculpted abs, his jeans molded to every muscle of his powerful thighs. My throat closes. I reach the doors, dive through, then grab the handle, and slide the door closed, only to encounter an obstruction. "No, no, no." I glance down to find he's planted his leg in the opening between the door and the frame. Shit, I tug on the door and he grabs it from the other side. Hell, I am no match for his strength. I release the door, then pivot and race around the bed, only he grabs me around the waist.

I shriek as he hauls me up and over his shoulder again. I yell, swing my fists and brush his side; my hair falls over my eyes, I brush it aside, find he's entering the bathroom. He kicks the door shut, lowers me to the ground.

"Strip," he orders.

I glower at him even as I squeeze my thighs together. "I will, if you will," I retort.

"Oh?" He smirks. "If you don't remove your clothes, I'll have to do it for you."

"Whatever," I snort.

"And I won't stop there."

"No?" My voice trembles and I purse my lips. Why the hell am I so nervous and excited at the same time?

"No." He looks me up and down. "I'll tie you up, blindfold you, and then I'll fuck you so hard, you won't have any choice but to obey me after."

Goosebumps flare over my skin and it's not only because I am wearing wet clothes. His filthy promises… It's decadent and completely wrong.

I tip up my chin, grab the bottom of my blouse and peel it off. His gaze drags to my breasts, down my navel, to my thighs. I toe off my sneakers. I unbutton my jeans, lower the zipper, then drag them down my legs to my ankles. I step out of them, along with my socks, then kick them aside. Goosebumps race across my skin. I straighten to meet that hot, hungry gaze of his. My throat closes and warmth suffuses my chest.

Shit, the way he's looking at me, like I am his favorite rock song and most hated melody, all rolled together.

"Take it all off," he commands.

I reach behind my back to unhook my bra and my breasts spill out. He inhales sharply. A flush steals up my throat. *Don't stop, don't, not now. Show him he doesn't scare you.* I drop the bra, then slide my fingers into the waistband of my panties. I slide them down, and his entire body stiffens. I kick aside my panties, straighten, and cry out to find he's stepped forward, into my space.

"D… Damian."

"Shh." He reaches out to push aside a tendril of hair that's stuck to my cheek. "So beautiful."

My knees tremble. I press them together to stop myself from losing my balance.

He drags his finger down the line of my throat, between my breasts, to my bellybutton. My toes curl. He pauses at the top of my pussy, and I shiver. An aching emptiness claws in my lower belly. It's always like this… Jesus, he only has to touch me and I am sure I am going to come apart or go right over the top, and he hasn't even touched me properly.

"Tell me what you want," he commands.

"No." My voice cracks and I swallow down the ball of nervousness that blocks my throat.

"You sure about that?" He sinks to his knees between my legs, fixes his mouth on my cunt.

I yell out, "Ohmygod!"

He grabs my butt, one large palm on each butt cheek, and squeezes.

A trembling sweeps up my back. "Oh," I gasp. "Oh!"

He plants his shoulders between my thighs so I don't have a choice but to part my legs, then he proceeds to lick me from my backhole to my clit, again and again. My entire body bucks; I dig my fingers into his hair and tug. He growls against my core, the vibration seeping into my center and mixing with the melting hunger inside that ebbs and flows and throbs in tandem to each suck of his mouth as he devours my pussy.

"Jesus," I throw my head back and pant.

He thrusts his tongue inside my channel and I moan.

He slides his finger in between my butt cheeks and fingers my puckered hole, and I whine. It's filthy, damn him. It's the part of me that I'll never get used to him touching, and yet… Oh, my… Shivers of pleasure trickle down my legs, up my spine, radiating out from where he's touching me, kissing me, biting me.

"Damian," I howl as he tugs on my swollen clit. "Damian."

He rises to his feet, carrying me by the tops of my thighs as he swivels around and backs me into the closed bathroom door. He reaches between us to lower his zipper and I glance down in time to see his cock spring out. Thick, large, with a vein running up the side, the swollen head is angry and throbbing and "Holy crap!" I gasp, "A piercing? You have a P/A! How the hell didn't I notice that earlier?"

"Maybe you were too busy?" I hear the smirk in his voice and know I should retort, but bloody hell… *Not only is Big Daddy D well-endowed, but also the best part of him wears a crown.*

Umm, hello, back up. I snort.

"What are you thinking?" He frowns.

"Umm… Just that…" I reach down and tug on his P/A. He growls and his dick lengthens. I swear, it lengthens further.

"Oh, wow," I gasp, "That's, uh, bigger than I thought."

"But you knew that already."

"There's knowing and, uh, seeing." I swallow, "How the hell did that…that monster cock of yours fit inside of me."

"Only one way to find out." He wraps his massive fingers around his thick dick…which stills does nothing to make it seem less threatening. If anything, it brings home just how large this man is… Everywhere… I steal a glance at his feet, still in his motorcycle boots… Yep, definitely big.

He pumps himself once from base to head and precum oozes from the tip. I swallow, my throat seems to dry up, and my core pulses, warming, throbbing, aching… I groan, "Please, Damian," I beg, "fuck me."

A shudder seems to grip his shoulders, "When you say my name, it fucking ruins me, woman."

He begins to push into me, then groans, "Fucking condom. I don't have one."

"I… I am on birth control."

"And I am clean."

I set my lips "A bit too late to worry about that," I mumble, "considering."

"I want you to know that what we have is different."

"That's what they all say," I scoff.

"Flower," he growls, "look into my eyes."

I peer up into his face, "There, happy?" I tip up my chin.

"Not until you tell me that you believe me."

"What?" I swallow, "What do you want me to believe?"

"That I've never felt like this with anyone before. I've never felt this connected to any woman." He thrusts his face into mine, so I have no choice but to meet his eyes, "Not until you."

"Not even," I lick my lips, "not even Riley's mother?"

"Not even her."

There's no hesitation in his tone, his gaze direct. The expression on his features, one of sincerity. Holy shit, he actually means it.

"Damian," I whisper and his control seems to shatter. His jaw tics and a vein throbs at his temple, then he pushes his hips forward and buries himself inside of me in one single thrust, and I scream again. *Ohmygod,* the thickness, that heaviness between my legs, it's like being impaled.

"Damian," I gasp again.

He grits his teeth; sweat beads his brow. He slams his big palm into the door by my side and I swear the entire barrier shudders. He's bigger, brawnier, than any man I've ever known… Than anyone I've ever met… Likely, he isn't aware of his own strength.

He draws in a breath and his chest expands, his shoulders still clad in his leather jacket seem to grow bigger, if that were possible.

Reaching up, I cup his cheek, "Why the hell do I feel so much for you?"

"The same reason I do?" He glares into my eyes. Anger rolls deep in their depths, and frustration and something else — the same confusion that's haunted me since I set eyes on him. And does that make it worse? Or better? God knows…

Except, something inside of me empathizes with him. "I know," I whisper, "it's not easy."

"Tell me about it." He chuckles, then tilts his hips and slips further inside my channel. A groan rumbles up his chest, "You're so tight, Flower."

"Oh." A trembling shudders out from the point where his massive cock disappears inside my aching pussy. "I thought you like to fuck hard," I mutter.

"I'm trying to be gentle."

"Who said I wanted gentle?"

"I don't want to hurt you," he insists.

"Too late." I slide my palm around his nape and tug until his face is right above mine. "I very much want to hurt you." I bury my teeth in his lower lip.

29

Damian

What the fuck? The coppery taste of blood fills my mouth, pain shivers down my spine, my dick lengthens, and my thigh muscles bunch. "Fuck," I snarl, "you're crazy, woman."

"*You* make me crazy," she replies against my mouth. She licks my wounded lip, swallows down my blood, and all my senses hone in on her.

My vision narrows, and a pulse throbs at my temples, across my eyelids even in my balls. "You've done it now," I grit out through clenched teeth. I shrug out of my jacket, suddenly burning up.

"Ooh," she bats her eyelids, "I'm soooo scared, I'm—" She huffs as I kick my hips forward and drive into her, burying myself to the hilt. She hits her head back against the door, "It's too much, too hard, too large, too everything—"

"Quiet," I order and she presses her lips together.

"Look at me when I fuck you," I growl, and color smears her cheeks. "Shit, you love it when I talk dirty, don't you?"

"What?" she squeaks, then lowers her chin. "Of course, not. What gave you—?"

I pull out, then thrust into her again and she moans, "Ohmygod."

"I'm right here," I answer.

"Jesus, you've got such a big ego."

"You're welcome, sugar."

She peers at me from under hooded eyelashes, "If you weren't so good at fucking, I'd take exception to your corny dialogue."

"You're welcome, again." I laugh. "And it's not corny, when it's the truth."

"Why you—"

I piston my hips, and sink into her with such force that the entire door shakes. She gasps, digs her heels into my sides, grabs onto my shoulders with such impact that my nerve-endings pop in response. "Shit." The pressure at the base of my spine builds in intensity, my vision tunnels, my cock lengthens... "Fuck," I growl. "Come with me, Flower." I thrust into her, my balls slapping against her inner thighs. "Come all over my dick," I command, and she shatters.

She cries out, arches her back, thrusts her breasts up and into my chest, squeezes her pussy around my cock and shudders as her climax crashes through her.

I watch her face, her flushed features, the beautiful column of her throat, the beads of water that dot her shoulders, the creaminess of her breasts, the swollen tips of her nipples. Leaning down, I suck on one and she shivers. I raise my face to hers. "Julia," I whisper, "open your eyes."

She flutters her eyelids, gazes at me with pupils so dilated that my groin hardens. I plunge into her again and again as my climax crashes over me. I erupt inside of her, shooting long streams of my release. She leans up, presses her lips to mine, offering herself up— her sweetness, her vitality, her life—and I know then, I can't see her again. I need to leave, need to get away from her before this...thing spirals out of control. Before I allow her further into my heart, my soul…my home… Introduce her to my daughter. *No, I can't do that.*

I pull out of her.

"What's wrong?" She scowls.

"I need to leave."

She stares at me, "What? You don't mean it."

I lower her to the floor; her knees seem to give way. I reach for her, then pull back. If I touch her, I am gone. I need to put distance between us. Fast. Reaching down, I grab my jacket and pull it on.

"You can stay here for as long as you want."

"I... I don't understand."

"The arrangement is over."

"So, do I get to meet your daughter?"

I look her up and down, "What makes you think you are worthy of meeting her?"

Her features crumple, "Asshole."

"Yep." I attempt to smirk, but it feels plastic. "That's me. You didn't think that I wanted more than to take your arse and your pussy... Couldn't get to your mouth, but..." I shrug, "not that it's much of a loss, considering you aren't even a great kisser." *What the fuck was that? What is wrong with me?*

She gapes. "Are you..." She shakes her head, "You're a horrible, horrible man."

I swallow the words I want to say and nod. "What-fucking-ever." I jerk my chin, "Would you mind getting out of my way? I need to get home to my daughter."

30

Julia

What the hell happened there? One second, he's inside me; the next, he can't get away from me fast enough. I sink down against the closed bathroom door. He'd fucked me, and I swear, it seemed to mean something to him. He'd said as much. Maybe too much, considering he'd gone and insulted me almost as if it were in self-defense, like he was getting in too deep and wanted a way out.

He'd lashed out at me in that typical Damian fashion, where he was trying his best to hurt me. And he'd succeeded. My lower lip trembles. Bastard had hit me where it hurt. How dare he? I fist my fingers at my sides. How dare he leave without a second glance? Was it that easy for him? Like I was another notch on his bedpost that he could fuck and leave?

But hold on, he said he hadn't felt like this with anyone before. That he'd never felt this connected to any woman as he had with me... Not even Riley's mother. And I believe him when he says that.

Is that why he's running from me?

From what I've pieced together, he'd dropped out of sight after Riley's mother left him — Again, how the hell had he kept that out of the papers? That's what must have prompted him to take a sabbatical, and focus on taking care of his daughter. And that had been a year ago. A year since he'd withdrawn from his gigs, to focus on bringing up his kid, to the extent that he doesn't even want a nanny involved. I chew on my lower lip.

Apparently, he is done with me, and my orgasms too… Hell, now *that*, I am going to miss. How he'd glare at me and the tingles would start in my belly, how he'd touch me and my nerve-endings would fire in hyperdrive, how he'd kiss me and I'd instantly grow wet, how he'd lick my pussy and... Oh hell. I bury my face in my hands. Why the hell did everything have to turn out to be so, so complicated? Why the hell had I accepted his crazy-ass proposition in the first place? What is wrong with me?

Money is important, all right, but it has never featured high on my priorities… I mean, I could definitely do with that infusion of cash to pay off the debts I racked up while traveling. Not to mention that I wanted the money to ease the retirement years of my mother. But hell!

I'd been swayed by the cash and screwed up the chance I had to really understand this man. Face it… He'd ensured that the money thing stood between us… He'd wanted our relationship to be transactional. I'd proposed a one-night stand; he'd turned it into something more. On the one hand, he'd wanted to spend more time with me, but on the other hand, he'd reduced it to something financial.

In fact, he'd gone to great lengths to ensure that he kept me out of his life, out of his house, out of his head and heart. And despite all that, he'd sensed the deepening connection between us. Damn it, when we fuck, it is more real, more primal, more electric than any experience in my life. And he senses it. He has to. No wonder he is running scared. Coward.

No wonder he'd walked out on me without a second glance. He'd had an escape clause all along — the fucking money. This was all an arrangement after all, something he could pull out of at any time. Just another business decision.

And hell… Those orgasms he'd wrenched from me? I squeeze my thighs together… No one else could give me those. He's spoiled me for any other man. After the complex, growling, broodiness that is Daddy Savage… No way, can I be happy with anyone else. Which means, I am, basically, fucked. Gah! My throat hurts and my head pounds. What the hell am I going to do now, huh? A shiver runs across my skin, and if I stay here naked, I'll freeze to death. I rise to my feet, stagger over to the shower.

Twenty minutes and a whole lot of hot water and tears later, I feel somewhat human. My head still hurts and my nose is stuffy, and my eyes must be swollen, but fine… At least I'm warmer. A chill grips me and I press my fingers together.

Okay, not really. Nothing compares to the warmth that comes off of Damian's big body. That man is a bloody furnace, and there is so much of him to go around, I could plaster every centimeter of my body to every centimeter of his and there'd be enough of his body left for me to press myself to his body twice over. *OMG, what am I thinking?* I have certifiably gone mad. My imagination is clearly in overdrive, or else I have OD'd on Damian enough that he's gone to my head and lodged himself under my skin, in between my legs, in my heart… *No, not there. Never there.*

I turn off the shower, wrap myself in one of the long, fluffy towels I find on one of the shelves and step out. That's when I catch sight of a bathrobe laid out on the bed. What the —?

So, he left me aching and angry, and yet, he'd stopped to ensure I had something to wear when I came out. How strange? I walk to the bathrobe, push my arms into the sleeves, and his scent teases my nostrils. My toes curl, my belly flip flops, and it feels like I am wrapped up in the man all over again. The pressure builds at the backs of my eyes again. *No, no, no, goddammit, this is not happening. I am not going to cry over him.*

Nope. I march back into the bathroom, notice that my wet clothes are gone. Huh? I head across to the kitchen, find that the washer-dryer is running. What the —? He ran a wash for me? And — the scent of coffee draws my gaze to the percolator, the coffee ready to be poured from the jug. He made coffee so I could have something hot to drink? Next to it is a covered plate, with a note.

Heat and eat this.

I trace the bold cursive and it blurs in front of my eyes. Why are you doing this Damian? You've been such a bastard to me, and yet, you want to take care of me. You don't want to introduce me to your kid, and yet, you treat me like I'm special. In fact, that's what you told me right before you decided to cut and run. You're a complete mystery, Big D… One I am going to solve.

The dryer beeps, and I retrieve my clothes from the washing machine, only to find them entangled with his. Guess he'd changed before he'd left? Of course he wouldn't have wanted to drive back in wet clothes, not to mention he had extra clothes in the closet.

I disentangle my blouse from his jeans, my jeans from his shirt. If only it were that easy to disentangle my life from his? Tears prick my eyes and I brush them away. Damn it, now I am getting sentimental about laundry?

Once dressed, I pour out some of the coffee, and carry it, along with one of the muffins that I'd heated up. I walk toward the work-table with the clay molding tools laid out. I set my coffee down, reach for the armature, the framework on which the sculpture can be molded. It's not what I'd normally use, but it will do. I reach for the ready-made moist clay in the tub on the side. Again, not what I'm accustomed to using, but hell, if it isn't of the finest quality money can buy. The man had certainly not spared any expense.

I walk over, pluck my phone from my bag, and pull up my favorite music mix. The haunting tunes of Damian's first album fill the air. Much better.

I pick up a fistful of the clay, shape it in between my palms, then get to work. I must lose track of time, for the next thing I know, I hear the door opening. I whirl around, to find Karina stepping through. Followed by Isla.

"What the hell?" My voice cracks. Shit, how many hours have I been here? My throat is scratchy, the way it gets when I am too focused on my art. "How did you two get here?"

Karina exchanges a look with Isla, then both walk over to me. "What are you working on?" Karina asks.

"Umm, it's not ready yet." I glance around, then grab the folded burlap cloth, also part of the supplies he provided. Goddamn it, did the man have to be so perfect? Only when it comes to being thoughtful in things outside of sex, that is… Okay, hold on, even during sex, he'd made sure to take care of my needs, made sure that I'd orgasmed… Hell, my life had become one long, hot, sweaty climax since I'd run into him… Except when he had commanded me not to come, of course. *Okay, stop. Don't think of him anymore.*

I place myself between the unfinished sculpture and my friends.

"Well?" I frown. "What are you doing here? How did you find me and —" I scowl at Karina, "How did you get a key to the apartment?"

She stares back at me.

"Right." I blow out a breath, "You're the security expert for the Seven so, of course, you have access to their properties."

"You don't have to sound so upset about it." She half smiles. "I haven't been inside his bedroom."

Right.

I dig my fingers through my now dry hair, then realize I must've gotten the clay in my hair. Crap. I glower at Karina's perfectly coiffed hairstyle. "Do you always have to look so perfect?" I glance out of the window at the pinkening skies, "So early in the morning?"

"I'm far from it." She peers into my face, then holds out the bag she's been carrying. "It's for you."

"What's that?"

"Open it."

I wash my hands in the bowl of water on the table and dry them, then take the bag from her, peek inside. "Oh!" I glance up at her. "You brought me clothes?"

She tilts her head, "He was most insistent and very detailed about what to get you."

"You mean… D… Damian?"

"Who else?"

I glance down at my clay flecked garments. Damn it, Damian, how the hell do you think of everything? No one else has taken such good care of me before. Why the hell do you have to make it so difficult for me to hate you?

Karina's features soften, "Why don't you freshen up and join us? And then we can talk?"

Ten minutes later, after a quick shower and wearing a fresh pair of jeans and a T-shirt that is a perfect fit—I wouldn't have expected less from him—I join the two girls in the kitchen.

Isla adds some chopped herbs to the frying pan.

"You're making breakfast?"

"I found the ingredients for a quick omelet." Isla divides the contents of the pan onto three plates and sets them on the counter. She follows up by placing a fresh croissant on each plate. "We picked these up on the way over, but, the entire kitchen is stocked, enough that if you planned to stay here, well," she glances at me, "you wouldn't need to leave this place for a week... Maybe longer."

"Oh." I slip onto one of the bar stools, reach for the cup of coffee that Karina hands me.

Isla raises her cup, "Salut, babe."

I clink my cup with Karina's, take a sip, and set it down. Then cut into the omelet. The flavors burst on my tongue and I blink. "Wow," I take another bite, "this omelet is—"

"Delicious." Karina nods.

I turn to Isla, and she raises her hands, "Not that I am not a good cook, but it's the ingredients. Everything is farm fresh, organic, top of the line."

"I am sure it is." Everything Damian owns is top-notch and he's choosing to share it with me. I set down my fork. "This doesn't make sense," I groan.

"What? The omelet?" Karina asks.

"No." I draw in a breath, then lower the glass. "Damian," I exclaim. "He…he's killing me with his consideration."

"Huh?" Isla exchanges a glance with Karina. "So, what's bothering you, babe?"

"Everything." I stab my fork into the omelet and play with it. "Nothing. I don't know." I drop the fork with a clatter.

"Eat first." Karina tucks into her own food. "Bitching about men is best done on a full stomach."

"Yeah." I half smile, then sample the croissant. "This is good," I tell them. "Thank you for bringing this. And thank you for making breakfast, Isla."

"Not a problem at all, when you're cooking in a kitchen that induces an orgasm by just being in the space," she retorts.

I choke, then reach for my coffee, and take a healthy sip.

Karina pats me on my back, "You okay?"

"Yeah."

"Something I said?" Isla watches me with a curious gaze.

"Orgasms," I mumble. "If there's one thing the man got right, it was that."

"I knew it!" Isla giggles. "How many O's have you had since you got together with that panty-melting hunk?"

"Too many to keep track of," I grumble.

"Ooh." Isla fans herself, "That's sooo hot; don't stop. At least, I can live vicariously."

"Get your own." I frown.

"I do, babe." She nods, "Ben keeps me happy."

"Ben?" Karina asks. "You have a boyfriend?"

"My vibrator."

I choke again, this time on the gasp that has me inhaling the spit in my mouth. Jeez. "Sorry," I finally manage to rasp.

"You named your vibrator?" Karina chuckles, "Good move."

"It makes the experience much more intimate, you get me?" Isla laughs.

"Oh, one dick's as good as another. The name only gets in the way," Karina jokes.

"Unless the name is Arpad, huh?"

Karina jerks her head in my direction, her features taking on a stunned expression, then she nods. "You're perceptive."

"You sound surprised." I take in her features. "Ah," I nod, "I see."

"What?" She tilts her head.

"You thought I was the nanny, so clearly, someone who doesn't have much ambition, or an IQ, for that matter. And then, of course, I'm screwing Damian so, well, how could I possibly be anything other than a bimbo, huh?"

Karina winces, sips from her cup, "Guilty."

"You're not denying it?" I blink.

"Why should I?" She glances between me and Isla, "I admit, that's what I thought about both of you, actually."

Isla gapes, "Gee, thanks." She frowns, "Straight talk is okay and all, but thank God, I don't suffer from that affliction."

Karina does a slow blink, then laughs, "I like both of you."

"Thanks," I mutter.

"No, really." She glances between us again. "I admit, I had you girls down as… Well, there's a type who hang around the Seven. You have to understand, in my line of business I see a lot of things—"

"You mean, thanks to the security agency you run?"

She nods. "It's a man's business I am in. I mean, what isn't? But this one, particularly. And then, having to make a success of it... I admit, it's probably increased my testosterone levels to a degree even I am not comfortable with."

I frown at her. *What a weird remark. Why would she say that?* "You… you want a child, don't you?"

Karina's shoulders jerk.

Isla makes a noise in her throat.

"I'm sorry," I mumble. "Guess the events of the last few days have me on edge… It's sent my empathy radar into overdrive, and I'm an artist… And a nanny… Means I sense things…" I shut up. "I didn't mean to pry."

"No, it's okay." Karina's lips twist. "I do want a child, more than anything, but there is no man on the horizon, so…"

"IVF?" Isla ventures.

"Maybe." She shakes her head, "I am trying to work up my courage toward it." She half laughs, "Seems I am more old-fashioned than I thought when it comes to these things."

Tell me about it. I thought I'd be alright with the strange association Damian had proposed. Turns out, I need more. I want to see him more often, spend more time with him, get to know what makes him tick, how he is when he sleeps, when he is composing, when he's taking care of his child.

"I need to get inside Damian's house."

Karina stares at me. "You know I can't help you with that."

"You can." I nod. What has gotten into me? I must have absorbed some of Damian's authoritarian attitude, for I hold Karina's gaze. "You believe in the sisterhood, don't you?"

She frowns. "I wouldn't have come this far if it weren't for my mother, and the women along the way who helped me," she says slowly.

"Take one for the team." I tilt my head.

"I can't put my professional reputation at risk. If word got out..."

"We'd never tell anyone." Isla mimes zipping her mouth and throwing away her key.

Karina folds her arms over her chest. "I can't believe you'd ask me to do that."

"What were Damian's instructions to you?"

"Instructions?"

"Yeah, yeah." I shake my hair from my face, "What did he tell you with respect to me? What is it that forced you to become friendly with me?"

Karina's face flushes. "I admit I befriended you because Damian wanted me to keep an eye on you, but honestly, the more I got to know the two of you, the more I liked both of you."

"We are highly likable." Isla laughs. That woman, she is as friendly as a puppy. She's already forgiven Karina for starting out this relationship with us under false pretexts. Me? I'm not giving in that easily.

"What else did he tell you to do?" I hold Karina's gaze.

She scrutinizes my features, "He told me to watch out for you, protect you —"

I nod, "Either you tell me how to get into his place, or I'll have to break in, and the walls around his place are really high."

"Hmm."

"I may hurt myself." I stab my tongue into my cheek. "And that would make Damian unhappy."

"Very unhappy," she agrees.

"So…?" I hold my breath.

"So," she raises her cup, "at least, let's finish breakfast first?"

I clink my cup against hers, "Done."

Several minutes later, she sets her coffee cup down next to her empty plate and leans forward, "Listen carefully…"

29th Dec

Damian

After leaving Julia, I'd called Meredith and asked her to stay the night. She'd agreed. Then I'd gone on a ride to clear my head. Turns out, that wasn't as easy as expected. My thoughts were filled with Julia, what she had come to mean to me, how I want her in my life… All of which is impossible.

By the time I'd made it home, it was dawn.

I'd jumped into the shower and changed into clean clothes, then walked into the living room to find Meredith waiting for me.

"You can't do this on your own, Damian." She folds her arms across her chest.

"I don't need anyone's help." I scowl at her as I pace the floor. Some of Riley's toys are scattered on the carpet. I pick them up and drop them into the box next to the settee. The pink hairband that she'd worn catches my attention. I pick it up, take in the shiny unicorn on it. "Girl's obsessed with fairytales and rainbows," I mutter. "And that damn Frozen." I shake my head, "I can't get the lyrics of the song out of my mind." I turn to Meredith, "Do you think Riley would enjoy the books as much as the movies?"

"Damian." She frowns.

I hum the tune from the theme song, then drag my fingers through my hair. "See?" I tilt my head. "That goddam tune is burned into my brain."

"Maybe you should try your hand at writing songs for kids."

I study her expression, "You think so?"

"You're a born father, Damian."

I swallow the ball of emotions in my throat. "You're being too kind."

"It's the only time you act human, when you talk about Riley."

I squeeze my eyes shut. "It's the only time I feel human." I shuffle my feet, "That's why, you see, I can't allow anyone else in. I can't let anyone else help me with this…situation I am in."

"You're going to have to give in and get help eventually. You can't go on like this."

"You're right," I thrust out my chest, "but surely, I am allowed to treat her as my little girl for a while longer."

Meredith's forehead wrinkles; she opens her mouth as if to say something then firms her lips. "I'll call later to check, in case you need my help with anything."

"Thanks." I walk toward her and kiss her cheek. "Thanks for everything. I don't know how I could have managed without you."

She pats my shoulder, scrutinizes my face. "Damian." Her forehead furrows, "You know how much I care about you. You know the Seven of you are the closest I have to family?"

I nod.

"If I hadn't come across you kids when you were picking fights on the streets after the incident, I don't know what I'd have done with my life."

"Meredith," I grip her arm, "you've been a quasi-mother to all of us.'

"I could never have my own children, but being with all of you has meant I haven't miss that part of my life as much as I would have."

I nod.

"And then there's Peter."

"Peter?" I frown, "Sterling's chauffeur?"

She nods, a gleam in her eyes.

"What does he have to do with…?" I stare. "Jesus, Meredith," I mutter. "You mean, you and Peter?"

"Don't tell me the lot of you didn't guess?"

"Hmm, well." My neck heats. "It's not like we talk about you that way, and besides, Peter…uh…"

"He's protective about you lot, too, huh?"

"Yeah," I nod. "Still, I mean," I shuffle my feet, not knowing what to say. It's a bit like finding out that your parents have sex. I mean, they do and that's how we were born, but somehow you want to pretend that they are these perfect creatures with no wants or passion or— "Hell," I roll my shoulders, "why are you telling me this, now?"

"Just so you know that we all have our secrets, Damian."

"Right." I tip my chin up and glance past her.

"And we all need help with our demons."

I scowl, "Why don't you tell me what's on your mind?"

"Julia." She stares up at me.

I meet her gaze. "Julia?"

"Let her in, Damian. She wants to be part of your life. She can help, if you let her."

"I don't need anyone's help." I step back, "This is something I need to deal with myself."

"Do you, though?" She reaches up and pats my cheek, "Don't delay until it's too late. Don't let Julia get away."

I blow out a breath. "Thanks for the advice."

"Now, I feel like I've been put in my place."

I stare at her in horror. "Meredith, no. You know you are much more than an assistant to all of us."

"Of course, I do." She chuckles, "And trust me, I won't take any lip from any of you boys, either."

"You're tough," I grumble.

"No shit." She laughs, then turns to leave. I wait in the doorway until she's driven off and the gates have closed behind her, then head inside.

Later that evening, after putting Riley to bed, I make my way toward the study at the far end of the ground floor. I check my phone to make sure my app is open and tuned into Riley's bedroom. Placing my phone upright on the table next to the sofa so I can see the screen as well as access it, I pour myself a whiskey, then sink down into the comfortable settee and grab my guitar.

I begin to strum the guitar, composing the song in my head.

Whisper your kisses in my ear
My lips on yours
As you fall apart all over my cock
As lust swells your eyelids
And your pussy weeps
As you come so prettily, I am sure that I will never feel as alive again…

I draw in a breath. Shit, that's bloody emo, and hot… And what the hell am I writing now? A lust song, an ode dedicated to the woman who's turned my life upside down. Who I need to stop seeing, stop thinking of, before she turns me into a bumbling idiot who'd give up his life for one more touch, one more fuck, one more time to sink my cock inside of her. "Bloody hell." I toss the guitar aside, rise to my feet and head for the snifter of whiskey, when the app on my phone beeps. I top up the liquid in my tumbler, head for the phone and snatch it up. The security app has a notification. I swipe to it and the image of a woman opening the front door and walking in fills the screen.

"What the—?" I take in the familiar tilt of her chin, her slender shoulders, the curved hips, the dark hair piled on top of her head. *What are you doing here, Flower, hmm?*

I track her progress across the living room, and into the hallway. She glances right, before turning the other way. She heads toward the study.

I glance up as she walks in.

"Hello, Damian."

31

____

Julia

Of course, I expected him to know when I had walked into his house. Just because Karina had given me the passwords to his gates and to his front door didn't mean Damian was going to be unaware of when I'd entered his domain. I fully expected him to be waiting for me… I hadn't expected the impact of how it would be to see Daddy D, in his own surroundings, in a pair of sweats and a thin black T that hugs his torso and clings to his abs and shows off the angle of his beautiful shoulders…

OMFG. A bead of sweat runs down my back. I glance around, taking in the cozy surroundings, the faded leather of the settee, the bookshelves, the drum set in a corner, a piano at the other side, with the thick rug in front of the fire that begs to be used and caressed. Like me…my skin, my heart. I rub the skin over my chest.

"You okay?" He frowns.

No.

No.

I nod, gesture to the space. "This is not what I expected."

"I didn't expect to see you here, either."

"Umm." I shuffle my feet. "Me, neither."

"And yet, here you are."

"You don't seem too surprised."

"I'm not." He frowns. "I suppose it had to happen."

"What?"

"You deciding to take a tour of my place, wanting to see how I live, wanting to get close to me. It's normal."

"It is?" I frown.

"Uh-huh." He rubs his chest and his biceps bulge. The sleeve of his T-shirt pulls tight against his muscles. Whoa! Surely, the cloth's gonna snap any second? I swallow.

"It's my overpowering charisma, my larger-than-life personality, my magnetism." He tilts his head. "Admit it, you had to see me again."

"I… I." I take a step inside, and stare at the rat's-ass of a man, every inch a rock star, with the tattoos that peek over the collar of his T-shirt. How weird. He's been inside me, and I haven't even seen him completely naked.

"What are you hiding?" I frown.

His features freeze, "What do you mean?"

"I've never seen you without your clothes." I take in the inverted triangle of his torso, the tapered waist, the corded thighs that stretch the material of his sweats, his feet…which are naked. My throat dries. His beautiful toes, large feet…and wide, with toenails that are blunt cut. I can't take my gaze off of them… My thighs clench. Jesus. Clearly, I have a foot fetish.

"I began sculpting you from memory."

"Excuse me?"

I jerk my chin up to meet his gaze, "I began working on your bust." *Why am I telling him that? Is it to try to catch him off balance? Is it to try to get my brain, which is stuck in some kind of Damian Savage sex-filled haze, to kickstart and function again?*

"You didn't need me to pose then?"

"Your features are etched in my mind." Heat sears my cheeks, but

I don't look away. *What the hell am I trying to do here?* Fessing up like that? Walking in here without a plan seemed all brave, but this, faced with six-feet four-inches of lethal alpha male, in his den… On his turf, where he knows the rules and I don't…? OMG… How stupid can I get? I take a step back; he shakes his head.

I angle my body toward the exit; he holds up his phone. He taps a finger on the screen and the door to the study begins to swing closed.

I yelp, leap toward it…too late. The door shuts with a snick. There's a click. Oh no, he locked it. He did. I know he did. I move forward, more out of habit than anything, intent on testing the handle to check if he did lock it, then stop. I won't give him that satisfaction. I will not repeat the stupid scene from earlier when I had tried to open the bloody door and had to give up and turned around to— Heat envelops me from behind. I gasp.

He tugs on my backpack and I allow him to lower it to the ground.

"Unbutton your coat," he orders.

I pause.

"Do it," he snaps, and all thoughts drain from my head. I reach for my coat, release the buttons. He reaches around, to pull the lapels aside. He lowers the coat down my arms, then eases it off of me.

I should feel cooler without it. Instead, the heat of his body cocoons me, thrums across my skin.

He pulls on the hair that I'd piled on top of my head, and the strands come lose and slither down and around my shoulders. Goosebumps pop on my skin. How can I be hot and cold at the same time? I curl my fingers into fists so he can't see how much I am trembling.

"Look at me," he whispers.

I shake my head.

"Please," he urges and I freeze. OMG, Damian… Asking me for something? That's a first, and somehow, so apt, in the quietness of this space, with the crackling of the wood fire in the background and the heat of his big body that burns me deeper than any flames ever could. It feels right to turn around, raise my gaze to meet his.

Cerulean, bright, blazing brighter than the fire I have seen in any kiln. What a strange thought. I bite the inside of my cheek.

"You're amused about something?" His beautiful lips kick up in a smile that mirrors the rightness I feel inside. Shit, what's wrong with me?

"Your daughter," I venture. "Is she asleep?"

"She's fine where she is."

His features take on that slightly remote expression I am coming to recognize, the one that signals he's put up a barrier between himself and the world, the one which is as clear as a sign that says 'fuck the hell off.' What the hell? Why did I have to go and blurt that out right then?

I glance at the settee and spot a few sheafs of paper with his writing on it. "You've been composing?"

He glances down at the pages, then sweeps them up and sets them aside. "They're not for public consumption."

"I'm hardly a member of the 'public,'" I make air quotes with my fingers. "Please?" I wheedle, "I want to read the lyrics."

"Not happening." He ambles toward the piano.

I reach for the pages on the settee and he clicks his tongue, "Don't even think about it."

I pout. Does he have eyes at the back of his head or what?

"Considering it was my orgasms that fueled the words,"—seriously can you believe this?— "you could at least let me take a peek."

"I explicitly forbid you from looking at the lyrics," he snaps.

And now, I definitely need to read them.

He saunters over to seat himself in front of the piano. That's when I bend down, grab the papers and glance over them quickly. Oh, wow! These are good...different...but so good. Better than anything I've heard him sing before.

He begins to play a few notes, and I place the pages back, then walk over to him. "Is that the tune for the new lyrics?" I ask.

"Maybe." He continues to play the instrument with those long thick fingers which shouldn't seem so at home at the keyboard, but they do. Gah! He can play me anyway, too. I shake my head, and clearly, his influence is rubbing off if I can't stop the word play on my own thoughts. I take in his features, his tense shoulder muscles, his spine which is ramrod straight. I reach him, place my hands on his shoulders and begin to massage. He stops playing. I dig my fingers into the knots, begin to ease them out. He grunts.

I drag my knuckles down either side of his spine, in the hollows between his vertebrae, and he heaves out a sigh. "You're good at this."

"Comes from all the clay I've molded," I say, only half-jokingly.

"Oh, baby, how I'd like to mold you," he smirks.

"Ugh," I frown, "you can't resist the bad puns, can you?"

"Do you blame me?" He chuckles. "When I find an opening, I take it."

Speaking of taking openings… *Noooo, stop, right there. Just because alphahole here likes to twist meanings out of words where none existed before, doesn't mean I should, huh?*

"I think you use it more as a diversion," I retort.

"Oh?" He lowers this chin, "How's that?"

"You're an asshole, that's for sure, but there's something inside of you, some mystery, something hurt maybe, something that keeps pulling me back even though I try my best to stay away."

"Like the Pied Piper?"

"You calling me a rat?" I bristle.

"In the story, the Pied Piper got all of the children to follow him too. Maybe *you're* the Pied Piper. But I was thinking of you more like a little mouse who has run amuck and turned my life upside down. You know, if you give a mouse a cookie, she'll never leave. No matter what you do to make her."

I slap his shoulder, "Seriously, you're horrible."

He chuckles. "Comes with the territory."

"How is it to be a rock star, with so many people eager to find out everything about you?"

"First," he holds up a finger, I am a reclusive rock star and second, that's why I am not on social media anymore."

"That's brave of you."

He folds his arms over his chest, "Are you being sarcastic?"

"No, really. How many celebrities would take that step, and risk alienating their followers?"

He drops his arms and rotates his shoulders, "You means the ones I still have left?" He chuckles wryly. "For a while, I felt unconnected to the songs I was creating. I hoped that if I disengaged with the world it would help me to look inward more, connect with my imagination once again." He laughs, "I can't believe I admitted to that aloud."

He rakes his fingers through his hair. "Also, this way, I don't have the incessant pressure to engage with my fans. I don't have to justify what I say or do. I don't have to worry about if I am pleasing people or not."

"And when you are on stage, what then?"

"Then I am ready to entertain, to be that other person. Still me, but different."

"I'd love to see you perform live."

"That's not happening for a while."

"No," I protest, "I've seen videos of your shows and you are incredible."

"It doesn't interest me anymore."

"Then what does?"

He looks over his shoulder, scrutinizes my features. He half turns, pushes back the bench, then wraps an arm around me and pulls me around to stand between his legs.

"You do."

"Oh." I stare at his gorgeous features — the high cheekbones, the hooked nose, that mean upper lip, the fat lower lip that I want to chew on.

"Like what you see?" He smirks.

"Very much." I swallow.

Heat from his big body pours over me, surrounds me, the strength of his dominance pushing down on my shoulders, holding me immobile as he urges me closer, closer.

"Open your mouth," his voice lowers to a hush and goosebumps pop on my skin.

I part my lips. Just like that, he leans up, slides his forefinger over my tongue and I suck on it.

His blue eyes deepen to that cerulean that sends a thrill right up my spine. I bite down on his digit and his lips twist. "Such a hellion."

He pulls his finger from my mouth, drags it down my chin, my throat, the valley between my breasts. He pinches my nipple and I yelp.

"Who does this belong to?"

You, it belongs to you, is what I want to say. Hah! As if I am going to make it that easy for him. "Who do you think?" I ask.

He peels back his lips, slaps my breast.

I jump, "What the—"

"Who do your breasts belong to?"

"Not to—"

He slaps my left breast, then my right, my left again.

I yell, "Stop, stop, you asshole."

"Alphahole," he snaps. "Tired of correcting you, tired of having you challenge me, go toe-to-toe with me. You think you can defy me and win, you thought wrong."

"Fuck off," I choke.

"Wrong answer."

He cups both of his big palms around my breasts and squeezes, like I am a shapeless mass of clay for him to mold, or a bust that he is sculpting. Okay, so it is my bust that he's massaging and kneading and pummeling like he can't keep his hands off of me. And I don't want him to stop touching me. I need him to stop teasing me, and fuck me, only I am not going to ask for it. Ever.

"You don't scare me," I blurt.

"Oh?"

I lower my chin, stare at his beautiful, cruel, mean features. "You can't make me submit."

He bares his teeth and I shiver.

Jesus, what the hell is wrong with me? I'd come here, wanting to push him over the edge… I hadn't realized that it's me that I'm challenging, that I want him to take me, show me how it could be when

I'm not thinking too much, simply taking what is in front of me. "Do your worst," I mutter.

He releases my breasts, only to grab my hips, spin around, and hoist me up and onto the wooden top of the piano.

I stare down at him, at his cold features, the stern lips, how he frowns at me as if trying to solve a puzzle. "Why are you here?"

"Why do you think?"

"I think you're trying to provoke me."

"Am I succeeding?"

"Maybe." He tilts his head. "Maybe not." He reaches forward, cups his big palm around my pussy. "Maybe you want to push me until I take you, so you can pretend you didn't really want it."

"I don't."

He laughs, "Your presence here says otherwise."

I swallow. *Can't refute that, can I?*

I glance away and he chuckles, "Thought so. Tell me what you want me to do and I will."

I bite down on the inside of my cheek.

"And if I don't?" I mumble.

"Then," he pushes back the piano bench and rises to his feet, "I am leaving; you can see yourself out."

He angles to go and I swoop down and grab his arm, "Please."

He glances down at my hand then back at me. I release my hold.

He glares at me, and my throat closes. He holds my gaze with his, raises an eyebrow, and I know then, if I let him leave now, he'll never see me again. He'll ignore me, walk away from me, never allow me to get close to him again, and damn it, I want it, just once. I want to feel the full power of his presence, the weight of his body on mine, his tongue dancing over mine, his fingers entwined with mine, his dick inside my pussy as he rams into me over and over again.

"Please," I swallow, "ruin me."

32

Damian

"You don't mean that."

"I… I do." She tips up her chin.

"You don't know what you're asking for."

"Don't I?" Her lips twist. She begins to unbutton her shirt.

I shake my head. "Stop."

"Make me." She reaches for the next button.

I swoop down and grab her wrist. "Told you not to do it."

"Oh?" She smiles wider. "What are you gonna do about it?"

I draw in a breath. She's teasing me, testing me, and I shouldn't give in to the allure of her body, her scent, the way she peers up at me from under heavy eyelids, then slides her palm between her jeans-clad thighs, "Don't you want this Damian?"

"Don't play with me," I warn.

She throws back her head, laughs in a sultry husky tone.

A ripple of lust pulses down my spine.

She brings her other hand up to cup her breast, "And this…? I know how much you'd like to fuck my tits, Daddy D."

"Daddy D?"

She blinks, "Ignore I…said that."

"No." I lean into her. She pushes her shoulders down into the lid of the piano. Her foot hits one of the piano keys and the sound rings out through the space. The vibrations roll up from the surface against where my thighs meet the slip of the keyboard. My groin hardens.

Hell, music and this woman. Together, they are a lethal combination. One I can't live without, the other I can't have enough of. One is my livelihood… The other my…life? What am I thinking?

She's only someone I find appealing, someone I need to fuck out of my system, someone whose orgasms unlock the dead place inside of me where I have hidden for so long. She brings me alive, and that's not a bad thing, considering I am finally able to write. She's the key to my muse and I need to keep her in that space. As long as I don't let her intrude into my everyday life, I'll be fine.

"So, you like role play?" I ask.

"I didn't say that."

"Don't lie," I snap at her.

She winces. "I… I'm not lying."

"Yes, you are." I lean over her, until my head is positioned right over hers. "Admit it."

"I… admit nothing," she whispers.

"Hmm." I lick her lips; she winces.

"Am I hurting you?" I peer into her eyes.

"No…no," she shakes her head.

"Then I need to rectify that."

"What—?"

I grab at the half-open fronts of her shirt and tug. The buttons pop off, she gasps, and her shirt gapes open in the front. I glance down at her beautiful tits that spill out from the top of her demi-bra. "So pretty." I pull the shirt apart, on either side of her, over her arms and hold her in place.

"D… Damian," she moans.

I stare down at the dark pink of her nipples visible through the almost transparent cloth. Hell, she's bloody gorgeous, so edible, a fucking sonnet that I need to memorize until I forget everything else. I bend down, close my mouth around one of the pebbled peaks.

She moans, the sound so hot, so needy, blood drains to my groin.

I bite down on her nipple and she yells, "Jesus."

"Not the name I want to hear," I growl, then turn my attention to her other breast. I tug on the nipple and she groans. "Oh…" she murmurs, "ohmygod."

"Try again." I release her shirt only to cup her tits, squeeze them together. I bury my face in the fragrant valley between her flesh, and her scent goes straight to my head. My cock throbs, my balls hurt... What the hell is Flower doing to me? I've never been this close to losing control, to forgetting why I wanted to make her come in the first place. I raise my head peer into her face. "You're driving me crazy," I mutter. "I need to fuck you out of my system."

"What?"

I nod. "I need to make you come over and over again, store up enough of your orgasms to last me a lifetime, and then I won't need to see you again."

Her forehead scrunches and her gaze narrows, "So, I was right?"

I tilt my head.

"You really have this thing, that my orgasms help you write."

"It's worth a try."

"At least, admit it." Her green eyes blaze. "Give me recognition where it's due."

"Why should I?" I drawl, and it's not because I don't want to acknowledge the role she's begun to play in my creative process, it's just… I have a thing to see her pissed off. It's so much more fun when she sets her jaw, curls her fingers into fists, throws a punch at me. So sweet. As if she'll ever catch me off balance.

"Wanna fight me, huh?" I smirk.

"What I want to do is kick you in your balls." She strains against me, pulls up her knee. I lean down and into the 'V' between her legs, massage her breasts with enough force that she groans, "What the hell?" She draws in a breath, and her chest heaves, more of her tits filling my palms.

My shaft hardens further, as I lean into the hollow between her thighs. Another note from the piano reverberates across the space. That was me, or more precisely, my cock, that rang that particular note.

What the fuck am I thinking? Clearly, she's getting to me, twisting up my thoughts…and my balls. And no way, can I let that happen.

"If you think I am gonna fuck you under the same roof as my daughter, you're wrong."

"Oh." She swallows. Her shoulders droop and her lips turn down, "I understand."

"You do?"

She nods. "I actually think you went up in my estimation when you said that."

"Don't give me too much credit," I release her breasts, take a step back, sink down onto the piano bench, "for it's not going to make me stop from giving you an orgasm."

"What?"

I grip her waist, pull her forward until she's balanced at the edge of the piano's lid.

Julia

The chords from the keyboard fill my ears; the vibrations roll up my legs, sink into my center. My core clenches. My pussy spasms. OMG, this is insane. I glance down in time to see him lower the zipper of my jeans.

"Damian what—"

He tugs on my jean legs, pulls them down past my knees, then lowers his face to my center. He draws in a breath, and his shoulders seem to swell. "Your scent, it haunts my dreams, laces my every waking moment. I want to write an ode to that sweet cunt of yours, do you know that?"

He hums a tune and the sub vocals ladder up my core, sink into the crevasses between my pussy lips, coil inside my womb. My thighs tremble. I raise my chin, glance up at the ceiling. What the hell is happening to me? I'd come here, hoping to meet his daughter, sure that I'd surprise a reaction out of him, definitely goad him into fucking me… But this…almost worshipful stance of his is…different. It's deeper than what I'd anticipated, more moving, and so, so arousing. I gulp, try to close my legs.

He clicks his tongue, "Don't hide from me, Flower."

He blows on my center, and the heat of his breath crawls into my secret space. A whine bleeds from my lips. I slap the back of my palm to my mouth. How can I sound so needy? So ready, so willing for whatever it is he wants to take from me.

He licks my core through the cloth of my panties and a shudder grips me. "Ohmygod," I moan. "Oh."

"Damian," he growls. "Say my name, Flower."

"Damian," I croak, and he stills.

I look down to find his gaze fixed on me. "You have no idea what you do to me, do you?"

"The same thing you do to me?" I venture.

"Which is?"

I frown. "Is that a trick question?"

"There are no trick answers." His lips curl, he dips his head, closes his teeth around my swollen nub that's outlined against the cloth, and my back shoots up and off the piano.

"Damian," I screech, "what are you doing?"

"What do you think?" He straightens, then holding my gaze, grips the waistband of my thin nylon knickers. He yanks and they snap; he pulls them off of me. Cool air brushes my lower lips a second before he bends and swipes his tongue from my backhole to my clit, and then again.

"Damian," I gasp.

"Shh!" he admonishes me. "Keep your voice down. You'll wake Riley."

Right. I bite down on my lower lip, curl my fingers into fists and swallow down another moan when he lowers his head between my thighs again. He closes his mouth around my clit and my back shoots up and off of the piano. "Ah!" I can't stop the moan that bleeds from me. He swipes his tongue between my pussy lips, then curls his tongue around the swollen nub of my clit and my eyes cross. I swear, they do. "Ohmygod."

I open my eyes, and he looms over me. He stuffs my panties in my mouth as I gaze at him wide-eyed. He puts a finger to his lips, then drops back into his seat. He forces his shoulders back between my thighs, forcing me to spread even wider apart, then closes his mouth over my pussy again.

A groan boils up, as I grip the edge of the piano and hold on.

Bloody hell, I'll never get used to how he aims for my throbbing core with a single-minded focus. How he slides his fingers around my upper thighs, holds me in place and licks me, and sucks on my pussy and fucks my channel with his tongue, in-and-out and in-and-out.

I slap my fingers against the wooden lid of the piano, dig my heels into the keyboard, and the music rises in a wall of noise that surrounds me, engulfs me, pours over me, as he tears his mouth from my center, replaces it with two-three-four of his thick fingers, all at once, and curves his digits inside, hitting that spot that only he is aware of, while he reaches up to pull the panties from between my lips. He thrusts his thumb inside my open mouth. "Come," he orders. "Come all over my piano."

I don't want to obey him. I don't want to give him what feels like something too personal, too intimate, to shatter right here under his roof, on his musical instrument that he plays with those skilled fingers… Oh, wait, that's me. It's my body he wields like it was contoured for his fingertips, that he can press, and dip into, and strum and spank into a miasma of broken notes and searing prose, his very own composition that he hates…and loves… And he does, in his own way. He just doesn't know it yet.

"Come for me, Flower." He lowers his voice to a hush and I am gone. The climax encloses me, sheaths me, throws me up high, then releases me, and I plunge down, down, down, back into his waiting arms, his teasing mouth, his wicked lips, that tongue of his that gives and takes from me. I crack open my eyelids and watch him watch me. He lowers his chin, licks the moisture that glistens on my inner thighs. He swallows, then rises to his feet. "Get dressed." He stalks away from the piano and heads for the door.

"Coming?" He glances at me over his shoulder, "I don't have all day."

Of course, not. I lower my feet to the floor, my knees buckle, and I grab at the keyboard. The rich tones of the keys fill the space.

His gaze narrows and he seems on the verge of saying something, then desists.

I shove my panties in my back pocket, zip up my jeans, then head over to where he holds up my coat. I thrust my arms through the sleeves, and he buttons me up, his forehead furrowed in concentration. When he reaches my chest, I step back. "I'll do it."

He glares at me and I subside. Damn it, when he looks at me like that, I can't deny him anything. Not even this small token of my defiance. Bah! What defiance. I had given in to his touch, come apart completely and he… He hadn't even broken a sweat. Had I been wrong to think he was falling for me? Wishful thinking, maybe?

He snatches up my backpack and offers it to me, then steps aside to let me pass. Only to guide me toward the living room. Guess he can't wait to get me out of here. I glance around the space, at the thick rug in front of the fireplace. My foot brushes something. I glance down at a doll which is face down on the carpet; next to it is a worn-out toy dog. I pick it up.

"Benjy." He clears his throat.

I stiffen. *Don't breathe; don't look at him.* Finally, he's revealing a little more about himself. *Let him speak. Don't say a word. Don't.* "Is that her favorite toy?"

"How did you know?" He frowns.

"It has a well-worn look about it. Also," I pat the toy's furry head, "I had one of my own that I held onto, into my teens."

"You didn't want to grow up, huh?"

"You could say that," I toss my hair over my shoulder, then shoot him a sideways glance. "Don't get any ideas, buster."

"Me?" He smirks. "Not likely. I am too busy trying to get my next album out."

"For which you need me as an inspiration, huh?"

"Don't get any ideas." He echoes my earlier words.

"Not likely." I head for the door, "You've made it clear what you want from me."

"And—?"

"And," I twist open the door handle, then turn to face him, "I decline."

"What?" He frowns.

"My orgasms are not for sale anymore."

His jaw tics, "Everyone is for sale."

"Not me; not anymore."

"I paid good money."

"Check your records, I've returned your payments."

He frowns, "And your debts?"

I raise my shoulders, "I'll live with them, pay them off over the next twenty years, like other people."

"You're not other people." He takes a step forward, then stops. "You're different."

"Yeah, that's why you treat me like I'm—"

"Special."

"Expendable." I toss my head.

"I let you into my home."

"I broke in." I set my lips.

"Why do you think Karina gave you the passcodes?"

"You…?" I blink, "You knew?"

"I was the one who encouraged her to share them."

"She deceived me?"

"Not her fault. She didn't know. Not really." He widens his stance. "I told her to do what was needed to ensure your safety. And clearly, giving you the means to enter my home rather than breaking in, was in your interest."

"You…you liar."

"Everything between us was true. Every time I touched you, I meant it. Every orgasm I drew from you was more than real…"

"I don't believe it."

"Don't tell me that you didn't feel it."

"What I feel is manipulated. You used your money, your dominance, to steer my life the way you wanted."

"I work with what I have."

"So do I." I draw myself up to my full height. "You want to see me come, yet you won't allow me to meet your daughter. What do you call that?"

"I am protecting her… Protecting you…"

"How is treating me like a second-class citizen, who you don't trust, protecting me?"

"I don't want you getting close to her, not when this relationship between us is fake."

"And who's fault is that?" I throw up my hands. "You could have let me in, allowed me to take care of her and do my job."

"Your job…" he smirks, "is to come when I command you to."

"This entire conversation is insane." I glance around. "In fact, why the hell am I here arguing with you, when clearly, you have no intention of doing the right thing."

"The right thing is for you to leave." He jerks his chin at the door. "Good bye, Flower."

A ball of emotions closes my throat. Why the hell does he have to call me by that stupid pet name? "I fucking hate you," I choke out the words. "I wish I had never met you."

"That makes two of us." His gaze sharpens. He glances over his shoulder, then back at me. Huh? Did he hear something I didn't? Was that his daughter calling?

"Have a good life." He turns to leave as I step over the threshold. The door snicks shut behind me. I stand there, stare straight ahead, my heart thudding in my chest.

I should go, should get out of there, should leave the rock star and his manipulations behind and live my own life, find my own way, look for another job as a nanny, as I sculpt on my own time. My life was complete, right? I had found my calling in the two things that spoke to me… A career, unorthodox as it may be, but I was able to follow my passion—both of my passions. How many can say that? And if there's no one special, too bad. I lower my foot to the first step, glance at the gates in front that are swinging open.

I should get into my car and drive away, leave the asshole who sees me less as a person and more as a—a thing to get his creative juices flowing—no pun intended.

I should…turn around, march inside, and confront him. And ask him why the hell did he insist on holding me at arm's length? Why did he never make love to me? Why did he create that damn studio for me? He had to have felt something… So, why did he allow me inside his home, only to turn me out again?

He wants me… He does… So, what stops him from claiming me as his?

I stiffen, stare at the path beyond the gates.

If I leave, this is really it. He'll let me walk away, no questions asked. I'll never see him again… Not even online, considering he isn't on social media anywhere. And he may not release another album again. Not if he's as blocked as he claimed. Which is a pity. The alphahole is bloody talented. He was meant to compose, to sing, to burn up the stage with his presence and dominate his audience, as he'd taken control of me…my reactions…my orgasms. And the truth is, no one can make me come like he does.

I owe it to myself… Well, at least, for the future of my sex life—which he's spoiled completely for me, now that I know how it could be with him. Aargh! I drag my fingers through my hair. What the hell do I do?

I step down, turn to walk away, then hesitate. So, he told me to leave, and what? I am going to obey him? I am going to turn my back on him? When had I ever done as I was told, huh? Not with my parents, and certainly not because a certain rock star has ordered me to. At the very least, he owes me an explanation for why he's turning me out of his life.

Turning, I key my password into the keypad, then push open the door and slip in.

33

Damian

"Fuck this shit." I raise the guitar by its neck then fling it aside. It hits the fire head-first and the flames flicker up its body. The blaze fills its sound hole, leaps up to wrap lovingly around the inlay. "Fuck." I curl my fingers at my sides. I'd let her go. I'd made her come, then hurt her with my words and escorted her out.

A noise reaches me… I jerk my chin toward Riley's room. What the hell is wrong with me? I'd flown into a typical spoiled rock star rage. I'd slipped up and made enough noise to scare my daughter. When will I stop being selfish? Stop thinking solely of myself, and put my daughter's needs first? I race toward her room, come to a stop inside the doorway.

"Angel?"

Riley blinks up at me from the bed.

"Daddy?" She frowns. "I am scared." She sucks on her thumb, and my heart stutters.

"Shh!" I walk toward her. "Daddy's here now; you are safe."

Her chin trembles. "Will you read to me?" She sniffles.

"Of course, baby."

I sink into the chair next to her, "Which story, honey?"

"Alice." She cuddles her kitty cat doll close, "Will you read Alice and the white rabbit?"

"Alice in Wonderland," I correct her.

"Alice in W a n d e l a n d," she pronounces, using the phonetic spelling.

"Good girl," I praise her.

"Story, Daddy," she prompts.

"Last one, Poppet." I take in her features, her pink cheeks, the tousled locks, "Then you have to leave."

"B...but, I don't want to go." Her lower lip trembles.

"I don't want you to leave either," I confess.

"So why are you sending me away?"

"Because," I swallow down the thickness in my throat, "because sometimes we all have to do the things that we hate, because it's the only way to move on. When the time comes, baby, we all have to leave."

"When will my time come, Daddy?" She rubs her cheek into her pillow.

My heart stutters. "Not for a long time, baby."

"Will you stay with me until then?" She smiles at me and a pressure builds behind my eyes.

I reach over and kiss her forehead, "I promise."

She yawns, snuggles into the bed. "Read to me, Daddy," she mumbles. "I love to hear your voice as I'm falling asleep."

I pick up the book and begin.

Alice sighed wearily. "I think you might do something better with the time," she said, "than waste it in asking riddles that have no answers."

· · ·

The earthy scent of clay mixed with the sweetness of vanilla reaches me. I stiffen, but continue to read out loud.

"If you knew Time as well as I do," said the Hatter, "you wouldn't talk about wasting it. It's him."

I hear the soft sound of her sneakers hit the floor as she takes a step into the room.

"I don't know what you mean," said Alice.

The floorboards creak as she walks toward me. I don't stop. I glance down at the book, the words swirl in front of my eyes, and I continue reciting from memory.

"Of course you don't!" the Hatter said, tossing his head contemptuously. "I dare say you never even spoke to Time!"

She draws abreast, pauses, then glances at the bed. "Damian," she gasps, "What's…what's happening?"

A tear runs down my cheek, falls onto the page of the book.

"Perhaps not," Alice cautiously replied: "but I know I have to beat time when I learn music."

"Damian?" She turns to me, "What is this?"

I place the bookmark in the right place, then close the book. "What do you think it is?"

"You…you're scaring me, Damian."

"Am I?" I rise to my feet, place the book back on the sideboard. "Why are you here, Julia?"

"I… I heard the noise of something crashing and ran back in. I wanted to make sure you were okay."

I turn to face her, fold my arms over my chest, "I am perfect."

She glances at the bed, then back at me. "You…you're not."

"What makes you think so?"

"Because." She swallows, angles her head in the direction of the bed, then back at me, "You know why."

"No, I don't."

"Don't make me say it, Damian, please," she begs.

"Say what?" I twist my lips, "What is it you want to say to me, Julia?"

"Damian," she shakes her head, "don't do this."

"Don't do what?" I roll my shoulders. "Don't do what, Julia?"

"Make me point out that…"

"That?"

"There's no one other than us in the room, Damian."

"Isn't there?" I walk toward the bed, glance down at the shape of the figure under the covers. "You mean this, don't you?" I rip the sheet off and Julia screams.

I snatch up the bolster and fling it aside, then grab the cushion from where it's placed on the pillow, and rip the cloth from it. Goose feathers dot the air like snowflakes. They float down over me, stick to my cheeks, cover the fabric of my T-shirt. I see her stuffed kitty on the floor and kick it aside.

"She's dead," I say, the coldness growing in my chest, reaching out, growing faster, harder, until it reaches my extremities. I lower my arms to my sides. "She's gone. My child… I couldn't save her. I wasn't there for her. Her mother took her and left, and I didn't stop her."

"Damian." She touches my shoulder and something inside of me snaps.

I turn on her, grab her by her neck and haul her close, "I was fine, getting along. I was ready to give up everything to spend time with her, take care of her for the rest of my life. I would have given up my career, my songs. I would have sacrificed myself for her, and then you had to do it."

"Wh…what?" She swallows. "What did I do Damian?"

"You swept into my life with your sassy comments, and your perky breasts, and your curves. You forced yourself under my skin."

"F…forced?" She frowns.

"Don't lie to me." I squeeze her neck and her gaze widens.

"Damian, stop." She scratches at my wrist. "Damian, please, you don't mean this."

"I mean it all." I nod. "It's because of you that I kept leaving her alone and coming to you. It's because of you that I realized that—"

I pause and take in her wide-eyed look of confusion.

"That I couldn't live like this."

"Like what, Damian?"

"Alone, trapped in my head. In the past, grieving for what may have been. One look at you, and I wanted more. I wanted a life with you, Julia. And I knew I didn't deserve another chance at happiness, not when my daughter would never see another day. She died and it's my fault. I'll never forgive myself…and now," I take in her beautiful features, her parted lips, her gorgeous tits that heave under her coat, "I am going to do my best to forget you, after…"

"After?"

"After I fuck you." I swivel around and thrust her backward.

34

Julia

"No, you can't do this." The backs of my knees hit the mattress and I tumble backward onto Riley's bed. I try to rise up, and he reaches down and flattens his palm against my chest.

"What's wrong?" he asks. "Don't want me now, Flower? You wanted me to fuck you, you were begging for it earlier. Now, when you know that I think of my dead daughter as still being alive, you don't want anything to do with me?" he growls.

"It's not like that." I push up; he shoves at me and I hit the bed with a thud.

He looks me up and down. "Take off your coat," he snaps.

"Don't do this," I beg him.

His lips curl and his eyes gleam. He rolls his shoulders, plants his fists on his hips. "That's not what you've been saying all these days, sugar."

"Don't call me that," I snarl back.

"Sugar?" He tilts his head, "Why not? You're deceptively sweet, you make people think you are innocent, that a little time in your presence won't hurt anyone. Then when their back is turned, you crawl under their skin, you ensure they grow addicted to you, can't live without you. Is that what you did to your last boyfriend too? Is that why he dropped you?"

"Fuck you," I spit out.

"Thought you'd never ask." He steps forward and I raise my foot and kick out. I catch him in the chest, and the man doesn't even stop. Bloody hell, he simply chuckles, then advances. I jump up on the bed, throw up my fists, "Don't you dare come closer…you…you twat."

"You have the twat, not me."

"What?"

"Twat," he replies, then stares down at my crotch. "It's another word for pussy."

"Oh?" I knew that. Of course, I did, so why the hell do my cheeks heat? We are past the kissing and touching stage. Hell, he's made me orgasm so many times, and yet he mentions the 'p' word and I am blushing like a virgin on her first date?

He rolls his shoulders, snaps his fingers at me, and damn it, I know then, that if I don't stop myself, he'll fuck me with such force that I'll feel like a virgin all over again. I squeeze my thighs together. Damnit, why am I turned on, when he's acting like a complete bastard?

"Let's fight," I suggest.

"What?"

"Fight," I hold up my fists, "a fair one, and winner gets—"

"Dibs on how to fuck."

I swallow.

"Where to fuck." He stares at my mouth, then at my breasts, before lowering his gaze back to my crotch, and… Jesus, I am completely wet, and this… This is all kinds of fucked up. He's just confessed that he's been babysitting his imaginary—scratch that, *dead* —daughter, in whose room we are, and on whose bed I am… And all

I can think of is how I want to shag her father. Aargh, this is… beyond messed up. I keep my fists raised, stay focused on him as he licks his lips.

"How many times," he raises his gaze back to mine, "to fuck."

My nipples harden. Heat flushes my belly, sears up my spine. Sweat pools in my underarms. Shit, it is getting too hot. I definitely need to take off the coat.

"Fine," I snap.

"Fine," he rasps.

I reach for the button of my coat, and he stiffens.

"Relax," I mutter, "you wanted me to take this off, right?"

"Hmm." He watches me from under hooded eyelids as I slip off the buttons, then shrug the coat down one shoulder. I peek up to see his lips parted, his chest heaving as he pays close attention to my every move. Hell, this…thing between us, it's potent enough that I have his complete focus. Or rather, he's tuned into every move of my body. Well, that's one thing I can use in my favor, right? I slide the coat down over the other shoulder. Then hold it out in front of me.

His gaze latches onto my breasts. His nostrils flare and his breathing grows ragged. He leans forward on the balls of his feet and his fists tremble—no, did they actually tremble? I cup one breast, play with my nipple and he swallows.

Oh, my. Why hadn't I realized before now that I have as much power as he does in this relationship? I mean, I knew he wanted my orgasms, but all along, his money had tilted the scale in his favor—or so I'd thought. Fact is, the money really doesn't matter. When it comes to this—me and him, in this room filled with memories and happiness and sadness… It is just us. A broken alphahole of a man and a woman hellbent to make it everything right for him… For me… For what we can have together.

I release the coat, then run my palms down the skin bared between my shirt and the waistband of my jeans. He growls. It literally rumbles in his throat. My heartbeat ratchets up; my pulse begins to pound. I slide my fingers inside my waistband.

His biceps bulge and he takes another step forward, until his knees are flush against the bed frame.

"Take off your T-shirt," I whisper. "Please, Damian."

He reaches behind himself to wrench his T-shirt up and over his head. I take in the broad expanse of his chest, the ripped planes, the eight-pack abs which I've seen online before, but I've only caught glimpses of the real thing. I can hardly count the time he begrudgingly opened his shirt, before taking my arse. "Oh! My God." Heat flushes my skin; my pussy clenches. I rake my gaze across the tattoo written along the inside of his left forearm. "Riley," I read the cursive.

He blinks, brings up his right hand to massage the skin over his heart. "Fight." He shakes his head, then holds up his fists again.

Well, hell, now I've done it. Whatever chance I had of taking him by surprise is gone. I hold up both of my fists. "Let's do this."

I throw a punch; he angles his body and avoids me easily. I raise my other fist and he tilts his head so my fist brushes the air near his neck. Damn it, this won't do. It won't. I take a step back, then another, and lower my fists. "Your turn." I jerk my chin, "Come on, give it your best."

He hesitates. "I don't want to hurt you." He frowns.

"But maybe I do." I race forward, kick out at him.

I'd been so sure that he would duck, and I'd been braced for that, but he doesn't. My foot connects with his chest and the momentum carries me forward. I crash into that hard barrier of him. He takes my full weight, staggers a little, then plants his broad palms on my hips to hold me in place. Only he crashes into the chair he'd been sitting on, which tips back, and he tips with it. The world tilts, and his big body pitches backward as he lands on the chair. He angles his body to take my full weight and the chair splinters. The back of his head connects with the floor with a thwack —and he does have a hard head, but hell, if that wouldn't have hurt.

He stays sprawled on the remnants of the furniture, his arms wrapped around me, my legs around his trim waist. *Thud-thud-thud.* I hear my heart thud in my chest. Or is that his? I turn my nose into the skin of his throat, draw in his scent. My head spins as all of my senses seem to open to absorb as much of him as I can.

"Damian," I whisper. He doesn't move. I raise my head to glance at his features, his closed eyelids, the dark lashes that are too long for a man, but which only enhance the masculinity of his features, the hollows under those spectacular cheekbones, that pouty lower lip, the tendons of his beautiful throat that move as he swallows.

I crawl up to cup his cheek, "Damian?" I rub my thumb under his eye and my finger comes away wet. I swallow. "Babe?" I mutter, "You okay?"

He stays silent. His arms hold me close, his heart beats against my breast, but his eyes remain closed. Another tear rolls down his face.

"Oh, hell." My throat constricts. I frame his face with both of my palms, "Hey, Big D, please…" I bite down on my cheek. *Please what? Please don't mourn your kid who you lost too early, the mother of your child who's no longer with you? The remnants of your past that you haven't been able to move on from?* "Damian, sweetheart."

I watch as he draws in a breath — his shoulders flex, his chest planes rise up and down. The rest of him is still, too still, locked in a place where he is alone with his memories, the sadness, the anger… Which is directed at himself, not at the world, or at me. That mockery, the jabs and digs… Not to mention, the crude puns he loves to lob — All of it comes from a place of self-loathing. And Jesus, I really should have been a shrink.

"D?" I pat his cheek, but he doesn't respond. My pulse begins to race and my heartbeat ratchets up. What the hell? "Are you hurt?"

I tilt his head one way, then the other. Hmm, his jawline really is spectacular. And his ears? They are perfect! Don't get me started on all that luscious hair of his that curls around his shoulders… *Hold on. Hello? Are you checking him for any possible wounds or are you checking him out? Uh…both? Can't it be both? No, it's wrong.* The man's down. Don't take advantage of him now.

But he's taken advantage of me all along. Besides, I need to pull him out of this funk he's fallen into.

I need to do something…anything, to pull him back to the present… I glance down at those sexy as f lips of his, and my belly trembles. *Don't do it, don't do it…*

Oh, what the hell? I am here, so is he, and he's alive, and I need to do something to comfort him… And I'm just a woman surrounded by a 100% macho male who, for the first time, is at my mercy. So, I do the only thing I possibly can in the circumstance.

I lower my lips to his. Soft and hard, at the same time. How can he be a confluence of so much? I lick his lower lip and he opens his mouth. I ease my tongue inside. Hot, sexy, dark and edgy, and for the first time, there's a hint of something more… Something…vulnerable. The band around my chest tightens. My core clenches.

I tilt my head and deepen the kiss. I hold his chin and press my lips to his, until my nose bumps his, and I draw in his breath, and inhale more of that spicy scent of his and my ovaries go into overdrive. I lean over him, dig my fingers into his hair and proceed to fuck his mouth with mine. My thighs tremble, I hook my knees over his hips for purchase, push my breasts into his naked chest, press as much of myself to him as I can, and lean in even closer. A shudder grips his body, his grip around me tightens, but he doesn't kiss me back. He allows me to assault his face as I press kisses to his mouth, nibble kisses up his cheeks, rain kisses over one closed eyelid, then the other, the salty taste of his tears clinging to my lips. Lick his forehead, bite the tip of his nose. My nipples harden and moisture pools between my legs. I push my pelvis forward, to cradle the tent in his crotch, but there's still no participation. I rub my core into the hard column outlined in his pants, bring my lips back to his, brush my mouth over his. Nothing.

I reach between us, slide my hand under his waistband. My fingers brush the crown of his cock, and two things become clear. One, he's not wearing boxers. Gulp. And two, the man is very much here and with me — at least the part of him that is under me is. I tug on his P/A and his entire body jerks. I wrap my fingers around his thick length — and OMFG, my digits don't meet around the circumference, and okay, so I have short fingers, but hell!

This…monster dick of his, once more, lives up to its reputation. I gulp again, and my throat closes. I squeeze the base of his dick, and I swear his shaft lengthens further. Oh, wow… That was instantaneous. I swipe my fingers from base to crown and the wetness of his precum greets me. My mouth waters and I groan as I close my eyes and lick my lips. Heat flushes my skin. Will he taste as good as he smells? I open my eyelids, stare into those blue eyes of his, which glare at me. He releases his hold on my waist, only to clamp his palm around my neck.

"You've done it now," he growls. "I am going to fuck your mouth."

35

____

Damian

What the hell is wrong with me? She's trying to comfort me and I…
can't stop myself from lashing out at her, pushing her away. It's
second nature. I want to open myself up to her, hold her close,
wallow in the sense of rightness that this moment holds…but I can't.
I won't. I deserve every second of unhappiness, of restlessness and
frustration, of berating myself for not making the time to take care of
my daughter when she was alive.

And now, Flower knows my secret. No doubt, she'll hate me for
it when she comes to her senses… But for the moment, she is here
with me, and I intend to make the most of it. I intend to lose myself
in her sweetness, her heat, the warmth of her mouth—yes, I heard
her moan, saw her lick her lips, and know that's what she wants
—,the tight grip of her cunt as she milks me. I want to forget everything that has happened and grab this moment for myself. I tighten
my fingers in her hair and her gaze widens.

"Damian," she gasps, then smiles before she slides down my body, until her face is level with my crotch. She pushes down the waist-band of my sweats and my dick bobs free. She tightens her hold on me, massages me from crown to base. She squeezes my swollen length and the blood empties to my groin.

"Suck me off," I order.

She holds my gaze, then lowers her head to close her mouth around my cock.

"Bloody fuck," I growl. She licks the crown, wraps her tongue around my piercing and my cock jumps in response. She tips down her chin, takes me in and down her throat, and I can't stop myself from thrusting forward. She swallows and stars burst behind my eyes. "What the fuck are you doing to me, Flower?"

I shake my head to clear it, glance down to where saliva drips down her chin. "You're killing me, taking everything from me." I scowl. She pulls back leaving a trail of wetness on my cock, and the sight of her lips wrapped around my thick length… It's everything. She bobs her head, takes me in again and heat coils in my belly. My balls tighten and pressure builds at the base of my spine. "Oh, hell." My vision tunnels, my lungs hurt, my thigh muscles bunch, but it's not enough. "I need to do this my way." I glare at her and she pales.

"You understand?" I ask.

She peers up at me, licks her tongue up the underside of my shaft. The hair on the nape of my neck rises.

"Nod your head if you do."

She doesn't respond.

I lower my chin to my chest. "Do it," I draw in a breath, "or walk away. Right now."

Her gaze flickers; she hesitates.

All right, then. I begin to withdraw, but she grips my length, then jerks her chin.

Something hot stabs at my chest. She's not leaving. Not yet. She's staying. For now, at least.

"You sure?" I snap, then curse myself. *Jesus, get a grip, asshole.*

She bobs her head, takes me down her throat again. The tight heat encloses my shaft and the muscles in my belly lock. "I gotta do this. Now." I thread my fingers through her hair, and pull back until only the tip of my cock is positioned between her lips.

"Ready?" I scan her features.

She licks the underside of my swollen head and the blood rushes to my groin. I push her forward until the base of my cock scrapes her lips, then pull her back, again and again. She grips my thigh with her other hand, stares up at me as tears leak from the corners of her eyes. I pull her back, then tug her forward, over and over again. More saliva drips down her chin, her pupils dilate until only a circle of green remains around the black of her irises, and I see myself through her eyes.

Depraved, filthy, selfish, the kind of man she should have never met. The kind she'll, hopefully, never meet again. I pull out of her so suddenly, she gasps. Then grip her under her arms and rise to my feet, bringing her up with me. I kick the chair out of my way, scoop her up and deposit her on my daughter's bed. She stares up at me from her prone position, watches me as I shove my sweats down and out of the way. I reach for my dick and pump it once.

Her gaze drops to my crotch. "Damian," she mumbles, "you're so big."

"I'm exactly what you need," I insist. "Are you ready for me?"

She nods, then reaches down to lower the zipper of her jeans. She pushes them down, along with her panties and sneakers, then parts her legs. "I want you." She holds out her arms, "Come to me."

My heart hammers in my chest. I rake my gaze down her swollen breasts, her slightly rounded stomach to the wet flesh between her legs, and damn it, I can't stop myself. I sink to my knees, and swipe my tongue up her pussy lips.

"OMG," she groans, "Damian, Damian…please… Damian."

I massage my throbbing girth, as I grip her thigh and hold her still and make love to her pussy, her cunt, her clit, that gorgeous hot channel between her legs into which I thrust my tongue—in and out, in and out.

"Damian," she screams, "I can't bear it, please, baby, please."

I rise above her, place one knee on the bed, then the other. I position myself between her legs, then thrust forward.

She screams, "Jesus." Her eyes roll back in her head, as I stay still, allowing her time to adjust. When she lowers her chin and holds out her hand, I twine my fingers with hers. I twist her arm over her head as I lean into her and sink in another inch, and another. She moans, and I kiss her breast, suck on her nipple as I hook my arm under her knee and drape her leg over my shoulder. The angle allows me to breach her further.

She gasps, "You're so deep inside of me, Damian…" She whimpers, "Please."

"I know," I whisper as I press little kisses to the pulse fluttering at the base of her neck, to her chin, her lips. "Take me, baby. Take all of me."

I pull back, then plunge forward so her channel sheaths all of me. Heat sweeps up my spine and my heartbeat ratchets up. The pulse thuds at my temples, my wrists, even in my balls. I tear my lips from hers to gaze into her eyes. "Look at me," I command.

Her breath hitches, she widens her gaze, and I discern the outline of myself in her eyes as I thrust forward into her with enough force that her entire body moves up the bed. I release her hands only to hook my arm under her other leg and place it over my other shoulder. "Hold on." I reach over to cover her breasts with my palms and squeeze.

She groans, and the sound lodges somewhere deep in my belly. I close my mouth over hers, then thrust into her over and over again. I swallow her every scream, commit her every moan to memory. I drag my mouth from hers, stare into her eyes and whisper, "Come."

36

Julia

I'm coming. I'm coming. I may have screamed that, or simply repeated it to myself over and over again. I curve my back and scream as the climax crashes over me. That blue gaze of his is burned into my head, the curl of his cruel lips etched on my heart as the orgasm slams into me. The aftershocks ripple up my spine; my limbs tremble as I cling to him with my legs wrapped around his neck.

His shoulders seem to swell; his biceps expand as he continues to plunge in and out of me. He impales with a thrust so hard that his balls slap against my arse. His dick seems to extend, his chest planes undulate, and a hoarse groan rips from him as he empties himself into me. "Fuck."

He lowers his forehead to mine and kisses me — slowly, gently, tenderly. He nibbles on my lower lip, licks the corner of my mouth, then buries his nose in my throat and inhales. He curves his palm around my breast, draws circles around my nipple, then the other. He drags his lips down my throat, to the valley between my breasts, smooths his big palms down my stomach, before he touches the part where we are joined. He glances up at me, his expression tortured.

"Damian?" I whisper, "What are you doing?"

"I'm sorry I deceived you," he searches my features.

"You didn't." I reach for him and he pulls back and out of me so suddenly that my pussy clenches on the emptiness where he'd been a millisecond ago.

"Where are you going?" I sit up, panicking, as he pulls up his sweatpants.

"Stay." He stabs a finger at me, then walks to the bathroom.

I hear the sound of the water running. A second later, he appears in the doorway. He walks over to me, then presses a cool washcloth between my legs. "Did I hurt you?"

His voice is bland. I glance at his features to find a mask, devoid of emotion.

"Damian, what's wrong?" I clear my throat, "Please, talk to me."

He cleans off the remnants of our joined cum from my thighs, then flings the cloth aside. He steps back, reaches for my clothes and hands them to me. "Get dressed," he orders.

I stare at him for a moment; he glances away. *What the hell?*

My heart begins to race. This is crazy. We just made love… Okay, we fucked, and it was insanely hot, and the orgasm? Why the hell does each one seem better than the last? And now, why is he turning away from me? I pull on my jeans, tie up my sneakers and straighten my shirt the best I can.

"Sit." He gestures to a chair, then walks around to the other side of the bed. Like that would put enough distance between us?

I watch him as he paces the carpet, Riley's now mussed-up bed between us.

"Do you want to talk about it?"

He pauses mid step. "About what?"

"This." I point at his daughter's bed, "How long has this been going on?"

"Since she died in a car accident, a year ago. Her mother drove her car with the two of them over a bridge."

"Oh, my God," I gasp. "I am so sorry, Damian. I can only imagine—"

He holds up his hand, then turns away. "Save your pity," he throws at me over his shoulder, "I've had enough of it."

I purse my lips, wait as he continues to pace, back-forth-back.

"Meredith—?" I finally venture.

"Is aware that I am in therapy."

"So, when she comes over to help—"

He nods. "It's the only way I can manage to leave the house, if I am confident I have someone at home with—" He squeezes his palms at his sides. "At home."

"I understand," I reply.

"Do you?" He tilts his head.

"Of course, I do." I tip up my chin, "You're in therapy and this is one way of helping you get through the ordeal. It may sound strange to an outsider, but grief can do the most bizarre things to anyone. I am happy she has been there for you when you've most needed support. I only wish—"

I draw in my inner lip, glance away.

"Tell me." His voice softens, "You know you can say anything that's on your mind to me, Flower."

I release the breath I'd not been aware I was holding. "I wish you'd let me in earlier. I wish you hadn't felt the need to hide the situation from me. I wish it had been me that you'd turned to for help."

His shoulders uncoil, and that's when I realize how nervous he'd been about sharing this part of himself with me.

"I… I do understand, Damian," I say softly.

"Do you?" He laughs. "The delusional rock star who messed up the only thing that was of any worth in his life."

"Don't say that." I frown.

He continues to pace back-forth-back as I track his movements. Finally, he stops, then turns to me. "What?" he barks.

"I didn't say anything," I point out.

"I am getting help for it," he clarifies.

"I don't doubt that." He glares at me and I tip up my chin. *Do not*

back off, not now. Don't look away. I hold his gaze as he takes a step
forward and comes around to stand in front of me.

"Does anyone else know about what you are going through?"

"The Seven are aware that Riley and her mother died in an accident." He rubs the back of his neck. "They helped me keep the news
from the media."

I can only imagine the circus it would have been if they'd found
out that, not only did he have a daughter and a girlfriend, but also
that they were dead.

"And your...uh —"

"Affliction?" He chuckles without humor. "Only Meredith and
Arpad are aware of the true extent to which I haven't been able to let
go of her." He hesitates, "And now...you. So you see, in my own way,
I have turned to you. Maybe from the moment I saw you... My
subconscious has known that I wouldn't have a choice but to let
you in."

My heart stutters. What does that mean? The fact that he
revealed his secret to me? Okay, to be fair, I had barged in on him,
had literally forced him to share this part of himself... But still... He'd
trusted me enough to be open about it. He hadn't hidden this
from me.

"I have a proposition for you." He turns to face me.

I grimace. "If you're going to offer me money again —"

"No money," he snaps. "I do need your time, though."

"Time?"

"And your orgasms."

"Orgasms?" I frown. "You're out of your mind, you know that?"
Oops. I wince, then look up to gauge his reaction before continuing,
"Sorry, but... It's one thing to believe that giving me orgasms fires up
your creative muse, another to —?"

"To?" He folds his big arms across his chest, and of course, I
clench my thighs. I take in the breadth of his shoulders, the smattering of hair across his chest that felt so good, so delicious when I
was pressed up against him.

"—to live it." I clear my throat.

"Are you complaining about it?"

"No." I fold one leg over the other and he lowers his gaze to my thighs. My pussy clenches and my toes curl. I fold my hands in my lap, wriggle around to relieve the gnawing that's creeping up in my core. "Umm."

"What then?" He frowns. "What do you want in exchange?"

"I want." I lick my lips. *Jeez, can I say it? Can I?*

"Say it." He slaps his hands on each side of the chair and brackets me in. "What is it? What do you need?" he peers into my eyes. "Tell me, I'll do anything."

"Anything?" I tilt my head.

His gaze narrows as he considers what I've said. "Anything," he confirms.

"Marry me."

37

Julia

"You did what?" Isla shrieks.

I stare at her from over my glass of wine—which she had brought over, because I've barely been in the apartment long enough to order in provisions since arriving from Australia. Not to mention, my time has been taken up by an alphahole of a rock star… The one who's agreed to become my husband.

"Yeah," I nod.

"And he…?" She takes a healthy swig from the wine glass, "He agreed?"

"He set a date and everything," I mutter. "And of course you're helping me organize the wedding."

She hesitates.

"You are, aren't you?" I frown.

"Of course I am." She nods, cautiously, "But you mentioned something about a date?" She swallows, "When...when is it?"

I open my mouth and she raises a hand, "No, don't tell me. Let me guess. It's next week?"

I shake my head.

She pales, "It's in five days?"

I raise my hand, palm face up.

"Four?" She gulps.

I stay silent.

She blinks rapidly. "Three days. Please tell me I have at least three days to organize this event?"

"Afraid not." I purse my lips.

She sinks back in her chair. "It's tomorrow, isn't it?" She wrings her fingers together.

"No." A chuckle wells up, and I swallow it down. I mean, this entire thing would be hysterical, except for the fact that it is my life and this is actually happening.

"It's the day-after-tomorrow."

"What?" She chokes. "You mean it's on New Year's Eve? Do you know what kind of a logistical nightmare this is going to be? Not to mention, having to organize your dress and the venue... How the hell am I supposed to manage everything?"

"About that." I grab my backpack, pull out his credit card and hold it up.

Isla snatches it out of my hand, "Now we're talking. Though I have to warn you, that all the money in the world, may not be enough to pull this off, given the crazy timelines."

"You're telling me," I mutter. "I asked him what the hurry was and he said," I raise my shoulders, "why delay?"

"Maybe he doesn't want to wait, in case you change your mind?" Isla offers.

"Not likely, considering I was the one who proposed." I huff.

"Maybe he doesn't trust himself to not change his mind...?"

I stare up and into Isla's shrewd gaze. "May...be," I concede. "More likely, he thinks money can buy anything." Typical Damian, to throw money at a problem and expect it to resolve itself. I wrap my arms about my waist. "Just like he didn't think twice before he commanded me to move into the apartment in The Shard, because *no fiancée of his is living in a crummy apartment.*" I air-quote his words.

I glance around the tiny one-bedroom, which is small, but comfortable… But it isn't mine. Which is fine. I belong nowhere, remember? It's why I had gone half-way across the world to find a place I could fit into.

I mean, sometimes you need to go full circle before you find where you belong… Which is where? In his arms, in his home, between his thighs as he wraps his massive arms around me and holds me down. *Argh! Stop.*

I bury my face in my glass of vino. "What the hell have I done, Isla?"

"Umm…seems you got yourself a hubby, Julia." She coughs.

I scowl back, "You're laughing at me."

"No," she shakes her head, "not really."

I frown.

She raises a shoulder. "Okay, maybe a little. You've got to admit, the situation is slightly humorous."

"Not from where I am," I purse my lips.

"Tell me what happened. Why don't you start at the top, hmm?" She drops her voice to a soothing tone and I give her a dirty look.

"What?" She throws up her hands, "I am only trying to help."

I drain my glass. "You can help by topping up my wine."

She reaches for the carton of wine, then turns it upside down. "Sorry, that was the last of it, babe."

"You'd think Amelie would have stocked up better, considering she was in the middle of a rollercoaster of a relationship with the doctor," I grumble.

"Maybe that's why there isn't enough wine here," Isla offers. "She probably drank it all as she came to terms with being hitched to an alphahole for life."

As I soon will be.

My heart begins to thud, sweat beads my palms, the wine glass slips from my grasp, and crashes onto the floor. Good thing it's plastic, huh?

I pick it up, then walk over to the garbage can and dump it in. I straighten, then stare out of the window. "Jesus, what a mess!"

"You should have thought of that before associating with one of the Seven."

"Hey, not fair." I pivot to frown at her, "You're the one who encouraged me to go for him."

"I meant that you shag him, not propose to him."

"Yeah." I hunch my shoulders. "Why the hell did I do that? More to the point, why the hell did he accept? Especially after he'd told me that he wasn't going to marry anytime soon!"

"He said that to you?"

"Yeah."

"And yet, when you proposed, he agreed?" She frowns.

"He did."

"Maybe he changed his mind?"

"Ha, that's not something Damian does. That man... Once he makes up his mind, nothing can sway him."

"Maybe this is different...?" she suggests.

"And maybe this is all a dream?" I wrap the strands of my hair around my hand and tug; the pain squiggles down my neck. Okay, so this isn't all a figment of my imagination. This is really happening. "Help me," I implore her.

"Maybe you could take it back?" She tilts her head, "Tell him it was all a mistake?"

"What was a mistake?" A new voice sounds from the doorway and I scream. So does Isla.

"It's me, girls." Karina holds up both of her hands. "Just me. Sorry, I guess I should have knocked."

"Or something." I frown. "How did you get in?"

She stares at me.

"Right. You did the security for this place, so you have all of the passwords."

She walks over and places a bottle of champagne—expensive by its label, no cheap almost-vinegar type plonks for Madam, here.

"Glasses?" she asks, then glances down at the plastic cups in distaste.

"Surely there's something better here?" She walks over to the shelves, opens and shuts a few, then produces glasses. The kind from which you drink water. "This will have to do."

She walks over as Isla pops the cork of the bottle. "Woo," she squeals, "that's a happy sound."

"Har, har." I slink down into my chair, "I am never going to be happy again."

"Because you're marrying the Rockausarus?" Karina asks.

"You mocking me?" I accept the glass from her.

"Not at all," she raises her glass, "I am here to commiserate."

Hmph, I frown as she throws back the contents of the glass.

"Not bad, but personally, I prefer vodka," she declares.

"You're certainly drinking it like it's vodka." I grimace.

"Old habits." She tips back her chair, fixes me with her gaze, "What the hell were you thinking anyway, proposing to him? If I'd known it would come to this, I'd never have given you the passcodes to the house."

"He wanted you to," I retort.

"Huh?"

"He set you up, coaxed you in the direction of parting with the information."

"So, he knew I'd…" She sits up straight. "Hell, I should have known he was playing me. These Seven…" She pours out another glass of champagne, then tosses it back. "I should have told you to stay clear of them."

"You've known them longer than us though, right?" Isla chimes in. "You and Arpad—"

Karina glares at Isla with murder in her eyes, but Isla, of course, ignores it. Or doesn't care. Maybe she notices, but continues anyway. That girl has no filter, honestly.

"—I mean, the two of you have that love/hate thing going on, which is hot," she continues.

Karina drains her glass, fills it up again.

I reach for the bottle and top up my own and Isla's. I mean, I want my share of this expensive shit, as well.

"Admit it. The two of you have a thing for each other." Isla chuckles. "What, with those horny looks you trade —"

"My looks are not horny," Karina's tone grows glacial, "and I'd rather shoot myself in the head than spend any time with that asshole."

"Alphahole," I automatically correct her.

"What?" She stares at me.

"He's trained you well, already," Isla murmurs.

"No, he hasn't." I jump up and begin to pace. Yeah, I'm mirroring what said a-hole rock star did earlier, but whatever. I am too agitated and I need to think, to come up with a solution. "And I really need to find a way out of this."

"Why?" Karina's voice rings out.

I stop, turn to stare at her. "What do you mean, why?"

"You took the bull by the balls —"

"It's by the horns," Isla pipes up. Both Karina and I stare at her, and she stares down at her drink. "Never mind. Proceed," she mumbles.

Ha, everyone here is a clown today, for some reason. After all, it's only my life that's going down the shitter.

"Can you explain your bull and balls reference?" I glower at Karina.

"It's bull and horns —" Isla ventures.

"Shut up," both Karina and I echo without looking at Isla, who coughs.

"Yeah, I want to hear your reasoning, too, Karina," she mumbles. "What did you mean by that?"

"Just that, you could do worse." Karina stares at me.

"She could do better," Isla huffs.

"Sure," Karina drags her finger around the rim of the glass, "considering he is famous, rich, handsome —"

"Career on the decline, may not recover after his last flop, has loads of issues —" Isla counts off on her fingers.

"How do you know about his issues?" I scowl.

"Tabloid speculation." She raises her shoulders. "Besides, no one

can get to be that successful without some skeletons in their closet…
And definitely not, one of the Seven."

"So, he does have issues?" Karina asks.

"Boy, does he," I nod.

"Good, so you can help him resolve them."

"Me?" I frown "How can I help him?"

"He feels something for you."

"She means, he's hung up on you," Isla adds.

"It's true. I'd say he's in love with you, except I don't believe in
that emotion."

"Wow." I look her up and down, "Now I see why the Seven trust
you with their security. You're pretty cut-throat, aren't you?"

"I do what I have to do to survive." Her features harden. "And I
have seen all kinds in this line of work. Which is why I also know
that there's something genuine between you and him."

"Is there?"

She nods. "Marriages have been built on worse." She licks the
champagne off her finger, then holds up her glass. "You two have a
lot more going for you."

"Like what?"

"You want security and he wants…" Karina shoots me a glance
from under her eyelashes, "Well, you know what he wants."

"You mean sex?"

"I mean, whatever it is that floats his boat, and which he, clearly,
is getting from you."

"What if he gets tired of me?" I wring my fingers together.

"Julia, Julia." Karina shakes her head. "You're a strong, beautiful, intelligent woman, and he's just a man who thinks with his dick.
Trust me, you know what you have to do to keep him hungry enough
so he keeps coming back for more. Besides, you love him."

I stare at her. "Shit, is it that obvious?"

"To us," Isla mumbles under her breath, "and only because we're
your friends…" Her voice trails off. She glances at me, then away.
"Sorry, babe, but yeah, it's kind of written all over your face. I mean,
that's why you proposed to him, right?"

Because I love him? I gulp down more champagne, then choke again. Bloody hell, I do love him. Only he doesn't... He can't possibly be in love with me. I am just the means to his relaunching his career. So why the hell did he accept? It makes no sense.

I shake my head. "No, no, no, this is all wrong. I should call him and tell him it was all a joke and that it's off."

"But you won't," Karina drawls.

I stare at her again. "How do you know?"

"Because you want him, and you have the courage to fight for him. Question is, will you act on that now?"

38

———————

Dec 31st

Damian

"This makes no sense." I glance down at my button-down shirt, my tailored slacks, that I'd paired with my sneakers, then up at Arpad. "What the hell are you smirking about, you douche?"

"Me?" Arpad straightens from where he's leaning against the window. "Maybe it's the venue?" He glances out and I know he's seeing the arena of Shakespeare's Globe with the three floors of seating.

"It's too small for the event, don't you think?" he drawls.

I glance up at him, "Ha! Sarcasm, huh?" I glower.

"Can't you take a joke?"

"Not right now." I glance around. "Where's my jacket? Shit have you seen my jacket?"

"It's with me, ol' chap." He thrusts the beaten leather jacket at me.

"Thanks." I slip it on, then smooth my palms over the sleeves. "How do I look?"

"Terrified."

I glare at him, and he chuckles.

"Relax," he takes a step back and looks me up and down, "You look like a rock star about to get married."

"Is that good?" I frown. "Is it too obvious that I didn't opt for something more formal."

"Nah," he scratches his chin, "maybe."

"Which is it?" I growl.

"Both?" He smirks. "Neither."

I scowl at him, "Enjoying yourself, brother?"

"You have no idea." He laughs. "I've waited years… Years, to get back at you."

"You mean for all the times I whipped your arse when we sparred?"

"You mean that I whipped yours, don't you?" He folds his arms over his chest.

"Let's say, we were evenly matched," I reply. "I'll give you that, considering I'm not in a mood to fight today."

"What kind of a mood are you in, huh?" He waggles his eyebrows. "Can't wait to see the wife, then?"

I frown at him, "Wife to-be, and this is all your fault."

"What, you mean for spotting the fact that there was something between the two of you before you realized it, and ensuring that she turned up at your doorstep?"

"I'll never forgive you for that," I growl.

"You're welcome." He nods.

"Oh, fuck off." I drag a finger under my collar. Shit, maybe the button-down was a bad idea. Why the hell hadn't I opted for my normal T-shirt and jeans?

"Don't even think about it." Arpad grabs the bottle of whiskey from the table, along with two glasses, then walks over. He hands me a glass, pours some of the amber liquid into it.

I sniff it. "Macallan's," I nod. Can't fault the man for his taste in whiskey, at least. I take a healthy swig, and the taste of oak fills my senses.

"Limited-edition," he adds. "Had a pal save one for me."

"No doubt." I toss back the rest of the contents, hold out my glass for more. He fills me up and I down that too. "More," I mumble. "Top me up."

"Easy, tiger," he cautions, "you don't want to be drunk for your wedding now."

"Don't I?" I mumble. "She blackmailed me into this."

"Did she?"

"It was either marry her or lose her."

"And you didn't want to let go of her?"

I stare at the contents of the glass; the amber sparkles under the watery sunlight. "Wonder if it will rain?" I glance up at the overcast sky.

"Now you're deflecting." Arpad shakes his head, "And PS, I thought you had more balls than this."

"What are you talking about?"

"No one's ever coerced you into doing anything you didn't want to do."

"Except the women in my life, huh?"

"Riley," he says softly.

I shoot him a glance, "Be very careful what you say next."

He leans forward on the balls of his feet. "I've never been a father. God knows, I can only imagine how it felt for you to have known her for such a little while, only to lose her, but you need to let go of her, bro."

"Don't talk about her as if she's—" My throat closes and a burning sensation fills the back of my eyes. Shit, what is this? Will I ever reach a stage when I'll be able to think about her without my heart breaking, without my stomach twisting itself up in knots, without every part of me insisting that I was in the wrong?

"She's gone, bro," Arpad says softly. "She's not coming back."

"Don't you fucking think that I know that?" My voice cracks, and I squeeze my fingers around the glass of whiskey. "If only I could turn back the clock... If only I'd taken the threats more seriously... If only I'd taken steps to protect them."

"It wasn't your fault."

"Of course, it was," I snap. "I was too focused on my next album, my career, my image. It was always the next thing. I didn't appreciate what I had in front of me—my daughter, my angel, the light of my life." I squeeze my eyes shut. "It's my fucking fault that she's dead."

I've said it… the dreaded 'D' word that I've never been able to enunciate before. "She's not with me anymore," I choke out the words. "I'll never be able to hold her again, smell that baby scent of hers, or teach her to ride a bike. Or whip her first boyfriend when he comes to pick her up on her first date. Fuck!" I fling the glass and it shatters against the floor. "Bloody fuck, what the hell am I doing here anyway? I should be home, working on my album, taking care of—"

I draw in a breath. I have to stop talking about her as if she is still here… My logical mind knows it. My brain insists on it…. But my heart… My soul… All of it, refuses to accept the irrefutable proof of what I face every day. My daughter, my child, my little girl, will never smile again, will never look at me, or call me Daddy, will never ask me for her favorite toy, or ask me to read to her again.

"Fuck." I drag my fingers through my hair. "This marriage. It's all wrong. I shouldn't be doing this."

"It's the one thing you should definitely see through," Arpad admonishes me.

"Oh, yeah?"

He nods. "This is your chance to put the past behind you, to finally move on with a woman who—"

"Sees this as, as much of an arrangement as I do?"

"It's a start." He surveys my features, "The attraction between you two is off the charts. It's definitely the right start for building a marriage."

"Since when have you become an advocate for the old ball and chain?"

"Since I saw you struggle and fail to get over your grief; since I saw you become a shadow of your former self; since I saw you begin to self-sabotage your own career."

"Self-sabotage?" I frown. "What do you mean?"

"You've been releasing your worst-ever work since their accident."

"Understandable."

"Is it?" He walks up to stand in front of me. "Or have you been using the grief as an excuse to not create? Maybe you don't want to give it your best shot. Maybe you can't stand the thought of being successful."

"Do you know how crazy you sound?" I chuckle.

"Is it though?"

He steps into my space, and I growl, "Back off, man."

"I won't," he snaps back. "It's time you stop punishing yourself for what happened."

"So, you keep saying."

"So, you lost something very precious to you —"

"You have no idea," I snarl. "No one… No one should have to bury their own child…."

"I know, I know where you're coming from."

He lays a hand on my shoulder and I shake it off. "No, you don't." I step back and begin to pace again, "No one can understand what I am going through."

"Maybe she can."

"Oh?"

"You found something that's very rare."

"What's that?"

"A chance at true love."

"Love?" I bark out a laugh, "Didn't know you believed in that emo shit."

"I don't," he mutters, "but Jesus, man, when I look at you and how you're wasting away your life... Hell, if I don't want it to work for you, if it drags you out of the spiral of self-destruction that you've been stuck in —"

"I was fine where I was."

"Were you now?" he raises an eyebrow, "Going off social media, dropping out of sight, and fueling speculation that you were losing your shit. Not to mention, not hanging out with the Seven like you used to."

"I was there for the others when they needed me. I got on the bloody calls with them and held their hands as they found their women."

"The bare minimum," he sneers, "and only because I didn't give you a choice."

"Get off my balls, man."

"No."

I glance around, curl my fingers at my sides. "I can't do this. This was a bloody stupid idea. Fuck my career, fuck the next album, fuck everything. I'm leaving." I head for the exit.

He plants his body in my way. "I am not letting you sabotage the one good thing that's come your way since the accident."

"You can't stop me," I growl.

"But we can."

I glance past Arpad as Edward walks into the room.

Of course, he's not alone. Sinner, Saint, Weston and Jace follow him. "Bloody hell, the only one missing is that joker Baron showing up, to complete this shit show."

"If that's what it takes," Arpad growls.

"What do you mean?" I frown.

"No one told him yet?" Edward ambles over to the arm chair in the corner and drops into it.

"Do you want to, or should I?" Sinclair drawls.

Weston and Jace take a stance by the door. Clearly, they don't trust my not making a break for it. Obviously, they know me too well. Shit. This is what happens when you have friends you've known since you were teens. They think they can take liberties with your life. Well, it is time to set them right. No one can make me do what I don't want to do. No one.

I glower at them, "You wankers thought it would be a good idea to stage an intervention?"

"Just returning the favor, ol' chap." Saint smirks.

He's referring to how the rest of us had cornered him when he'd been in the middle of his courtship with Victoria. We'd been his sounding board as he'd explained all the justifications for why he wanted to fake-marry her… We'd goaded him along, steered him onto the right path, which was to put the ring on her finger, and well, hell, look at the two of them now. In happily wedded bliss, with a kid on the way.

"Oh, no, no," I shake my head, "this isn't the same situation as you and Victoria."

"Oh, no?" He folds his arms over his chest. "Pray, tell me, what's different here?"

"You married her to get to the Mafia," I point out.

"I married her because," he shuffles his feet, "because I love her."

"You barely knew her." I scowl at him. "No way, could you have fallen for her so quickly."

"Couldn't I?" He draws in a breath. "I knew from the moment I laid eyes on her that she was the one for me. I kept fooling myself otherwise, but I knew." He slaps his chest, "Deep inside, I knew, brother. It took me long enough to admit it, after I put her and our child in danger. I don't want the same to happen to you. It's why I'm telling you—"

"What?" I growl, "Confess to feelings I don't have and marry her?"

"Marry her because she's the only thing standing between you and complete destruction. Besides," he looks me up and down, "you have feelings for her."

"I don't," I growl. "She's simply a means of accessing my muse."

"Didn't Shakespeare marry his muse?" Arpad pipes up.

"What's that got to do with anything?" I crack my neck, "And what was it that you guys were going to tell me before we were side-tracked?"

Arpad glances at the others, "Shall I?"

Sinclair nods, "Go ahead."

"Baron contacted me." Arpad declares.

"What?" I blink. "Baron? Our Baron? The one we haven't seen in nearly a decade?"

"Know of another?" Edward leans forward in his seat, "Go on, tell him the rest."

Arpad pulls out a sheet of paper from the pocket of his slacks, "Of course, the douche used snail mail. Not like it's going to stop us from trying to track him down."

"We've tried and failed so far," I point out, "What's new now?"

"What's new is that he's addressed this communication to all of us, sans you." He jerks his chin at me.

"But you're reading it to me?"

"He wants us to share this with you."

"Well, spare me the suspense," I mumble, "not that I am fucking interested or anything in what he has to say."

"So, you don't want to know how his advice to you is to not marry her."

"Hold on," I pause, "I decided to get married two days ago, and he's found out about it and had enough time to send Arpad here a letter stating I shouldn't do so?"

"Seems like it." Arpad nods.

"Something doesn't feel right about this."

"You think?" Sinclair smirks.

"It means he's not far off." I glance around at the faces of my friends, "Likely in this city. Close enough to keep tabs on us."

"So we think," Edward agrees.

"Why would he do that?"

"Who knows why Baron does anything?"

"Isn't he over-dramatizing this entire incident thing, considering it wasn't he who got the worst of the experience?" I glance at Edward, who pales.

He rises to his feet, walks over to me, "You have something to say?" His jaw tics. "Something you want to get off your chest, perhaps. Considering you escaped the incident, more or less intact, only to fall apart at the first sign of a personal tragedy."

"What do you know about personal tragedies, huh? You, who took the easy way out, and decided to leave the world and its day-to-day matters behind, after all? You renounced everything and ran away, Edward. You left it to the rest of us to hold each other up. You weren't here when we went off on the bender, when Saint got into such intense fights it was clear he had a death wish, when Sinclair decided to pursue business success to the detriment of everything else, when Weston fell apart after his father died, when I lost my..." I swallow, "lost my daughter and her mother, and knew it would change me forever. I needed you then Edward, and where were you? You were off in some monastery somewhere, trying to find yourself."

"I would have been no good to you if I had stayed," Edward mumbles. "Hell, I was so out of my head with pain, I was no good to myself in the state I was."

"So were all of us," I growl. "But we stayed on, we helped each other, we worked through our crises."

"You had each other. You didn't need me." Edward's throat moves as he swallows. He glances around the room, "Isn't that right, fellas? You had the six of you—"

"Five," Arpad cuts in. "Baron cut and ran not long after. He'd have stayed, if you had."

"Wait, so this is all on me?" He stares at the assembled men. "Weston? You're the most level-headed of these tossers. Do you feel the same way?"

Weston snorts, "Me, level-headed?" He scratches his beard, "Maybe in comparison to the rock star hellbent on self-destruction, with his continuous string of failed concerts and the worst-performing Christmas single in history—"

"Hey," I protest, "it wasn't that bad. In fact, it hit number one—"

"In what, the worst Christmas songs of all time?"

"Close," I mumble. "It was called the least festive song ever, I believe. At least, get your facts right. And weren't we talking about how Father, here, did the vanishing act on all of us?"

"You're deflecting, Savage," Weston admonishes. "And for the record, yes. If you'd stayed, Edward, things would have been different.'

"Hold on, hold on." Edward throws up his hands, "Why is all of this coming out now? Why have none of you mentioned this to me earlier? And hey! You guys had each other, while I was away dealing with my own shit, alone."

"Your choice," I growl. "If you'd stayed, we could have dealt with it together, as a team, as we always did."

"Except you didn't." A familiar voice rings out. I turn as Julia glides into the room. She's wearing a simple white dress that covers her from throat to wrists, tucked in at the waist, clinging to her thighs as she walks, before flowing down to swirl around her ankles. She looks ethereal and beautiful and completely not what I expected. She's worn her hair piled up on her head and my fingers tingle to pull out the pins and have the strands scattered around her shoulders, her back, over my pillows. I'd lean down and sink my nose into the glistening locks and draw in that sensuous, exotic scent that is so uniquely Flower.

"What are you doing here?" I growl.

"Have you told them?" She moves closer, her features serene, those green eyes darting between the others, then back to me. "Tell me, Damian, do they know?"

"About what?" My heart begins to thump in my chest. *Why is she here? What is she going to share with the rest?* I allowed her a peek into the part of my life that is a secret from all of them, except Meredith… Hell, not even she knows the extent to which I have been caught up in my grief, unable to move forward… Until Julia had flounced in and shined a spotlight on the dark recesses of my mind. "What are you talking about?" I snap.

"You know." She tips her chin up.

"Do I?" I tilt my head, take in the set of her jaw, the nervous tremble of her fingers as she clenches them together in front of her. "What are you doing here, anyway? It's bad luck for the groom to see the bride before the wedding."

"Thought you didn't want to get married," Arpad coughs into his hand.

"Yeah," Edward nods, "thought you were going to call it off?"

"Call what off?" Julia glances around at them. "What's going on?"

"You tell me, Flower." I drawl, "To what do I owe the unexpected appearance of my fair bride to-be in what, I confess, is a break with tradition that even I find surprising."

"What's surprising is that you haven't revealed your secret to them," she retorts.

"Secret?" I curl my fingers at my sides. A bead of sweat drips down my back. Not that the Seven wouldn't understand why I had to keep the memory of Riley alive a little longer, but hell, some things… Some things are sacred, you know what I mean? And no one…is allowed in. And I had let her peek in where no one else had, and now I am going to pay the price. "My secret?" I glare at her.

"Of course, babe." She pauses in front of me, then places her hand over my chest. "Shall I tell them?"

39

Julia

"What?" He lowers his voice to a hush, "What are you going to tell them, Flower?"

I tip my chin up, gaze into his beautiful features. His jaw tics; a nerve throbs at his forehead. He watches me like the predator he is, a man lost in the darkness that comes to the fore in his stage performances. If I'd wanted to know what troubled him most, what drove him to leave the frantic lifestyle he used to have, only to drop out of sight, I know the reason now. And he thinks I am going to reveal his secret to the world?

"What do you think?" I mutter. "Want to take a guess at what it is?"

"I think," he snaps, "it's time for us to leave." He swoops down to grab my wrist, but I swerve to the side.

"Hold on," I yelp, "I haven't told them yet."

"And you won't, either." He stalks to the door, pulling me in his wake. I dig my heels into the wooden floor, stumble against him.

He turns, rights me by the shoulders. "Hell, you okay?" He scrutinizes my features, his eyes filled with concern that takes my breath away.

"Y…yeah," I stutter." Let me just complete what I have to say?"

He schools all emotion from his face. "No." He glares at me. "Don't do it."

"I… I have to," I mumble, "I don't have a choice."

"You always have a choice," Damian snarls. "I knew I shouldn't have trusted you." He releases me so quickly that I lose my balance once again. This time I right myself.

"You're right." I flip my hair over my shoulder. "But it's too late now." I turn, face the rest of the Seven. Saint widens his stance, Sinclair sets his jaw, while Arpad glowers at me. Weston, Edward and Jace, who's lurking in the far corner, survey me with something like confusion.

"You should know—" I draw myself up to my full height. "You should know that—"

Behind me, I sense Damian's body grow rigid. The anger rolls off of him in waves and slams into me. My thighs tremble and my core melts… Jesus, the fact that even his anger turns me on so is depraved. I stare around the room, take in another breath, "You should know that he's writing again, and his lyrics are nothing short of genius."

"Knew it!" Arpad stabs a finger in Damian's direction. "Those words on your phone were yours, weren't they?"

"Who's writing?" Edward rises to his feet. "Is it Damian, you mean?"

"Lyrics?" Weston gasps in mock horror.

"Genius?" Saint's brow furrows.

"We talking about the same person here?" Sinclair finally drawls.

"Totally." I flex my fingers, which tremble. "You should read some of what he's written. It's vintage Damian Savage. The kinds of words which broke hearts and made his early album a cult hit—"

"Hold on," Damian snaps from behind me. "You read what I wrote."

"Oops," I curls my fingers at my sides, "I shouldn't have said that, huh?" I turn to him, "I can explain—"

"You read my work when I specifically told you not to."

"D… Damian… No, it's not like that."

"Then what is it like, huh?" He closes the distance between us and the tips of his boots brush against my stilettos. Yeah, I'd actually decided to pull out all the stops, gone in for the entire bride-in-white look. Not that the man has noticed, apparently, for he hasn't said a word on that. Not that I'd allowed him to, considering I'd pulled this crazy stunt on him.

"Damian," I whisper, "let me explain."

"Oh, you will." He curves his fingers about my shoulders, then lowers his forehead to mine. "Later, when we are alone, you can tell me all about your little spying trip in my space.

"I told you it's not like that," I insist. "I didn't go into your studio."

He frowns down at me. "Still lying to me, I see?" His gaze darkens. He releases me, then turns me around to face the rest of our very interested audience.

"Well, now that the bride to-be is also here, we may as well as commence the ceremony."

"Hey, hold on, you weren't going to start without us, were you?" Summer marches in, Victoria at her heels.

Isla races inside, "Hey, has anyone seen Julia? I can't find her in the dressing room and—" she steps inside and spots me, "Oh, hell, Jules, what are you doing here?"

I bite the inside of my cheek. What should I say? I did something stupid? I got cold feet, and decided to come in search of my bridegroom—stupid I know, but too late—and found he was getting cold feet too, and that had made me angry. I knew I had to do something, but then the guys had begun to rib him, and well, I had to step in. Damn it, why do I feel so protective about this alphahole, when, clearly, the tenderness is something that is not yet reciprocated?

"She's exactly where she should be," Damian's voice rings out in the silence.

I glance sideways at his countenance. The skin around his lips is stretched tight and that vein at his temple is throbbing with such vehemence, I swear it's going to pop.

"Damian," I whisper, and he tightens his hold on my shoulder.

I wince. "Ouch," I protest, "you're hurting me."

"Good," he hisses under his breath, then glances back at Isla. "Change of plans. We are getting married here."

"What?" I gasp.

"Here?" Isla pales. "B…but the press who've been invited?"

"Fuck the press," Damian growls.

"Now, now, ol' chap." Arpad steps forward. "Let's think this through. You need the press."

"I've done without them for this long," Damian barks back.

"And this is the start of a new chapter in your life. It's why you agreed to invite them here… To witness you taking the first steps to your reformation," Edward adds.

"Says the man who couldn't wait to turn his back on the world," Damian snorts.

"I cannot believe you just said that," I gasp at him. "Honestly, Damian, you need to apologize."

"What?" He glowers down at me from his superior height, "No."

I tip my chin up, stab a finger into his chest, "You tell him how sorry you are."

He scowls.

"Right now," I hiss at him.

"Fine," he hisses back, "but you're going to pay for this."

"Oh?" I flutter my eyelashes, "I'm counting on it."

His blue eyes blaze with those familiar sparks, his nostrils flare, he lowers his head, and I'm sure he's going to kiss me, or yell at me, or both. Instead, he brushes his nose up the side of my throat, and I shiver. He releases me and steps back.

"I apologize." He nods in Edward's direction, "I was out of line."

Edward seems taken aback, then he glances between us. "Don't say it because your wife to-be asked you to," he sneers. "I can live without your fake repentance."

"Jesus," Damian swears, "does everything have to be so…so… packed with OTT sentiment with you?"

"That's me," Edward's lips curl, "I'm an OTT kind of guy."

"Huh?" I stare at the Father. And I'd always thought him to be a mellow kind of guy. Guess I thought wrong. Still waters always do run deep, apparently.

Isla's phone rings. She switches it off, then walks over to us, "You guys, if you're sure you don't want the press to be witness—"

"I'm not—"

"I'm sure," Damian snaps at the same time.

I stare up at him; he ignores me.

"Tell the press they'll get to do a short q-and-a with us after the wedding, as man and wife."

As man and wife. Of course, he would say that, rather than husband and wife. Gah! Big picture, Julia. He means to go through with it then. After everything I heard earlier, when I'd been sure that he would back out… He throws me for a loop again. Apparently, my little scene had worked. Too well. Now I am well and truly stuck.

"B…but," I force the words out, "what about the guests?"

"Ohmygod, the guests." Isla digs her fingers into her hair. "What do I do with them?" She stares between us. "Don't tell me you're not going to let them witness the wedding after they agreed to attend, and at such short notice?"

Damian widens his stance; his muscles tense.

"Let's allow the guests in," I plead with him. "It's not fair that I asked Isla to help organize the wedding, which she pulled off in less than two days—"

"More like twenty-four hours," Isla pouts. "I should have known none of the Seven would do this the normal way. Have any of you all heard of planning things and not getting married on a whim?"

"Uh, I think I am the one to blame this time," I offer.

"You. Him." She scowls at Damian. "Once you women hook up with the Seven, it's like everything changes. All of you expect the world to bow down to you."

"So, what's wrong with that?" Damian frowns down at her, and honestly, he's being serious. Like, totally serious, here.

OMG. I dig my elbow in his side. "Stop," I reprimand him. "You're not helping."

"So?" He turns that blue gaze on me, "What do you recommend?"

"I recommend that we go ahead with the wedding, as planned—"

"No."

"Then we invite the guests up here instead?"

"Hmm. Let me think." He taps a finger against his cheek, gazes into the distance, "Not happening."

"What?" Isla gasps.

"No," I protest. "Don't do this. It will, likely, destroy your career."

"Which I stopped giving a fuck about a long time ago."

And I should too…but apparently, I can't. This man. He's too bloody talented to hide away from the world, and somehow, now that I know his secret… Not that it means I have any power over him… In fact, quite the opposite… I feel like I am responsible, somehow, for making sure he shares his talent again with the world… Hence, when he'd suggested inviting the press and the guests to the wedding, I had gone along…

All of this was his plan, and now he doesn't want to go through with it, settling instead, for a more intimate affair, which honestly, is what I prefer too… But the backlash from the press and the guests who, I am sure, would only be too happy to spread more rumors about Damian's downfall… And which bothers me more… And which—

Hold on! Why the hell am I so upset about it, somehow, while this man…? He stands there watching me watch Isla have a nervous breakdown?

I lean up on tip-toe and tug at his sleeve. He lowers his head. "Please," I whisper, "for Isla's sake. Let's, at least, invite the guests up."

"For Isla's sake?"

"Yeah."

"So. It's another favor."

"Actually, you're doing yourself a favor by agreeing to have them here—"

"Then, no." He straightens.

"What?"

"You heard me."

I open and shut my mouth, curl my fists at my sides, then mutter, "Fine, fine, it's a favor to me."

"To be repaid in full, as I want, when I want, how I want…?" He leans in closer, "In whatever form I want?"

I swallow, hesitate.

He turns to me, places his palms on my shoulder.

"Agree now, or forever hold your peace." He meets my gaze, "Well?"

40

Damian

Yes, it's a dick move—me arguing with her when she's trying so hard
to save this shamble of a ceremony that I don't give a fuck about…
And yes, it had been my idea to invite the press and the guests…
Nothing like giving them a ringside view to my downfall, huh? After
all, that's what I do best, right? Allow the world to sit centerstage as
I detonate before them.

So why the hell is she so hellbent on saving my career? My reputation. As if she cares? Is it the money? The opportunity to rub
shoulders with fame? Perhaps the chance to take credit for resur-
recting a rock legend… More like a rolling stone that had gathered
too much moss, excuse the sorry pun. And while we're at it, also
excuse me for not being more trusting for how she begs me to go
through with this sham of a wedding. One she'd initiated, by the
way, so why the hell should I comply with what she has in mind?
Unless… Well… I can use the situation to my own advantage, which
you bet I am going to do.

"What is it to be, then?" I rake my gaze over her features. "Tell me, Julia. Yes or no? Are you in or out?"

She draws in a breath and her lips tremble. She glances around the room, no doubt, takes in the expressions of the rest of the Seven —whose opinions matter, of course, but not as much as she thinks. They're my friends, my brothers in arms, but none of them have been through what I have. To have bounced back from the incident only to have my soul shattered all over again? Well, let them try to recover from losing a part of themselves as I had. I guarantee they wouldn't have made it as far as I have. Which isn't saying a lot, considering I've managed to screw up my life completely. And even now, when I should be thanking my good fortune that she came along, here I am, screwing it all up, all over again, and I can't stop myself.

She glances at Isla, then back at me. "Yes," she mutters, "I'll do as you please."

"Good." I take in her pale face, her huge eyes, the hair piled on top of her head. I reach down and she flinches, as I pull the pins from her hair.

She gasps and I hear a few murmurs from the women as her hair tumbles around her face. I arrange it about her shoulders to my satisfaction, then nod. "That's better." I lean down and kiss her cheek. "You're a good friend," I whisper in her ear before I tug on her earlobe, and she gasps.

"Just don't expect me to be the same," I growl. Her shoulders tremble. I step back, turn to Isla, "You can ask the guests to come in here, and we'll have a meet and greet with the press later."

Her forehead scrunches, then she nods, "Fine." She turns to leave.

Amelie walks up to Julia, "Let's get you freshened up, okay babe?" She hooks her arm through Julia's and leads her out, with Victoria and Summer at her heels.

I glance around the room, take in the expressions of the rest of my friends. They glare at me as if it's my fault. "What?" I rake my fingers though my hair. "I'm doing my best," I growl.

"It's not enough." Edward frowns.

"Do better then," Arpad snaps.

"Now, it's my fault?" I snap

"Always."

"You bet."

I stare at the traitors, "Whose side are you on?"

"Hers," they reply in one voice.

I dig my fingers into my hair and tug, "You guys can't be serious."

"*You* can't be serious, you complete ass." Arpad stalks forward and grabs my collar.

"Hey," I protest, "What's wrong with you?"

"What's wrong with you?" he snaps back. "The woman's in love with you, you shithead. She's trying to save your bloody soul—which is a lost cause, if you ask me, but whatever—and this is how you repay her?"

"How?"

"You know how." He drags me up by my collar, "You're being a complete, unreasonable prick—nothing new and I don't care— Hell, none of us cared if you stayed where you were, hiding behind your wall of grief like a coward—"

"I'm not a coward," I argue.

"Oh," he laughs, "that's not what I see."

"Don't say it," I warn him, "don't…"

"It's clear as hell that you want her by your side, even as you do your best to push her away. You want her to help you see the light, yet you do everything possible to drag her down into the darkness with you. Just like you've held the rest of us at arm's length, but here's what you should understand…"

"What?" My heart begins to race. There's a ball of fucking emotions in my throat that won't go away as much as I swallow. "You may as well as complete your little speech," I say through gritted teeth.

"We're not going anywhere," Arpad snaps.

Behind him, Edward chuckles. Sinclair and Saint stare at me with determination in their eyes. Weston folds his arms over his chest and raises one eyebrow. Jace crosses his legs, leans against the wall. "You heard the man," he says.

"That woman is worth ten—"

"A hundred—" Edward chimes in.

"A hundred," Arpad corrects himself, "of you." He nods. "And she cares about your fucking black heart—God knows why—and the rest of us can see what you can't."

"What?"

"That you love her, you prick."

"No."

"You fucking care for her for the first time since…"

I stare at him.

"Since your daughter died."

I squeeze my eyes shut. "It never gets easier," I mutter. "It's fucking killing me, man, that I'll never be able to read to her again, kiss her cheek, smell her baby scent, teach her to ride a bike, buy her a dog, run with her across the heath, buy her makeup, fight off the boys who dare glance at her… F-u-c-k, I'll never get to see her again and it's eating me from the inside! I can't go on."

"You must."

"It's tearing me apart… This… This thing is so real, I can see it, feel it, touch it… This horrible nothingness that's gnawing at me… It's tying me up in knots." I lower my chin to my chest, "It's suffocating me slowly."

"Write it out."

"Eh?" I glare at him, "You think I haven't tried."

"You have your muse with you now."

"Hmm."

"You and she both said you're finally writing."

"It's all crap."

"Not from what she said." Edward moves toward us.

"It is," I insist.

"That's for us to decide," Arpad replies.

"Right." I snort. "The day I show my early ideas to you knobheads will be when I know I've finally lost it."

"Not us. Share it with her." Weston closes the distance to us. "Trust me, bro, having your woman by your side is like no other feeling on earth. The trust, the selflessness of what she brings to your relationship, how she reacts to your creative output, will be the most honest, the most loving, yet the most critical. You can trust her."

Can I?

"If I, the most cynical mofo on this side of the Atlantic, found my soulmate, I believe there is hope for you." Sinclair stalks toward me. He wraps his arms around me and Arpad. "You gotta believe in her, believe in yourself. You have to get through this."

"The wedding?" I mumble.

"That, too," Edward closes in from the other side to grip my shoulder, "and the grief that you have been holding inside and not sharing with us…"

I frown.

"You don't have to allow us in. I mean, as your priest, I'd love for you to confide in me. But as your friend, hell, if I want to peek into that twisted heart of yours." He chuckles.

"Thanks, man." I grimace.

"But you can open yourself up to her."

"Right." I crack my neck, "Who are you guys and what have you done to the Seven?"

"I can't speak for the others, but personally, the love of a good woman changed me." Saint's lips twist. He prowls forward and grabs my neck to pull me toward him, then smashes his forehead to mine.

"Ow," I half yell, "What the hell, you dumbfuck? That hurt!"

"Good." He smirks. "Had to find the fastest way to get some sense through that thick skull of yours."

"What-fucking-ever."

Arpad laughs; the others chuckle.

"Now what?" I protest. "What is it you guys are trying to tell me?"

"Something that even that tosser Baron realizes, and he isn't even around." Jace joins us to complete the strange whatever-it-is that is going on here.

"Which is?" I finally ask.

"That you love her."

"You can't live without her."

"You need her and you better not fuck this up."

"You better take this opportunity and run with it and turn your life around or else—"

"Fine, fine," I half yell. "You guys are scaring me, with this weird emo, group hug thing."

"Group hug?" Arpad snorts. "What is a group hug of alphaholes called anyway?"

"A hole in the heart?" Weston offers.

"An alpha pit?" Edward grimaces. "Maybe not."

"Shitholes?"

Arpad laughs, "Forget I asked. The fact is, we may act like we don't give a fuck—which often, arguably, we don't—but in this instance, we're not giving you a choice, man. You're going to embrace this chance and make the fucking most of it."

"Stop yelling in my ear; I can hear you just fine," I grumble.

"It's time." Arpad glances around the group, "Shall we show this chap we mean business?"

My heart begins to race, adrenaline laces my blood, and I sense their intent a second before the tossers haul me up and carry me, up and toward the sliding doors of the room that opens out onto the rooftop where the tables have been laid out for the reception later. Beyond that all of London can be seen; but that's not what interests me as much as the glimmer of blue in the center… A fucking pool.

"Don't you fucking dare, you wankers, you dicks, you… pratholes."

I hear their laughter as I fall through the air.

41

Julia

"You ready?"

Isla straightens from where she's righted the hem of my skirt. My very short skirt that comes up to mid-thigh. I shuffle my feet—now clad in leather boots that come to over my knees. And the heels? Well, let's just say I feel like Wonder Woman right now, or Lady Gaga in her heyday… God knows, I need the confidence of both, rolled up together, to walk into that room. I stare at the double doors that are currently closed, and gulp. My fingers tremble and I clench them together. No flowers… Okay, so no real flowers. Instead, I have a bouquet of flowers made out of long-life clay, the kind that will last a long time, and become a true family heirloom. Something I hope to, one day, pass down to my children… When I have them… Me and Damian and our children. Jesus, will I have his kids? Will this marriage, that came out of nowhere—so what, if I had initiated it?—result in something that will last at least as long as this clay flower bouquet? Or will it wither away like those made of real flowers? Destined to be pressed into the pages of a book and be remembered for its shortness, the intensity with which it took place, only for things to implode? Are we destined to become a fly-by-night headline of the paparazzi? Here today, gone tomorrow? With not even the printed word having recorded our brief encounter? St-o-p right there. Talk about having an overactive imagination, huh? Jesus H, I need to get out of my head.

"Is it too much, you think?" I glance between Isla, who's listening to something on her ear piece, to Summer, who looks me up and down, to Victoria, who flanks me, serene as always, in her pale green gown. They'd all agreed to be bridesmaids and walk me up the aisle, more out of encouragement than tradition. Not that anything about this wedding is old school. Far from it.

"You look like a rock star's bride." Victoria smiles at me.

"Is that good?" I wonder aloud.

"You look perfect." Summer smiles at me, her pale pink gown molding her slim curves and setting off her dark hair with the pink tips that she recently added. Her eyes gleam and she chuckles as she looks me up and down, "Karma had this couriered to me. Thank God, I got it to you in time."

"Karma?" I frown. "She's—"

"My sister." Summer nods. "She's been holed up with her Italian hunk forever." Summer flicks her hair over her shoulder. "If she doesn't show herself soon, I'm going to have to go to Sicily and find out what she's hiding."

"You think she's hiding something?"

Summer's forehead furrows. "It was a figure of speech, but now that you mention it, I wonder if there isn't a grain of truth to it."

"What are you going to do?" Isla asks her.

Summer wrings her fingers together. "The last time I spoke to her, she sounded odd. I asked her if something was wrong and she dismissed it, saying she was down with the flu." Summer rubs her fingers over her forearm. "As sisters, you know, we've always shared everything, but I simply can't get over this niggling instinct that there's more than she's letting on. Know what I mean?"

No, not really. I am an only child, so I've always wanted the kind of relationship with a sibling that Summer talks about, but I've never had access to it. Which is why, maybe, I love kids and want my own family… And now I'm getting married… And hell, I am starting this chapter of my life on a big fat lie. Shit, shit, shit, I can't stop the sobs that grip me.

"Ohmygod," I hear Isla gasp aloud, then she steps up to wrap her arm around my shoulders. "Babe, what's wrong?"

"N… nothing," I blubber.

"Something is." Summer walks over to rub my back, in slow steady circles, "It's okay, honey, let it all out. So much has happened in the past few days, it must be catching up with you."

"Well, I wish it had caught up with me later. I need to feel stronger, I do, but damn, if everything doesn't seem…like…like…"

"It's all out of control?" Amelie joins us. She holds out a wad of tissues and I grab them, dab at my eyes. "Yeah," I sniff. "I mean, what if he hates me for what I'm making him do?"

"You did the right thing," Amelie insists.

"I know, but what if he never forgives me for it?"

"He will," Isla replies. "Maybe not immediately. I mean, when did a man recognize when something good happened to him, huh? Not even when it hits him over the head, does he admit that it's the right thing for him."

I blow my nose, then look for a way to discard the tissues. "Here," Isla holds out another tissue and I drop them in there. She wraps them up, then carries them over to the wastebasket. "Look, babe, if you don't feel this is the right thing for you, we can call it off."

"What?" I blink.

Isla glances at Summer, who nods, "Sure, doll, you say the word and we'll take care of the groom. Not to mention, the alphaholes in there. We'll hold them off—"

"And the press and guests," Victoria adds. "We'll take care of them all, if you want to leave."

"Oh," I swallow, then glance around their faces. Do I want to do that? Do I want to get the hell out of here? Out of what could be the biggest mistake of my life, or the biggest opportunity to…to find true love, to find out what makes Damian tick, to figure out how to help him, to help myself by helping him... Yeah… I know, it's warped… But something about this man... Since I'd first seen him in person, I'd known there couldn't be anyone else for me. I need to… Want to hold up a mirror to him, to show him the man I see, the soul he hides from the world... The words that he writes when he's alone, the melodies that bleed from his fingers when he thinks no one hears, the… Tenderness that he has yet to show me with any consistency, but which I know is hidden under that veneer of alphaholeness he likes to draw around himself like a cloak, because I've seen glimpses of it… Unless I am mistaken about him? And my instinct says, no, I'm not. That things will somehow work out… *Will they?*

I drag my gaze across the faces of my friends, "Will it all work out?"

Victoria moves forward and wipes a tear drop from my cheek, "When I married Saint, I thought it was the end of life as I knew it, and I was right."

"You….you were?"

She smiles, a secret uplift of her lips that hints at so many things, I can't put a name to all of the emotions. "Turned it, was the start of my best life, my only life, the dream life I wanted, but thought I'd never have. The Seven, you see… They under-promise and over-deliver."

"You make it sound like a business transaction," I tilt my head.

She chuckles. "Maybe it is. They, together, have interests in one of the biggest financial services companies in the country. Making money is a passion for them, pushing things to the very edge is their specialty, and then there is the non-profit they started together."

"Is that FOK media?" I remember reading about it in the press.

"FOK media," she nods, "the full name of which is, Full of Kindness."

"You're kidding?"

"Nope." She laughs. "It's a nonprofit that identifies and manages upcoming fresh talent. They extend interest-free loans to the most deserving ones, to start their own businesses.

"The Seven instituted that?" I start.

"Yes..." she smiles, "stuff they don't like to talk about, but which you'll find out as you get to know them better."

"O-kay." I scan her features, "What are you trying to say?"

"Give Damian a chance. Get to know him. While this is not a traditional arranged marriage, in some ways, you are marrying a stranger."

"Except he isn't," I say. "Not really."

"Exactly." She pats the space above my heart, "Where it counts, you know."

"Yeah," I swallow, "you're right. I do know him. I know that he's not as self-destructive as he wants me to believe, not as cruel as he tries to portray himself, not as…lacking in heart as he often signals with his actions, not as," I swallow around the lump in my throat, "not as much of an alphahole as the persona he portrays to the world." I stare into her face. "So… You're saying, there's a chance that things will work out?"

She wipes a stray tear off of my cheek, "Only one way to find out, babe. You ready to go in now?"

42

———

Damian

I tug on the sleeve of my button down, then glance at Arpad, "How do I look?"

"Your usual sorry self." He grins.

"Jesus, why the hell did I bother to ask?" I glance forward through the now-open doors onto the rippling waters of the pool where I had been unceremoniously dunked and held captive by the rest of my ex-friends… Yep, I've officially disowned them, as of fifteen minutes ago — when they'd not allowed me out of the pool until I'd promised I'd go through with the ceremony… Which, to be honest, I had no intention of skipping. Not after that promise I'd obtained from Flower. And while I had been upset with her having sneaked a peek at my work — How the hell had she come across it, anyway? — it had, more, been surprise at her coming to my defense in the face of the rest of the Seven turning on me. Including that bastard Baron.

Bastard knew exactly what to say in his letter. He'd goaded me, knowing I'd do the exact opposite of what he suggested. I curl my fingers into fists.

How the hell had he found out about my upcoming nuptials anyway?

A mystery that Arpad has taken upon himself to track down, given the letter had been sent to him.

I roll my shoulders in the perfectly-fitted tux—which Edward had produced, along with the rest of this tailored suit that I am wearing. Seems this is his wedding gift to me. He'd had it arranged, right down to the formal shoes. I glance down at my feet. I am actually wearing Italian-fucking-loafers. When was the last time I put on such formal wear? At Stella and Riley's funeral.

I draw in a breath, waiting for that familiar pain to stab at my chest... And it does, and my guts churn, and my belly coils in knots, and yet… Somehow, I also swallow down the taste of my grief and turn to where the rest of the men are lined up to my left. "I'm going to get back at you guys," I warn.

"Looking forward to it, brother," Arpad chuckles.

"Better make sure it's not an empty threat this time, Savage," Jace laughs, before blowing a kiss across the space to his wife Sienna, who just walked in with their newborn in a sling. The tiny baby looks fucking sweet, I'll admit. How the hell can I even look at the kid without tying myself in knots like I used to, huh? Apparently, sharing my grief, first with Julia, then with Arpad and the rest of this lot, seems to have loosened something inside of me. Maybe there is hope for me? Perhaps I can get past the darkness that has gripped me for so long?

"You okay, Savage?" Saint asks.

"Yes." I shake my head, "No. Shit…" I drag my fingers through my still damp-hair… Yeah, I'd managed to jump into the shower in the changing rooms by the pool, which is where I'd also gotten dressed. My wedding day and I am actually dressed in a formal tux —something which is so far from my own style that, honestly, I have to ask… How the hell did this happen?

"Also, you're welcome," Sinclair drawls.

"For what?" I scowl.

"For making sure you turned up for your own wedding, you shoe stain."

I wince, "Getting creative with your insults, finally, I see?"

"Getting antsy as the time draws closer, I see?" Arpad chuckles. He pulls out his phone and snaps a shot.

"What the fuck?" I mutter. "You're in disgustingly good humor."

"Unlike you." Edward smiles from his place in front of me. "Not long now, Savage." He smirks. "Any last wishes before this last step?"

"Hey," I protest, "you're my priest, for fuck's sake—"

"No swearing," he says mildly.

"And you smirked," I accuse him. "Didn't think you had a mean bone in your body."

"Much you don't know about me." Edward's eyes gleam. For a second, I am sure I glimpse something beyond the affable, if quiet, priest and friend I've known for so long—something darker, more violent… Unpredictable? Hell, I should know. I was—am—the same.

"Jesus, Ed," I mutter, "you're going to get into so much trouble one of these days."

"Nothing I can't handle." His smile widens as he stares past me.

"Straighten up, Savage," Arpad calls out to me.

"What?" I tug down the lapels of my shirt. "What's wrong?"

"The doors are opening."

"Shit." I curl my fingers into fists at my sides. I've faced a crowd of millions at Wembley Stadium, so compared to that, this should be a moon walk—I mean, cake walk—right? There are, what, fifty handpicked guests, at the most, in the room, all of whom I know, in one capacity or another. So why the hell are my palms damp? My stomach churns; my guts heave. "Fuck, I am going to be sick," I mutter.

"You're not." Arpad laughs

"Wait until it's your turn, you prick," I growl.

"Na-a-ah." He waggles a finger. "Not falling for the oldest trick in the book, my man. Besides, I am going to have my hands full, seeing how you cope."

"Ha-fucking-ha." I widen my stance, push my shoulders back. *Easy now. This is a walk in the park, a simple ceremony. A few minutes and it'll all be over. All you have to do is —* I turn toward the doorway, and that's when my world turns upside down.

What the hell is she wearing?

Julia steps into the room and a hush descends. The guests stop talking, sensing the presence of an angel. A goddess? The epitome of femininity, who is every fantasy I ever had. She takes a step forward and the long sweep of her leg gleams in the sunlight that chooses that moment to stream down from the open window. The ray spotlights her, bounces off the tiny stars in the thin veil that floats above her face, and entwines with her dark hair that cascades about her shoulders. The lace of her bodice encircles her neck and flows down to meet the beading that starts above her breasts; the corset cinches in, showing off her impossibly small waist before flaring over those gorgeous hips and ending at mid-thigh.

Slim thighs, made for being wrapped around my waist, the muscles moving and giving as I haul her up against the nearest door and pin her to it with my cock buried inside of her. "Fuck," I swear aloud and Arpad elbows me in the ribs. *Get your mind out of the gutter this once, will you?* But how can I stop the lascivious thoughts that run through my mind as she glides closer, closer, her arms encased in that same ivory lace that sets off the creamy skin I'd caressed not so very long ago?

And now she is baring her body to the people here. My muscles tense, my groin hardens, and something primitive coils in my chest. Lust? Jealousy? Possession? How dare she reveal herself in front of the world when the only person who is allowed to see her, feel her, hold her, make love to her, is me? *She's mine. All mine.* And no way, do I want anyone else laying their gaze on her beauty. So what, if they appreciate her? Too bad. *She belongs to me. Only me.* I take a step forward and Arpad grabs my arm.

"What are you doing?" he mutters.

"What?"

"You okay, Romeo?"

"Huh?" I shake my head to clear it. "You can let go of me. I am not going to do anything stupid.'

"You sure?" He leans in close then brushes some imaginary dust off of my shoulder. "You're not going to pick her up and run out of here, or something?"

I had considered it. I flex my fingers, feel my pocket. Good. My surprise is still there. "Nah," I wrench my shoulder from his grasp, "I'm done running." I glance up at my bride, who walks past the gathering and toward her future, "Besides there's something I need to complete first."

"You not going to do anything stupid, are you?" There's a note of concern in Arpad's voice.

"Can't promise that," I allow my lips to curl, "but whatever I do, it will make for a great headline." I focus on looking relaxed, lock my gaze with my bride's.

She comes to a stop in front of me, tips up her chin.

I glance down at the green eyes that stare up at me through the barrier of her veil. I take in her flushed features, the quivering lips, the upturned nose.

I glare at her; she trembles. She gulps, tips up her chin. I reach for her veil and raise it over her head. A sigh runs through the audience.

I bend down, press my mouth close to her ear. "Nothin' lasts forever," I whisper, and the bouquet slips from her fingers.

43

Julia

The bouquet slips from my nerveless fingers. He swoops down and grabs it before it can hit the floor. A ripple runs through the crowd. Yeah, talk about unorthodox weddings, huh? Other than the fact that I am dressed like Axl Roses' freakin' bride from November Rain, and that Damian has changed into a tux — sans tie — and fitted dress slacks, complete with pointed Italian loafers and a blue handkerchief tucked in his left breast pocket, which means that he looks like James Bond — Daniel Craig not Pierce Brosnan — with that hard jaw, mean lips and piercing blue gaze of his, which had eaten me up from the moment he'd turned and stared straight at me.

For a second there, his entire body had tensed, his features had taken on an expression of... Shock? Lust? Need? Ha, I must have been dreaming. Damian f'ing Savage would never need anything from me. No, he'd demand and simply take; and I'd let him. When it comes to the rock star, I can't say no, and hell, if that isn't the reason

I am standing here, even after that cryptic statement of his: *Nothin' lasts forever.* Does he mean us? This marriage, this relationship that never was? I open my mouth to ask, when he shakes his head.

"But—" I protest and he turns and hands the bouquet over to Isla, who steps up to take it. She moves away, and Damian faces forward. I clasp my fingers together, follow his lead to face Edward.

He glances between us, then gestures to the crowd behind us, who subside.

"We are gathered here today to celebrate the union of Damian Savage and Julia Child Andrews.

I cringe. Yep, not making that up. That really is my middle name, and now you know who my mother's hero was—a travesty, considering I can't cook… Unless you count baking clay a form of cooking, which, coming to think of it, it is.

"I believe the couple would prefer to recite their vows to each other directly, instead of having me officiate?"

We would? Eyes wide, I stare at Edward, then shoot a sideways glance at Damian who nods.

"Why didn't you warn me?" I hiss at the rock star, who curls his lips.

"You didn't ask."

"You could have told me," I whisper-scream.

"You're the one with all the answers." He turns to me, "I am sure you'll think of something. Meanwhile…"

"Meanwhile?" I mirror his stance. "What's happening, meanwhile?"

"Meanwhile, I say my vows, of course." He smiles.

"Vows?"

His grin widens. He holds out his hand, palm face up. "Take it," he coaxes me.

I glance down at his hand, then up at his face, "Is this a joke?"

"I've never been more serious." His features grow intense and his gaze narrows. He jerks his chin, and damn it, but I can't refuse him. I place my hand in his.

His warm fingers dwarf mine. He rubs his thumb over the back of my hand and my pulse rate ratchets up. His lips curl and I know he's aware of exactly how his proximity affects me. Jerk. I try to pull my arm away and he curls his fingers around my hand, holding me in place.

Then he pulls out a piece of white ribbon from his pocket.

Huh?

He proceeds to wrap the ribbon around our joined hands, once, twice, thrice, then he raises his gaze back to mine, "You changed my life from the moment I met you. When I look into your eyes, I see my future. All I want is to hold you and protect you through sickness and sorrow, through happiness and life's challenges. I promise to always take care of you, to be there for you when you need me, and when you don't, I promise not to be an ass."

The audience laughs.

"I promise to cherish you and shield you, and walk by your side through life's ups and downs. Say you'll be mine, Julia. Only mine."

I stare up into those piercing blue eyes; the darkness in his irises deepens with an intensity that's so palpable, my knees tremble. The heat of his big body reaches out to me, envelops me in a warm embrace—solid, dependable. In that moment, I believe his words, the honesty that thrums in the space between us. The vibration of something powerful, something bigger than either of us, grips me. I curl my fingers about his hand, or as much as I can reach of his broad palm.

"I will," I whisper, and his features seem to take on an expression of relief. Huh? Did he think I would refuse him and flounce off? If he only knew. "I promise to walk by your side through the good days and the bad, through ups and downs. When things get tough, there's no one else I'd rather turn to than you. When the moments of celebration arrive, there's no one else I'd rather rejoice with than you. When my spirits nose dive, and that happens quite often, I warn you—"

There's a titter from the assembled women.

"—there's no one else I'd rather have to cheer me up than you." I swallow, place my other hand over our joined palms, "for, I love you."

His throat moves as he swallows.

"I have loved you, Damian Savage, from even before I knew who you were, and when I laid my eyes on you, there was no one else."

His face pales.

"There can be no one else."

His features harden.

"But you. Only you, Damian."

Silence descends.

I glance up as he holds my gaze. A vein throbs at his temple. The skin around his eyes tightens. He searches my face with such single-minded concentration, I am sure he's memorizing my features.

"I now pronounce you husband and wife." Edward's voice sounds like it comes from somewhere far away. "You may kiss the bride."

He places his free palm over mine, then tugs. I lean in, raise my chin as he lowers his face to mine. Closer, closer. Not breaking the connection between our eyes, he presses his lips to mine.

Soft, sweet, he holds his mouth in place as he shares my breath, and holds my gaze. He's so close, I can discern the golden dot in the iris of his left eye. The crease of fine lines that radiate out from the edges of his eyes, the single grey hair at his right temple. And it's the most intimate moment of my life. And the most erotic. More than all the times that he's fucked me… For this time… Something feels different, almost as if he means his vows, as if he's trying to tell me something with his body language.

He wraps his other arm around my waist, pulls me to him. My lips part and he slides his tongue over mine. A shiver runs down my spine and desire flares low in my belly. A moan swells up my throat. An answering groan rumbles from his chest. This… This, I know. This dance is familiar. Whatever our differences, our bodies have always been in sync. I expect him to deepen the kiss, to ravage my mouth and take…and take… And he pulls back.

Huh? I flutter open my eyelids to find him staring down at me with something like wonder and bemusement and heat. I rise up on tip-toe, try to reach his mouth again.

He chuckles, then lowers his lips to mine and kisses me — softly, deeply, nerve-wrackingly, heartbreakingly, genuinely… Oh, I don't have the words to describe how it feels when he coaxes me to open my mouth and swoops his tongue inside to drink from me, suck from me, mold my body to his as he ravages my mouth, and I want him. Oh, how I want him, right there, in front of everyone. I moan, and he brushes his lips over mine again.

"Julia," he whispers against my cheek, "my beautiful bride, I—"

A shot rings through the space.

Damian

I hear the shot a second before she gasps. Her gaze widens.

"Julia?" I frown down at her.

"Damian." She shudders. "Damian, I love you."

"I know," I snap.

Her knees buckle and I twist our joined hands behind her and haul her even closer. She's so damn slim, I can barely feel her weight. "Julia, what's wrong?" I growl. Around me, the scene explodes and I am aware of the rest of the Seven moving to plant their bodies between us and the source of the shot. "Julia?" My heart begins to race and my pulse thuds at my temples. "Julia?" A wetness bleeds into my hand. I raise it, and I know what it is even before I spot the scarlet on my fingers.

"Oh, my fucking god! Julia, you're hurt."

Her eyelids flutter. "Why are you always so angry?" she whispers. "Is it me? Do you hate me Damian?"

"No." I shake my head; my throat closes. I try to yank my hand free of the binding that ties me to her and the goddam ribbon refuses to give. "Fuck, fuck, fuck."

"Don't swear." She half smiles.

I tug again and manage to pull free. I wrap my arms around her, cradle her against my chest, and she glances up at me. "I love the view from here," she says.

"And I love you," I cry out. "Julia, baby, I love you. You hear me?"

"I know." Her voice is serene. She raises a hand to my face and cups my cheek. "My beautiful man." She closes her eyes and my heart explodes in my chest.

"No!" I howl. "Fucking fuck, Julia, don't you dare die on me! You hear me?" I shake her bodily, and she coughs. She opens her eyes and I draw in a breath. The oxygen rushes to my lungs and for a second the world tilts. I righten to find she's staring up at me.

"Damian?"

"I'm here."

"Don't let go of me," she whispers.

"I won't; I promise."

She closes her eyes again, her black lashes a dark fan against her white skin. *No, no, no.* "I will not let you die. You hear me?" I scream. "Don't you dare leave me. Not after the promises you made, Julia, Flower… Please, baby."

There's a commotion, another shot going off. I gather her close, turn my back on the rest of the audience, blocking out the room… Everything else… The world.

Why didn't I learn my lesson? I lost my daughter and found Julia and refused to acknowledge what she meant to me. I'd waited until the last moment to tell her I love her. I had failed my marriage vows, broken them within seconds of making them. Typical.

"Damian?" There's a touch on my shoulder and I shake it off. "It's Weston, let me take a look at her."

"No." I shake my head, refusing to relinquish my hold on her. If I do, I'll never see her again.

"Rockstar, let me help her. I'm a surgeon, remember?" Weston's words cut through the chaos in my head. I glance over into his calm features. I know him. I can trust him with my Flower.

He nods and I lower Julia to the floor.

I kneel next to her prone body, watch as he pulls off his jacket and presses it to her wound, to stem the bleeding.

"Damian," someone grips my shoulder, "the intruder has been apprehended."

I glance up into Edward's face. "I want to see him."

Edward nods.

"I want to see the face of the motherfucker who dared take away the most precious thing in my life. I want revenge," I state in a voice that's so calm, so precise. *How the hell am I even alive when my darling wife, the love of my life, is gone?*

"I'm not sure that's advisable—"

"I will not stop until I have my revenge. You understand?"

He nods.

"Damian," Arpad squats down next to me, "the ambulance is here."

There is more commotion behind me, then a paramedic looms over us. "We need to look at her, Sir."

"No." I spring to my feet and grab the paramedic's collar, "Don't you fucking touch her."

"Damian," Arpad hauls me back, "they need to help Julia."

"Julia," I swallow, "my Flower, my wife."

"Yes," he grips my shoulder, "let them examine her."

The paramedic reaches for her and I shove away his hand. "No. Please," I beg, "don't take her away from me."

Edward grips my other shoulder, "I promise, they won't."

"No," I growl, "I don't believe you. I don't believe any of you. I need to be with her. She asked me to stay with her. I can't allow her to leave. You understand? She's all I have left, and I love her, and I didn't realize it until now. Do you understand, I—?

Edward's hand connects with my cheek and the shock of it—not only the physical impact of the slap, but that it's Edward behaving out of character again—is enough for me to loosen my grip.

Arpad and Edward drag me away. Weston steps back and the paramedics move in.

My friends keep ahold of me and I watch as one paramedic takes over trying to stem the bleeding from the wound while the other fits an oxygen mask over her face.

They strap her onto a stretcher, begin to carry her away. Edward coaxes me to follow and I force myself to put one foot in front of the other.

Isla stops us, "The press conference, the reporters…"

"Fuck the reporters," I growl.

"Let's not alienate the press," Arpad cautions.

"Fuck that," I snap, "My wife was just shot and you think I care about the world?"

He grips my neck and forces me to meet his gaze, "Take two hours," he says. "Then, you need to talk to them. Julia would want you to do this."

Right. I draw in a breath, force myself to focus, focus. "At the hospital," I finally mutter, "I'll issue a statement in two hours."

Isla nods and darts off.

I head for the doors, supported by Arpad and Edward on either side, like the fucking loser that I am. I can't even walk on my own, it seems. I twist away from their grasp; they don't protest. I stalk forward, my friends in tow, past the few remaining guests, out the open doors, down the steps, toward where the paramedics are loading in the stretcher with my life, my heart… How am I even breathing right now?

I stumble and Arpad rights me, "You okay?"

No, I never will be again.

I reach the ambulance, grab hold of the handle to pull myself inside, when another woman stops me. "The cops will need to speak with you."

I stare at her, not able to place her features.

"Karina?" Arpad steps forward.

Karina glances at him; her features tighten. "The cops," she repeats. "They need his statement."

"Not now, we need to go to the hospital," I snap.

Arpad shoots me a warning glare.

I hold his gaze for a second, then turn to Karina, "At the hospital, after the press conference."

She nods. "Three hours, no more. Also," she scowls, "the shooter was the same man who broke into your place a few months ago."

A paramedic interrupts, "Sir, we need you to get in so we can close the doors now.

"Motherfucker," I say to Karina as I pull myself into the vehicle. "I am going to make sure he goes down for a long time."

"You do that, Rockstar." She turns and heads toward the waiting cops .

I sink down into the seat next to Julia and hold her hand.

As the doors begin to close, Arpad calls out, "I'll be right behind you."

44

Julia

The darkness is so soothing, it envelops me, cocoons me. I want to stay here, and yet, something niggles at my subconscious mind. Him. Where is he? I reach for him and find nothing. Panic grips me… I need to go to him. I can't leave, not now, not when he said he loves me. He LOVES me. Of course, he'd said it under duress… On my last breath… Last breath? No, I am not dying, am I? I can't die. I don't want to die. Goddam it. I snap my eyes open and the light blinds me.

"Ow," I protest, "I hate fluorescent lights."

"Julia?" The light cuts out, to be replaced by his face—his hard chin, those high cheekbones, the skin stretched across it, now pale and with hollows under those beautiful eyes. "Julia?" His stern lips form my name and I watch, fascinated at the few grey hairs that thread his stubble.

"You're old." I cough, and my voice sounds strange, even to me.

"You're back, Julia." He turns my palm, the fingers of which are entwined with his, I now realize. He lowers his head and presses his lips to my knuckles. "Thank God, you're back."

"Where did I go?" I frown.

"Nowhere," he places his other palm over mine and presses our joined palms to his cheek, "you were right here with me, all this time."

"Where am I?" I glance around, taking in the fixtures, the clean lines, the fluorescent lights above — I had been right about that — the screen which monitors my heartbeat... Oh. "I'm at the hospital?"

He nods, "Do you remember what happened?"

I turn to him, "I was shot?"

"Left shoulder, the bullet scraped the skin."

I try to raise my left hand and a dull throbbing sensation shoots down my back. I glance down to find my arm is in a cast. "Oh," I swallow. "But I am okay?"

"More than fine." He cups my cheek, turns my face back to his. "You are going to make a complete recovery."

His blue gaze is clear, almost innocent. His hair is disheveled, the wrinkles at his eyes more prominent. The tendons of his throat move as he, once more, presses his lips to my fingers. "Damn it, Flower, I thought...you were... That you were..."

"Dead?"

He winces. "Told you never to say that word."

"And I am telling you now that I am not going to let you go so easily."

"Huh?"

"We just got married! You didn't think I was going to pop off and allow you to walk away a free man?"

He laughs, "I'd forgotten how sassy you can be sometimes."

"Sometimes?"

"Okay," he concedes, "most of the time."

"Wow." I blink at him, and he frowns.

"What?"

"Nothing."

"Tell me," he coaxes. "What were you thinking?"

"Just that, you've never agreed to my point of view so easily."

He rubs his cheek against my fingers. "Don't get used to it," he mutters.

"Of course, not." I glance at the sleeve of his tux, now ripped over his right shoulder.

"Your jacket is torn."

He glances at it, then back at me, "The same bullet that grazed you—"

"Tore through your sleeve?"

He nods.

"Ohmygod." I grip his fingers with my other hand. "Ohmygod, Damian, it could have hurt you."

"Instead, it's you who took the bullet. Meant for me," he mutters, a strange expression stealing over his face. "If something had happened to you?" His features contort. "If anything had happened to you, Flower… I'd have… Never recovered from it. I'd have killed myself."

"Hush." I place my fingers over his lips. "Now who's talking about the 'D' word, huh?"

His mouth twists. "I am allowed."

"Not on my watch." I smile.

"About that," he looks to the side, then back at me, "I have something to tell you."

The hair on the nape of my neck rises. I peruse his features, the vein that thuds at his temple, his eyes, which are clear with a decision that he'd made at some point in the last few hours while I was out cold. He strokes my hand with a fervor reserved for near-death experiences which, yeah, I admit, I'd been through. But I am here and alive and so is he, so why does he harden his jaw, lower his forehead to our joined hands as if paying homage, right before he leans over and kisses my brow? His touch——gentle, soft, caring… So not like the Damian I know.

"Baby?" I whisper, "What's wrong?"

He releases me and sits back in his chair. Why is he putting distance between us?

"Damian?" I plead, "Speak to me. Tell me what you're thinking."

"I'm sorry," he says.

"For what?"

"You're going to hate me, but later, when you are happy, and with a family of your own, you'll know that I was right."

"About what?" I try to sit up, but the goddam pillows are all at the wrong angle. "And I want to have a family with you, Damian. You know that."

"I know," he nods, "and so did I, but that was before."

My heart begins to race so fast, I am sure I'm having a cardiac. Good thing I am in a hospital, huh? And no, I am still breathing. No other pains or anything, so not a heart attack. Just this stupid oaf, trying to pull another alphaholish stunt on me, I think. "Stop it," I growl.

He looks at me with so much helplessness, so much anguish, so much regret that tears fill my eyes. "Damian, no," I choke out. "Don't do it."

"It's done." He half smiles. "I am getting the marriage annulled."

"What?"

He nods.

"This was all a mistake."

"But you love me."

"I do." He looks down at his lap, studies his hands. "I've never loved another woman as much as I do you."

"Then?" I stare, "Why… Oh!" I draw in a breath. "Oh. That's why you came to this stupid-ass decision."

The look of bewilderment on his face would be amusing if I didn't want to strangle him right now. "What do you mean?" His jaw tics. "And it's the right decision."

"It's clear that you are running scared. Typical," I snarl. "All you men who talk big and have larger-than-life personas and are fucking dominant and don't hesitate to take what you want, and when it comes to the real stuff, when the rubber hits the pavement—"

"The road," he corrects me, "when the rubber hits the—"

"Whatever!" I yell. "When it's time to face up to your true feelings and make tough decisions, you're the first to blink." I snort. "And who, exactly, is this the right decision for?" I push myself to an upright position, succeed this time, then wince when my shoulder protests.

He reaches for me, and I slap his hand away. "Don't you dare touch me."

He doesn't glare at me, simply folds his hands back in his lap, and damn it. Damian, alphahole Damian, being compliant... Bloody hell. My belly knots and the band around my chest tightens. This is not good. Not good at all.

"I made this decision in a cogent frame of mind and it's right for you," he states.

"You mean it's right for *you*," I spit out. "You're so fucking selfish. Why didn't I realize that? You're doing it just to save yourself heartbreak. So you don't have to experience the highs and lows of a relationship. You'd rather not try. You prefer to give up a chance at true love and a marriage and all the experiences you could have because... You. Are. A. Coward."

"I'm not—"

"You are," I snap. "In fact, you are so afraid of heartbreak, that you've been using your daughter as a shield all along. By pretending Riley is alive, you protect yourself not only from the pain of losing her, but also from the pain of losing anyone else."

His features harden. "You don't know what you're talking about."

I shake my head, "That's where you're wrong. I know you better than you know yourself. And, it's only now that I'm realizing why I proposed to you."

"Because you love me?"

"You actually have the audacity to throw that in my face, now?"

He glances away, then back at me. "You love me; that's why you asked me to marry you."

"Not only," I snarl. "I proposed to you, because I knew you didn't have the guts to ask me to marry you. Because I knew if I left it to you, you'd put it off, or never come around to it, or always have an excuse as to why it wasn't right for us. You'd always reduce what we have to a transaction or something where our feelings were irrelevant. It's why I took the opportunity when I saw it. Because I knew you loved me, even before you told me. Before you could even admit it to yourself. Because I *know* we are right for each other. We'd be so amazing together, Damian."

"You're wrong." His jaw firms, "I am completely wrong for you. In fact, I am the last person you should associate with."

I gape at him, then throw up my one good arm, "You're pathetic, Damian Savage, you know that? You're a wuss."

He winces, then straightens his shoulders. "Now you know." His lips twist. "Now you realize why there can't be a future for us, in any form."

I open and close my mouth. "Really?" I stare. "You're doing this now? After everything we've been through, you're backing away?"

"This is the only way."

"It's not." My eyes begin to burn.

"It is."

"Don't do this." I reach for him and he pushes his chair back.

"You promised you wouldn't leave me," I choke out through a throat gone dry.

"And you know, I never keep my promises." He holds my gaze, leaving me in no doubt of his intent. His eyes are clear, his expression vacant.

Asshole. How can he do this? How can he be so calm when my entire world is collapsing around me? "I hate you," I cry. "I wish I'd never met you in person."

"Good." He nods, as if this were his intention all along.

I gape at him. "That's all you have to say to me?" I sputter.

"Not only." He rises to his feet. "You can keep the flat." He pivots and stalks to the door, and damn him, but I can't let him go, not without saying or doing something to hurt him as much as he's hurt me.

"Tell Riley I said goodbye."

He pauses mid-step. His big body jolts as if I'd just whipped him or shot him all over again. He stays there immobile, a beat, another. Then straightens up to his full height.

"Goodbye, Julia." He heads for the doors and walks out.

45

Damian

I stare across the garden at the greenhouse. The greenery creeps up the transparent panels of the walls, to crisscross the area. It lends a spider-web kind of appearance to the entire space. A bit like my life right now. Only difference is, I am caught in a web of my own making.

How could I have fucked things up so royally? I had married her, and she had almost died. That… That says it all. If something had happened to her…? I could have never forgiven myself. For a second there, when I'd said my vows, I'd almost believed that I could make a go of it, have a happily ever after. Who the hell had I been kidding? Those kinds of happy endings don't exist for assholes like me who can't put a step forward without getting it all wrong.

There's a noise behind me. I turn to find Arpad leaning against the door of my studio.

"You?" I growl.

"Expecting someone else?"

"You're on the wrong side of the door," I mutter.

"You're on the wrong side of life, you bloody coward," he roars.

"Tell me something I don't know." I cross the floor to the settee in the far corner and sink into it. Then lift my bottle of whiskey in his direction, "Want some?"

He frowns. "Christ, Savage, it's not even noon."

"It's noon somewhere in the world."

He glares at me. "Pull yourself together."

"What does this look like?" I swig from the bottle of liquor.

My stomach protests; I ignore it. I deserve to be stinking drunk, enough that I wipe out the memory of her eyes, her face, how she'd paled when I'd announced that I was getting the marriage annulled. Hell. I raise the bottle of whiskey and swig from it again.

"Are you done destroying what little there is left of you?"

"Done?" I laugh. "I'm barely getting started." I tilt the bottle to my lips, suck on empty air. "Shit." I glance around, then lean over to place it right next to its twin, equally empty, as are all of the others that I have arranged in a line on the coffee table in front of me. "You have to admit I'm at least a tidy drunk," I mumble.

"What you are, is a bloody pussy."

"No argument from me on that." I stagger to my feet and weave my way to the bar, where I reach for another bottle of whiskey. A hand stops me… Not mine… Which means it must belong to that ass, Arpad. I follow the arm attached to it, to the face of my friend, who glowers at me. "What?" I groan. "Can't a man enjoy his liquor in peace, at least?"

He snatches the bottle from me. I reach for another. He pushes that out of my reach and I stumble around the bar toward the bottles placed against the wall.

"Don't do it," he snaps.

I raise my middle finger in the air. "I just did it."

I hear him move; the hair on the nape of my neck rises. I know he's coming for me, and I turn, but hey, guess what? All the liquor I drank has, in fact, slowed down my reflexes. Imagine that? He grabs me by my shoulder and begins to haul me toward the door of the study. "What the fuck man?" I protest, "What the hell are you up to?"

"Thank me for the fact that I still care enough to come here and haul your ass away from the path of self-destruction you are on."

He shoulders open the door and marches me down the hallway.

"So, what's new?" I laugh. "It's what I do best. Destroy everything good that ever comes into my life."

"What the hell, Savage?" He releases me so quickly that I stumble, then right myself.

"Hey, watch it," I mumble.

"No, you watch it," he yells.

My ears begin to ring. "Pipe down, man," I mutter. "If you make too much noise, you'll wake up Ri—" *Shit.* I flatten my lips.

"Riley?" His features take on a stricken look. "Damian… What are you talking about? Riley's gone. Your daughter's dead, Damian."

Of course, I know that, and yet hearing it from his mouth, makes it seem all final and real and I know then that she is never coming back. She's never going to be with me again. She's gone, and so is my love, my Flower, my Julia. She's gone, and it's my fault.

I straighten, "Thanks for letting me know." I brush down the front of my sweatshirt. "You can leave now."

"Damian, don't do this. Let's talk, at least."

"Since when do you believe in talking, huh?" I chuckle. "Thought you preferred to speak with your fists?"

"You're right." He widens his stance. "Let's take this outside, shall we?"

"Fuck that." I raise my fists, throw the first punch. He ducks. I see two of him and I think, maybe, I managed to brush the side of his face… At least, I think I did, then he plants his fist in my side and pain slices through me. I yell, "What the fuck!"

He throws another punch. I swerve, bury my fist in his stomach. He groans, doubles over. I grab his shoulders, double my knee up and into his chin, but he's too fast. He twists his shoulders, breaks free, grabs me around the waist and throws me over his shoulder. I land on my back, my head connects with the floor, and sparks explode behind my eyes. White noise thuds in my ears.

I open my eyes and see her. Green eyes, lush pink lips, that beautiful thick hair of hers flowing down toward me. "Damian?" She smiles, "What are you doing down there?"

"What are *you* doing here?" I ask.

"I belong here." She laughs. "And you belong with me." She holds out her hand. I take it.

"I love you, Damian," she whispers.

"Damian?" Hard fingers grip mine. "Damian, you with me, buddy?"

I snap my eyes open to find Arpad looming over me.

"Where did she go?" I frown.

"Who?" He hauls me to my feet.

My guts churn and my belly twists. "I think I'm gonna be sick."

Fifteen minutes later, I accept the cup of coffee Arpad hands me. I take a sip and wince when the liquid burns my lip. I deserve it, of course. That, and every punch that Arpad got in. Not that I'll ever admit that to the bastard.

"Why the fuck did you come by anyway?" I mutter.

"The cops had a breakthrough with the intruder." He tilts his head.

"Oh?"

He nods, "Turns out..." He stares at me, "You ready for this?"

My heart begins to beat faster. "What is it?" I set my jaw.

"Go on; I can take it."

"He confessed to running Stella's car off the bridge."

"What?" The breath rushes out of me and I clutch the edge of the table as if it's the only thing tethering me to this world. "He caused the accident that killed—" I can't bring myself to complete the statement.

"Seems that way." He reaches over to grip my shoulder, "Sorry buddy, I know it's a lot to take in."

I dig my fingers in my hair and pull, "And all along, I've been thinking it was my fault. That I should have stopped her from leaving after we fought. I thought if I had asked her to stay a while longer, somehow the accident would have been averted." I lower my hands to my lap, suddenly exhausted. "It wasn't me." I stare at him. "But why the hell would he do that? Why would he kill my daughter? My little girl... "Why?" My voice cracks and I curl my fingers into fists.

Arpad shifts uncomfortably. "I caught up with the other guys, and we think—" He straightens, looks me in the eye, "It's a possibility—nothing's confirmed—but we believe there's a good chance that—"

"The Mafia are involved," I finish for him.

He nods.

"Motherfucker." I slam my fist into the table and the coffee slips over the sides of our mugs. "We need to do something about this. Need to track down whoever is the brains behind this. The asspricks turned our lives upside down with the incident and now... This?" I crack my neck. "The day I get my hands on whoever is behind this," I take a deep breath then let it out, "I am going to kill the bastard."

He smiles grimly, "Get in line. At any rate, the shooter's going down for a long time for what he did."

"And the link to the Mafia? Are the police aware of it?"

He shakes his head. "Our pact on that stays in place. We keep the cops out of it and go after the Mafia ourselves. I've taken it on myself to spearhead the efforts, and by the way, you're welcome."

"For what?" I crack my knuckles, "It's about time you pulled your weight on this."

He gapes at me, "Seriously? After everything I've done for you, that's all you have to say?"

I laugh. "What else do you want me to do, kiss your feet?"

"A thanks about now would not be remiss, you wanker." He stares at me, then takes a sip of his own coffee. "At least, I can't fault your taste in this stuff." He swallows another mouthful. "You still buying that fancy Colombian coffee?

"Nope." I stare at him. "This one's Black Ivory. You know, the coffee they make from the beans that Thai elephants shit out?"

He gags, "What the fuck?" He slaps the cup on the island. "You're shitting me."

"That was the elephant shitting, actually," I retort.

He stares at me. I hold his gaze for a full second before I chuckle.

"Asshole," he growls. "Apparently, your sense of humor is still intact." He reaches for his cup of coffee, then thinks better of it. "Now that you've had your fun and games, ol' chap—"

"My fun and games, is it?" I growl. "You're the one who came into my house and proceeded to rough me up." I touch my nose—which had, thankfully, stopped bleeding after the shower and after the icepack I'd applied to it—and wince.

"Someone had to do it." He chuckles.

"No doubt, you were the first in line," I grumble. "What about the rest of the Seven?"

"What about them?" He shrugs, "They know the two of us have a special bond, considering—"

"Considering when we were kidnapped the bastards had us beat the shit out of each other on every possible occasion, until only one of us was left standing? Yeah." I roll my shoulders. "We survived it, though."

"Did we?" He stares across the table at me. "Sometimes I wonder how we would have turned out if we hadn't been kidnapped."

"And I wonder how it would have been if Riley hadn't died."

He starts, then takes in my features.

"I know... Hell, we all know how tough it's been for you since you lost your daughter, but that's no excuse for what you did to Julia."

I squeeze my eyes shut.

"You need to get your shit together and make it up to her."

"Don't tell me what I have to do to get my woman back," I snap.

"Someone has to. Considering you've got the attention of the entire media. For a man who's not even on social media, you sure manage to grab the headlines."

"Might have something to do with the fact that I recounted an annulment instead of a tête-à-tête with my newly-married bride at the much-delayed press conference that finally took place at the hospital." Yeah, I'd done that.

He laughs. "You have balls. I'll give you that. You faced them, told them the truth, misguided as it was."

"Fuckers wanted a scandal. They got it." I raise my shoulders. Fuck, if I care what the media wrote about me... But since I have their attention... I have them primed for what is going to come next. I am going to use them to get back the one thing that matters to me the most.

"Give Karina my thanks for helping out with the cops." I nod at him.

"Tell her yourself." His jaw hardens.

"Oh?" I take in his features. "What happened? You two not talking?"

"There's nothing between us," he mutters.

"That's not what I asked."

He scowls. "That's all I'm going to say on the matter."

"Hmm." Whatever there is between the two of them, it is going to turn out to be bloody entertaining to watch as it plays out. Meanwhile, I have my own shit to sort out. Namely, one gorgeous, green-eyed, dark-haired, curvy sprite to whom I have a lot to make up. I place my cup on the island, then walk past him toward the door.

"Hey," Arpad calls out, "what are you going to do now?"

"Something I should have done a long time ago."

46

Julia

I drag the needle across the surface of the clay, smoothing away some of the excess material. My hair falls over my face and I shove it out of the way. I need to get this done if it's the last thing I do. After that horrible debacle of a wedding that shouldn't have been. Thankfully, I don't have a ring from it to remember him by. Of course, he hadn't gotten a ring. Why would he? The biggest douchebag rock star in the world, and I had to fall for him. On the other hand, I have nothing to remember him by. Which is good, right? It means I can go on with my life.

Luckily, the press hadn't known who I was. They'd tried to come sniffing around after the press conference Damian had held at the hospital—or so Isla and Karina had informed me. Karina had made sure I had the maximum security possible, and even then, a journalist had been caught snooping in the corridor outside my room. She'd made sure to hustle him away, then helped me disguise myself and leave the hospital. I'd wanted to go to my apartment, but she'd told me it wouldn't be safe. The press had gotten wind of it and had parked outside. So, I'd agreed to return to Damian's apartment at The Shard. Only for the time-being, and only until this entire sordid scandal blows itself out. Oh, and this was only after she'd confirmed to me that the camera in the flat —yeah, the one in the mirror, as I had suspected—had been disabled.

As for the scandal involving me and Damian, the articles which mentioned my name were taken down almost as soon as they went up. That must have cost him a fortune... Good... I hope it cost him a lot more than the money he'd offered to pay me when we'd first met. The later articles in the media don't mention my name.

Of course, the guests and the press who'd been invited to the wedding know who I am. They know it's me that the media is talking about every time there's mention of 'the woman' Damian had married and broken up with in the space of a few hours. A few very intense hours, during which time, he'd vowed to take care of me, to cherish me, protect me, to love me…

He loves me. He'd confessed that right before he'd walked out. And I know it's true. That ass. My fingers tremble, as the sculpting needle slips from my hand, marking the surface of the likeness I've been working on. Argh! I can't do anything right, can I? I slap the sculpting tool down on the work-surface, then glance around the space. I am in Damian's apartment, surrounded by the memory of how he'd fucked me, working on his bust, and I think I am going to get over him here? Ha! Fat chance. I've set myself up for failure, as always. I cover the piece I am working on.

I head to the bathroom to wash my hands. Then grab my purse, and coat, change into my sneakers, and march out of the apartment. I leave the building and keep going. I need to simply get away from everything that reminds me of him… Need to move out as soon as possible. Need to… Forget how he kissed me, touched me, shared his secrets with me… Told me how he'd loved his daughter… Allowed me a glimpse of how he mourns for her.

Jesus, the man had taken the passing of his daughter to heart when he hadn't been fully over being kidnapped as a child himself.

Still, none of that forgives what he did to me. It doesn't. So why the hell am I still thinking of him?

I stalk past the homeless man on the sidewalk who calls out to me. "Hello there, young lady."

"Hello," I mumble back.

"I have something for you."

"Not interested," I snap.

"I promise, it's something you need to see."

"I promise it's not anything I need in my life right now."

"It's from Damian."

"Eh." My feet skid on the pavement, I stumble forward, manage to steady myself, then turn around. "What did you say?"

"It's Damian." He holds out his phone to me. "You should see this."

I stomp back, grab the phone—guess homeless people do own phones, right? I'm not being judgmental or anything—open my mouth to ask, but he tips his head to the screen. "Don't miss it," he says.

I glance down, catch a glimpse of Damian on the feed of his social media account, huh? When did he reactivate that? He's in what I recognize as his greenhouse. I peer at the screen, taking in the shrubs, the flowers…the yellow daffodils that grow in profusion from the pots, the hanging urns, the trough in the background. It's early in the year for them, so how did he manage to coax them to blossom from almost every available surface?

He stares into the screen and I swear it's as if he's glancing straight at me, into my eyes, my soul.

"This is for you, Riley." He strums his guitar, then begins to sing.

Would you know me
    If I saw you from afar?
    Would it be the same
    If you held my hand again?

. . .

I must stay on
    And live as if it counts,
    Even though nothing matters
    Now that you are gone.

For I won't see you run across a field,
    Grow up to become a teen,
    Smile up at me
    As I kiss you goodnight.

I'll move forward,
    Through seconds, minutes, days…
    'Cause I know I just can't stay
    Hidden behind the veil.

Time. Will it heal?
    Can it conceal?
    Will it allow me to embrace
    What you meant to me?

Can I ever forgive myself
    For not knowing you better?

He stops playing, stares into the camera. "My name is Damian Savage, and I am a failed rock star. I was also once a father." He swallows, "I lost my daughter, Riley, in a car crash that also killed her mother."

I gasp. Oh, my God, he's sharing his story with the entire world.

"That was a year ago." The tendons of his throat flex. "I have mourned her since. I opted to stay in my grief, unable to let go of her memories and move on. I was on a path to self-implosion until an angel crossed my path."

I clap my palm to my mouth. Oh, wow, what is he saying? What is he doing?

His lips kick up, "She was the most incredible thing that had happened to me in a long time. One look at her and I was gone. I knew she was it for me. The chance to crawl out of the darkness I had spent so long in." He pauses, "But you know me." He raises his arm. "Asshole that I am, I fucked it up." He grips the neck of his guitar. "I hurt her. I allowed my flower to wither without keeping up my promise to protect her from the elements. I failed her."

A ball of emotions chokes my throat.

"I walked away from her. I broke her heart. I failed myself." His jaw tics. "You told me, Flower, that I was a coward, that I could not face up to the reality of my emotions." He draws in a breath, "You're right." He leans forward, the skin around his eyes stretching. "This is me saying that you were absolutely, 100% accurate. About everything." He chuckles. "I suck, babe. I am not worthy of your attention. Not at all… But if you're listening to this, and I hope you are… And if anything in what I said strikes a chord, then come to me." He seems to choke, "I'll be waiting." He swallows. "I love you."

The camera switches off.

I stare at the blank screen. "How dare he?" I scowl. "How dare he do this?"

"Impressive, huh?" The homeless man crows, "A rock star laying out his heart like that on social media?"

"A gimmick. That's what it is," I rage.

"Is it?" He frowns, "The man sounded sincere."

"He's a bloody liar," I growl. "How dare he…he do this?"

"Maybe he wants you back?" The homeless man ventures.

"The bastard left me…" I begin to pace, "and now… Now… He dares go on record, in front of everyone and…"

"Profess his love?"

"Exactly." I grip the phone in my hand. "That…that conniving, full-of-himself, ready to spot a chance to promote himself—"

"Hold on." The homeless man blinks. "It took courage to do that.

Maybe he wanted you to know he meant it and this was his way of showing how serious he was?"

"By professing to love me on social media?"

"Considering he hasn't been on social media in over a year, is there a better way he could have shown how important you are to him?"

"He could have called me."

"Would you have taken the call?"

"N…no." I stare down at my shoes. "But d…did you hear him?"

"I did," he nods, "I think he meant every word."

"He asked me to come to him…"

"Right before he said he loves you."

"I never doubted that," I growl.

"So then?" He stares at me.

"So what?"

"What are you still doing here?" He raises an eyebrow.

"Why the hell should I go to him? He should come to me… That… That ass."

"Aha," he exclaims.

"What's that 'aha' for?" I say suspiciously. "I don't like the sound of that 'aha' at all."

"So, you have as much of an ego as him, huh?"

"Of course, not," I counter. "I mean, I do… But not as much as him."

"So, you're going to let your ego get in the way?" He raises an eyebrow, "Everything you want is right there, and you're going to do a 'Damian' and flounce off?"

"He wouldn't flounce," I point out. "And you don't play fair."

"Ha," he chortles, "knew it. I knew you were a better woman than that…douchebag of a rock star."

"Hey" I snap, "Don't call him a douche."

His eyes twinkle.

I flush. "Fine, you've made your point."

"Go on, then." He nods, "Go get your man."

I turn to leave, and he calls out, "My phone."

"Oops! Sorry." I pivot, hand the phone over, then begin to run.

Hold on… The phone… It was a top-of-the-line, latest model iPhone. A homeless man couldn't afford that, could he? I stop, turn around and find... He's gone? Hell. I glance around to find he's hurrying up the street. And why the hell had I spilled my guts to a stranger? Why had it been so easy to talk to him? Why the hell had he felt so familiar? And how the hell had he known that Damian had been talking about me, huh?

"Hey," I call out, "who are you?"

He pauses and looks back. "No-one of consequence."

"I don't believe that," I shout back.

"You have a date with a rock star. Don't be late," he admonishes, then turns and continues to walk away.

"Weird." I shake my head, then spot a cab. "Taxi," I hail the driver, who pulls up to the curb. I grab the handle, open the door and slide in. "How fast can you drive?"

47

Damian

I place my guitar on the settee that I had pulled into the greenhouse with Arpad's help. Before leaving, he'd also helped me arrange the daffodils about the place in such a way that they couldn't be missed. He'd offered to help shoot the video but I'd refused. Somehow it hadn't felt right having anyone else in this space with me as I prepared for the most important performance of my life. Now it is done; the video is out there. My song, that I'd been working on for the past few days—the one I had started writing, not quite sure what it was about… I still don't dare pull apart what the words mean. Being with Julia has given me the courage to push forward, to trust my instincts again. If I could make her come, if I could coax her to fall apart so beautifully under my fingers, then I can trust myself to pour what I feel into words… I can trust the world to understand what I mean… And if they don't… If they hate it… Well, then… I've done my best. I've given myself in the truest way an artist can do, and the rest… Well, it is out of my hands anyway.

I rise to my feet and begin to pace… It has only been ten minutes since the video went live; my phone had begun to buzz almost immediately. No doubt, the media is reaching out.

It looks like I'll need to reach out to Summer and take her help in managing my PR, after all. After years of turning my back on everything career related, while pretending to go on as if I weren't self-sabotaging myself, guess it's time to face the music after all—pun intended.

I glance at the feed of the security camera pointed at my gate. Where is she? Why hasn't she come yet? A car drives up to the gate, an unknown car, and a man—a reporter?—gets out. I watch as the guards that Karina posted at my gates ask him to leave. At least, I won't be bothered here. I'd known once the video went live that the press would be all over me. It's why I'd ensured there was extra security. It's also why this is the safest place for me to be now… And I had asked her to come—I stiffen.

I had asked her to come to me. After I'd walked out on her, I'd still demanded that she return, that she take the initiative. Shit, I really am a complete prick. A wanker of the first order. Why the hell should I expect her to come? Am I hiding again, in my fortress, trying to avoid the real world? No, that's not it. I had gone live to the world for the first time… Hell, I had set up my social media profiles again, just for that. I am going to face the fallout from this, one way or the other…so. No, it's not…that…but clearly, I hadn't been thinking right… I have to make amends for what I did. I have to go to her. I stalk out of the greenhouse to the garage, where I climb onto my motorcycle. Kicking it to life, I gun it down the driveway, through the space between the still-opening gates. I spot one of the security guards racing for his car to follow me as I drive past the cars pulling up. More media, no doubt. I race toward Julia.

Half an hour later, I pull into the parking garage of The Shard. I park my bike, wrench my helmet from my head, and race for the elevators, bursting into the apartment a few minutes later. Even before I cross the floor of the living room, I know it's empty. "Fuck!"

I walk over to the bedroom, check the closets; they're empty. I check the bathroom—there is no sign of her toiletries. I stalk over to the terrace by the pool—also empty. I walk back to the living room, glance about the space. "Fuck, fuck, fuck."

I missed her. Again. I should have come earlier. Should have not walked out on her at the hospital. Should have held her close and never let go, and now… It is too late. "F-u-c-k!" I fling my helmet on the floor, where it bounces once before rolling to the side. I tear off my gloves, then dig my fingers in my hair and tug; pain lances across my scalp. My knuckles hurt and my face still hurts from the earlier altercation with Arpad. My chest hurts.

I stare about the room, wanting, needing, something to vent my anger on. I stalk toward her worktable, where she's covered something with a burlap cloth and pull it off.

"What the—?" I stare at the likeness of myself.

I'd known that she was working on it... and while it is me… There's no mistaking those familiar features, the hair, the mouth, those ears...Yet, it is not. I look larger than life. A dominant male, one with intent writ in every nook and crevasse on his face, and yet, those eyes… There's something in them I don't see often. Something I don't allow myself to feel…

Hope. A light in the darkness, a simple optimism that things will get better, there will be a tomorrow and things are always meant to be as they are now. I can't take my gaze off of the sculpture, which she created from memory, and her bare fingers.

I gulp. A hot sensation stabs at my chest. Jesus, I've been such a fucking fool. A complete and utter wanker. I reach out a finger to touch the sculpture when I hear her voice.

"It's not that great, I know... I've been working on it. I'm just not that good yet—" I turn on her and she stops.

"You're right; it's not great." I stare at her and she tips her chin up.

"I… I hope you don't mind that I worked on it." She swallows. "I did ask you to pose but then… Things happened and—"

"I do mind," I snap.

She freezes. "I didn't realize it was such a big deal to you that I captured your likeness."

"It is though." I stalk toward her, and she takes a step back. "It's a very, very big deal that you spent your time molding a piece of life-less clay into my features."

"Fine," she says stiffly, "I'll throw it away."

"You will not," I growl.

"No?" She scowls. "You're confusing me now."

"Good," I come to a stop in front of her, "because you've confused me from the moment I set eyes on you."

She draws in a breath then surveys my features. "Why are you here, Damian?"

"Why do you think?"

She walks past me, heads for the bust, "I… I don't know." She drops her backpack on the ground next to her, shrugs out of her coat and flings it aside. "Either way, I am done here."

"Are you now?"

She nods. "You made it very clear to me in the hospital that you didn't want anything to do with me."

"Did you see the video that I recorded?" I glare at her.

"What if I did?" Ignoring the bust, she walks over to the potter's wheel that I had set up for her, in my apartment, where she still is. She flips the switch so it begins to turn, then grabs a lump of clay and places it in the center of the wheel.

"You have nothing to say about it?" I frown.

"It was a beautiful song, if that's what you want to know. The lyrics made me cry. It brought out all of your pent-up grief over Riley in a way that is deeply moving," she replies, her tone sincere. "I think it's your best work so far."

"Thanks to you," I reply. "You showed me how to dig deep inside and channel my emotions into words. If it hadn't been for you, I couldn't have written that."

Her shoulders freeze. She leans forward, dips her fingers into the bowl of water and cups it around the clay. The thrum of the wheel fills the space; the slurp of her flesh against the clay reaches me. I prowl over to her, watch over her shoulder as she bends in concentration, her gaze focused on the beauty taking shape under her fingertips. She scoops up some water, dribbles it on the clay again.

I reach past her, dip my fingers in the bowl of water, then splash it in her face.

"Hey," she protests, "don't do that."

I cup more water in my palm, hold it over her hair. It drips down her face, splatters on her shirt, molding the fabric to the curve of her breasts.

"What the—" She glances down at herself, then flicks her hand and clay splatters across the front of my jacket.

"Stop that," I admonish her; just as the clay instantly droops in the center of the wheel.

"Look what you did now!" she cries.

"Hmm." I glance down at the wheel, then back at her, "Maybe I should rectify it?"

"What do you mean?"

"Scoot forward."

"What?"

"Do it," I order.

She scowls, then moves closer to the worktable.

I shrug off my jacket and toss it aside, then swing my leg over the seat.

48

Julia

He fits his big body behind mine in that narrow seat and the heat of his body instantly envelops me. His powerful thighs bracket me from either side. He has to bend his knees to fit into the space, and the result is that he squeezes me even tighter in the 'V' between his legs.

"Wh…what are you doing?" I gulp.

"Nothing." He leans forward and the planes of his chest mold against my back and the hardness at his crotch throbs against my hips. I'm instantly wet.

"Damian," I protest, "I…need to continue with my—"

His warm breath whispers against my ear and I shudder.

"Continue with your—?" he prompts.

"With, uh—" I glance down at the now-shapeless piece of clay. What was I going to do? Oh, yeah, I was going to pretend to work on my next piece, in the hope that he'd leave, but clearly, he's not. "With my work," I respond.

"You go right ahead, Flower," he murmurs, "I am going to be an innocent spectator."

"Innocent, my ass." I swipe up the clay, mash it up, then smack down the ball as close to the center of the wheel's base as I can. With the weight of my body acting as a brace, I begin to mold the clay.

He watches from over my shoulder for a few seconds, then reaches out to align his arms over mine. The skin of the insides of his arms slides over mine; I shiver. He wraps his big palms over each of mine, that are wrapped around the clay. A ripple of sensations bursts from the contact and travels up my arm. My nipples harden; my inner thighs flex. "Damian," I whisper.

"When you say my name like that," he swallows, "I'd do anything for you. I'd tear the world down to protect you…. I'll never forgive myself for putting you in a position where someone could hurt you."

The intensity of his tone whispers across my nerve endings. All of my senses seem to pop at once. "That wasn't your fault," I reply.

"If I hadn't agreed to marry you, if I hadn't decided to turn the entire ceremony into a media circus, you wouldn't have been shot."

"It was barely a scratch." I can't stop the faint smile from curving my lips. There—this is the Damian I've come to know. The sensitive, caring man under all that bluster he wears for the outside world. The part of himself that he's revealed to me over and over again, only to retreat. "Besides, you forget something."

"What's that?" He crowds me further, if that were possible, so his front is plastered to me from chest to crotch, his thighs molded to mine, his arms and fingers flattened to mine…

I am surrounded by him, drowning in that edgy masculine scent of his. My mouth waters, and I swear, if I turn my head and offer him my lips, he'll take them at once… But not yet. First, I need to tell him something. "You didn't have a choice," I declare.

I sense him scowl. "About what?" he asks.

"I wouldn't have taken no for an answer," I retort.

The muscles of his thighs flex, his shoulders inch forward and his entire body seems to curve around me, protectively, half-threateningly… In that way that is overpowering and dominant and oh-so sexy.

"Is that right?" he purrs.

I nod. "I would have married you, one way or another."

There's silence, filled only with the smooth clatter of the wheel.

Then he laughs. A glorious, easy, mirth-filled laugh that rolls across my body, and arrows straight to my core.

"I have no doubt." He places his chin on top of my head. "I knew you were going to be trouble. I just hadn't realized how persistent you were going to turn out to be."

"Someone had to be," I mutter, "considering you refused to acknowledge what was there right in front of you all this time."

He places his mouth close to my ear, "And what was that?"

"That you can't live without me."

"Oh?"

"That you need me."

"Hmm."

"That you're the only one for me."

His fingers squeeze mine and the clay tumbles over again. "Now look what you've done," I huff. "I'll have to start all over again."

"Will you let me do the same?"

I freeze, stare at the shapeless lump of clay on the wheel that swirls in front of me. "What do you mean?" I whisper.

"I mean, can we start over again, you and me?"

There it is. The words I wanted to hear, and it's a start, but I want more.

"When you said your wedding vows, did you mean them?"

"You know I did." He reaches past me and throws the switch that shuts down the momentum of the wheel.

In the silence that descends, I can hear my heartbeat. Or is that his? "And yet, you walked away from me. You left me when I needed you most."

"I had to," he insists. "Don't you see? If I had let you stay, I would have only hurt you more. The way I hurt my daughter. Hell, even the mother of my child, who I should have treated better."

My belly clenches and a burning sensation fills my chest. Shit, why am I jealous of a woman who is already dead?

"None of that was your fault."

He laughs, the sound hard. "My rational mind realizes that, but tell that to my heart, Flower. The thought of being without you, of living with the guilt of something happening to you is a powerful motivator. It makes me want to spirit you away somewhere, away from the eyes of the world, where nothing and no one can harm you."

I close my eyes; my pulse thuds at my temples. This man. Only he can string together words to form a sentence that punches me straight in the gut. I turn my face, so my lips are next to his. "Then do it," I say. "Hide me away where no one else can see me but you, no one else can touch me but you, no one else can make love to me but—"

He closes his lips over mine.

49

———————

Damian

I'd raced to her with the intent of talking to her, making sure she knows how I feel, but one glance at her gorgeous features, a whiff of that delectable feminine scent of hers, a single touch of her skin, and I am a goner. I need to hold her close, kiss her lips, nibble my way down her body and lick my way up every single curve to reassure myself that she is still with me. I slide my tongue inside her mouth, suck on her essence and kiss her, drawing her breath into every part of me. The blood rushes to my groin, the pulse pounding in my balls. I cup her cheek, hold her in place as I kiss her. She moans low in her throat, strains against my chest. I fold my arms over hers and wrap them around her body, holding her immobile. She wriggles her hips, thrusting back and into the cradle of my hips. I can't stop the growl that rips from me. "Jesus, Flower, you're so damn responsive."

She arches her spine back, rolls her head into my shoulder. I release her arm, only to cup her breast and squeeze.

She whimpers and the sound goes straight to my head. I pinch her nipple through the wet cloth that clings to her curves and she cries out.

"Who does this belong to?" I ask.

"You, Damian," she mumbles.

I drag my hand down to cup the flesh between her legs. "Who does your pussy belong to, Flower?"

"You," she gasps. "Only you."

"You drive me crazy, you know that?" I growl.

She moans again, turns her head, reaches for my mouth with hers, but I pull back. I reach over, scoop up some of the slip and smear it across her chest, around her breasts, outlining her nipples. I survey the results, then nod. "Now that's my idea of a bust."

She glances down, then chuckles. "Not very artistic, but it'll do."

"I've been dying to do that since you first told me that you were a clay artist."

"So, I'm an artist now, huh?"

"You were always one to me," I say. "You were always more creative than me," I correct myself.

She turns around, takes in my features, "You don't mean that." She frowns. "Your songs, your words…"

"Are meaningless without you." I hold her gaze. "I began a band out of some twisted sense of rebelling against the world, and what it had done to me."

"The incident?" she ventures.

"I was older than the rest of the Seven, when we were kidnapped. Not as susceptible to the mind games, and physically, in better shape."

"That's why they made you fight?"

"For their pleasure." I stare out of the window. "Initially, they pitted me against Arpad. We had to fight until one or both of us lost consciousness. It became a game for the two of us, how to keep hitting each other, without hurting the other too much, but making it believable enough for our kidnappers to buy it. When they caught on, I took the blame for it."

"You?" She swallows.

"Arpad was much smaller than me at that time. No way, would he have survived whatever twisted plan they had in mind."

"What…what did they do next?" she whispers.

"They blindfolded me, took me to an underground fighting ring, where they pitted me against men stronger than me. I fought them, of course. I wouldn't back down. I wasn't going to die there, that much I knew."

"Then you were found?"

I nod. "The cops got a lead, tracked us down, sprung us, we went home, end of story."

"Or the beginning?"

I draw in a breath, glance down at her. "The rest of the Seven went through a lot more mind games than me. No wonder it warped them completely."

"But the experience changed you too…"

"Of course." I wipe my hand across my face, "I came out full of anger and with a taste for sparring, which you already know."

"But it hurt you in ways you didn't realize…" She presses her palm to my cheek and I turn into her touch.

"Not until much later. Apparently, the shock of what had happened to me manifested with another trigger."

"Riley," she replies.

"My daughter," I nod. "When I confirmed that Stella was pregnant with my child, it was a complete shock." I rub the back of my neck. "I wasn't ready for a family, or for a relationship with her, but I knew I had to do what was right. I wanted my daughter to have a stable home, but I knew I couldn't be around to provide it. So, I found an apartment for the two of them and I paid for whatever they might need so that Stella could take care of Riley."

"So, did you see Riley on weekends?" She tilts her head, "Or on certain days of the week, maybe?"

I shuffle my feet. "We didn't have a formal arrangement, as such. My career was just taking off. I spent more time away than at home. Whenever I was in town, I made it a point to see both of them, but with the schedule of tours I had, it became more and more infrequent." I rub the back of my neck. *Bloody hell, I'd been such an ass.* I could have gotten to know my daughter better; instead, I'd run from my responsibilities.

"Stella became increasingly frustrated. It wasn't enough for her that I provided all the material requirements for her and Riley."

"She wanted more?"

"Understandably," I reply. "I thought I had been clear from the beginning. I wasn't interested in a serious relationship with her, but I can see where she might have started to believe I might come around to the idea. She was the mother of my child, so we functioned as co-parents, but only insofar as I paid for everything and she took care of Riley."

She stares at me and I wince, "I know, I know." I rub the back of my neck, "I thought if I threw enough money at the problem it would suffice, that I could buy my way into my daughter's life." I raise my hands, "It was a mistake." *One I have regretted every day since.*

"We began fighting more. I barely saw Riley, even when I was in town, preferring to conform to my rock star image by carousing about town."

"I saw the headlines," she remarks.

I grimace. "It wasn't pretty. Then, after one particularly vicious argument, during which she told me exactly what she thought of my fathering skills, she took Riley and walked out. I think she had planned to leave Riley with me for the night, but I was such a jerk... She accused me of being insensitive. She told me that paying for everything wasn't enough. I needed to be more present in my daughter's life."

I press the heels of my palms to my eyes.

"She threatened to take Riley and leave me. Told me I probably wouldn't even notice. The worst thing is, she was probably right. I was furious. I knew she was upset and I shouldn't have let her drive. But I was so angry." I squeeze my eyes shut. The ball of hurt in my chest grows bigger, wider, until it seems to consume all of me and I shudder. Tears prick the backs of my eyes. "I should have stopped her. I should have been the father Riley needed me to be. Instead, on her sixth birthday, I stood over a rock with her name engraved on it, and cried."

She makes a sound deep in her throat. "Oh, Damian." She wraps her arms around my neck and pulls me close until our lips meet. She kisses my mouth, my cheeks, reaches up to kiss me across my closed eyelids.

"The memories of those we love don't fade; they become a part of us. They're imprinted in our cells, in everything we do, and as time passes, everything you do, they do with you," she whispers against my skin. "You did the best you could at the time; it does no good to look at the past and berate yourself. You need to forgive yourself for what happened, Damian."

"I'm sorry I tried to make our relationship transactional, sorry I tried to turn what was between us into a business arrangement. Can you ever forgive me for that, Flower?"

"Shh!" She presses her fingers across my lips, "It's forgiven. You are a good man Damian, and you tried your best to be a good father. We can only work in the moment with the information we have. The rest is not really in our hands, is it?" She cups my cheek, "Behind that alphaholish persona is a sensitive man who feels deeply, who cares a lot about those in his life. It's what makes you the kind of artiste whose words resonate with millions. Don't ever lose that, Damian."

I glance down into her serious green eyes, "When did you become so wise?"

"Just the life I've lived, I guess." She laughs lightly. "I ran away to broaden my horizons, and came back with the realization that everything I needed was right here." She takes my hand and places it over her heart, "Know what I mean?"

"I do." I tuck a strand of hair behind her ear. "Will you ever forgive me, for everything I put you through?"

"On one condition." Her lips kick up. "Make love to me."

50

———

Julia

His gaze intensifies. He lowers his head and kisses me—softly, sweetly, then with increasing urgency. The world tilts and I open my eyes to find he's on his feet. He lifts me up, then walks inside to the bedroom. He lowers me to my feet in front of the bed, then whips off his T-shirt.

I rake my gaze down his ripped eight-pack and gasp. "What's that?"

His lips quirk, "What do you think it is?"

I close the distance to him, then run my fingers across the cursive tattooed over his heart.

The font is the same as the one he'd used to ink Riley's name on his forearm.

"You inked my name on your chest?" I finally ask.

"I got it before the wedding and never got to show it to you. Every time I saw it, it only made me feel worse about walking out on you the way I did."

"Oh." My heart flips in my chest.

"I didn't realize what I was going to do, not until I'd walked into the tattoo parlor and found myself under the needle. I knew then, what I wanted inked into my skin. I hadn't even told you how I felt yet, but somehow, it felt right, you get me?" He tilts his head, "I had to do something to show you that you are part of me. Then," he squeezes his eyes shut, "I walked out on you at the hospital." The tendons of his throat move as he swallows. "When I realized what a fool I'd been, how I'd hurt you, even that gesture didn't seem enough."

"That's why you declared your feelings on social media?" I raise my gaze to his.

He cracks open his eyelids and that fiery blue gaze of his fills my line of sight. "I had to do something to make up for the anguish I caused you."

"What you did," I swallow, "it was incredibly brave of you. And moving… No one's ever done something like that for me," I glance back down at my name written across his chest, "or like this."

"And no one else ever will."

I lean up on tip-toe and kiss him. "You're crazy, you know that?"

"Crazy in love with you." He deepens the kiss, then bends his knees and grips the backs of my thighs. I climb him, wrap my legs around him, throw my arms around his shoulders and open my mouth to him.

He reaches the bed, lowers me onto the mattress then follows me down and covers my body with his. I cling to him, dig my heels into his back, drag my fingers down his thick neck.

He leans back, then reaches between us to grip the lapels of my shirt. He rips it and I gasp.

"Old habits." His lips kick up. "I'd apologize for it, but I happen to know that it turns you on."

I chuckle, "So bloody cocky! Even when you're apologizing to me, you're full of yourself."

"And you love it." He lowers his head and kisses me deeply.

I reach down between us, unzip his pants. "Take them off," I demand, "I want to have you naked on me."

He raises one eyebrow, but complies.

I release him long enough for him to straighten. He toes off his boots, then shoves down his jeans and his boxer briefs. He stands still, allowing me to appreciate the full expanse of his chest, his narrow abdomen, the thickness of his cock that juts up against his lower belly, those powerful thighs, peppered with hair, the thick calves, and those beautiful feet that move toward me as he takes a step forward. He reaches down, pulls off my sneakers and socks, then unzips my jeans and pulls them off. I pull off the remains of my shirt and toss it away then lie back as he looks his fill. He rakes his gaze down my breasts, to the hollow between my legs. His nostrils flare. He curls his fingers around his thick shaft and pumps it once. The piercing glints against the almost-purple flesh. Moisture glistens at the tip and an answering dampness pools between my thighs. I part my legs, hold out my arms. "Come to me, baby, please."

He swoops down, covers my body with his. Oh, that solid weight of his. I've missed it. I draw in a breath and my senses explode with his scent. My core clenches and I can't stop the groan that bleeds from my lips. He pushes up on his elbow, reaches between us to grip himself, and positions his dick against my entrance. He peers into my face, holds my gaze. "I love you," he whispers, then pistons his hips forward, impaling me.

A jolt runs up my spine as the width of his hips forces me to widen my stance even more. "Ohmygod," I gasp, "Damian."

He grips the back of my thigh, loops my knee over his arm, and folds my leg up and to the side.

The new position allows him to slide in even deeper, until he bottoms out against my pelvic bone. Ripples of heat, sensations of pleasure, coil in my core and I swear more moisture fills my channel.

"I can't," he says through clenched teeth, "can't hold on Flower. You're too tight, too much."

I take in the gleam of sweat on his forehead, the color that smears his cheeks, the tendons of his throat that strain, as he holds himself immobile.

I flex my inner muscles around him and a growl rumbles up his chest. "Julia," he warns, "if you do that again, I—"

I clench around his cock and a shudder grips him. His shoulder muscles bunch and his lips twist, "I am going to fuck you now, babe." He pulls out, then thrusts forward with such force that my entire body moves up the bed. He plunges into me again and again, and the bed slams into the wall.

"Damian." I lock my arms around him, strain against his massive chest, as he pounds into me.

He lowers his forehead to mine, stares into my eyes. "Come with me," he commands as he buries himself inside me with a powerful thrust that sends a jolt of pleasure twisting up my spine. I throw my head back, tip my chin up and can't stop the scream that boils up. He closes his mouth over mine, absorbs it as I shatter completely.

He pumps into me again and again. His muscles tense, his shoulders bunch under my arms, then with a hoarse cry, he empties himself inside of me. His climax seems to go on and on, as my body trembles in the aftermath of my own orgasm. I hold him close as he buries his face in the crook of my neck. His big body covers mine as his muscles twitch with the aftershocks.

Finally, he flips onto his back, and takes me with him so I am positioned on his chest.

I press my cheek into the hard planes, count the beats of his thundering heart, as he folds his arms about me, enclosing me in his heat.

"Thank you," he whispers, and twines his fingers with mine.

"For what?" I turn to stare up at his face. This view... I'll never get used to it.

"For being yourself," he replies. "For putting up with me. For taking me back."

I chuckle. "OMG, the alphahole being this polite?" I shake my head, "I bet it's going to be sunny today."

As if in response, sunlight slants in through the windows and lights up the space with a bright yellow glow.

"The bust?" he asks after some time has passed. "I want it."

"It's terrible," I tell him. "I can do better than that."

"It's perfect." He smirks, "You didn't think I was going to allow you to throw away my likeness, did you?"

I slap his shoulder.

"No, seriously." He opens one eye. "You cut through all of the macho bullshit and revealed a part of me that I have never acknowledged."

"It's your strength," I say quietly, "that you feel things so deeply. It's what makes your work so different."

"Only as long as you are with me." He cups my cheek, "Say you'll be by my side, wife?"

"Wife?" I blink. "The marriage?"

"I didn't annul it." He swallows.

"You didn't?" I sit up. "But the headlines?" I ask.

"All speculation. You know how the journalists are." He pulls me back to his chest.

"And you encouraged the conjecture?"

"I didn't do anything to stop it. I was too busy beating myself up for not being able to protect you."

"But you told me..." I frown.

He shakes his head.

"But—"

He presses his finger to my lips, "I tried... God help me, I truly wanted to, but I couldn't bring myself to do it." His tone dips. "You belong to me, and while logic told me that I had to let you go, my heart... My heart insisted I shouldn't." He frames my face, and gazes into my eyes. "My soul was already yours. You're my muse, Flower. You are inside of me, imprinted in my every cell, you are the reason for my existence."

Warmth fills my chest. I stare up, knowing that he's speaking the truth, that he's never been this open, this completely bare as he is in this moment.

"I belong to you and there is no way I could knowingly sever the bond between us." His lips kick up in a smile that illuminates his features. "Besides, you don't think I'd let you go, not after I have you where I want you, do you?"

"And where is that?"

"By my side; always mine."

EPILOGUE

Julia

For Riley Alice Savage who loved this park
Forever in my heart

"It's beautiful." I glance from the epitaph on the bench in Waterlow Park to the stern profile of the man at my side. Damian stares down at the bench, his features reflecting complete focus. His gaze is trained on the bench, yet his eyes are unfocused. Is he recalling her as he last saw her, the day her mother took Riley from him and left? Or is he remembering the happier times when he read to her, played with her in this park, watched movies with her? He's told me that those were the best times they had together as father and daughter, when he'd put her to bed and read to her.

"She was beautiful." He exhales, then turns to me, "You're beautiful." His lips tip up. "Riley will always be with me." He wipes the tear that slides down my cheek, "But you Flower, you are my present and my future."

"Oh, Damian." I rise up to my tip-toes and press my lips to his throat. I wrap my arms around his neck, bury my face in his chest. His heartbeats mirror mine as he folds me in his arms. He kisses the top of my head. "I mean it Julia. I am never letting you go."

I tip my chin up, peer into his gaze. "There's nowhere else I'd rather be than right here by your side."

He presses his lips to my forehead, "I love you Julia Child Andrews." He peruses my features, an intent look in his eyes.

My heart begins to race and my pulse rate ratchets up.

He releases me, only to slide his hand into his pocket. Then he bends his knee into the ground, holds up a ring, "Be mine."

"Oh." Sensations course through my veins and my stomach trembles. I glance down at the platinum ring with the emerald in the center, surrounded by tiny pink stones. It is simple, joyous, gorgeous, and so utterly charming and so...so perfect.

He holds out his palm and I place my hand in his. He slips the ring onto my finger. "The green is for your eyes, the pink..." he swallows, "the pink is for —"

"Riley," I whisper.

He nods. "She'd have loved to meet you. She'd have loved you."

"I would have loved her. And I love you, Damian." I swallow the ball of emotions in my throat. "You think she'd have approved of us?"

He rises to his feet and pulls me to him. "She'd have enjoyed getting to know you better." He presses another kiss to the top of my head. More tears prick the backs of my eyes. Oh, hell, the last thing I want to do is to blubber. I wind my arms around his lean waist and press myself closer.

We stay that way for a few seconds...maybe minutes. Around us, the wind whistles through the leaves. The screams of boys playing ball reach us, then the barking of a dog, which fades away. Silence a beat, another.

"I'm sorry I didn't tell you about her earlier," he says. The vibrations of his deep voice, rumble up his chest. "I wanted to... Many times, I wanted to share everything about my life with you... But it felt too early, and I didn't want to scare you off... God knows, I was trying to figure out what I felt toward you myself."

"I think... I may have subconsciously guessed," I finally breathe out.

He stills, then pulls back enough to glance down at me. "You did...?" He frowns.

I tip my head back, "Not consciously. I mean, I wanted to meet Riley, but every time I asked about her, you kept deflecting, and that only made me more curious."

"Of course, it did." He chuckles, "I should have known that a sassy little thing like you would not have stopped until you'd uncovered the truth."

"I am sorry I burst into her bedroom like that... I shouldn't have invaded your privacy but—"

"I'm glad you did." He smirks, "You can invade my privacy anytime you want, baby."

"Argh." I shake my head. "Guess that's a sign that you're feeling yourself again, huh?"

"When I'm with you, I always feel like I have everything."

"But I want more," I whisper.

"You do?"

I nod, then reach up and whisper into his ear, "I want your child, Damian."

His shoulders bunch and his features take on a strange look, one I can't decipher. "Damian," I mumble, "I... I'm sorry if I hurt you. If it's too soon, I understand. It's just, I've always wanted a big family and—"

"Yes." He nods.

"Yes?"

"I want you to have my child... My children, Flower." He cups my cheek, "I've never wanted it with anyone else, but with you...it feels right. You're the woman I've been waiting for my entire life."

"And Riley's mother?" Shit, why did I ask that? I shouldn't have, but when it comes to Damian, I have no filter. I seem to blurt out whatever's floating around in my subconscious with him, which is probably a sign that I trust him... Which is good, right?

"She wasn't you." He peers down into my eyes, "I never missed her when I was away from her, never wanted to spend every night with her, never feel like a part of me was missing when she wasn't in the same room as me." The skin at the edges of his eyes crinkles, "But you... You, my Flower, are the most important thing in the world to me. I can't live without you. When I thought I had lost you, it felt like I had cut out a part of myself. No worse, it felt like I was dying inside, like I was —"

I slap my palm over his mouth, "Shh, no D word, remember?"

He kisses my fingers and all of my nerve endings seem to come to life. He wraps his fingers around my wrist and lowers my palm to his chest.

"Say you'll never leave me."

"Never."

"Say, you'll always be mine," he demands.

"Yours," I whisper. "Always yours." I tip up my chin, meet his searing gaze. "You sure do have a way with words, Mr. Savage."

"It's because of my muse, Mrs. Savage."

I shiver... That's me. He's referring to me. OMG, I am married to a rock star. The man who half the world's female population covets, and the other half, well... They are, clearly, blind.

"Do I know this muse?" I giggle.

"Want to meet her?" He waggles his eyebrows, "She inspires me most when she's naked and spread over my lap, so I can spank her until she's wet, right before I turn her over and make sweet love to her."

Heat blooms between my thighs. "What if she wants to be fucked instead?" I squeeze my legs together.

His grin widens. "That can be arranged too." He leans down and kisses me again, hard, then turns and leads me down the hill. "To think, I have Arpad to thank for you showing up at my door," he mutters.

"Wait, what?" I gasp, and turn to him, "What's Arpad got to do with anything?"

"Asshole called up your agency and asked for you to take on the assignment as my nanny."

"What?" I gape, "So it was him—?"

"Yep," he nods. "In a way, I am grateful to him. If he hadn't sprung that on me, we wouldn't be here today."

"He's a good friend." I reach up and he dips his chin, closing the height-gap between us enough that I can touch his face. This casual gesture of affection, this ability to touch him anytime I want... Wow, it's something I'll never take for granted. "He knew you were hurting, that you needed a reason to come out of the dark place you were in. He saw the opportunity and took it."

"Hmm. Perhaps you are right." He rolls his shoulders.

"I am," I say with a smug smile. "Thanks to him, your video went viral; with your song already making it to the top of the charts in the country."

Yep, the notoriety of the supposed annulment, within hours of being married, followed by his from-the-heart song and declaration of love, had broken the internet.

"I am not complaining, though that's not why I did it," he replies. "And the song was all you. You inspired me, Flower.

My heart feels like it's going to burst. As closed off as he'd been earlier, he doesn't hold back now. He cuts out his heart and offers it to me every opportunity he gets. My hard-ass, sensitive artist of a rockstar. There are so many layers to him that not even a lifetime will be enough to get to know him. He'll always manage to surprise me at every turn, and God, I can't wait to experience this beautiful life of ours together.

Stupid tears fill my eyes and I blink them away,

"The song..." I glance up at the view of his hard jaw. "It was more than beautiful... it was—

"It was probably the first completely honest piece I ever wrote." He pauses, turns to me. "Was it cathartic? Yes. Could I have done it without you? No. Every time I saw you come apart under me, Flower... It healed something inside of me. The honesty of your response to me, the way you looked at me, how you held on to me and allowed me a glimpse of your soul as you shattered... It loosened the walls I had built between me and myself..." He laughs, "Am I making sense?"

"Yes," I whisper, "more than you know." I flatten my palm against his chest, "It's the same for me. When I am with you, I feel free. I feel supported enough to be able to explore my own creativity."

"We're good for each other." His grin widens.

"Told you so." I chuckle.

"Remind me never to get on your bad side, babe."

"As long as you don't forget to bring your mean side to bed."

He slaps my arse and I jump. "Hey, what was that for?" I protest.

"Enough dallying, woman. Let's get going. We need to make an appearance at Sinclair's place before I can drag you back home and ravish you."

"Do we?" I pout, "Couldn't we give it a miss?"

"We'll put in a quick appearance." He pulls me into his side. "I promised the guys I'd be there. Besides, I need to pay back Arpad for what he did to me, and I promise, you'll want a front seat for what's going to happen next."

Epilogue 2

Karina

Why the hell had I accepted the invitation to this New Year's Eve party? Technically it's past the New Year, but the Seven, minus Baron, had spent New Year's Eve first at the hospital in solidarity with Damian; and later, trying to console the rock star, who'd shut himself off, before emerging with the track that had changed every-thing. So, today is the official party, to stand in for the New Year's bash.

I ring the doorbell of the townhouse on Primrose Hill. This isn't my scene, at all. So what if the Seven are my best—read: only—clients right now in London. It is because their business is too important to lose, that I had moved half-way across the world from LA. It is thanks to their security concerns for themselves and their growing circle of friends and family that I am making enough money to be able to grow my business. So yeah, that is my answer. That's why, when Sinclair Sterling, business man extraordinaire, who, together with the Seven, owns one of the biggest financial services companies in this country, had asked me to attend this event, I couldn't refuse.

I blow out a breath, then straighten when the door is flung open.

Light spills out, along with laughter and the clinking of glasses. The hum of conversation envelops me with almost as much warmth as the wide smile on the face of the woman who stands in the doorway. "Karina." Summer Sterling grins up at me, her impish smile lighting up her face. "You came."

"I could hardly refuse your husband," I mutter.

She laughs, "Sinclair can be persuasive."

"That's putting it mildly."

She chuckles, then pulls me into a hug, "Happy New Year. It's wonderful to have you here with us today."

"Ah." I pat her shoulder. Awkward... That's me...with any kind of demonstration of affection. Comes from being the daughter of a single parent, who also happened to be a career military man.

Summer steps back, then links her arm through mine. A liveried man darts forward to shut the door, "Sorry I didn't get here in time, Madam." His rich, plummy accent has me staring at him.

"It's alright, Jeeves," Summer sings out, "I prefer to get the door for my friends anyway."

"Very good, Madam." He stands to attention as we walk past him.

"Is his name really Jeeves?" I whisper to Summer.

"No, but that's what I call him," she whispers back.

"Honestly, Summer." I stare down at her.

"What?" She raises her shoulders. "It suits him. Besides, it gives me the perfect excuse to practice all of my Bertie Wooster trivia questions on Sin."

"You mean Sinclair Sterling unbends enough to answer them?"

"He's still in training." She nods, "But he'll get there."

I laugh, "You're good for him, you know that?"

"Those of the Seven who've gotten hitched have been lucky in finding the right women."

"And who is that?" I ask, "The right kind of woman for one of the Seven?"

"Someone who can hold her own, who doesn't hesitate to go toe to toe with them and challenge them, who doesn't back down when they go—"

"All alphahole on you." I nod.

"See, you know what to do. So, what's stopping you?"

"What do you mean?" I frown down at her.

"I mean you and Arpad. What's stopping the two of you from—?"

"Kar-e-e-na." I look up to find Julia walking toward me.

"Hey," I wave back. "How are you?"

"I'm very good." She beams, "Also, I have news for you."

"I knew it!' Summer squeals. She grabs Julia's hand, "OMG, he did it? You guys are back together?"

Julia's face breaks into a wide grin, "Yes... Yes, we are."

"Congratulations!" Summer exclaims. "About time Damian did the right thing.

"This is amazing news." I smile, "I am so happy for you, Jules."

"I couldn't have done it without your help." She grips my shoulder, "Thank you, Karina."

"I didn't do anything," I mutter.

"You put your job on the line when you gave me the access codes to his house."

"Nothing that he didn't want happening." I stare past the women to the congregation of men at the bar. Weston's behind the counter serving, Damian's typing out something on his phone, while Sinclair and Saint, are engrossed in discussion.

"Where are the rest of the Seven?" I ask

"You mean Arpad?" Julia's lips quirk.

"I mean—" My phone buzzes and I pull it out of my handbag.

Arpad Ahole: The security camera on my yacht is not working. You need to check it out right away.

Me: I'm at a party

Arpad: I don't pay you to drink on my time. I need this fixed
ASAP.

"What the hell?" I huff

"What's wrong?" Julia turns to me.

"Nothing." I grouse. I drop the phone in my bag, then reach over
to grab a glass of champagne from a passing waiter.

"Wait... What did I miss?" Isla walks over to join us. "Who's
engaged? Whose wedding do I need to plan next?"

"Not mine, thank you very much," I assure her.

"That's what you say now." She looks me up and down,
"Speaking of, you look awesome, girl. I don't think I've ever seen you
in a dress before."

"It's not an attire that's suited to my line of work exactly," I reply.
Running a security agency means being on call 24/7, and the physical
nature of the work involved means pants are more practical outfits.

"Just take the compliment, already," Isla teases.

"You're right." I nod, "Thanks." I run my fingers down the fabric
that clings to my figure, "I quite like the results, actually."

"Has Arpad seen you in this outfit yet?"

I blow out a breath, "Okay, stop. He's my employer, and he hates
my guts."

"Maybe he's secretly in love with you," Isla counters.

"No, thank you." I hitch my handbag over my shoulder. "I want
nothing to do with him or the Seven."

"And us?" Summer grins. "What about us?"

"You girls are the best," I say sincerely. "These alphaholes don't
deserve you."

"Hear, hear." Victoria walks over and embraces me warmly.
"Shall we toast?" She raises her glass of water, "To girlfriends."

"To women who know what they want," I raise my glass.

"To alphaholes who know what *we* want." Julia chuckles.

"To us." Isla raises her glass and we clink.

"Am I too late for the toast?" Meredith walks over, champagne
glass in hand.

"How are you?" Julia cries.

"Much better, now that I know Damian came to his senses and made things right with you." She chuckles, then nods at Julia's ring, "Told ya, you'd get your HEA."

"You did." Julia laughs, "Thank you for all of your help."

Something passes between the two of them, then Meredith leans over and hugs Julia, who returns the embrace. The two women hold onto each other for a few seconds.

Finally, Meredith, pulls back, and wipes a tear from her cheek. "I am truly happy for you and Damian." She raises her glass. "A toast," she declares, "to the bad boy rock star and the woman who brought him to heel."

"Hear, hear." Summer raises her glass, "To Julia." She glances between us, "Let's down this in one, ladies."

"To Julia." The others raise their glasses. That's when my phone buzzes again. I pull it out.

Arpad Ahole: I trust you are en-route to my yacht to fix the camera? Else...

Me: Are you threatening me?

Arpad Ahole: Call this your first and last warning. I set off at dawn. The work had better be complete before that.

What the hell? What's wrong with this guy. I grip the phone, contemplate dropping it on the ground and smashing my heel into it —but that's not going to solve anything. Bet the bastard would find another way of reaching me. Instead I drop my phone in my bag. "I've got to go."

"No." The women look at me with varying expression of disappointment.

"Sorry, apparently, the a-hole has found a new way to make my life miserable."

I glance around for a place to put the glass. Isla takes it from me.

"Thanks," I flip my hair over my shoulder. "This shouldn't take too long..."

To find out what happens next read Arpad and Karina's story in The Billionaire's Baby

Read an excerpt from Arpad and Karina's story

Karina

"Gah, I could punch you right now, Wolfgang." The female announcer snaps.

"Problem is, that's not all you want to do with me is it?" Wolfgang retorts, "And Ivy?" There's a pause when I swear I can imagine him lean in closer to her, "The name's Wolfe."

"Errm." Ivy clears her throat over the airwaves, "so that's our favorite TV trope, brought to life by Wolfe and I... which sounds like something out of Red Riding Wood."

"Hood." Wolfe chuckles.

"That's what I said." Ivy huffs. "Red Riding Hood. So as I was saying, that's our favorite TV series trope, can you guess what it is? This is Ivy—"

"—And Wolfe." The male announcer interjects.

"And we are so very pleased to be guest hosting the Evening Show on your fave Smile London FM. Email us, call us... tweet us and let us know—"

I lean forward and shut off the car radio. What a bunch of twerps those two were, firstly the attraction between them was off the charts. Secondly they had no idea about it and were clearly dancing around it, all but punching each other in the face with the force of the tension building between them. Thirdly... well... if they didn't sort it out they were going to blow up on the show in front of everyone. No doubt smack each other in the face before smacking each other on the lips. Ha! I snort aloud. Good to know my sense of humor was somewhat alive... especially considering I had to spend the evening fixing up security on the boat of Mr Full of Himself Douchecanoe. Arpad f'ing Beauchamp. A man whose demeanor was every bit as pompous as his name. Yeah he came from old money, la-dee-dah, like I cared, but to see him stomp around with that giant stick up his ass you'd think he was conscious of his status every single second of his life. Which he admittedly was. Which was why he'd ordered me to get to his boat and fix the security camera on it that had stopped working before he set sail to whichever island it was he was sailing off to next.

Lifestyles of the rich and famous and all that.

Some of us minions had to spend our evenings working, others partied till dawn then sailed off into the sunrise. Of course so I was his security consultant and admittedly he and the rest of the Seven paid me a lot… like a l-o-t enough for me to leave my life in LA and move to London and ensure that their security detail was top notch.

The Seven had been kidnapped as pre-teens by the Mafia. They had escaped but not without the psychological scarring that came with that kind of experience and a life-long goal to get even with the perpetrators; with it the need to guard against any kind of fall out, i.e. the Mafia attacking them or their loved ones not to mention the fact that a few of the seven had met and married the women of their dreams ergo; more people to protect from a security stand point, which meant… I had never been busier. From finding the right talent to add to my team, to constantly upgrading the security details for the ceremonies when any of them decided to get married, the last being Damian, the rockstar who married his almost-nanny and produced a single that had knocked the socks off every single critic and countdown chart.

So yeah, couldn't complain, my bank account was happy… which means I should be happy, only I am not. I am not one to rest on my laurels, not one to bask in my success… I know what I wanted next, a family of my own. Good news is that I was already working on it.

In fact I had a date tomorrow night to fire the first salvo in that direction. No pun intended. I snort aloud. I just had to get through this last chore on my list and then I could get some rest and be ready to get started on this latest project.

I ease the car into the parking lot of St. Katherine's Dock, then grab my bag with all my tools and head down the line of gleaming vessels.

Trust London's wealthiest to bag a spot in the center of London to park
their toys. I search for one yacht in particular… what had he called it?

Heartbeat. A weirdly sentimental name for someone who was
known as Killer… not because he killed in real life but for the killing
he'd made as an Angel Investor. Yep, that's how Arpad f'ing
Beauchamp had made his money.

Investing behind those who had the ideas but not the finance
wherewithal to bring them to fruition. He had a knack for spotting
talent I'd give him that…. And that's all I'd ever concede and definitely not to his face. The man had a mean streak a mile wide, if any
of our brief interactions was any indication. Rumor has it he didn't
even spare the women he dated… but then the women he was interested in were known for their taste in men who took charge in the
bedroom… and pushed things beyond the point of comfort to put it
mildly. Good thing I wasn't one of them.

I prefer my men amenable and food spicy. See, the thing with
food? It never let you down. Finding the best restaurants in town
and eating out was a particular fancy of mine. Table for one please,
oh yeah, nothing like the silence of my own company to unwind in
the evenings. I wasn't lonely, just alone, and there was a difference
between those two words now, right?

I reach *Heartbeat* and clamber overboard, then walk over to the
cabin and key in the password. Letting myself in I glance around and
press what I think is the light switch. Bingo. The door locks shut
behind me as I glance around the space. Whoa, this was a yacht?
More like a floating mansion. It had seemed reasonably sized from
the outside, but in here… wow! I walk down the steps to the sunken
living room. Plush leather seats span one entire side, with a coffee
table in the center, and a flat screen on the opposite wall. I walk
through to a kitchen with a galley and an island table. The gleaming
kitchen equipment was top of the line and would rival any five-star
hotel I was sure. Not that any of it has ever been used, of course not.
Mr Alphahole here would never deign to step into a kitchen, he
probably travelled with an entire crew to fetch and carry for him.
Bet he spent his time jerking off to porno that he'd watch on that

screen while he shoved his hand down his pants and… please…
argh! Don't go there.

I walk past the kitchen and push the sliding doors apart to find
omg! A complete full furnished massive bedroom. Complete with a
king size bed that took up almost all the center of the room. On the
far end a door that I assume leads to the bathroom. There's a second
door beside it that must lead to a walk in closet? Huh, did he have
one on the boat as well. On the other side is a table and next to it a
neat pile of what looked like a rope, tacked to the wall. A rope? Huh,
how weird.

I glance around the room, take in the massive sliding doors
beyond it showed a view of now darkening water, rays of sunlight
from the setting painted the sky a burning red and orange.

I stare at the bed again… *leave, turn and leave, right now.* Come on,
surely a sniff won't hurt, hmm? Also there are no cameras in the
bedroom, so he'll never find out right? I cross the floor, walk around
the bed and run my hands across the pillow. Soft… Egyptian cotton
thread count innumerable no doubt. Only the best for the asshole
after all. I grab a handful of the sheet and pull it up to my nose.
Notes of bergamot and cloves, cinnamon and something dark,
musky, edgy… something dangerous. I'm instantly wet, what the
hell?

How can his scent turn me on so? And when I loathed the man?
And his attitude, and his entitled mindset. The way he thinks he
could boss me around, and expect me to drop everything and prioritize him beyond anything. A shiver runs down my spine. Only my
sense of hate getting the better of me, of course. That's why my
stomach flutters, that is the only reason my heart beats so fast in my
chest. Shit, now I was turning myself on, and that wouldn't do, not
when I had work to do. I pivot, then retrace my steps toward the
cabin, and head for the captain's area. There at the extreme right I
pull up the controls for the security camera—there's only one and it's
focused on the doorway, there's a second one focused on the living
room. Of course they are used only when the boat was docked. I get
to work fixing the controls… and am done in fifteen minutes. There,

that was easy. It took more time to drive here through the late evening traffic.

I stretch and yawn, suddenly tired. It's been a long day, long week, long year actually setting up business in this city. But I am in a good place, confident my business was going to do well. I pack up my tools, head for the door, then hesitate. Should I? Why not, it shouldn't matter. I pivot head back for the bedroom, when fireworks go off outside. I glance out the large windows and admire the spectacle. So damn beautiful. If only I had someone to hold my hand while I enjoyed it. Nah, doesn't matter. I have me... don't I. I yawn again. Shit, I really as beat. I turn, pass by the bed, then hesitate. Wouldn't hurt to take a quick nap, huh?

Surely, the a-hole wasn't going to come back before the morning and I'll be long gone by then, right? I place my bag on the floor next to the bed, toe off my shoes, then slip into bed... on the side where I am sure he sleeps where the scent is most potent. I draw up the covers to my chin and OMG. Goosebumps flare on my skin, It's as if I am surrounded by him, as if he's cocooned me with his body, and he's all around me, with me, in this bed. A delicious warmth envelops me, I close my eyes and let sleep take over.

A loud creak tears through the silence in my mind. I sit up, my heart pounding in my chest. My pulse rate ratchets up. My eyes strain through the darkness. Where the hell am I? The entire room seems to tilt. I scream and slide off the bed. I hit the ground on my ass, roll over to hit the glass wall of the cabin. I turn press my nose into the transparent barrier and stare out. Darkness broken only by the white tipped foam that crashes again the side. I scream, scramble back until I hit the bed. The boat. I am on the boat which is no longer harbored. It's at sea, with me on it. The entire yacht creaks again, the walls seem to groan the boat lurches up and I hold onto the edge of the bed, anchor myself as it seems to grunt and screech like a living thing, then straightens. Silence, for a second. The hair on the back of my neck rises, I smell the ozone in the air, then the boat groans, and hurtles down.

The momentum carries me forward toward the wall. I throw out my hand, manage to grab the edge of the bed, hold on a the boat seems to sink through space, then hits something — the water I presume? — with a crash. The sound echoes in my ears, reverberates down my spine. Then the vessel tilts in the opposite direction. I glance out the window of the cabin and scream again. Water. So much water, I am surrounded by a wall of water. What the hell is happening? How did the boat get here?

I hit the ground on all fours crawl my way up to the door. Grabbing the handle I pull myself up, then twist the knob open. I lurch forward as the entire boat goes into another incline. Damn it. I race forward, throw myself onto the couch in the living room and hold on until the boat rightens again. Then cross the living room, up the steps toward the captain's cabin. That when I see the man silhouetted against the wheel.

He's wearing shorts that cling to his tight ass. And what an ass it is. The fabric outlines the indentation on each side, only to stretch across the girth. The waistband shows off his inverted V figure and his back… I gulp. The planes of his back flex and buck like a living thing as he grips the wheel of the boat, widens his stance and leans into the next wave. The next wave… OMG it's a huge, huge WAVE… I glance up and cry out as I realize he's driving the boat straight up the crest of a monster of a wall of water. There's a crash of thunder, then lighting flickers beyond the boat and I gasp again. An entire sea of darkness, capped by a furious whites, and in the foreground his massive shoulders that bunch and knot as he grapples with the wheel, holds the boat on course.

Another clap of thunder in the distance, and the alphahole — for it is him, Arpad f'ing Ahole, the bloody owner of this boat, my crazy ass employer, my frigging boss who's driving this boat straight into the storm.

He throws back his head and laughs. What the hell? Is he crazy? Does he have a death wish or something? I stomp forward to ask him just that, when the boat groans and begins to slide back, taking me with it. My legs seem to go out from under me. I scream as I hit the decking and roll back. The boat pitches and I am thrown against the wall. Darkness envelops me.

When I open my eyes again, I am back in the bed, in the bedroom of the boat, the sheets pulled up to my chin. Huh? Was it all a dream? I sit up and my pain slices through my forehead. I groan, fall back against the pillows.

"Take it easy." A low voice rumbles across the space. I glance over to meet familiar gray-blue eyes. "You?" I cough. "What the hell are you doing here?"

"It's my boat?" He leans forward and my gaze takes in his bare chest, the sculpted eight… no.. ten… no, twelve pack? Nah… not possible no one has a eight pack do they?

"Enjoying the view…?"

I tip my chin up, meet his gaze.

"I've seen better." I lie.

He chuckles, "You must be feeling better, though I admit I preferred it when you were flat on your back in my bed, naked."

I peek under the sheet. "What the hell?" I gasp, "where are my clothes?"

"Had to take them off, since they got wet when I was dressing your head wound."

I touch my forehead and pain flashes behind my eyes. "Ow." I gasp.

"Let me see that." He leans over me and his scent intensifies. His chest planes ripple, his biceps bunch as he reaches across.

I pull away, and he frowns. "I won't hurt you."

Why don't I believe you?

"Unless you want me to?" His lips twist, "Do you want me to, hurt you, my little stowaway…?"

To find out what happens next read Arpad and Karina's story in The Billionaire's Baby

Read an excerpt

Karina

"Gah, you're a frustrating man, Wolfgang." The radio announcer groans. "You know that?"

"Exactly why you like me." Wolfgang chuckles. "And Ivy?" There's a pause when, I swear, I can imagine him leaning in closer to her. "The name's Wolfe."

"Errm," Ivy clears her throat over the airwaves, "so that's our favorite TV trope, brought to life by Wolfe and me…which sounds like something out of Red Riding Wood."

"Hood." Wolfe chuckles.

"That's what I said." Ivy huffs. "Red Riding Hood. So, as I was saying, that's our favorite TV trope. Can you guess what it is? This is Ivy—"

"—And Wolfe," the male announcer interjects.

"And we are so very pleased to be guest hosting the Evening Show on your fave, Smile London FM. Email us, call us…and let us know—"

I lean forward and shut off the car radio. What a couple of twerps those two are. Firstly, the attraction between them is off the charts. Secondly, they have no idea about it and are clearly dancing around it, all but punching each other in the face with the force of the tension building between them. Thirdly…well…if they don't sort it out, they are going to blow up on the show in front of everyone. No doubt, smack each other in the face before smacking each other on the lips. Ha! I snort aloud. Good to know my sense of humor is somewhat alive… Especially considering I have to spend the evening evaluating and repairing security on the boat of Mr. Full-of-Himself-Douchecanoe, aka Arpad f'ing Beauchamp.

A man whose demeanor is every bit as pompous as his name. Yeah, he comes from old money, la-dee-dah. Like I care. But to see him stomp around with that giant stick up his ass, you'd think he's conscious of his status every single second of his life. Which, he probably is. Which is why he'd ordered me to get to his boat and fix the security camera on it that he claims has stopped working before he sets off to whichever island it is he is sailing off to next.

A camera, which had been set up by someone else before I came on board as his security consultant.

Some of us have to spend the evening working; others party till dawn, then sail off into the sunrise. Of course. Admittedly, he and the rest of the Seven pay me a lot… Like a l-o-t; enough for me to leave my life in LA and move to London to ensure that their security detail is top notch.

The Seven had been kidnapped as pre-teens by the Mafia. They had been rescued, but not before it had left them with a burning need to get even with the perpetrators of the incident. It also means that the men are ever vigilant about the Mafia attacking them or their loved ones. That's why they had asked me to increase the security on them and their families. Add to that, the fact that most of the Seven had recently met and married the women of their dreams... And it means I have a shitload of people to protect, from a security standpoint.

Which means… Yeah, I have never been busier. From finding the right talent to add to my team, to constantly upgrading the security details for the ceremonies when any of them decide to get married—the latest being Damian, the rock star who married his almost-nanny and produced a single that knocked the socks off of every single critic and countdown chart.

So, I can't complain. My bank account is happy…which means I should be happy. Only I am not.

I am not one to rest on my laurels, not one to bask in my success… I know what I want next—a family of my own. Good news is, I am already working on it.

In fact, I have a date tomorrow night to fire the first salvo in that direction. No pun intended. I snort aloud. I just have to get through this last chore on my list and then I can get some rest—and god knows, I need it—and be ready to get started on this latest project.

I ease the car into the parking lot of St. Katherine Docks, then grab my bag—which, while being stylish enough to take to a party, is also spacious enough to hold my emergency tools—and head down the line of gleaming vessels. Trust London's wealthiest to bag a spot in the center of London to park their toys. I search for one yacht in particular… What had he called it?

Heartbeat. A weirdly sentimental name for someone who is known as Killer… Not because he kills in real life, but for the killing he makes as an Angel Investor in Silicon Valley. Yep, that's how Arpad f'ing Beauchamp makes his money.

Investing in those who have the ideas but not the financial wherewithal to bring them to fruition. He has a knack for spotting talent, I'll give him that…. And that's all I'll ever concede, and definitely not to his face.

The man has a mean streak a mile wide, if any of our brief interactions are any indication. Rumor has it, he doesn't even spare the women he dates… But then, the kind of women he prefers are known for their taste in men who take charge in the bedroom… And push things beyond the point of comfort. Good thing I am not one of them.

I prefer my men amenable and my food spicy. See, the thing with food? It never lets you down. Finding the best restaurants in town and eating out is a particular fancy of mine. Table for one, please. Oh yeah, nothing like the silence of my own company to unwind in the evenings. I am not lonely, just alone. And there is a difference between those two words, right?

I reach *Heartbeat* and clamber overboard, then walk over to the cabin and key in the password. Letting myself in, I glance around and press what I think is the light switch. Bingo. The door clicks shut behind me as I glance around the space. Whoa, this is a yacht? More like a floating mansion. It had seemed reasonably sized from the outside, but in here… Wow! I walk down the steps to the sunken living room. Plush leather seats span one entire side, with a coffee table in the center, and a flat screen on the opposite wall. I walk through to a galley that has an island table, but only one chair. Huh? That's weird. Doesn't he entertain on the boat? Bet he does, so what's with the lone chair?

On the other hand, the gleaming kitchen equipment is more what I expected. It's top-of-the-line and would rival any five-star hotel, I am sure. Not that Mr. Alphahole, here, would ever deign to step into a kitchen. He probably travels with an entire crew to fetch and carry for him. Bet he spends his time jerking off to porno that he watches

on that screen as he shoves his hand down his pants and… Please…
Argh! Don't go there.

I walk past the kitchen and push the sliding doors apart to find—
OMG! A complete, fully-furnished, massive bedroom. Complete
with a super king-size bed that takes up almost all of the center of
the room. On the far end is a door that, I assume, leads to the bathroom. There's a set of mirrored doors beside it that must lead to a
walk-in closet? Clearly, he's spared no expense in doing up this
space. Everything is gorgeously designed, if space efficient.

On the other side of the cabin is a narrow freestanding table, and
on it, a neat coil of what looks like… A rope? How weird. I move
closer, then reach out and brush my fingers across the cord. It's soft
to the touch, almost sensual, the material reddish in color, with
sparks of gold flecked through it. I bring it to my nose and sniff. An
edgy, almost nutty scent tugs at my nostrils. My core clenches. Wow,
what the hell does he use this for anyway?

I step back, glance around the room, take in the massive, sliding
glass doors. Beyond them is the view of the now-darkening water,
rays of sunlight from the setting sun painting the sky a smoldering
red and orange.

I stare at the bed again… *Leave, turn and leave, right now.* Come on,
surely, a sniff won't hurt? Besides, there are no cameras in the
bedroom. At least, there were none indicated on the security detail
for this boat I'd inherited from the previous agency... So he'll never
find out, right?

I cross the floor, walk around the bed and run my hands across
the pillow. Soft… Egyptian cotton, thread count innumerable, no
doubt. Only the best for the asshole, after all. I lean over, bury my
nose in the pillow... Don't judge.

Notes of bergamot and cloves, and something dark, musky, edgy
—something dangerous—envelops me. I'm instantly wet. *What the
hell?*

How can his scent turn me on so? And when I loathe the man?
And his attitude, and the way he thinks he can boss me around, and
expect me to drop everything and prioritize him above everything

else. A shiver runs down my spine. Only my sense of hate getting the better of me, of course.

That's why my stomach flutters. That is the *only* reason my heart beats so fast in my chest. Shit, now I am turning myself on, and that will not do. Not when I have work to do. I pivot, then retrace my steps toward the cabin, and head for the captain's area. There, at the extreme right, I pull up the controls for the security cameras.

I get to work fixing the controls…and am done in fifteen minutes. There, that was easy. It took more time to drive here through the late evening traffic.

I stretch and yawn, suddenly overwhelmingly tired. It's been a long day, long week, long year, actually, setting up business in this city. But I am in a good place, confident my business is going to do well. I pack up my tools, head for the door, then hesitate.

Should I? Why not? It shouldn't matter. I pivot and head back toward the bedroom, then glance out the large window and admire the spectacle. So damn beautiful. If only I had someone to hold my hand while I enjoy it. Nah, doesn't matter. I have me…don't I? And my love for yoga. The only way I know how to unwind. I roll my shoulders, and my muscles protest. Shit, I am too tense.

I place my handbag on the bed stand, then raise my arms high above me. The skirt of my dress pulls tight against my thighs. This won't do. It's why I hate wearing dresses. Damn. I pull off the dress, drape it over the foot of the bed, then kick off my heels and walk over to the center of the room.

I face the window of the yacht, then raise my hands again, bring them down, flow down onto my hands and the tips of my feet, then push up into a downward facing dog. I hold the pose for a few seconds, until my hamstrings burn, my biceps stretch, give. I rock back and forth, then swoop up, back to downward facing dog, then jump forward, straighten. Take a breath in and out, then repeat the process.

By the time I'm done with my routine, my muscles are limber, sweat beads my forehead. I wipe it off, then stretch and yawn. A pleasant tiredness buzzes in my blood.

Yeah, I could rest for a little while, then get out of here.

Hold on, bad idea. *Honestly, are you actually thinking of staying on here for more time than is absolutely essential?*

I reach for my dress then stop, glance at the bed. It looks so comfortable. I yawn again. Coming down from a yoga routine always relaxes me so much. My limbs grow heavy, my eyelids seem to be weighted down, and I can barely keep them open. I could nap in the car, of course...but it's almost dark and that doesn't sound safe. And I know it's not safe to drive home without catching a few minutes of shut-eye.... I sneak a peek at the bed again; it looks so comfortable.

Just a short nap. That can't hurt... Can it? It'll rejuvenate me enough for the ride home which, again, I am in no condition to navigate when I am this exhausted.

I slip into the bed and draw the covers up to my chin. His dark scent wraps around me. Goosebumps flare on my skin. It's as if I am surrounded by him, as if he's cocooned me with his body, and he's all around me, with me, in this bed. Should I set an alarm on my phone to wake up? Nah, I'll be fine. It's only a quick nap, after all.

Besides Arpad a-hole isn't going to come back before the morning, and I'll be long gone by then...

A delicious warmth envelops me and I close my eyes.

A rumbling creeps into my consciousness and I push it away. I press my cheek into the soft pillow, draw in that scent of bergamot and cloves. His scent. Mmm. A languid heaviness tugs at my limbs. My muscles relax and I drift off again. Until a loud creak tears through the silence in my mind. I jackknife up to sitting position, my heart pounding in my chest. My pulse rate ratchets up. I strain to see through the darkness. Where the hell am I?

That's when the entire room seems to tilt. I scream and slide off the bed. I hit the ground on my ass, roll over to hit the glass wall of the cabin. I turn and press my nose into the transparent barrier and stare out. Darkness, broken only by the white-tipped foam that crashes against the side. I gasp, then scramble back until I hit the bed. The boat! I am on the boat, which is no longer harbored. It's at sea, with me on it.

The entire yacht creaks again, the walls seem to groan, the boat lurches up, and I hold onto the edge of the bed, anchor myself, as it seems to grunt and screech like it's possessed, then straightens. Silence, for a second. The hair on the back of my neck rises, I smell the ozone in the air, then the boat groans, and hurtles down.

The momentum carries me forward toward the wall of the cabin.

I throw out my hand, manage to grab the edge of the bed, hold on as the boat seems suspended in space, before it hits something — the water I presume? — with a crash. The sound echoes in my ears, reverberates down my spine. Then the vessel tilts in the opposite direction. I glance out the glass wall and scream again. Water. So much water, I am surrounded by a wall of water. What the hell is happening? How did the boat get here? I hit the ground on all fours, crawling my way up to the door. Grabbing the handle, I pull myself up, then twist the knob open. I lurch forward as the entire boat goes into another incline. Damn it. I race forward, throw myself onto the couch in the living room and hold on until the boat rightens again. Then cross the living room, up the steps toward the captain's cabin.

That's when I see the man silhouetted against the wheel. He's wearing shorts that cling to his tight ass. And what an ass it is. The fabric outlines the indentation on each side, only to stretch across the girth. The waistband shows off his inverted V figure and his back… I gulp. The planes of his back flex and buck as he grips the wheel of the boat, widens his stance, and leans into the next wave. The next wave… What the — ? It's a huge, huge wave. A behemoth of a WAVE. I glance up and cry out, for he's driving the boat straight up the crest of a monster of a wall of water. There's a crash of thunder, then lightning flickers beyond the boat and I gasp again. An entire sea of darkness, capped by furious white tips, and in the foreground, his massive shoulders that bunch and knot as he grapples with the wheel, holds the boat on course.

Another clap of thunder in the distance, and the alphahole — for it is him, Arpad f'ing A'hole, the bloody owner of this boat, my crazy-ass employer, my frigging boss, who's driving this boat straight into the storm.

He throws back his head and laughs. What the hell? Is he crazy?

Does he have a death wish or something? I stomp forward to ask
him just that, when the boat groans and begins to slide back, taking
me with it. My legs seem to go out from under me. I scream as I hit
the decking and roll back. The boat pitches and I am thrown against
the wall. Darkness envelops me.

When I open my eyes again, I am back in the bed, in the bedroom of
the boat, the sheets pulled up to my chin. Huh? Was it all a dream? I
sit up and pain slices through my forehead. I groan, fall back against
the pillows.

"Take it easy." A low voice rumbles across the space. I glance
over to meet familiar grey-blue eyes.

"You?" I cough. "What the hell are you doing here?"

"It's my boat?" He leans forward and my gaze takes in his bare
chest, the sculpted six-...no, eight-pack? Nah...not possible. No one
has an eight-pack, do they?

"Enjoying the view?"

I tip my chin up, meet his gaze.

"I've seen better," I lie.

He chuckles. "You must be feeling better. Though, I admit, I
preferred it when you were flat on your back in my bed, naked."

I peek under the sheet. "What the hell?" I gasp, "Where are my
underclothes?"

"Had to take them off, since you bled all over them from your
head wound."

I touch my forehead, and the pain flashes behind my eyes. "Ow,"
I moan.

"Let me see that." He leans over me and his scent intensifies. His
chest planes ripple and his biceps bunch as he reaches across.

I pull away. "It's fine," I grumble, "it's just a bump. It's not
bleeding."

"I won't hurt you," he rumbles.

Why don't I believe you?

"Unless you want me to..." His lips twist, "Do you want me to,
hurt you, my little stowaway?"

"What?" I scowl, "Of course, not."

"Then why are you here?"

Arpad

"Not by choice." She tips her chin up. "Trust me, I'd rather be a million miles away."

I grin. "And yet, here you are."

"I came in to check the security cameras—which are working now, by the way. The next thing I know, I am waking up to the apocalypse." She scowls. "What the hell were you doing driving the yacht into a storm?"

"What the hell are you doing on my boat?"

She reddens. "I checked the camera—which is functional, by the way—you can thank me later—" She tosses her hair and winces. "After which, uh, I guess I was too tired, and decided to work out?"

"Work out?" I drum my fingers on my bicep. "Exactly how did you decide you were going to work out."

"I was tense, and decided I need to do a quick yoga session."

"Hmm." I rub my chin, trying to understand this. "So, you decided to do a quick yoga workout, dressed in…" I glance at her dress laid out at the bottom of the bed.

"No, I took off the dress," she mutters.

I tilt my head. "Good thing. I don't like that color on you anyway."

She gapes, "You don't?"

I shake my head. "Black doesn't do you justice. You're such a fiery personality, you need to wear red."

"Red?" she murmurs.

"Yep," I bend over her and lean in enough to share my breath with hers, "it brings out the highlights in your hair."

"Oh." Her pupils dilate and her breathing goes ragged. She inches closer, close enough for her breasts to graze my chest. And damn it, I'm instantly hard.

I straighten and she blinks, as if coming out of a trance. I can't stop the smirk that curls my lips. "Your heels," I murmur, "you took them off as well?"

"What?" She straightens, then glances around her, "Sorry, what did you say?"

"Your stilettos," I point to where I'd placed her footwear by the side.

"Right," she swallows, "of course, I took them off."

"And then you proceeded to work out in my cabin?"

"It was just a basic routine with few stretching poses." She blinks rapidly, "You know, like downward facing dog?"

Oh baby, I'd love to downward dog you. The thought of having her balanced on her hands and toes, butt in the air…tits thrust out as she arches into the pose… I clear my throat. *Jesus, is it hot in here or what?* I widen my stance. "So, you came into my cabin, where you shouldn't have been in the first place, did a quick workout, then crawled into my bed?"

She wrings her fingers together in front of her.

I stare at her.

She flushes. "In my defense, I wanted to find out if the living quarters were secure or if you needed a camera or something here as well so—"

I hold up my hand, "Hold on, back up. So, you came into my bedroom to check if there were cameras…and then what? You decided to stay on?"

"Not really." She hunches her shoulders. "I came in here and it was so calm, I decided to do my yoga routine. Then, the bed was so inviting, and I was so tired, and I might have uh, decided to take a nap…"

"A nap?"

She nods. "Yeah, stupid idea, but I was exhausted and I didn't think you'd be back for a while," she mumbles, "and besides, you owe me for coming in and fixing your security camera, on what should have been an evening off."

"Had plans, huh?"

"Kind of." She sits up. "Shit, what time is it?"

I raise my shoulder, "Beats me."

"Where's my phone?" She glances round the space. "Please, please I need my phone."

"Phone?"

"So, I can check the time." She spots her bag on the table, and her features light up. "Can you get me my bag?"

"Why?"

She scowls at me, "So I can get my phone from it, you ass."

"Get it yourself," I drawl, then drop into the chair and lean back for good measure.

"I don't have any clothes on."

"So?"

She gapes. "You're a complete alphahole, you know that?"

"I'll take that as a compliment." I smirk.

"Oh, F off." She pulls the sheet up and around her shoulders, then swings her legs over, and hitching up the sheet, walks over to the table. Still holding the cover, she manages to grab her bag, unzip it and pull out her phone. "What the hell?" she yelps. "It's almost 10 am."

"It is." I tip back my chair, watch her as she waves her phone in the air.

"Turn this boat around."

"No."

"I have to get back."

"Too late."

"You don't understand," she snarls. "I have somewhere I need to be."

"So do I." I scratch my chest and her gaze drops there. She swallows. I drag my hand down to my waist and her breathing grows shallow. Hmm, interesting. Apparently, little Miss Perfect here is not as impervious to my presence as she'd like me to believe.

"Don't do that," she mutters.

"What?"

"That entire showing-off-your-torso thing."

"Was I?"

"You were, and you know it." She tips her chin up. "I demand that you get back to land right now."

"It's that important, huh?" I frown at her.

She tosses her hair back from her face. "Of course, it is. That's what I've been trying to tell you all this while."

"Why don't you tell me what made you get that tattoo, first?"

She scowls, "What tattoo?"

"How many tattoos do you have?" I smirk.

She opens her mouth, and I raise my hand. "Yes, I saw it, when I took off your underwear. Deal with it."

Color smears her cheeks.

"You're a piece of work, you know that?"

I chuckle, "That's not the answer to my question."

She tugs up the sheet then, purses her lips. I wait as she seems to consider her options. "So, if I tell you the rationale behind the tattoo, you'll take me back to land?"

I shrug.

She glowers at me, then snaps back her shoulders. "The line you saw that I had tattooed... It's from my favorite poet."

If you but knew the flames that burn in me which I attempt to beat down with my reason.

I recite it at the same time as her.

"You know the poem?" She frowns.

"Pushkin." I nod. "I know who wrote it. I want to know why you have it tattooed on your back." I hadn't missed the cursive written on one side of her spine; it was beautiful, evocative and unexpected... And yet, exactly the kind of verse I'd expect her to love. Deep, intense, yet fiery and passionate. It is so much Karina, that I have to find out more about it. "Well?" I lift one eyebrow. "Why did you get it?"

She draws in a breath, then glances away. "Because I was so

rebellious as a kid and it got me into so much trouble. I got it to remind myself that it's okay to pick my battles. I don't have to win everything. Just the important ones, you know?"

I stare at her. "You don't like to lose," I mutter, and she tips up her chin.

"Neither do you," she states.

"Which leaves us at a stalemate."

"Which leaves you on the yacht, and me back on land," she insists.

"No," I drawl.

"What?" Her features tighten. "You promised to take me back."

"I did no such thing."

"B... but..." she stutters, "you said...."

"No, I didn't." I waggle my finger at her.

"You...you liar," she chokes out.

"Wrong—" I swallow down the chuckle that bubbles up. Karina —angry, all flashing eyes, and glowing skin. My god, the adrenaline from the chance to spar with her is better than the thrill of closing a killer deal in Silicon Valley. "I didn't say anything. You asked if I would take you back if you told me about the tattoo. I shrugged and you assumed that meant yes." I pretend to yawn. "You need to pay more attention to the details, doll."

She walks over to the side-table near the bed, places her phone on it, then swivels to stand over me. "What the hell is wrong with you?" she demands.

"What's wrong is that you are naked in my bedroom and I haven't touched you yet."

She frowns. "Don't try to intimidate me, you ass."

"Oh, you'll know when I'm trying to intimidate you, Stowie."

"Stowie?" She blinks. "I have a name, you know."

I look her up and down, "I'm not in the habit of remembering the names of my hired help.

"Hired help?" she splutters. "How dare you?" She launches herself at me, and hits my chest with such force that the impact knocks me and the chair over.

I land on my back; my head connects with the hard floor and her knee connects with my stomach. "Uff," the breath rushes out of me. She scrambles to get away, and I grab her around the waist, flip her over onto the ground and lean over her. "There… Much better," I mutter.

"Let me go." She makes that little snarling sound at the back of her throat again. How cute.

"Now, now, is that any way to thank your savior?"

"Savior?" She huffs, "More like a kidnapper."

"If the title fits." I raise my shoulders. "I did patch you up, and put you to bed."

"So?" She snorts.

"And saved you from being lost at sea in a storm."

"You were saving your own hide, you… You complete tosser."

"Apparently, living in London has improved your insults, at least."

"It's done nothing for your attitude, you bastard."

I click my tongue, "I think I need to wash out your mouth." I stare at her lips. "Or maybe I should shut you up another way, hmm?"

"Don't you dare." Her golden eyes blaze at me.

"You have no idea what I am going to do."

"Don't I?" she mutters. "You were thinking of kissing me."

"Hmm." I lower my face until my nose bumps hers, "Now that you mention it…" I hold her gaze and the gold of her irises deepen to a burnt amber. "Fucking beautiful," I mutter.

She blinks. "You don't have to flatter me."

I take in her features, the slope of her creamy shoulder, the shape of her curves so soft and under me. "The first thing you should know about me," I growl, "is that I never lie."

"What's the second?"

"I never back away from a challenge."

She purses her lips. "I am not challenging you."

"Hmm, I could have sworn that's what your earlier words sounded like."

"I was simply asking you to turn the yacht back and drop me off."

"Can't, babe."

Her gaze narrows. "You don't understand. I need to be back by 5 pm."

"Hot date?"

She glances away, then back at me. "Something like that," she mutters. "It's just...someone I have to see."

My gut twists and something hot stabs at my chest. "Drop him," I command.

"What?"

"Whoever it is, you're not meeting him again."

She opens and shuts her mouth, "You're completely off your rocker."

Tell me about it. Why the hell do I care who she's going to see? It's not like I have a claim on her. Still, when I'd tucked her into my bed, something had felt right about it. And not just that she had her eyes closed, and wasn't glaring at me like she wanted to rip my head off, which is her natural response whenever she sees me. So why the hell am I still holding her down, with my hips between her legs, my groin flush against hers, my chest wearing the imprint of those beautiful breasts? "Stay with me, for the next thirty days," I snap.

"What?"

"That's how long this trip is for."

"You're joking."

"Told you, I never joke."

"Get off of me." She slaps at my shoulder.

"Not until you give me your answer."

"Then my answer is no."

"Refuse me and I'll strip the contract for the security details for the Seven from your company."

"You can't do that." Her features twist, "You wouldn't dare do that. I'll take you to court."

"Don't dare me, Stowie."

"Don't call me that."

"What would you prefer?"

"My name, for one, you ass. You can call me Karina. On the other hand," she pushes up against me, "don't call me at all."

"I prefer Stowie." I take in her flushed features, the pulse beating at her throat. "So what do you say? Do we have a deal?"

"No."

"I am not letting you up unless you agree."

"What is this? Compulsion?"

"Coercion." I allow my lips to kick up in a smirk. "Or would you prefer seduction?" I lower my gaze to her lips. "Will you taste as sweet as you smell or will you be as prickly as your demeanor, hmm?"

"You'll never find that out." She makes a noise deep in her throat, and the sound travels straight down my spine. My groin hardens. Bet if I look down, I'll see the crotch of my pants tented. She must sense it, or rather, feel the thick length jab into her stomach, for her gaze widens. She gulps, the sound audible in the silence.

"Thirty days," I stare at her parted lips, "during which we explore this chemistry between us. Then we can go back to our individual lives as if nothing happened."

"Thirty days." Her tongue darts out. "That's it? And we both walk away?"

"Seven-hundred and twenty hours to explore each other." I peer into her face. "That's forty-three-thousand two-hundred minutes to give into the attraction between us and find out exactly what it holds."

She blinks, then shakes her head. "You mean we shag each other, don't you?"

"Not giving it names, babe. Why don't we let nature take its course?" I glance up into her eyes. "With a little help from us, of course."

Something passes across her face, an expression I can't quite discern. "What?" I scowl, "What is it?"

"Thirty days." She nods. "I'll agree, but I have a condition of my own."

To find out what happens next read Arpad and Karina's story in The Billionaire's Baby

Read an excerpt from Karma and Michael Byron's story in Mafia King

Karma

"Morn came and went—and came, and brought no day…"

Tears prick the back of my eyes. Goddamn Byron. Crept up on me when I am at my weakest. Not that I am a poetry addict, by any measure, but words are my jam.

The one consolation I have, that when everything else in the world is wrong, I can turn to them, and they'll be there, friendly steady, waiting with open arms. And this particular poem had laced my blood, crawled into my gut when I'd first read it. Darkness had folded into me like an insidious snake that raises its head when I least expect it. Like now. I'd managed to give my bodyguard the slip and veered off my usual running route to reach *Waterlow Park*.

I look out on the still sleeping city of London, from the grassy slope of the expanse. Somewhere out there the Mafia was hunting me, apparently.

I purse my lips, close my eyes. Silence. The rustle of the wind between the leaves, the faint tinkle of the water from the nearby spring.

I could be the last person on this planet, alone, unsung, bound for the grave.

Ugh! Stop. Right there. I drag the back of my hand across my nose. Try it again, focus, get the words out, one after the other, like the steps of my sorry life.

"Morn came and went—and came, and brought no day…" My voice breaks. "Bloody, asinine, hell." I dig my fingers into the grass and grab a handful and fling it out. Again. From the top. I open my eyes, focus on a spot in the distance.

"Morn came and went—and came, and…."

"…brought no day."

I whip my head around. His profile fills my line of sight. Dark hair combed back by a ruthless hand that booked no measure.

My throat dries.

Hooked nose, thin upper lip, a fleshy lower lip, that hints at hidden desires. Heat. Lust. The sensuous scrape of that whiskered jaw over my innermost places. Across my inner thigh, reaching toward that core of me that throbs, clenches, melts to feel the stab of his tongue, the thrust of his hardness as he impales me, takes me, makes me his.

"Of this their desolation; and all hearts
Were chill'd into a selfish prayer for light.."

Sweat beads my palm; the hairs on my nape rise. "Who are you?"

He stares ahead, his lips moving,

"Forests were set on fire —but hour by hour
They fell and faded —and the crackling trunks
Extinguish'd with a crash —and all was black."

I swallow, squeeze my thighs together. Moisture gathers in my core. How can I be wet by the mere cadence of this stranger's voice?

I spring up to my feet.

"Sit down."

His voice is unhurried, lazy even, his spine erect. The cut of his black jacket stretches across the width of his massive shoulders. His hair… I was mistaken. There are strands of dark gold woven between the darkness that pours down to brush the nape of his neck. My fingers tingle. My scalp itches.

I take in a breath and my lungs burn.

This man, he's sucked all the oxygen in this open space, as if he owns it, the master of all he surveys. The master of me. My death. My life. A shiver ladders its way up my spine. *Get away, get away now, while you still can.*

I take a step back.

"I won't ask again."

Ask. Command. Force me to do as he wants. He'll have me on my back, bent over, on the side, over him, under him, he'll surround me, overwhelm me, pin me down with the force of his personality. His charisma, his larger-than-life essence that will crush everything else out of me and I… I'll love it.

"No."

"Yes."

A fact. A statement of intent, spoken aloud. So true. So real. Too real. Too much. Too fast. All of my nightmares… my dreams come to life. Everything I've wanted is here in front of me. I'll die a thousand deaths before he'll be done with me… and then, will I be reborn? For him. For me. For myself. I live first and foremost to be the woman I am… am meant to be.

"You want to run?"

No.

No.

I nod my head

He turns his head and all of the breath leaves my lungs. Blue eyes, cerulean, dark like the morning skies, deep like the nighttime, hidden corners, secrets that I don't dare uncover. He'll destroy me, have my heart, and break it so casually.

My throat burns. A boiling sensation squeezes my chest.

"Go then, my beauty, fly. You have until I count to five. If I catch you, you are mine."

"If you don't?"

"Then I'll come after you, stalk your every living moment, possess your nightmares, and steal you away in the dead of midnight, and then…"

I draw in a shuddering breath; liquid heat drips from between my legs. "Then?" I whisper.

"Then, I'll ensure you'll never belong to anyone else, you'll never see the light of day again, for your every breath, your every waking second, your thoughts, your actions… and all of your words, every single last one, will belong to me." He peels back his lips, and his teeth glint in the first rays of the morning light. "Only me." He straightens to his feet, and rises, and rises.

He is massive. A beast. A monster who always gets his way. My guts churn. My toes curl. Something prial inside me insists I hold my own. I cannot give in to him. Cannot let him win whatever this is. I need to stake my ground in some form. *Say something. Anything. Show him you're not afraid of him.*

"Why?" I tilt my head back, all the way back. "Why are you doing this?"

He tilts his head, his ears almost canine in the way they are silhouetted against his profile.

"Is it because you can? Is it a… a..." I blink, "a debt of some kind?"

He stills.

"My father. This is about how he betrayed the Mafia, right? You're one of them?"

All expression is wiped clean of his face, and I know then I am right. My past… Why does it always catch up with me? *You can run, but you can never hide.*

"Tick-tock, Beauty." He angles his body and his shoulders shut out the sight of the sun, the dawn skies, the horizon, the city in the distance, the whisper of the grass, the trees, the rustle of the leaves... All of it fades, and leaves me and him. Us. *Run.*

"Five." He jerks his chin. Straightens the cuffs of his sleeves.

My knees wobble.

"Four."

My heart hammers in my chest. I should go. Leave. But my feet are welded to this earth. This piece of land where we first met. What am I, but a speck in the larger scheme of things? To be hurt. To be forgotten. To be brought to the edge of climax and taken without an ounce of retribution. To be punished... by him.

"Three." He thrusts out his chest, widens his stance, every muscle in his body relaxed. "Two."

I swallow. The pulse beats at my temples. My blood thrums.

"One."

Michael

"Go."

She pivots and races down the slope. The fabric of her dress streams behind her, scarlet in the blue morning. Her scent, lushly feminine with silver moonflowers, clings to my nose, then recedes. I reach forward, thrust out my chin, sniff the air, but there's only the green scent of dawn. She stumbles and I jump forward. Pause when she straightens. *Wait. Wait. Give her a lead. Let her think she has almost escaped, that she's gotten the better of me… As if.* I clench my fists at my sides, force myself to relax. *Wait. Wait.* She reaches the bottom of the incline, turns. I surge forward. One foot in front of the other, my heels dig into the grassy surface as mud flies up, clinging to the edges of my £4000 Italian pants. Like I care? Plenty more where that came from. An entire walk-in closet full of tailor-made clothes, to suit every occasion, with every possible accessory needed by a man in my position to impress… everything, except the one thing that I have coveted from the first time I had laid eyes on her. Sitting there on the grassy slope, unshed tears in her eyes, and reciting… Byron? For hell's sake. Of all the poet's in the world, she had to choose the Lord of Darkness.

I huff. All a ploy. Clearly, she'd known I was sitting near her… No, not possible. I had walked toward her and she hadn't stirred, hadn't been aware. Yeah, I am that good. I've been known to slice a man from ear to ear while he was awake and fully aware. Alive one second, dead the next. That's how it is in my world. You want it, you take it. And I… I want her.

I increase my pace, eat up the distance between myself and the girl… that's all she is. A slip of a thing, a slim blur of motion. Beauty in hiding. A diamond in the rough, waiting for me to get my hands on her, polish her, show her what it means to be… dead. She is dead. That's why I am here.

Her skirts flash behind her, exposing a creamy length of thigh. My groin hardens; my legs wobble. I lurch over a bump in the ground. The hell? I right myself, leap forward, inching closer, closer. She reaches a curve in the path, disappears out of sight. My heart hammers in my chest. I will not lose her, will not. *Here, Beauty, come to Daddy.* The wind whistles past my ears. I pump my legs, lengthen my strides, turn the corner. There's no one there, huh?

My heart hammers, the blood pounds at my wrists and my temples, and adrenaline thrums through my veins. I slow down, come to a stop. Scan the clearing.

The hairs on my forearms prickle. She's here. Not far. Where? *Where is she?* I prowl across to the edge of the clearing, under the tree with its spreading branches. *When I get my hands on you, Beauty, I'll spread your legs like the pages of a poem. Dip into your honeyed sweetness, like a quill into an inkwell, drag my aching shaft across that melting weeping entrance.* My balls throb. My groin tightens. The crack of a branch above shivers across my stretched nerve endings. Instinctively, I swoop forward, hold out my arms. A blur of red, dark blonde hair, skirt swept up in a gust of breeze. She drops into my arms and I close my grasp around the trembling, squirming mass of precious humanity. I cradle her close to my chest, heart beating thud-thud-thud, overwhelming any other thought.

Mine. All mine. The hell is wrong with me? She wriggles her little body, and her curves slide across my forearms. My shoulders bunch, my fingers tingle. She kicks out with her legs and arches her back. Her breasts thrust up, the nipples outlined against the fabric of her jogging vest. *She'd dared come out dressed like that…? In that scrap of fabric that barely covered her luscious flesh?*

"Let me go." She whips her head toward me, her hair flowing around her shoulders, across her face. She blows it out of the way. "You monster, get away from me."

Anger drums at the backs of my eyes; desire tugs at my groin. The scent of her is sheer torture, something that I had dreamed of in the wee hours of twilight when dusk turned into night. She's not real. Not the woman I think she is. She is my downfall. My sweet poison. The bitter medicine I must imbibe to cure the ills that plague my company.

"Fine." I lower my arms and she tumbles to the floor, hits the ground butt first.

"How dare you?" She huffs out a breath, her hair messily arranged across her face.

I shove my hands into the pockets of my fitted pants, knees slightly bent, legs apart. Tip my chin down and watch her as she sprawls at my feet.

"You… dropped me?" She makes a sound deep in her throat. So damn adorable.

"Your wish is my command." I quirk my lips.

"You don't mean it."

"You're right." I lean my weight forward on the balls of my feet and she flinches.

"What… what do you want?"

"You."

She pales. "You want to… rob me? I have nothing of value. I'm not carrying anything… except." She reaches for her pocket.

"Don't." I growl.

"It's only my phone."

"So you say, hmm?"

"You can…" She swallows, "you can trust me."

I chuckle.

"I mean, it's not like I can deck you with a phone or anything, right?"

I glare at her and she swallows. "Fine… you… you take it."

Interesting.

"Hands behind your neck."

She hesitates.

"Now."

She instantly folds her arms at the elbows, cradles the back of her head with her palms.

I lean down and every muscle in her body tenses. Good. She's wary. She should be. She should have been alert enough to have run as soon as she sensed my presence. But she hadn't. And I'd delayed what was meant to happen long enough.

I pull the gun from my pocket, hold it to her temple. "Goodbye Beauty."

TO FIND OUT WHAT HAPPENS NEXT READ KARMA AND MICHAEL BYRON'S STORY IN MAFIA KING

READ SUMMER & SINCLAIR STERLING'S STORY IN THE BILLION- AIRE'S FAKE WIFE

READ AN EXCERPT FROM SUMMER & SINCLAIR'S STORY

Summer

"Slap, slap, kiss, kiss."

"Huh?" I stare up at the bartender.

"Aka, there's a thin line between love and hate." He shakes out the crimson liquid into my glass.

"Nah." I snort. "Why would she allow him to control her, and after he insulted her?"

"It's the chemistry between them." He lowers his head, "You have to admit that when the man is arrogant and the woman resists, it's a challenge to both of them, to see who blinks first, huh?"

"Why?" I wave my hand in the air, "Because they hate each other?"

"Because," he chuckles, "the girl in school whose braids I pulled and teased mercilessly, is the one who I—"

"Proposed to?" I huff.

His face lights up. "You get it now?"

Yeah. No. A headache begins to pound at my temples. This crash course in pop psychology is not why I came to my favorite bar in Islington, to meet my best friend, who is—I glance at the face of my phone—thirty minutes late.

I inhale the drink, and his eyebrows rise.

"What?" I glower up at the bartender. "I can barely taste the alcohol. Besides, it's free drinks at happy hour for women, right?"

"Which ends in precisely" he holds up five fingers, "minutes."

"Oh! Yay!" I mock fist pump. "Time enough for one more, at least."

A hiccough swells my throat and I swallow it back, nod.

One has to do what one has to do… when everything else in the world is going to shit.

A hot sensation stabs behind my eyes; my chest tightens. Is this what people call growing up?

The bartender tips his mixing flask, strains out a fresh batch of the ruby red liquid onto the glass in front of me.

"Salut." I nod my thanks, then toss it back. It hits my stomach and tendrils of fire crawl up my spine, I cough.

My head spins. Warmth sears my chest, spreads to my extremities. I can't feel my fingers or toes. Good. Almost there. "Top me up."

"You sure?"

"Yes." I square my shoulders and reach for the drink.

"No. She's had enough."

"What the—?" I pivot on the bar stool.

Indigo eyes bore into me.

Fathomless. Black at the bottom, the intensity in their depths grips me. He swoops out his arm, grabs the glass and holds it up. Thick fingers dwarf the glass. Tapered at the edges. The nails short and buff. *All the better to grab you with.* I gulp.

"Like what you see?"

I flush, peer up into his face.

Hard cheekbones, hollows under them, and a tiny scar that slashes at his left eyebrow. *How did he get that?* Not that I care. My gaze slides to his mouth. Thin upper lip, a lower lip that is full and cushioned. Pouty with a hint of bad boy. *Oh!* My toes curl. My thighs clench.

The corner of his mouth kicks up. *Asshole.*

Bet he thinks life is one big smug-fest. I glower, reach for my glass, and he holds it up and out of my reach.

I scowl. "Gimme that."

He shakes his head.

"That's my drink."

"Not anymore." He shoves my glass at the bartender. "Water for her. Get me a whiskey, neat."

I splutter, then reach for my drink again. The barstool tips in his direction. This is when I fall against him, and my breasts slam into his hard chest, sculpted planes with layers upon layers of muscle that ripple and writhe as he turns aside, flattens himself against the bar. The floor rises up to meet me.

What the actual hell?

I twist my torso at the last second and my butt connects with the surface. *Ow!*

The breath rushes out of me. My hair swirls around my face. I scramble for purchase, and my knee connects with his leg.

"Watch it." He steps around, stands in front of me.

"You stepped aside?" I splutter. "You let me fall?"

"Hmph."

I tilt my chin back, all the way back, look up the expanse of muscled thigh that stretches the silken material of his suit. *What is he wearing? Could any suit fit a man with such precision?* Hand crafted on

Saville Row, no doubt. I glance at the bulge that tents the fabric between his legs. *Oh!* I blink.

Look away, look away. I hold out my arm. He'll help me up at least, won't he?

He glances at my palm, then turns away. *No, he didn't do that, no way.*

A glass of amber liquid appears in front of him. He lifts the tumbler to his sculpted mouth.

His throat moves, strong tendons flexing. He tilts his head back, and the column of his neck moves as he swallows. Dark hair covers his chin — it's a discordant chord in that clean-cut profile, I shiver. He would scrape that rough skin down my core. He'd mark my inner thighs, lick my core, thrust his tongue inside my melting channel and drink from my pussy. *Oh! God.* Goosebumps rise on my skin.

No one has the right to look this beautiful, this achingly gorgeous. Too magnificent for his own good. Anger coils in my chest.

"Arrogant wanker."

"I'll take that under advisement."

"You're a jerk, you know that?"

He presses his lips together. The grooves on either side of his mouth deepen. Jesus, clearly the man has never laughed a single day in his life. Bet that stick up his arse is uncomfortable. I chuckle.

He runs his gaze down my features, my chest, down to my toes, then yawns.

The hell! I will not let him provoke me. Will not. "Like what you see?" I jut out my chin.

"Sorry, you're not my type." He slides a hand into the pocket of those perfectly cut pants, stretching it across that heavy bulge.

Heat curls low in my belly.

Not fair, that he could afford a wardrobe that clearly shouts his status and what amounts to the economy of a small third-world country. A hot feeling stabs in my chest.

He reeks of privilege, of taking his status in life for granted.

While I've had to fight every inch of the way. Hell, I am still battling to hold onto the last of my equilibrium.

"Last chance —" I wiggle my fingers from where I am sprawled out on the floor at his feet, "—to redeem yourself..."

"You have me there." He places the glass on the counter, then bends and holds out his hand. The hint of discolored steel at his wrist catches my attention. Huh?

He wears a cheap-ass watch?

That's got to bring down the net worth of his presence by more than 1000% percent. Weird.

I reach up and he straightens.

I lurch back.

"Oops, I changed my mind." His lips curl.

A hot burning sensation claws at my stomach. I am not a violent person, honestly. But Smirky Pants here, he needs to be taught a lesson.

I swipe out my legs, kicking his out from under him.

Sinclair

My knees give way, and I hurtle toward the ground.

What the —? I twist around, thrust out my arms. My palms hit the floor. The impact jostles up my elbows. I firm my biceps and come to a halt planked above her.

A huffing sound fills my ear.

I turn to find my whippet, Max, panting with his mouth open. I scowl and he flattens his ears.

All of my businesses are dog-friendly. Before you draw conclusions about me being the caring sort or some such shit — it attracts footfall.

Max scrutinizes the girl, then glances at me. *Huh?* He hates women, but not her, apparently.

I straighten and my nose grazes hers.

My arms are on either side of her head. Her chest heaves. The fabric of her dress stretches across her gorgeous breasts. My fingers tingle; my palms ache to cup those tits, squeeze those hard nipples outlined against the — hold on, what is she wearing? A tunic shirt in a sparkly pink... and are those shoulder pads she has on?

I glance up, and a squeak escapes her lips.

Pink hair surrounds her face. *Pink? Who dyes their hair that color past the age of eighteen?*

I stare at her face. *How old is she?* Un-furrowed forehead, dark eyelashes that flutter against pale cheeks. Tiny nose, and that mouth —luscious, tempting. A whiff of her scent, cherries and caramel, assails my senses. My mouth waters. *What the hell?*

She opens her eyes and our eyelashes brush. Her gaze widens. Green, like the leaves of the evergreens, flickers of gold sparkling in their depths. "What?" She glowers. "You're demonstrating the plank position?"

"Actually," I lower my weight onto her, the ridge of my hardness thrusting into the softness between her legs, "I was thinking of something else, altogether."

She gulps and her pupils dilate. *Ah, so she feels it, too?*

I drop my head toward her, closer, closer.

Color floods the creamy expanse of her neck. Her eyelids flutter down. She tilts her chin up.

I push up and off of her.

"That… Sweetheart, is an emphatic 'no thank you' to whatever you are offering."

Her eyelids spring open and pink stains her cheeks. Adorable. Such a range of emotions across those gorgeous features in a few seconds. What else is hidden under that exquisite exterior of hers?

She scrambles up, eyes blazing.

Ah! The little bird is trying to spread her wings? My dick twitches. My groin hardens, *Why does her anger turn me on so, huh?*

She steps forward, thrusts a finger in my chest.

My heart begins to thud.

She peers up from under those hooded eyelashes. "Wake up and taste the wasabi, asshole."

"What does that even mean?"

She makes a sound deep in her throat. My dick twitches. My pulse speeds up.

She pivots, grabs a half-full beer mug sitting on the bar counter.

I growl, "Oh, no, you don't."

She turns, swings it at me. The smell of hops envelops the space.

I stare down at the beer-splattered shirt, the lapels of my camel colored jacket deepening to a dull brown. Anger squeezes my guts.

I fist my fingers at my side, broaden my stance.

She snickers.

I tip my chin up. "You're going to regret that."

The smile fades from her face. "Umm." She places the now empty mug on the bar.

I take a step forward and she skitters back. "It's only clothes." She gulps. "They'll wash."

I glare at her and she swallows, wiggles her fingers in the air. "I should have known that you wouldn't have a sense of humor."

I thrust out my jaw. "That's a ten-thousand-pound suit you destroyed."

She blanches, then straightens her shoulders. "Must have been some hot date you were trying to impress, huh?"

"Actually," I flick some of the offending liquid from my lapels, "it's you I was after."

"Me?" She frowns.

"We need to speak."

She glances toward the bartender who's on the other side of the bar. "I don't know you." She chews on her lower lip, biting off some of the hot pink. How would she look, with that pouty mouth fastened on my cock?

The blood rushes to my groin so quickly that my head spins. My pulse rate ratchets up. Focus, focus on the task you came here for.

"This will take only a few seconds." I take a step forward.

She moves aside.

I frown. "You want to hear this, I promise."

"Go to hell." She pivots and darts forward.

I let her go, a step, another, because... I can? Besides it's fun to create the illusion of freedom first; makes the hunt so much more entertaining, huh?

I swoop forward, loop an arm around her waist, and yank her toward me.

She yelps. "Release me."

Good thing the bar is not yet full. It's too early for the usual officegoers to stop by. And the staff...? Well they are well aware of who cuts their paychecks.

I spin her around and against the bar, then release her. "You will listen to me."

She swallows; she glances left to right.

Not letting you go yet, little Bird. I move into her space, crowd her.

She tips her chin up. "Whatever you're selling, I'm not interested."

I allow my lips to curl. "You don't fool me."

A flush steals up her throat, sears her cheeks. So tiny, so innocent. Such a good little liar. I narrow my gaze. "Every action has its consequences."

"Are you daft?" She blinks.

"This pretense of yours?" I thrust my face into hers, growling, "It's not working."

She blinks, then color suffuses her cheeks. "You're certifiably mad—"

"Getting tired of your insults."

"It's true, everything I said." She scrapes back the hair from her face.

Her fingernails are painted... You guessed it, pink.

"And here's something else. You are a selfish, egotistical jackass."

I smirk. "You're beginning to repeat your insults and I haven't even kissed you yet."

"Don't you dare." She gulps.

I tilt my head. "Is that a challenge?"

"It's a..." she scans the crowded space, then turns to me. Her lips firm, "...a warning. You're delusional, you jackass." She inhales a deep breath before she speaks, "Your ego is bigger than the size of a black hole." She snickers. "Bet it's to compensate for your lack of balls."

A-n-d, that's it. I've had enough of her mouth that threatens to never stop spewing words. How many insults can one tiny woman hurl my way? Answer: too many to count.

"You—"

I lower my chin, touch my lips to hers.

Heat, sweetness, the honey of her essence explodes on my palate. My dick twitches. I tilt my head, deepen the kiss, reaching for that something more… more… of whatever scent she's wearing on her skin, infused with that breath of hers that crowds my senses, rushes down my spine. My groin hardens; my cock lengthens. I thrust my tongue between those infuriating lips.

She makes a sound deep in her throat and my heart begins to pound.

So innocent, yet so crafty. Beautiful and feisty. The kind of complication I don't need in my life.

I prefer the straight and narrow. Gray and black, that's how I choose to define my world. She, with her flashes of color—pink hair and lips that threaten to drive me to the edge of distraction—is exactly what I hate.

Give me a female who has her priorities set in life. To pleasure me, get me off, then walk away before her emotions engage. Yeah. That's what I prefer.

Not this… this bundle of craziness who flings her arms around my shoulders, thrusts her breasts up and into my chest, tips up her chin, opens her mouth, and invites me to take and take.

Does she have no self-preservation? Does she think I am going to fall for her wide-eyed appeal? She has another thing coming.

I tear my mouth away and she protests.

She twines her leg with mine, pushes up her hips, so that melting softness between her thighs cradles my aching hardness.

I glare into her face and she holds my gaze.

Trains her green eyes on me. Her cheeks flush a bright red. Her lips fall open and a moan bleeds into the air. The blood rushes to my dick, which instantly thickens. *Fuck.*

Time to put distance between myself and the situation.

It's how I prefer to manage things. Stay in control, always. Cut out anything that threatens to impinge on my equilibrium. Shut it down or buy them off. Reduce it to a transaction. That I understand.

The power of money, to be able to buy and sell—numbers, logic. That's what's worked for me so far.

"How much?"

Her forehead furrows.

"Whatever it is, I can afford it."

Her jaw slackens. "You think… you —"

"A million?"

"What?"

"Pounds, dollars… You name the currency, and it will be in your account."

Her jaw slackens. "You're offering me money?"

"For your time, and for you to fall in line with my plan."

She reddens. "You think I am for sale?"

"Everyone is."

"Not me."

Here we go again. "Is that a challenge?"

Color fades from her face. "Get away from me."

"Are you shy, is that what this is?" I frown. "You can write your price down on a piece of paper if you prefer." I glance up, notice the bartender watching us. I jerk my chin toward the napkins. He grabs one, then offers it to her.

She glowers at him. "Did you buy him, too?"

"What do you think?"

She glances around. "I think everyone here is ignoring us."

"It's what I'd expect."

"Why is that?"

I wave the tissue in front of her face. "Why do you think?"

"You own the place?"

"As I am going to own you."

She sets her jaw. "Let me leave and you won't regret this."

A chuckle bubbles up. I swallow it away. This is no laughing matter. I never smile during a transaction. Especially not when I am negotiating a new acquisition. And that's all she is. The final piece in the puzzle I am building.

"No one threatens me."

"You're right."

"Huh?"

"I'd rather act on my instinct."

Her lips twist, her gaze narrows. All of my senses scream a warning.

No, she wouldn't, no way—pain slices through my middle and sparks explode behind my eyes.

To find out what happens next read Summer & Sinclair Sterling's story in The Billionaire's Fake Wife

Want to be the first to find out when L. Steele's next book releases? Subscribe to her newsletter on her website

BONUS SCENE

A month later

Damian

"Wake up, Alice dear!" said her sister. "Why, what a long sleep you've had!"

"Oh, I've had such a curious dream!" said Alice, and she told her sister, as well as she could remember them, all these strange Adventures of hers; and when she had finished, her sister kissed her, and said, "It was a curious dream, dear, certainly: but now run in to your tea; it's getting late."

So Alice got up and ran off, thinking while she ran, as well she might, what a wonderful dream it had been.

I shut the book and glance at Riley.

"That was beautiful, Daddy." She smiles, "I love it when you read to me."

"I know you do, honey." A tear runs down my cheek.

She reaches up and wipes it off, "Why are you sad, Daddy?'

"Because you're going to leave me, baby."

She shakes her head, then presses her fingers to the space above my heart, "I'll always be here with you, Daddy."

I can't stop the chuckle that tumbles from my lips, "When did you get so wise, huh?"

"I get it from you, Papa."

I cover her hand with mine, press her palms into my chest. "Stay," I whisper, "don't leave me."

She pulls her hand out from under mine, "I have to go. You know that."

I nod.

"But now you won't be alone, ever again." She leans close and whispers in my ear, "I like Juliet, Daddy."

"Her name's Julia."

"I like her." She nods. "And my baby brother."

I frown. "Baby brother?"

"Oh." She slaps her hand over her mouth, then steps back. "I have to go."

I watch as she heads toward the door, my little princess, my very own Alice setting off on her adventures.

She pauses at the door, then glances at me over her shoulder, "I am happy, Daddy."

"I know," I whisper.

She slips out of the room.

I stay there watching the space, waiting... Waiting... A shadow falls in the doorway, then Flower steps in. She draws her lower lip between her teeth, shuffles her feet. She has one hand behind her back, as if she's hiding something from me.

"Damian..." She tugs on her earlobe, "I have something to tell you."

Up next The Billionaire's Baby - Arpad & Karina's story

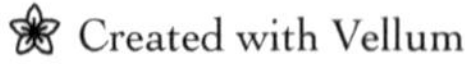 Created with Vellum